PRAISE FOR HAYDEN SMITH'S DEBUT NOVEL, NINE EXPENSIVE FUNERALS, THE FIRST IN HIS TOM O'BANION MYSTERY SERIES

With *Nine Expensive Funerals,* Hayden Smith has written a stunning page-turner of a murder mystery. Not only is this novel tightly and expertly plotted, but it is also rife with literary references that are pleasant to the ear....Unlike almost any thriller I've read, Smith gets us to fall in love with his characters. I really like Michael Connelly's Harry Bosch, but I don't love Harry. I do, however love Tom, Fred, Maria, and Doug. Hayden Smith builds suspense from the very first page onward. I simply couldn't put this book down and recommend it without reservation.

Charles W. Brice

I was born on Muskegon's East side in 1936. I grew up in that wonderful town. As I read this gripping tale of scheming and murder, I was constantly pleasantly surprised by the local content of streets, restaurants, factories, businesses, and landmarks, some now gone but not forgotten....Thank you, Hayden, for a great read and re-kindled memories.

Lou Schulist

Smith's use of a clean narrative style will sweep you through a couple's surprising journey.
Bear River Review, Monica Rico — Editor-in-Chief

I enjoyed the book very much. Couldn't put it down, powered through it in a day and a half. So, naturally you would have to say it held my interest. I usually like protagonists to have flaws which must be overcome to get a satisfactory conclusion. I think Tom fits the bill here.
Philip Smith

I'm from Muskegon and Hayden Smith is a friend. With that being said, two thumbs up for Hayden's new political murder mystery story. Set in early 1960s Muskegon, MI, the story weaves a suspenseful tale of greed and deceit by a powerful group of business owners dead-set against well-intentioned and dedicated community leaders....A number of twists, turns and surprises make this a page-turner. Readers will enjoy this book even though not familiar with Muskegon. In fact, it may even cause some to plan a visit to West Michigan.
Larry Zadonick

I bought the book, read it, and loved it — to the extent that I ignored my dog, the phone calls, any chores that needed doing, and about everything else....I really liked Tom and the two sets of in-laws who supported about every decision he made. The good guys were people of honor and integrity, the "bad guys" appropriately evil and amoral.
Dr. Carol Thompson

ALSO BY HAYDEN SMITH

Tom O'Banion Mystery Series

Nine Expensive Funerals

Vengeance Served Cold

VENGEANCE SERVED COLD

TOM O'BANION MYSTERY SERIES
BOOK 2

HAYDEN SMITH

Vengeance Served Cold is a work of fiction. Names and characters are the products of the author's imagination. Any resemblance to actual persons, living or dead, is entirely coincidental. Any references to events, establishments, organizations, locales, or corporations are intended only to give this novel a sense of reality and authenticity and are used fictitiously. All of them existed in the time setting, early 1960s. Some no longer exist today. All other events, establishments, organizations, locales, and corporations portrayed in this book are figments of the author's imagination.

First Trade Paperback Edition published September 2022
First e-book Edition published September 2022

Cover by: Rocking Book Covers
Lighthouse logo by: VendeDesign
Author photo by: Kenny Hekhuis Photography

ISBN 978-1-7359983-2-9 (Trade paperback)

ISBN 978-1-7359983-3-6 (e-book)

Library of Congress Control Number: 2022913491

Published in the United States of America by: The McKinley Company

This book is dedicated to my children, grandchildren, and great-grandchildren.

You are my joy, my raison d'être.

1

———

Tom was enjoying the crackling fire, taking away the chill from the blustery March Lake Michigan winds that whistled loudly around the small bungalow. His stereo radio played soft and easy jazz for the dinner hour. He laid his book down — *I'd better get something cooking.*

An insistent loud knock on the door made him jump. He thought, *that sounds like a Doug knock.* When he opened the door, sure enough, Doug stood there with a large Scrib's pizza and a cold six-pack of beer. "Let me in, this March wind has a nip to it."

"Welcome, pizza guy, get yourself in here. Let me take that pizza while you get your jacket off. I didn't know you were coming tonight. I'm glad you're here."

Doug smiled. "A little surprise. I thought you might like an old friend for company. And I'll bet you haven't had dinner yet."

"Nope, just thinking about it. Do we need to heat that up a little?"

"It's piping hot now, so let's get to it."

After setting up TV tables, they sat by the fire and were quiet while they went after it.

After his third slice, Doug asked, "How is Maria today? I assume you went to see her. Is she still in a coma? How long has it been now?"

"I was with her a good part of the morning. It will soon be six months. She seems restless and the nurses tell me that's a sign that she may be waking up. We'll see but I've had a feeling about her waking up for some time now."

Tom was reaching for his last slice of pizza when the phone rang.

He hurried to the phone table and picked up. "Hello."

"Tom, this is Jim Johnson. Something has come up that I need to talk about with you. I don't want to do it over the phone. I know it's short notice, but I wonder if I might drop in."

"Of course, Jim, come on over. By the way, Doug is here. Will that be all right?"

"I think so. I'll see you in about a half hour."

After he hung up, Tom sat back down on the sofa and looked at Doug, "I wonder what is going on that the chief couldn't wait until tomorrow."

Doug murmured, "I was puzzling over that too. Is it okay that I'm here?"

"If Jim said it was okay, I'm sure it is. I'm still on temporary status as a detective in training. I finished my state police program and almost done with my Master's in Choral Conducting. And to answer your unasked question, what will I do then? Truth is, I don't know yet."

Their conversation continued as they cleaned up all but two pieces of pizza in case Jim might want some.

Tom let the chief in a few minutes later. "Welcome, Jim. Can I warm up some pizza for you and get you a beer? You remember Doug, don't you?"

Jim shook hands with Doug, then chuckled. "I'd better not have pizza. Martha's holding dinner for me. I told her I would be home between 7:00 and 7:30, and it's already 7:15. We better get to business."

Doug asked, "Chief, would you like me to leave?"

"No, Doug, but I will ask you to keep this to yourself until it hits the *Chronicle* tomorrow and even then, don't talk about some of what you will hear, except with Tom."

He continued, "Tim Samuels is dead. He was shot early Friday morning at his office. He was always the first in, so there were no witnesses. You remember that he was in the Group of Nine — that group of 'community leaders' that were involved in the plot to get the former mayor to back down and eventually were charged with conspiracy to commit murder when the mayor was killed."

Tom and Doug started with questions when he paused.

Jim slowed them down saying, "We don't have a clue about who did this or if it is related to what went down last fall. It may be something else in Tim's past. The forensics and autopsy aren't done yet. We'll see what that tells us."

Tom asked, "What will you do next and how can I help?"

Jim replied, "I haven't figured that out yet. But late this afternoon this showed up in the mail." Jim pulled a letter out of his pocket along with two pair of police evidence gloves. He continued, "It was addressed to you, Tom, but we were concerned about what might be in it. We took the liberty of opening it and finding nothing bad in it, had it checked for fingerprints. Nothing there. There is more analysis we can do yet at the state police lab. For now, I'd like you, Tom, to put on these gloves, take it out of the envelope, and read it aloud."

The message was made with cut-out letters glued to an otherwise blank piece of typewriter paper. The words read, "O'Banion, Samuels is number three. You are on the list as well and I want you to know I'll get to you after I get the rest."

Tom gasped. Doug shook his head. "Jim, do you think this means what seems obvious at first reading?"

"Tom, I'm afraid it does. It sounds as if someone is out to get the other six members of the Group of Nine plus you."

"Why do you suppose I am on the list?"

"I'm not sure, Tom, but I suspect it has to do with how you broke the case wide open with your great detective work."

∾

"ARE you going to reassemble the task force?"

"I will soon. We'll start off with the original members — Mark Bergstrom from my office, Dave Smithson of the Michigan State Police, you, and me."

Jim continued, "Doug, I don't want anything about this letter to get out. No one else should know yet. You and Tom can talk about it, but no one else. Understood?"

Doug nodded. "I've got it, Chief." But his thoughts went, *I wonder who shot this Tim. And Tom's name was on that list. I'll have to protect him. I thought the Group of Nine was taken care of when they were tried for their involvement in the death of the mayor, Fred Thomas. Why would this be happening now?*

"Tom, wasn't the Group of Nine tried for their part in Fred's murder?"

"No, they were indicted but haven't been tried yet. Their attorney, Harold Evans, has been delaying for reasons that I don't know. Judge McVie and DA Harvey Swenson are likely the only other two who know why he's delaying. The last I heard, their trial will be sometime in the next month. Why do you ask, Doug?"

"Just curious. You know me. And you just cleared it up even though I still don't understand it."

2

Tom finished his final for his 9:00 a.m. class at Grand Valley State. He had been allowed to take it early — the end of March — because of his years of teaching and conducting at the high school level. He just needed his grade on this keystone conducting final with all the faculty there and he would be finished. Graduation was in May, and he would have his Master's in Conducting.

As he drove home to Muskegon, he thought, *I better stop and tell Maria.* Even though she was still in a coma, Tom just knew in his heart that she would wake up soon. In the meantime, he needed to keep her up to date with what he was doing.

Twenty-five minutes later he was walking into the long-term care section of Hackley Hospital. That's where Maria had been transferred when it was obvious that it would be a while yet. Passing the nurses' station, he asked the head nurse, "How's my girl doing today? I have some good news for her. I want to tell her this is a special day."

"She's doing great. Her therapy is working, and her muscle tone is improving so that when she wakes up, she won't take long to get active again. We've noticed a lot of change. Tom, you should try to talk to her doctor soon. Maria is showing some new signs now that she might be coming out of the coma soon. Some arm and leg restlessness and eye movements. He can tell you more about what the changes might mean."

Tom walked on into Maria's room saying, "Good morning, darling. Just finished my last final and in May I'll have my Master's. That gives us more options. I can apply to community colleges now, too. You have your Master's in theatre, so we can look for jobs together. So, time to wake up! I love you. Wake up, sweetheart," he pleaded.

Her nurse assured him, "She hears how much you love her. I can tell you do."

"You're right. She's my everything." And then to Maria, "This was just a quick visit to tell you the news. I'll see you this weekend for some longer, quality time, sweetheart."

He stopped by the nurses' station on his way out. "I'm going to be working with the police department again for a while. Here's their phone number to add to the others. By the way, would you put this picture up in Maria's room? It is one of her favorites from our engagement dinner last summer. I want it to be the first thing she sees when she wakes up."

"Of course, Tom, I know just where to put it."

TOM STOPPED at the police station on his way home through downtown. He waited a few minutes for the chief's meeting to end. Jim came out and beckoned to Tom, "Come in, Tom. I've been in touch with Dave Smithson and he's assembling a team. It will likely be many of the same people. We decided that, like last time, it will be fewer in number until we get a handle on what and who we'll need."

Jim continued, "Let me give you a quick catch up, not much specific information yet."

"Any news about the weapon, Jim?"

"Not yet. We know it was a rifle. But we should have some more forensic data by our first meeting on Wednesday. That may help clear up some of the uncertainty."

"Jim, what's happening with the rest of the Group of Nine?"

"As you know, three of them are now dead. We still don't know who was responsible for their deaths. The rest are all lying low waiting for their trial. I called each of them about Tim Samuel's murder. I thought they should hear it from me. And though I told them we were once again convening the task force they didn't stop asking questions. Each seemed afraid he might be next."

Jim continued, "I haven't told them about the threats in the message yet. If the threat is real, they should be told. I want to talk with the judge, the district attorney, and the group's attorney about whether to tell and, if they should be told, who should do it. I don't want to cause a problem with the legal process. So, the first item for the task force is to examine all the evidence we have and decide if the threat is real or the work of a crackpot case follower. Either way, when they hear the threat, the group members will react, maybe run, go deeper into hiding, or demand police protection."

Tom stated, "If they know, they may change their plea, thinking that a prison term might be safer than the risk of being killed."

"I agree. Now, how about the meeting, Wednesday at 10:00 a.m.? Will you be able to make it?"

"Sure thing, Jim."

"Good, we'll see you then."

3

When Tom showed up on Saturday morning to see Maria, her nurse aide exclaimed, "Here you are again. She hasn't changed much since yesterday but if you tell her, she'll know you are here and with fresh flowers."

Tom answered, "I was sitting out at the Ovals, just thinking about her, our future, and what I should do when that day comes when she wakes up. As always when I'm there, I am certain that she will be awake the next time I come. I never let any other possibility creep in. So, I decided to come in and see her bright and early this morning. And here I am."

The nurse aide murmured, "You are always welcome. Just leave her flowers on her table and I'll put them in fresh water after you leave. She has her physical therapy in about fifteen minutes. You better hurry down there. You know the way."

As Tom went in her room, he saw that the picture was on the wall where Maria would likely be looking when she woke up. He turned to Maria. "Good morning, darling. I brought you some flowers. Wake up and look."

Tom continued, "I have some more good news. Now that I'm done at Grand Valley, I'm free to do some work around our home. You made suggestions when we were dating, and I can start on some of them. It needs to become more 'ours' so that when you wake up and come home, you'll have some surprises. I'll share some of what I'm doing until you wake up. Come home to me, darling. I'll be heading home now, but I'll see you again later today and tomorrow. I love you. Wake up, darling."

Tom bent and kissed her forehead as he said the last words. His eyes were closed during the kiss, so he didn't notice the slight flutter of Maria's eyelids. He turned and headed down the hall to leave, his shoulders drooping a little that Maria was still in the coma.

When the nurse aide saw him leave, she went to Maria's room to put the flowers in water. When she finished filling the vase in the bathroom, she was startled by a sound from Maria's room. Thinking someone must have come in, she looked in the room only to see there was no one else there. She heard the noise again. It was Maria. Her voice was so light, husky, and delicate from no use, she could barely hear it. When she turned to look more closely, Maria's eyes were open, but then shut again right away. Not wanting to leave, she pressed the call button and said to the charge nurse, "Sandy, Maria is waking up! She just spoke, opened her eyes, and her hands are moving a little. Please try to catch Tom. He just left."

Sandy raced to send the orderly to catch Tom. Then she also called the entrance desk to get them to stop Tom as she hurried to Maria's room. When she reached the room, Maria's eyes again popped open, and she whispered, "Where's Tom? I thought he was just here."

Sandy commanded, "Stay with her. I'm going to call her doctor." She almost ran back to the nursing station, she was so excited. The receptionist at Dr. Franks' office told her he was with a patient and would call back. Frustrated, Sandy told her that this was really important — his patient just woke up from a coma.

As she turned to go back to Maria's room, the phone rang. The security guard at the front desk caught Tom before he left, so he was on his way back up. She hurried back to find Maria still opening and closing her eyes. Maria asked again, "Where's Tom?"

"He's on his way back. He should be here any minute," Sandy assured her.

Sandy told her aide, "Wait in the hall and keep Tom out. I want to talk to him before he comes in."

When Tom came, the aide had trouble keeping him out. She called out to Sandy who came out and pulled the door closed. "Please go back into Maria's room and record everything that is happening. Dr. Franks will need to know it all."

Sandy then led Tom to a private consulting room. "Tom, I know you want to be in there right now. But there are some things I need to remind you about."

"Why can't I go right now?"

"I know you want that. You will in a few minutes. Just keep these few things in mind. Maria will be anxious, frightened, and likely not remember why she is here. We don't want to shock her and risk her going back to sleep. There is a neurology resident on the way, and she'll be assessing Maria with some standard questions."

"What kind of questions?"

"Things like what her name is, what year, month, and time it is, who is the president. And she will evaluate whether Maria can follow simple commands like raise her hand, touch her nose, and close her eyes — just to see how things are working. Don't be surprised at anything that happens. Maria may be able to do more than you think, or she might not be able to do as much as we want yet. Don't reach out too quickly. If she wants you to touch her, then approach slowly and talk softly. All right, let's go in."

When they entered the room, Maria looked up and held out her arms. "Tom, why did you leave?"

"I thought you were sleeping. I'm so happy you are awake." Tom swiped his eyes to brush away the tears of joy that were running down his cheeks. *Oh Maria, you're awake! I've been praying for this for a long time.*

Maria whispered, "Where am I, Tom, and why am I here?"

"You were hurt, and you needed the rest and special care, so you're in this special part of the hospital. But now you're awake! And you're getting better!"

The charge nurse came back in. "Dr. Franks is on his way and should be here about 10:00 a.m. Tom, can you sit here with Maria and her nurse aide until he gets here? Dr. Franks ordered some routine medical tests, so you'll be interrupted a time or two while they do them. Maria, the tests are just routine."

Tom looked at Maria and held her hand to his face. "I'm not going anywhere." He smiled as Maria reached out with the other hand and he took it into his. He looked at Sandy. "I want to call some people and let them know, her parents, my parents, our friends — Doug, and Nancy, Maria's best friend at the high school. Should I call on this phone or somewhere else?"

"It's all right to call from here. Keep your voice on a low and even keel. No loud sounds. And if they decide to visit, be sure to tell them to stop and talk to me before they come to her room. I would wait until the neurology resident is with her and then make the calls while he is here. On second thought, why don't you make the calls when the resident is here doing his exam and use the small conference room down the hall?"

Tom turned back to Maria whose eyes were now closed. In alarm, he looked up and asked, "Is she okay?"

"She's fine. She'll open them again soon. There, see what I mean. Hold her hand and just be here when she looks up. She needs you near her."

The neurology resident knocked and came in. Sandy motioned to Tom to leave with her. Tom turned to Maria saying, "I have to go out to the other room for a few minutes. While I'm out I'll call your parents and let them know the good news. I won't be long." He kissed her forehead. "I love you. I'll be right back."

Maria got agitated as Tom turned to leave. The resident stopped Tom. "Wait, Tom, stay where Maria can see you and hold her hand if she wants you to. It may relax her more and keep her that way until our examination is done." Tom turned back to Maria and held out his hand. Maria calmed down and gave Tom's hand a squeeze.

The resident stepped close to the bed and took Maria's other hand. "Maria, I'm going to ask you a few questions. No answers are wrong. This isn't a test. We need to get some information from you, okay?"

After about ten minutes of questioning, he stopped. "Maria, you are doing great. I think we'll stop for now and I'll come back in when Dr. Franks gets here. So, if you feel the need to rest your eyes a little and rest your voice, it's okay. Tom will be right here with you until we come back in."

Maria motioned for the resident to come closer. "Could Tom call my mom and dad now?"

"Let me talk to the charge nurse and Dr. Franks and see what they say. For now, Tom, Maria needs you right here. Maria, I promise you we'll let your parents know before I go. Let's see what Dr. Franks and the staff think about all this."

When everyone left, including the nurse aide who said she would be right back in about five minutes, Maria beckoned, with a little finger wave, to Tom and whispered, "Come closer, sweetheart."

Tom was startled but he leaned in. She touched his face. "Kiss me before she comes back."

"Should we?"

"Kiss me quick. Gently please." Tom touched his lips to hers. When he opened his eyes, hers were closed. Tiny tears glistened in Maria's eyes, but she wore a big smile. It was a little crooked, but it was beautiful. Then Tom started smiling, they both laughed.

The nurse aide came back in, took one look, and asked, "What have you been up to? It's okay, I won't tell."

Maria giggled. "It was my first kiss in six months. I can't stop smiling."

Tom had a big smile. "Me either."

"I feel like I'm hungry but somehow it feels different. I can't describe it. It's almost like I forgot what hunger feels like."

The aide, with a twinkle in her eye, said, "If you behave while I'm gone, I'll go tell the charge nurse and maybe they can get you a little soup or something." She left smiling, *thank heavens — these kids just got their miracle.*

4

S ara arrived on time to meet with her dad's attorney, Mr.
Roberto Moretti. They connected after the funeral service for
her dad. He told her then that her dad had changed the will
after her mother died so that Sara and her grandmother were the
sole inheritors of his considerable estate. When her grandmother
died, she became her dad's only heir.

He told her that Joe had a separate account and accountant for
the restaurant, and that her dad was scrupulous about not mingling
funds. There had been an independent auditor called in, so the
house, business, and the cars were free and clear of any association
with the Group. He told her he talked to Chief Johnson and was told
that the police or district attorney had no claim to the money made
by her dad's restaurant business.

There had also been a substantial insurance policy with Sara as
the only beneficiary. She was able to use this money for living
expenses while waiting for the baby to be born. Her dad had also
helped her find some help at the Catholic Home for Unwed Mothers.

Mr. Moretti asked, "How are you and your little girl?"

She replied, "We are both doing just fine. I named her Arianna
Maria, the nuns helped me choose it. She was born in Hackley

Hospital. We're living in the Home while I finish high school. She is now a little over six months old and is my little sweetheart.

"When the insurance money came in, I moved to Catholic Central High School. I just couldn't go back to Muskegon High after everything that happened there. The nuns at the Home helped me make the transition. I'll graduate in June of this year, and I'll be eighteen in August. At that time, the two of us will move back into my parents' house since I'll be an adult. I'm not sure what is ahead yet for the two of us or how much Bob wants to be involved."

He asked, "Has he seen her, held her? Are the two of you talking and what kind of talking is it? You two were pretty close when you were in high school."

She was indignant. "Of course he has seen her. And yes, we talk. I don't want to push him. I still love him. I think when he comes home for the summer, we can start dating again and see what happens. Both of us are a little more mature now and maybe what we had before will rebloom. If we take it slowly and just let things happen naturally, we'll know if it is right."

Mr. Moretti smiled. "You've matured a lot and are taking your responsibilities seriously. I'm proud of what you are becoming, and I know that your dad would be proud of you as well."

"I know he would be. He and I grew close after Mom and Grandma died. He was a good daddy. He just made a mistake lining up with the Group of Nine. I have some questions for you."

She went on, "You've talked to the police and specifically to Chief Johnson. Do they know what poison killed Dad yet and who did it to him? Is there anything new?"

Mr. Moretti smiled again. "Wow! That's a handful of questions. Let's see. You know he was poisoned. Someone put the poison in his glass of milk. That suggests that he was poisoned by someone who knew him well enough to know he often had a glass of milk just before bed."

"A lot of people knew that. It was common knowledge among our friends."

"Yes, but most of those who knew would not likely kill him. It was a fairly common poison, so it is hard to track down people who might have bought some. So, no, they are no closer to finding the killer yet. Not a lot new, but there may be soon. If you haven't heard yet, the chief has started the task force again. They want to get a handle on this before it gets out of control. You'll likely see it in tomorrow's paper. Tim Samuels, another member of the Group, was shot and killed yesterday. That's now three gone out of the nine. How'd I do?"

"You did well. But I have two more questions. Am I in danger? And do you think Chief Johnson would release Dad's rifle? It was pretty special to him, and it's the gun that he taught me to hunt with. I'd like to have it if I can. I may want to do some more hunting someday."

"You should talk with the chief about that. Unfortunately, I don't know if you're in danger and he's the one to ask about the rifle."

"Okay. I'll call and make an appointment with him."

Mr. Moretti paused. "I have a question for you and some advice. Do you mind?"

"No, of course not, ask and advise away!"

"Now please don't be upset. Have you told Bob how well off you are?"

She was startled by the question. "No, I haven't. I don't know exactly where we stand right now, and I wouldn't want that to influence his feelings about me or Arianna. He likely suspects. He knew Dad owned the restaurant and figured that would become mine. What is your advice?"

"After hearing you talk today about your future and seeing what you have done, you don't need it, but here it is, give your new relationship some time to grow back, as I think it will, before you tell him. I think you'll know when the time is right. If you want to talk about it before you tell him, come see me. There are some legal protections we can take, but we won't do that unless you first talk it over with Bob and feel like it is the right thing to do."

"Thank you, Mr. Moretti. You've been such an immense help to me."

WHEN SARA LEFT HIS OFFICE, she looked around, as she always did, to see if there was anyone sitting in a car or standing near her car. The first time she met with Chief Johnson, she asked him if she was in any danger. He answered that he didn't think there would be any reason for concern. Then he said that just to be extra cautious, Sara should be on the alert for anything that made her uneasy and let him know. She had built that habit.

Today was different. She was driving to her cabin in the woods on Scenic Drive and didn't want to be followed. Dad had bought her an identical hunting rifle to his and it was stored at the cabin. Now she wanted it in the car. Dad had showed her how to store it in its sleeve under the back seat. When it was secure, she went back to the Home and Arianna.

5

When Tom greeted Gerri, the chief's secretary, she said, "That's great news that Maria woke up! The chief is on the phone, but he'll be in the conference room soon for the meeting. And Tom, he hasn't said anything about Maria yet. He wanted to tell them all at one time."

"Yes, it is good news. Thanks for asking. It's going to take some rehab time, but she'll soon be home again. Are we meeting in the same conference room as before?"

"You are. Dave Smithson and Mark Bergstrom are already there. They're expecting you. Jim will be in shortly."

Tom greeted Dave and Mark, helped himself to some coffee, and did some catching up. He respected Dave and Mark — they were great colleagues, and he was looking forward to working with them again.

The chief came in and along with him were several other members of the office staff. "Good morning, everyone. Before we start our meeting, I have some good news. Only Gerri and I know at this point. With Tom's permission, I'm going to let him share it with us. Tom, spread the good word."

Tom smiled, eyes sparkling. "My Maria woke up from the coma on Friday."

There was a round of applause, and the comments and questions started.

Tom held up a hand, saying, "I'll share what I can with you. They were doing a lot of tests over the weekend. From those and her doctor's assessment, there are reasons to believe she will have a full recovery. It is going to take time, but it will happen. Her voice is weak from disuse, she is still on a feeding tube, but with liquids she is learning to swallow again. They even had her sitting up on Saturday and standing up on Sunday. They have been doing passive muscle exercises, so her strength should come back quickly. With her progress on Monday and Tuesday, they think now she'll soon be home and change to outpatient therapy. We haven't told our parents yet because the doctor wants to give her a little more time to get settled, so I'd appreciate it if you wouldn't share the news with anyone else."

Tom teared up, gathered himself, and said with a big smile, "My Maria is back!"

After some final questions, the chief cut it off. "Let's get this meeting started. I'll step out for a minute to see what's going on out there. I'll bring Gerri back with me so she can take notes. Get yourselves a fresh coffee and we'll be right back. We'll have Pete Thompson covering the switchboard, so he may pop in."

When they returned, the chief said, "I got a phone call from Sara Antonelli. I haven't seen her in sometime. She said she had seen her attorney and at his suggestion, she has some questions including if and when she could have the gun back. It was special to both of them as he taught her to hunt with it. I have to think about that before I see her later this week."

Tom asked, "How is she doing? I haven't seen her since she had the baby. We had a little chat then. She told me she was living in the Catholic Home for Unwed Mothers and was going to stay there until she graduated from high school. She is doing catch-up on her studies and should graduate in June. I wouldn't mind catching up with her and Bob. I know Maria will have questions too."

Jim replied, "She sounds good to me. She told me her little girl, Arianna Maria, is a little over six months old now. I'll tell her you asked about her. Is it all right if I tell her Maria is awake?"

"Please do."

Mark asked, "Isn't she the girl who took you to court?"

"She is but that's all behind us now. Maria and I had some good conversations with her after the trial was over. She apologized to me from the witness stand. She was given probation for the perjury charge. She should be about done with that by now."

"That's gracious of you, Tom." Dave smiled. "You're a better man than I am."

"I'm sure that's not true. As I said, it's behind us. Maria and I have too much to look forward to since she's awake."

Jim said, "Here we go. Going to go back to last Friday night. I went to see Tom on my way home to tell him about what we learned that day. Tim was always the first into work, so there were no witnesses. Remember that he was in the Group. That's three of the nine. Then this morning, we received new forensic information about Larry Olsen's death."

Pete stepped in. "Chief, the attorney for the Group is on the phone, has some questions...what should I tell him?"

Jim looked at him, annoyed. "Pete, tell him I'm meeting with the new task force and that I'll get back to him shortly, and close the door on your way out."

Jim turned back. "Larry Olsen's car had multiple dents in both the bumper and the driver's side rear panel. There were wood chips on both locations, so we surmise for the moment that a vehicle with a wood bumper helped push him off the bridge and into the lake. The tire skid marks showed sudden moves by Larry's car. We think that he is murder number three of the Group of Nine."

The chief didn't hear the door now closing quietly as Pete walked away.

"And here is a possible decisive factor that these deaths might all be related. Friday morning, we got this in the mail. He/she addressed it to Tom. The message was with cut-out letters glued to an otherwise blank piece of typewriter paper. The words read, 'O'Banion, Samuels is number three. You are on the list as well and I want you to know I'll get to you before I'm done.' There was no forensic information on the note, no fingerprints, no odors, no indication of source."

Mark wondered, "And we still don't know if it is one person killing them all, as the note would seem to imply. Or is it several different people, as the varied methods would suggest?"

The men took that in with shakes of their heads and a look at Tom.

Dave asked, "Why did he or she send it here instead of directly to Tom?"

Jim continued, "We talked about that in-house. We think, at the moment, that it may be that he/she wanted us to learn of it as well as Tom. The fact that Tom is on the team with us is not well known. That tells us something, but we are not sure what. One of our early tasks is to evaluate this letter and determine if the threat is real or the work of a crackpot case follower. With the added information about Larry Olsen, we are leaning toward a real threat. And, if so, someone wants revenge."

Dave added, "I'm a little surprised that the post office delivered it what with all those pasted on numbers and letters on the envelope."

"They didn't mail it here. A watchful sorting clerk spotted it, took it to the postmaster, and he brought it over himself."

Jim added, "I'm checking all the legal bases to make sure what I can tell the rest of the Group. When they learn about the note and the addition of Larry Olsen, making three gone, they may start pushing for police protection. All of them told me that they were laying low, but all this raises the threat level."

Dave asked, "Since I'm over in Lansing, I haven't heard. When will their trials be?"

∼

Jim told them, "I've spoken to the district attorney about that. He says they have been taking their time, making sure their cases are airtight. These events may change the timeline when the Group has all this information. So, are there any questions about the note, anything you noticed that we might have missed? Dave, do you think your forensic team in Lansing might have some new trick up their sleeve in regard to the note?"

Dave answered, "I'll check it out with them. If they would like to have a look, when could it be available?"

"I want to show it to the District Attorney and to the Judge as well. Meeting with both of them should give me all I need about the legalities. I also need to discuss protective custody with them. Do we put them back in here or hire some guards for each of their homes?"

"Here is what I would like each of you to do. Put your heads together about what you have learned. Gerri will stay here until lunch and put your comments in the transcript. Then later this afternoon she will have the transcripts ready for you. Would you all like some lunch brought in or would you like to work it out yourselves?"

"We'll let you know when we finish up with Gerri."

Jim continued, "Just one more thing. I sometimes get a feeling about an investigation. I am more than uneasy about this one. I have the notion that if we don't move fast, we may have more deaths on our hands since the timing has escalated. The only thing that could slow it down is if we get all of them in protective custody. Please keep that in mind as you start. I would like for us to meet next Monday, but it would not surprise me that it might be Friday. Tom, I know you want to spend time with Maria, just give us as much time as you can. We need your thoughts."

Pete got off duty and stopped by his favorite tavern where there was a pay phone and called Larry Olsen's wife. "Mrs. Olsen, this is Pete Thompson."

She asked, "Why are you calling? You must know that Larry was found dead in his car. I don't need or want to talk to you."

"You might change your mind if you knew what I know. Larry's death was not an accident. The forensic evidence says that he was pushed off that bridge by another vehicle with a wooden bumper. They are now calling him the third member of the Group who is dead."

"What's going on with the rest of the Group?"

"I don't know but I could find out for the right price."

"What do you mean? I thought you were doing this as Larry's friend."

Pete said, "I was, but he's not here now."

"Just go away and leave me alone. I want nothing from you."

Tom walked into the rehab center and was greeted by the staff shouting, "Hurry, Tom, she's waiting to have lunch with you. She's having some broth, but we have a sandwich for you."

"The charge nurse will be in soon. She wants to have a little talk with you both."

Maria was sitting at a little table for two. Her walker was by her side, and she had a gait belt around her waist and the chair back. Tom, like a magician, pulled a single red rose out of his inside jacket pocket and handed it to her. "Pour toi, ma Cherie, tu es belle."

She blew Tom a kiss. "You remembered, didn't you! Won't you join me, monsieur?"

Her nurse aide took the rose and put it in a bud vase, placing it in the center of the table. Tom raised his glass of water, her nurse aide put Maria's glass in her hand, supported it with her own and they toasted.

"To you and your recovery, sweetheart."

Maria still needed help with her spoon to have her broth. Tom took his time with his sandwich. Even with help, Maria would often spill a little. She frowned and concentrated harder.

"Patience, Maria. You are doing well."

Maria tired quickly. Her aide murmured, "You are doing fine. Let's get you back to bed. Dr. Franks and the charge nurse will be here at 2:00 p.m. for a conference. It will be with the doctor, the charge nurse, you, Tom, and me. Maria, that gives you time for a quick half hour nap. Tom can sit right here with you."

Maria fell asleep quickly with Tom holding her hand.

WHEN HER AIDE WOKE MARIA, there was Tom at her side still holding her hand. The rest of the conference group were sitting around the foot of the bed, so Maria didn't have to turn her head a lot. Maria at first looked a little bewildered. She tightened her grip on Tom's hand, and asked, "Why are we all here? Is there some bad news?"

Dr. Franks quickly replied, "No, Maria, only good news. We want to let you know how well we think you are doing. I'll start off. Your tests show that your body is recovering quickly. You are making remarkable progress. In the five days since you woke up, you have been walking a little, you are strong when you sit up. You are still on a liquid diet but that will change in the next few days."

Maria interrupted to say, "But it seems like it is taking a long time."

Dr. Franks continued, "Maria, you were in a coma for almost six months. Please don't be discouraged, you are young and in good health. You will come along more quickly as your strength increases."

"But, Dr. Franks, it isn't fast enough for me. You are all lovely people, but if you don't mind, I'd rather be home with Tom. We have a life to live and no time to waste getting to it."

They all smiled broadly and gave her a round of applause.

Her voice faded and some of the words were mumbled. She asked, "How long before the mumbling will stop?"

Dr. Franks smiled. "With that spirit of yours, and the determination you are showing, it won't be long. Seriously, Maria, you are coming along well. Be patient. Sometime next week, we'll have you walking the halls with the walker. But for a few more days, just keep walking around your bed and before you know it, you will make it all the way around and to the door."

"When can I get rid of all these tubes and other paraphernalia?"

"We'll see when that comes, but a week or two at least."

"Doctor, could I have some light reading? I want to start using my eyes and my mind."

"There's that spirit again. I'll see what we can find. Would you also like to listen to some music?"

"Oh yes! I miss hearing music even though Tom sings to me often." She laughed and then asked, "Can I start having other visitors? Like my mom and dad? And Tom's parents?"

"How about this weekend? Just make it with no more than two people at first, later on as you get stronger, maybe a small group. We'll let you know. Maria, I can see that you are tiring. We're going to let you rest. I'll take this gang with me."

Seeing her face and her look to Tom, he added, "Don't fret. Tom will be right here when you wake up. As soon as you are sound asleep, I'm going to set him up in a room with a phone to call everyone with the news. I know it's been hard to keep it from them, but the time is right now. He won't be gone long, maybe fifteen or twenty minutes. You've normally been taking half hour naps. So, we'll have him back here when you wake up."

TOM WAS SET up in a consultation room where there was a phone and a chance for some privacy. He started with Maria's parents. "Hi Pop, this is Tom and I have some good news. Maria is awake and talking, a little whispery and slurring her words a bit. But talking! She is very weak, but Dr. Franks says all her medical signs are good. She is still somewhat confused at times, but she is showing flashes of Maria. They told me she is going to be fine, but it will take some time. Dr. Franks wanted us to wait to tell you until he was more confident she was out of the woods."

Mrs. Vitale was crying. Pop was trying to console her and talk to Tom. He asked Tom, "When can we come to see her?"

"I'll try to set it up for tomorrow. I need to talk with Dr. Franks as soon as I get done. So, tomorrow! I have more calls to make. I'll call again tonight."

He called his mom and dad with similar reactions. He promised a more detailed call later that night as well.

Tom decided to wait until later in the afternoon when Doug and Nancy were home from school. He would call Nancy first because that would be a short one. Doug would take some time as Doug would be full of questions. Maybe Doug could come for a late dinner and some conversation. He knew Doug would need it.

Tom hurried back to Maria's room to find her sleeping soundly. He sat down beside her, took her hand, and waited.

6

Gerri buzzed the chief, "Sara Antonelli is here for her appointment."

"Come in, Sara. It is so good to see you. How are you and how is that little girl of yours? She must be about six months old."

"She is a little over six months and not a little spoiled. She has the nuns and other staff at the Home wrapped around her little finger. She is chattering away and remembering Bob when he comes to see her."

"It's not my business, but anything else going on with you and Bob?"

"Mr. Moretti asked me the same thing. My answer is that I don't know yet. I think I still love him, but he has been away to college for almost a year. We talk now and then when he comes to see Arianna, but we have agreed to take things slowly and see what happens. We will know if it's right."

"You told me when you called to meet with me that you had some questions. I set aside as much time as you want unless we have an emergency and that's not likely."

"All right. Here goes. Do you have any information about the poison that killed Dad and who did it to him? And I saw in the *Chronicle* that another member of the Group was shot. Do you think it was the same person that killed both of them? If it was, why did they use different methods? Dad may have had the responsibility for the finances, but he was not that important in the Group. He told me that himself. Do you have anything new on his case?

"I also wanted to know if you're done with Dad's gun yet. It was special to him and me — he taught me to hunt with it. I got my first buck with it. I'd like to have it back if you are done with it."

"Okay, let me take them in order. We know what the poison is. It is a readily available poison commonly used around farms. That means it won't be easy to track down the killer by looking at who bought some recently. We're not very close to figuring out who might have done it, we have some theories but no suspect yet. We'll find him. As to anything else happening, there are some things and you will be reading about them in tomorrow's *Chronicle*, I guess I can tell you. We got the forensic evidence that someone pushed Larry Olsen's car into that lake south of town, so Larry is now officially number three. I activated the task force again."

Sara's mouth dropped and she blanched. "Am I in any danger?"

The chief put out his hand. "I've told you before and will say it again. There is no reason for anyone to think you were a part of this, so whoever it is, they won't think of you. Relax, Sara, you are safe."

Sara looked up at him. "Could the person who is doing the killing be one of the Group members?"

"Why would you think that?"

"One day Dad told me he wished he had never linked up with them. About two weeks before he was killed, he sat me down and gave me instructions on what to do if anything happened to him. I already knew Mr. Moretti, and Dad said he would take care of everything. He said he had already talked to Roberto about making sure he would look out after me. And he has. What I think is that Dad felt someone in the Group would come after him."

"Sara, you are safe. Just to be extra careful, I'll have a car go by every now and then. Are you still in school?"

"I am, but I do most of my work at the Home. Catholic Central High, thanks to the nuns, is taking good care of me."

"I will have a car drive by the Home at random times. Please let me know if you see anything that seems strange to you. I'll also call the director of the school, Sister Charlotte, and let her know about the drive-by and why it is happening."

Gerri buzzed him, "George Anderson is on the phone and desperate to talk with you. What should I tell him?"

"Tell him I'll get back to him within five minutes. Sara, are you feeling better about this?"

"Yes, thank you. But I am so glad you are sending the car by. That name, George Anderson, is familiar to me. I think he was the head of the Group. I never trusted him."

"Forget about him. He will be going away for a long time. By the way, I'll let you know about your dad's gun. I have to make that call. Thank you for coming in."

_____

7

Sara knocked and went in to see Sister Charlotte. "You know I'm going to graduate soon, and when I'm eighteen, I'm ready to move out with my little Arianna. I can't thank you enough for everything you've done for me and Arianna."

"We will miss you, child, and little Arianna. We know you have to start building a life. Your friend, Bob, her father, do you know what is going to happen with him?"

"No, Sister Charlotte, not yet. Bob will be home from college for the summer, soon now. We'll have some time to figure it out."

"Do you care for him enough to marry him?"

"I think so, but I want to spend some time with him so I can be certain. He sure does love his little girl.

"Sister Charlotte, I have to do some research at Hackley Library. Do you think someone could watch over Arianna until I get back? I should be about two hours, so I'll be in time for dinner."

"Of course, the sisters love watching over her." She called for her secretary and asked her to let the nuns know they would be watching Arianna. "Sara, we'll see you for dinner."

∾

SARA WALKED up the wide staircase into the library and as always was awed by the inspiring design. Charles Hackley's architects designed it to be a great quiet place to work, read, or just even think. She stopped by the librarians' desk before she went to the study area. "Pardon me, I'm going to be doing some research. I know where most of what I need for my Muskegon history paper but before I start, I would like to see your reverse directory. Could you show me where to find it?"

The librarian replied, "That gentleman is using it right now," pointing to a man at one of the tables in the study area. "I'll bring it to you when he brings it back."

Sara exclaimed, "I know him. That's Doug, er, I can't remember his last name. He's the orchestra conductor at Muskegon High School. I wonder what he is doing with a reverse directory."

"He might ask you the same question. Here he comes now."

Sara stammered, "Hi, Mr. Doug, sorry, I don't know your last name."

"Hello, Sara, how are you doing? I haven't heard much about you lately, just that you had your baby."

The librarian took the reverse directory and gave it to Maria. "You'll be the third one to ask for that today. There was another lady earlier this morning. We're having a run on it."

"Sara, could I ask, what do you need with a reverse directory? Sorry, it's none of my business."

"I told Sara you would ask that. By the way, what is your last name? I'm Darlene."

"Well, Darlene, my name is Doug McDermott and I'm pleased to meet you. And Sara, can we talk somewhere when you get done? I'll find a phone booth, call Tom, I mean, Mr. O, and we can all catch up. By the way, did you know that Maria is no longer in a coma? She's in a rehab facility and soon will be just like new."

"I hadn't heard. I'm staying at the Catholic Home while I finish my schooling. I graduate soon and then will move out in August when I turn eighteen."

"Well, maybe when Maria is better all four of us can have dinner sometime. I know they would like that."

"I'd like that, too. I'll let you know when I can get a sitter and I don't have any homework. Glad to hear Maria will be all right."

As he walked out to his truck, Doug thought, *I wonder what she wants from the reverse directory. And what is she up to? I'll just stay here and see where she goes from here. And who used it earlier this morning? I wonder who that could be.*

He didn't have long to wait. Sara came out of the library in about fifteen minutes. Doug slouched down in his truck until she was in her car and moving. He thought, *the first time in a while to use my skills in tailing a car.* He learned that skill and others a number of years before at the Agency. He was still one of their off-the-book assets.

He followed with some vehicles between them until she turned into a street in North Muskegon that Doug knew. He had just looked it up. It was the address of George Anderson of the Group of Nine. She didn't go into the driveway but continued on past a house or two and sat looking at the house. Doug went on by and found a spot where he could watch her and be ready to follow again. Sara started up again, passed where Doug was sitting, and went on up toward Scenic Drive. Doug followed, thinking, *I'll bet I know where she is headed now. It would be to the other address listed for George Anderson.* He followed her to the second address and waited while she sat checking it out. She turned around and headed back. He followed her next to the Catholic home. Doug drove by but committed the location to memory. He headed home wondering, *just what is this woman up to and is there someone I should tell.*

8

When Sara left his office, the chief called George Anderson and asked, "What can I do for you, George? I'm not sure I should be talking with you without your attorney."

George asked him, "What are you doing about whoever is killing all these men from our group? What are you going to do about protection for the rest of us? Our attorney will be calling you to set up a meeting to raise the same questions. Well, what about it?"

"Now just calm down, George. By the way, how did you know there are three gone? The information about the third one hasn't been released to the paper yet."

"I still have my sources, Jim. They keep me well informed. I'm asking you again, when are you going to get us some police protection? Our attorney, Mr. Evans, is seeing the district attorney about it as we speak and will be calling you shortly."

"George, would you do something for me? Call the others in your group and tell them I'll have an answer as soon as I talk to the district attorney and your attorney. We plan to have a protection detail for each of you. I'll be bringing all six of you in to stay here Friday night, so you'll be safe. The protection detail should start Saturday morning if I can get everything worked out."

George answered, "All right, Jim. We'll do it your way. But I'm not coming to stay in your jail. By the way, I'll be calling you from a different number when I call you back sometime tomorrow. I'm going into hiding until I hear from you."

"You're not leaving town, are you?"

"No, Jim, I'm not about to leave town and lose all that bail money. All the money we made so far is legal and above board, purchases and sales of properties, so we are looking to get it back when this mess is cleaned up. If I end up in prison, my family will need it. Just call me as soon as you can. I'll just be up at our cabin on Scenic Drive. Let me give you the address and phone number. Our housekeeper will be at the house in the morning if you need anything else."

He hung up. Jim sat thinking. *That's the first I've heard anything about legality of the money being held as bail. I'd better call some people to find out.* He hit the buzzer and asked Gerri to come in.

"Gerri, I need to make some phone calls. Would you get them for me in this order — DA Harvey Swensen, Judge McVie, and Al Svenson, the new interim mayor? Then will you call the members of the task force? We have to meet again on Friday. Early afternoon would be good. This can't wait..."

Within five minutes, Gerri transferred the first call to his office. "Good morning, Harvey, we have a situation. We now have three members of the Group killed by person or persons unknown. The task force is back to work on the murders. The rest of the Group is demanding police protection. Do you see any legal problems with that? And also, the heirs of those who are now dead are asking for the bail money. What are the legal concerns with that?"

"No, I don't see any legal problems with the police protection. If you need some temporary funds for new temp officers, the city council might need to get into that. You might want to talk to the judge about all that. By the way, Evans, the Group of Nine attorney, just left, so he'll be calling you soon."

"He's on my list to call. I was thinking we ought to have a meeting with him, Judge McVie, and you to talk about all of this."

Jim continued, "I'm calling the interim mayor today. He will know if there is a fund somewhere that can be tapped for the extra help. Is your schedule open to a meeting?"

"I don't have any trials going on, so I can be flexible enough. So, it will be a meet with you, the Judge, Evans, and me. Right?"

"Right. I'll have Gerri let your secretary know the day and time."

The next caller was Harold Evans. "Chief Johnson, what is happening to get my clients' protection solved?"

"Harold, it's Jim, please. We might as well be friends while we try to work through this. I'll be talking to Judge McVie this afternoon and I just talked to the district attorney. I'm also talking with Al Svenson to get funding for the protection details. I hope to have that all worked out this afternoon and the details can be in place by Saturday morning. In the meantime, I want to make sure the rest of the Group is safe, so I'm inviting, insisting, that they spend the night in the police station for their protection on Friday night.

"We also have another issue to discuss — the bail funds for those who are now dead. We need to figure out when, and whether, we can release the funds to their families.

"And, if you haven't heard, the task force has been reinstated and is hard at work to find out who is responsible for the killings. Is your schedule open to a meeting with us tomorrow?"

"We do have a lot to discuss. When do you think it will be?"

"My hope, Harold, is tomorrow or the day after at the latest. I'll have Gerri let your secretary know."

"Thanks, Jim, for your efforts. I look forward to hearing from you."

Gerri popped in. "Judge McVie has about ten minutes if you call right now. He is on a short recess."

"Shift the interim mayor, Al, to the last call and get the Judge. And thanks, Gerri."

Judge McVie asked, "Jim, what's going on that is so important?"

He told the Judge what had been happening and outlined what

he thought were the two primary questions. He also said he had assumed all should be at the meeting.

"I appreciate you thinking ahead about that. The four of us will be all we need. I have some time tomorrow morning so we could meet for two hours or so. Will you come here?"

"We will see you at nine tomorrow morning. I'll let the others know."

The phone rang for the last call. Jim said, "Thanks, Al, for returning my call." He outlined the problem and need for extra police as a protection detail. "Would you check with whoever to see if we can find funds and, on this end, I will start looking for people to fill temp positions? Thanks, Al."

9

Bob was home a day early from college. He called Sister Charlotte first thing and was told that Sara wasn't there but would be leaving at 7:30 a.m. for a half day at school tomorrow morning. If he wanted to catch her before she left, he would have to get there early.

Sara left the Home for what might be her last time there. Much depended on what happened this morning. Sara left for school about 7:15. It was a good thing that Bob got there a little early. He just pulled up to park when she got into her car. He watched her drive away. She was so focused that she didn't notice Bob's car. He quickly reversed out of the parking lot to follow Sara to school to talk to her about their future. *I just want to see her for a few minutes this morning and set up a lunch date.*

Sara stopped by a pay phone, made a phone call, and then continued off toward North Muskegon. Bob thought, *this isn't the way to school.* He was so intent on his mission and not being caught that he didn't notice the pickup truck that was following him.

Doug, in the pickup truck, had been waiting since 7:00 a.m. to see if he could figure out what Sara was up to. Now he was following two vehicles, neither of which was aware of him. He thought, *that looks like Bob Fowler in that second car. I wonder what the two of them are doing.* When Sara stopped at the phone booth, he saw the second car pull over, so he cruised slowly by and parked in the drugstore lot just beyond the phone booth. Sara made a call, got back in her car, and continued on Ruddiman Road toward Lake Michigan. Bob followed her with one car between them. Doug let two more cars go by, then he pulled out.

When the caravan arrived in North Muskegon, Sara turned right on E. Circle Drive, followed it until it turned into W. Circle Drive, then stopped a short distance away from George Anderson's home. She waited, and ten minutes later George came out and headed towards Scenic Drive. George didn't notice Sara's car as she lagged behind him several car lengths.

When George Anderson reached the driveway to his cabin, he drove right on in. Doug and Sara knew this was the driveway for George's cabin on Scenic Drive. Sara pulled into the driveway and cut the motor. She was just sitting in the car when Bob went past and parked on the roadside just past the driveway. He quickly jogged back to where Sara was parked and hid in the trees to see what she was doing. He arrived just in time to see Sara get out and retrieve a rifle from a hiding place under the back seat. Sara made sure the gun was loaded and was standing there looking down the driveway with the rifle in a hunting position but hadn't moved yet.

Doug saw Bob jogging, so he stopped a little further down, grabbed his handgun from the glove compartment, and quietly hustled back to George's driveway. He was in position to see both Sara and Bob. Doug was as startled to see Sara with the rifle as Bob. It was obvious that Bob hadn't known about the rifle.

Bob walked into the open. Sara heard his footsteps and started to lift the rifle. "Sara!" She jumped at Bob's voice. He kept coming, reached her side, but didn't try to take the rifle from her. She lowered the rifle down. He continued softly, "What are you going to do with this rifle?"

She teared up. "Bob, I might have shot you. How did you get here?"

Bob said, "Don't cry or move, Sara. I'm here for you. I was outside the Home and when you took off, I decided to follow you to school so we could talk. I didn't know what was going on when you didn't head to school, so I kept following you. What are you thinking? Again, what are you doing with the rifle?"

She burst into tears and said, "George Anderson killed Dad and I'm going to shoot him."

"Sara, listen to me. You can't do that. You can't take the law into your own hands. What about Arianna, what about me...and our marriage?"

Now Sara was sobbing. Bob said, "Sara, please, put the gun down on the ground."

"I just couldn't do it. Here, take it. I couldn't... I was about to put it back when you showed up."

Doug stepped out of his hiding spot behind them and as they both gaped at him, he walked over to Sara, held out his hand, and took the rifle from her. Sara sobbed even harder now. Bob took her in his arms, and she sobbed as if her heart was broken. When she quieted, they both looked at Doug. She asked, "Mr. McDermott. What...how..."

"Sara, I've been watching over you. Think of me as your guardian angel."

"Why? I don't understand."

"What addresses do you think I was looking up in that reverse directory? I've been suspicious of George for some time now. You know that Tom and I are good friends, and we talk about a lot of things. Tom doesn't tell me more than he knows is okay, but I put some things together and here I am."

Doug continued, "Now, I think we should get out of here and find a nice warm restaurant. We can talk about all this and figure out what to do."

"Am I going to be in trouble? And what about my rifle?"

"I'll stow it for now. When we have our dinner with Tom, I'll give it back. And as to trouble, that's what we are going to talk ab—"

They all heard the three quick shots from the direction of

George's cabin. Bob said, "Somebody else must be out here with a rifle."

Doug was quick. "That's not a rifle, it's a handgun. Get out of here. Whoever that is, he will be charging out of this driveway pretty soon and we don't want to be here. Just follow me, we'll go back toward North Muskegon, but we'll turn off first before we get down there. A left onto River Road will take us to old U.S. 31. Just keep following me, there's a little place on the corner of Lake Street and Whitehall Road. I know the owners — they'll give us some privacy. We'll talk this through."

Doug started back to his car at a jog. "I just heard a car start up. Sara, back out of the driveway, pull over on the side of the road like you're looking for wildflowers or something. Wait until you see my pickup, then follow me. Come on, we're parked at the same roadside park just around the corner. Hurry now!"

A half hour later they were settled at a booth in a back corner. They ordered some coffee and breakfast. While waiting, Bob asked, "Okay now, we know there is more to you than being a teacher. Tell us who you really are, Doug."

Doug grinned. "Why, I'm just a high school orchestra conductor."

They laughed nervously. Doug smiled. "You're right. There is more. I love my orchestra and the students in it. But I've had a few other careers before I started teaching. I can't tell you everything but here it is. Before coming to MHS, I was for several years an asset for a government agency — I can't tell you their name. But you can't say anything to anyone about me. In time, I think I will have to tell Chief Johnson about my past, but even then, I won't tell him everything. I can't...the agency has a strict code of secrecy."

Doug dropped all levity and said seriously, "Now here's the hard part for the two of you. Listen carefully, you were never there, never out on Scenic Drive this morning. Can you do that?"

"But that's not true. And there are three vehicles tracks and three sets of footprints."

"No, you see, I'm going back out there and under some pretense or other, I will clean up all the tire tracks and pick up anything you may have dropped. You were never there! Understand? Never. I just happened to get here at the same time you did. We decided to have breakfast together."

Doug went on. "Why are you here, Bob? Aren't you still in classes at MSU?"

"I am, but I asked permission to come here today. I only missed two classes and I'm doing okay in them. I told them I was on a special surprise mission to see Sara and my daughter, Arianna."

Bob stammered, "But what are we going to tell Sister Charlotte if she asks if I caught you at school? I talked to her last night, and she told me you were going to school early. I tried to get there before you left but I just missed you."

Doug cautioned, "You just need to get your story straight and make sure you stick to it. Can you do that?"

When they both nodded, he said, "Sara, you saw Bob behind you, you stopped and decided to skip and have an early breakfast here. And you just happened to run into me. And so, we all decided to have breakfast together."

Relieved, they both relaxed a little. But Sara still had a question about the morning and the possible death of Mr. Anderson. "How do we handle that?"

"Just act surprised. I repeat, no one will ever know anything different."

"One more thing, Bob, you said this was a surprise visit. I heard one word out there that popped out in your conversation."

Sara smiled. "I heard it too. What about that, Bob?"

"Doug, would you mind getting three orange juices?" As Doug hurried away, Bob slipped a little box out of his pocket, opened it toward Sara, got down on one knee, asked, "Sara, will you marry me?"

"Yes!"

Then they were standing, hugging, and Doug shouted to the owners, "How about that! My friends just got engaged."

"We could celebrate with a toast. Is that what the orange juice is for, Bob?"

"I think neither of you is old enough for alcohol. Congratulations on your engagement."

While Doug was paying the bill, the couple was back at the table holding hands. Doug returned and said, "I'm seeing Tom later today, but I'm not saying anything except I bumped into you two skipping school and decided to have breakfast together. Here's my phone number. Why don't you call me? We'll find another time to talk next week. Maria isn't strong enough yet, but we four can meet. Okay?"

10

Doug watched them leave, smiling at their happiness. *They'll be busy for a while.* He went back north to a farm store they passed on the way in. He bought four small barrels and a rake. He drove back to the entrance to George's cabin. He wanted to go back and take a look around. He thought, *maybe I didn't latch the tailgate well enough, and it popped open, the barrels rolled out.* That would be his story if anyone saw him. He heard nothing from the direction of the cabin. He wanted to go back there, but that would be too much to explain to the chief.

He lowered the tailgate of the truck, rolled the barrels out at various locations near the driveway. He took the rake out and erased Sara's car tracks with a sideways motion of the rake. He was about to do Bob's tracks when he heard a car approaching. He grabbed one of the barrels and threw it into the bed of the truck as the car went by. The driver waved and went on.

He erased Bob's footprints and put one more barrel in the truck. Taking his rake, he walked back through the woods to where he and Bob had parked and erased their tire tracks. He loaded the last two barrels and rake into the truck, closed the latch, and headed home by the same route as that morning.

When he was home, he called Maria's room at the rehab center, identified himself, and asked how Maria was doing. When they wanted to know more about him, he said, "I'm the orchestra conductor at Muskegon High School, I worked closely with both Maria and Tom."

Maria's aide exclaimed, "Yes, Doug, I've heard them talking about you. Maria is asleep right now and Tom left for the police station. He said he would be there most of the afternoon."

"Thank you. I'll try there."

Doug called the police station and asked for the chief. Gerri responded, "He's in a meeting right now and asked not to be disturbed."

Doug asked, "I was told at the rehab center that Tom would be there."

"He is. He is in the meeting."

"Would you ask him to call Doug when he is finished, please? Thank you."

"You're welcome, Mr. McDermott."

WHEN GEORGE GOT to the cabin, he parked in the carport and entered the side door. The minute he walked in he felt that something was different, almost like a presence or something. He had a handgun that he kept in a kitchen cupboard and felt he better get it before he started looking around. He walked into the kitchen and there was Anna Olsen standing on the other side of the table. She had a gun pointed at him, safety off. He said, "Anna, what are you doing here with that gun? Anna, just put it down and let's talk."

"How did you know I would be coming up here?"

"I called your housekeeper yesterday and asked if I could come this morning and talk to you. I told her I had some good news and wanted to surprise you. She said you were leaving the house for the weekend and that you would be back on Monday morning. I put two and two together and here I am."

Anna went on, "George, you and I are going to talk. I have some questions. You can just stay right where you are. I found your gun and emptied out the bullets, even the one in the chamber. And don't think about moving --I really can shoot. Larry made sure I know how to use a gun and a few other things. He thought it might come to this someday. He was right."

She continued, "Better still, sit down on the floor over there, back against the wall under the wall phone. And don't try to reach for that phone, I've cut the line already. Go ahead, sit down."

"Now, George, I got here pretty early, and I looked around. And guess what, there is a pickup truck out there with a damaged wooden front bumper with some missing pieces. It was just like Chief Johnson said when he called me to tell me Larry had been run off the road. Somebody killed him and it was you, George."

George interrupted, "I had to do something. I could tell Larry was weakening and might lose it. Then I got word that he was getting ready to leave town. I have sources all over and I couldn't take a chance. When I caught up with him at the gas station, I figured I could do it and not have to hurt you or the children."

"How thoughtful of you George. Didn't you think we would be hurt when he died? We just wanted to leave and never come back. You didn't let us. I lost my husband, and my girls have no dad. Ah, ah, ah, just sit still. I'm a good shot, Larry made sure of that."

"Anna, I can make it worth your while. How much do you want to just go away?"

"Don't call me Anna. I don't want your money. One more thing. What about poor Joe Antonelli? Larry told me he thought you were getting suspicious of Joe. Were you the one who poisoned him? Clever of you to use different methods on each of them."

"Yes, I did Joe. He was falling apart and then he turned on all of us. He deserved it. I need to get on my feet. I'm not comfortable on this floor."

He struggled to get up and just as he did, she fired three shots, a quick two in the heart area and a few seconds later, the last one in his forehead. He fell back down where he had been sitting. Mrs. Olsen waited for a long time and when he didn't move, she checked his pulse. She took the note out of her purse. It was made of plain white paper and with cut out letters on it. She quickly wrote something on the back of the note. She put the note on the kitchen table with the saltshaker holding it down. She went around the kitchen wiping down any place she might have touched, including the saltshaker and the doorknob at the back door where she had broken the window and made her way in.

Leaving by the way she came in, she brushed her footsteps and vanished into the woods. It was a bit of a hike to the entrance to Duck Lake Park where she left her car — no one would ever think to look there.

When Tom called, he was still at the station. Doug asked, "Tom, I need to talk with you. Can I come for dinner tonight? I have some things I need to talk about. I'll bring Doo Drop takeout."

"Sounds great, Doug. I'll stop at the rehab facility on my way home. Make it about 7:00 p.m. and I'll have some beer or wine, your choice. I can catch you up on how Maria is doing. She is making remarkable progress. See you at 7:00."

Doug walked in on time with perch, French fries, and onion rings. Tom said, "I have a good white wine chilling or beer. Which is your preference?"

"The wine sounds great. There's that good jazz station again."

"It is. What's up with you?"

"Tell me how Maria is doing while we get dinner on the table. You said good progress?"

Tom smiled. "She is sounding more and more like herself every day. Her voice is slowly getting stronger, she is walking with the cane about ten yards down the hall and then back. Her aide is with her, pushing her feeding and medication IVs. If she has any distance to go, to a test or something, they take her in a wheelchair. The doctor says that will continue for a few more days. She is still weak but improving every day. She said to tell you hi and she'll be looking for you when you can come by sometime."

"That's sounds terrific. Give her my best, please."

They toasted Maria's progress and started in on the perch and fries. Doo Drop was always the best. After they were well into the meal, Doug said, "I heard you were back to work on the task force again. What's going on?"

"No, you don't. I'll tell you before you leave. I need to hear what you were so anxious to talk about when you called this afternoon."

"After we clean up, can we take our wine in the living room? Then I'll get started on my stories."

Tom topped off their wine glasses and they settled in by the fireplace.

Doug turned to him. "There are two separate but related things to tell you. I'm leaving the high school. I've already told John Mann, the principal, and he told the superintendent. They are posting the job all over the state and don't think they'll have any problem replacing me. I'll finish the semester and graduation and then leave sometime in late summer or early fall before school starts."

"When did you decide this and why didn't you talk to me about it? And what are you going to do?"

"Hang on, Tom. I'll answer all your questions. I haven't told you before since I only made the decision a week or so ago. You were pretty busy with Maria waking up and I didn't want to add to your load. You just told me that she is going to be as good as new soon, so now it is time. I didn't talk to you before for much the same reasons."

"So, why now?"

"Part of the why is what Maria said to both of us when they let you go. Muskegon High School isn't the same without both of you. By the way, congrats on finishing your master's degree in conducting."

"Thanks, I'm glad it's done. It will make our search to find something where both of us can teach easier. So, what's the other part of why?"

Taking a sip of his wine, Doug went on. "You know I was in the military but what you don't know is that after my two-year enlistment was up, I won a spot as a special services soldier. I spent two years with them, the first six months being trained at The Farm as it is sometimes called."

"Isn't The Farm a part of the CIA or the FBI or something like that?"

"I can't say. Secrecy agreements and all that. Anyway, I spent the next year and a half on various overseas assignments. I took to it and made a good record. They didn't want me to leave. But when I persisted, I was told that some people wanted to talk to me. Long story short, I signed up for another two years as an asset for one of the agencies. Again, I can't tell you who it is. They sent me back to The Farm for another six months of advanced training. I was an asset, well paid, by the way, and actually stayed on for six years.

"During my first two-year enlistment, I also got my master's in orchestra conducting and led the Army band on my base. So, I decided, in my early thirties, that it was time for a quieter life and maybe a family, and I wanted to teach. Next thing you know, I was at Muskegon High School having a great time with students. It was just what I needed and wanted. Then first Maria showed up and you a year or two later, my life was made. I had the quieter life but no wife and family."

"Doug, I always noted how you took in a room and were aware of what was going on around you. I kind of figured out that you had some training that built that habit. But what's the reason for leaving now?"

"Part of my training was to stay aware of what was going on in the world that might open up to a mission. So, I became an insatiable reader of foreign affairs news. The Cuban Missile crisis was last November, so I was on the alert. Then I read about what was starting to stir up in East Asia, specifically in Vietnam. The next thing you should know is that the agency called. They wanted me back. I was adamant at first that I was happy where I was and out of shape. I told them that I would think about it and asked what was happening in Vietnam. They started sending me data on that situation and I got another phone call last spring near graduation. I took a trip out there during the summer. The trip to see my parents was an excuse to get out of town. I wasn't ready to talk to anyone here yet. We had some long talks at the agency about Vietnam and other hot spots that I didn't know about. So, I told them I wanted another school year to think about it. Then in the fall, things started heating up, you and Maria were in danger. I told them I couldn't leave while you needed me. Now that things are getting better..." He stopped when he caught Tom's expression. "What's up, buddy?"

"Things have busted loose again. We now know that three of the nine are dead, murdered by shootings, poisoning, and being pushed off into a lake. We are trying to figure out how to protect the rest until we can get them to trial. And all the time we are waiting for the next shoe to drop."

"Does Maria know you are back on the task force?"

"Yes, she does and, for some reason that I can't figure out yet, is in favor of it."

"That's a big change for her."

"It is, but I can't talk to her more about that until she is a lot better. So, mum's the word when you see her."

"I'm going to tell Jim, the chief, about my background. There may be some way I can help. It may be just keeping you alive and that's enough. You are on that list — along with the rest of the Group. Any chance Maria's in danger? You know I would protect you both."

"I'm sure Jim will welcome your help especially if you tell him about all your experience. I don't think Maria's in danger, but I'm keeping a close eye on her. Are you ready to see Maria yet?"

"Not yet. Let's wait until she is stronger. Just tell her I'm so glad she is doing well. And keep my background quiet until I talk to the chief."

12

Monday morning, 8:00 a.m. sharp, Doug walked into the police station. He went to Gerri, introduced himself, and asked if he might have a few minutes with the chief this morning. "I don't have an appointment, but it is important. He knows me and that I'm Tom O'Banion's friend. I could wait or come back when he's available."

"He's reviewing his schedule for today and planning the week ahead. His first appointment isn't until 9:00 a.m. If you could wait for twenty minutes or so, he might be able to fit you in. I'll alert him that you are here. Can I get you some coffee?"

"That would be great. Black, please. And thank you for working me in."

Gerri got his coffee and buzzed the chief. "Jim, there is a Doug McDermott here who says you know him as Tom's friend. He would like to have a short talk with you."

"I'll be with him in ten minutes. Thanks, Gerri."

Jim came out a few minutes later. "Doug, come on in."

After closing the door, he said, "Well, Doug, what's up? What about school?"

"I called them to let them know I would be there just before second hour. They'll cover for my first hour. Thanks for seeing me, Chief."

"Please call me Jim. Let's have it."

"Okay, Jim. Tom and I were talking last Friday night. He filled me in as much as he thought he could. I told him what I'm going to tell you." He handed his agency creds over.

"This looks official, Doug. What agency is it?"

"I can't tell you that, Jim. It changes depending on who I am working with at the moment." He went on with the story he had told Tom, his years of experience, his skills, and finally that he had planned to return to that life last year. "But when the mayor was killed, then Tom and Maria were shot, I couldn't leave my friends until this thing with the Group of Nine was done with. I will be going active again next summer assuming it is settled by then."

"Why are you telling me all this now, Doug?"

"I want to help however I can. I'm not trained as a detective, but I have skills that I've developed over the years through training and experience. I'm going to be protecting Tom and Maria no matter what. Mr. Mann knows that I'm leaving in the fall and the board is already looking for my replacement for next fall. If I need to, I'll leave sooner and let them fill in with a substitute. The board agreed to that if it is needed. So, Jim, here I am. How can I help?"

"Talk about manna from heaven. I can use you. I'll bill you as a consultant to oversee the protection of the remaining five members of the Group. That way, you can keep an eye on your friends as you oversee the protection detail. I'm working on getting funds for that detail from the city, so maybe I can pay you something too."

"Expenses will be enough. Do you have the men for the detail yet?"

"Not yet, but I have a list of retired police officers from all the communities around here. It will be easy to find enough. A group of us met with Judge McVie last week and have all the legalities worked out. By the way, are you armed?"

"I have military handguns and a military rifle. I hope I won't need all the ammunition I have. All of this is securely locked up in a military installed lockbox in my pickup. I can show you the registrations if you need me to."

"You won't need that. I'm amazed that you have kept this quiet. Why now?"

"I'm military through and through and we don't leave friends who need us. That's what it comes down to. I think presenting me as a consultant in the protection business is a good idea. I've got to keep my agency connections under wraps."

"No problem. We'll make sure that is kept secret. I would like to introduce you to the task force members at a meeting this afternoon." His buzzer sounded. He picked up the phone and Gerri said, "Chief, you better take this call. It's George Anderson's housekeeper, Mrs. Martin, and she is quite upset."

"Hello, this is Chief Johnson, Mrs. Martin. How can I help you?"

"Mr. Johnson, I'm concerned. Mr. Anderson left Friday morning and said if anyone called that he would be close by but would be back early this morning. I've called the cabin where I thought he might be but there is no answer. I'm really worried about him. Mrs. Anderson is out of town visiting her sister, but I don't want to bother her yet."

"Mrs. Martin, thank you for calling. Let us take care of it. We'll get right on it and let you know what we find out. You just stay there, do your work, and if we haven't called you by this afternoon, please call my secretary, Gerri, and let us know where we can find you. We'll call when we have something."

He buzzed Gerri and she stepped into his office. "Gerri, get Mark for me please and get me the address for George's cabin. It's in his file. Oh, and Doug here is going to be working with us part time in a special role. Please get his contact info before he leaves. One more thing, call the number given for the cabin."

"You don't waste any time, Jim."

"I'm afraid we may have another member of the Group in trouble."

Gerri came back into the office. "There's no ring through on that phone. It's like it isn't connected. And Mark is on his way."

Doug stood up. "Jim, I need to get to school."

"Gerri, please call the task force members and have them in for a meeting later this afternoon. We may have another situation to deal with. And, Doug, why don't you drop by on your way home."

13

Jim briefed Mark on the phone call from George's housekeeper. "It may be nothing except that the phone wasn't working right according to her. We'd better check it out. Take a patrol officer with you. Don't go through North Muskegon. One of their patrol cars might spot you and wonder why you are in their city. Find an alternate route from Old Highway 31. Check it out on the big county map, but my recollection is that his cabin on Scenic Drive is out past the state park and before Duck Lake. I'll make some calls and find out who has jurisdiction. I would like to know what is happening before the press gets wind of it. And Mark, I have one more thing to tell you. I have been thinking that I need a second-in-command. As of today, you have been promoted to Lieutenant. Your new responsibilities and increased pay start now. Pick yourself a man to take with you and check this out."

"I don't know what to say except thank you. I appreciate your confidence in me."

Mark picked Officer Don Phillips, a newly pinned Sargent, and filled him in on the details. They checked the address on a large county map and got a general idea where the house was. "It looks like the cabin is before the Duck Lake Park entrance. The residents out on

Scenic Drive usually have the house numbers well displayed. We'll go up Old U.S. 31 and pick up Scenic Drive north from there. Let's go."

After they passed the state park entrance, they slowed down and watched the numbers. "Mark, we're getting close. There it is. No gate and it's a gravel driveway. I wonder how far back it is."

Mark stopped at the entrance, "Don, let's each take a side, watch for anything that doesn't look natural. We'll take it slow. It's pretty damp out here, must have been some showers — we didn't have any where I live. It might wipe out any tracks, but we could get lucky. We should have our guns ready. No telling what we will find."

After about a quarter of a mile in, they saw the cabin. The driveway curved around so one didn't have to back up and turn around. Don said, "That looks like a small house instead of a cabin. There's a car in the carport."

Mark added, "And there's a pickup here in a turnoff. We'll check them both out later." They stopped, took out their guns and walked up to the front entrance. Mark knocked, knocked a second time, and finally shouted, "Police officers, open up." No response. He checked the door. Locked.

Mark motioned Don to follow and watch their backs. They approached the entrance from the carport and Mark knocked on this door and repeated, "Police, open up." Again, the door was locked. The way to the back was blocked by a lot of shrubbery — if there was another door back there, it would be hard to get to.

Looking in through the windows in the door revealed nothing. They returned to the front and followed a path around to the back on the other side to see an elevated deck facing the lake. Going up the stairs to the deck, Mark approached the door. "Don, be ready. The glass window on the back door is broken. Someone came in through here."

Each took a side, knocked again, and called out. Nothing. Mark tried the knob. The door opened, they went in, Mark first, Don to the other side, guns at the ready. The first thing they noticed was the odor. Mark said, "Over there, on the floor by the phone, he's been dead a while now. Let's check the rest of the house."

One at a time, they checked both bedrooms, the living room, and bathrooms. "All clear, Don. That fits with what the housekeeper said that he was alone. Mrs. Anderson is visiting a sister somewhere out of town. Let's walk the perimeter again, check out the vehicles. Let's stay on the cobblestone path that we came back here on. Rain probably wiped out footprints. But let's be careful about it."

They went all the way around to the carport, felt the car hood, cold. Also locked. Then both went together to the clearing where the truck was parked. It, too, was cold. Mark noted that the truck had a thick wood front bumper. After checking it out, he said, "We may have found the vehicle that Larry Olsen was pushed off the road with. We'll see what the forensics says."

He continued, "Back into the house to check the phone out."

As they walked back on the cobblestone path, Don said, "Look here, Mark. The phone feed has been cut near where it goes through the wall."

"You might make detective someday if you keep picking up details like that. This was done carefully so that even if George came in around this way, he wouldn't have seen it. I'm surprised you did. Nice work."

Mark continued, "Let's get back inside, I want to have a better look at the body. At first glance it appeared that there was more than one shot."

They entered off the deck again and approached the body. Mark told Don, "Look here, there were three shots, two grouped closely on the left side, probably got the heart with one or both, and the third one was right in the center of the forehead. Not much blood from the head shot. It could have been delayed from the other two. Whoever did this is a good shot."

"I wonder if he was trying to get to the phone when he was shot."

"Good observation, but I don't think so. See he looks like he was sitting here, tried to get up and got shot for his trouble. The head shot was likely from anger and making sure he was dead. Again, we'll see what the forensics team says. Now, Don, you have a decision."

"What's that?"

"Do you want to stay here while I make a call from a pay phone? You okay with that, or would you rather make the call?"

"You don't have a police radio in your unmarked car?"

"I do, but I don't want to use it. We need to get some more people out here before we take a chance with somebody hearing the call on a scanner."

"I'll be okay. You go ahead and make your call. Mark, look here, on the kitchen table. A note held down by the saltshaker. It has funny printing on it."

"Good eye, Don. Don't touch it." Mark made a mental note of what it said.

Mark went on, "I suggest you take one of these deck chairs with you and camp out on the front stoop. You've got a good field of vision and with the door unlocked now, you'll be able to get back into the house if anyone but me shows up."

Mark drove back to the Red Rooster Tavern. He knew there was a pay phone outside. He and his wife were there for a country music show a while back. They often had good groups playing here.

14

"Gerri, Mark here. I need to talk to the chief right now. We have another body out here."

"He's on the phone with the interim mayor. I'll get him right off and get you on."

She buzzed the chief, then knocked on the door. She heard the chief say, "Excuse me for a second, Al. I'll get right back to you."

Gerri put a note in front of him. "Mark has another body and is holding for you."

"Al, that's good news about the funds. I'll call you back tomorrow for details. We have a situation here, so I have to go. Thank you, Al." Jim hit the button for the other line. "Mark, what's up? Are you on a safe phone?"

"Yes, I am, Chief. This is the pay phone outside the Red Rooster Bar. Jim, George Anderson is dead. He took two bullets in the heart and for good measure one in the middle of his forehead."

"Sounds like someone was angry and wanted to make sure he was gone."

"I think that as well. Here's the other thing, there was another note made like the first. This one said, 'Number four. Getting closer, do you feel it, Tom?' And another thing, George has a pickup truck parked out there with a dinged-up wood front bumper. When the forensic people get to it, we may find George was the one who pushed Larry into the lake.

"There's more, Jim. But it can wait. We need to get a lot of people out here fast before there is a leak to the press. Do you know who has jurisdiction out here?"

"It is the county sheriff department. They are open to letting us continue as first agency on it since it pertains to a case we're working on. We'll see how that goes. I'm sure we'll get along fine. We'll have the state police forensic team as we did with the others."

"Jim, I better get back with Don. This is a first for him in this situation. He's doing great."

"You know what to do, Mark. We'll have you some help within the next half hour or so."

~

MARK WENT BACK down the driveway. Don was sitting on the front stoop, gun out until he saw that it was Mark.

"Anything going on, Don?"

"Not a thing."

"Let's get some yellow tape around the scene. We'll put a ring around the house including the carport and the deck. Then we'll put another ring around the pickup truck. The rain likely washed out any tracks, but we still have to check. So, we want to protect anything that might be there."

They had just finished the second side and were about to go back to the house when the first squad car showed up followed by the coroner in his hearse.

The coroner asked, "Is there room for me to turn around or should I back in?"

Mark introduced himself and Don. "You can drive straight in. There is a circular driveway in the front of the house. Let's get this done before too many others come."

The hearse stopped just past the front stoop. Mark said, "Just follow me in, Doc. The body is in the kitchen."

The coroner got right to work. He made notes of the placement of the three shots, noting to Mark, "There's a lot of blood from the chest on down to the floor. Not much from the head. That likely means that the first two shots, maybe even the first, killed him. The heart stopped pumping after it emptied itself out. The head had no blood left to bleed out."

Mark jumped in. "I kind of figured that time spacing of the shots. This was a pretty good marksman. Do you have any idea when he was shot?"

"When the heart emptied out, the rest of the blood in the upper chest drained by gravity and so ended all around him on the floor. On the time question, my estimate until I get him to the lab, is sometime today, probably quite early in the morning."

"That fits with what his housekeeper told us. She said that he left early this morning and likely went straight here. The killer must have been waiting for him. We found where he broke the door glass on the back door and reached in to unlock it. His killer probably was in the kitchen where the side door from the carport comes in. George likely made a move to the phone, but the killer had already cut the wires to the phone. We think the killer made him sit on the floor so they could talk. When George tried to get up, I suppose to fight back, he was shot."

The coroner said, "That's some analysis, Mark. The only thing you might have missed is the angle of the bullets."

"How do you mean?"

"There is a slight upward slant to the path of the bullet. Again, I'll know better in the lab. If it is true, then George got all the way up on his feet and he's a tall man. I'm five foot ten and when I met him, he stood a good two or three inches taller than me."

"That means that the killer was a short man."

"That's good, Mark. But there is another possibility. A woman may have done this."

"Now that complicates things. I would never have thought of that. How long will it take you to verify it?"

"If I can get out of here in the next half hour, I can have it for you early afternoon."

"Okay, Doc. Tell me what I can do to help you. I already have pictures of the way we found him, so that much is done. I hear someone else outside. I'd better see who it is."

"Help me get the body laid down and I can do the rest until it's time to carry him out."

They laid him out parallel to the wall the phone was on. Mark took the time to put the note in an evidence envelope, put it in his pocket, and went outside. Don was talking to someone from the sheriff's office and other cars were coming down the driveway.

Don told Mark, "This is a patrol officer for the sheriff's department. He was cruising north of here on Scenic Drive."

After introductions, Mark asked, "Did you get a call from the sheriff on your radio?"

"Yes, I did. But your chief told him to have me find a pay phone and call in to the sheriff. He told me to get out here and let him know what was going on. Look, I know you are taking first lead on this, all I want to do is get some info for the Sheriff."

The additional cars coming down the driveway were mostly from the Muskegon Police department, but Dave Smithson was among them. Mark thought, *he's a welcome sight. We will find more clues together.*

Dave told him, "Jim thought I might be able to help, so here I am."

"Glad you are here. We'll get all these troopers walking the sides of the driveway and into the woods looking for footprints. The rain probably messed them up, but we have to look." He told Don to walk widening circles around the property doing the same thing. "The killer might have walked out to another property. We may get lucky."

They saw the coroner come out the front door. He asked, "Could I get some help now to put the body in a body bag and carry him out to the hearse?"

Mark looked at Dave. Dave nodded. "Doc, we'll do it. Have you found more that we should know now?"

"Maybe a couple of things. Wait until we get inside."

When they got to the body, Doc said, "See the position of those small sticks in the wounds. Look at the angles. I'm about ninety percent certain, the shooter was shorter than George. And notice that there are powder burns around the wound in the forehead. The killer was up close when the last bullet was fired. This killer likely was angry, probably checked his pulse, and then, for good measure, put the gun to the forehead and shot the last time."

"Our task force will be meeting at 3:00 p.m. today. Any chance your report might be done by then?" Dave asked.

Doc said, "It's 10:00 a.m. now. I can have a preliminary report to you by the time the meeting starts." He zipped up the body bag.

"Let's get you on the road."

As he drove away, Mark added, "Dave, I have things to show you." They walked out to the pickup truck and took Dave around the front. Dave took one look at the bumper with several gouges and some scrapes. "Dave, this truck is registered to George Anderson. I think he is the one who pushed Larry Olsen into the lake. We have pictures of the bumper, but we need to get both truck and car towed to the station.

"One more thing to show you, Dave. Let's go back inside and sit in the living room. I want to be ready to move back to the office as soon as Don is finished with his walk around."

"What do you have?"

"There was another note like the last one. Strange letters pasted on the paper which said, 'This makes four. Five to go plus you, Tom.'"

"Mark, why is this person so intent on getting Tom?"

"We're not sure. We're open to any and all ideas about this."

"There's something new about this note. Apparently, they had some conversation before he was shot. The killer couldn't resist writing what George said before he died, maybe before he was shot. Notice on the back of the note. Without crazy letters and paste, it was just written. With a ball point pen, the killer wrote, 'Before I shot him, he told me, he was the one who pushed Larry Olsen into the lake, and he was the man who poisoned Joe Antonelli. He kept saying he couldn't trust either one of them.'"

"Do your people have a writing analyst, someone who can tell things about handwriting?"

"We do. I can either get one up here or take the sample to Lansing."

Mark continued, "We'll let Jim make that call."

Don walked in. "Mark, there was nothing except one spot that somehow was sheltered from the rain. The print isn't very clear, but it has some distinguishing parts. We'll get a better look when we get the picture printed."

"Good work, Don. I'll be leaving with Mark soon to go the task force meeting. I'll be leaving you in charge. When they all come in and report to you, find one who can stay with you and let the rest go. Remind them not to say anything to anyone about where they have been.

"Put padlocks on all the doors. We've been pretty lucky about the press but still it might have gotten out. Once I get back to a pay phone, I'll call the chief and tell him where we stand and ask him to have someone order up two tow trucks to get the car and truck. You and whoever you pick to stay with you can leave when they do. If for some reason the tow trucks can't come until tomorrow, I'll have the dispatcher call you and send someone to relieve you. We'll see you back at the office."

15

Bob and Sara drove into the parking lot of the Home and walked to Sister Charlotte's office. When they were admitted, Sister Charlotte took one look at them and said, "Why don't you shut the door behind you and tell me what has brought all this joy to your faces?"

Sara's face was beaming. "It shows that much, Sister?"

"It does, my child. Tell me about it."

Sara went on, "Sister Charlotte, I owe you an apology. When I saw Bob behind me, I stopped to find out why he was here. When he told me he needed to see me and to talk about us and our daughter, I couldn't go on to school. So, I skipped school."

Sister Charlotte said, "I heard. They called me. So, go on."

"I called Muskegon High School and asked for Mr. Doug McDermott. He's the high school orchestra conductor. I bumped into him at Hackley Library when I was there doing research. He told me then if I would like to talk to him or Mr. O, our choir director, to let him know. He agreed to take the day off and told us to meet him at his favorite restaurant in North Muskegon. He would buy us breakfast and listen to us. So, I parked my car in the school parking lot and rode with Bob to the restaurant."

"Someone at school saw you pick up your car this afternoon. Go on."

"The owners, Doug knows them well, fixed us a grand breakfast. We had a good talk. Doug could see, and told us so, that we had something going. We told him about our little girl, Arianna, and how Bob felt about her. He asked Bob why he was here and not at school in East Lansing."

Sara continued, "Bob told him he wanted to see me and had something to say to me. Doug, I mean, Mr. McDermott, asked him, 'Do you want some privacy?'"

Bob piped up, "I told him to stay right there and be a witness. Then I asked him to order us three glasses of orange juice."

Sara interrupted, "I asked Bob what he was doing. He said, 'Be patient, darling. Look, he's bringing them back.' I turned to watch Doug set the orange juice on the table and then turned back to Bob and there he was on one knee holding a ring in a plush box!"

Bob faced Sara and repeated his proposal, "Sara, will you marry me and make us the family we are supposed to be? And at the same time, make me the happiest man in the world."

Sara smiled broadly. "I asked Doug, 'Did you two set this up?' Doug told me it was all Bob's idea. That's why he came home early from college."

"Well, sweetheart? Let me hear your answer again."

Sara looked at Bob with stars in her eyes, "Yes! And next thing you know, we were hugging, Doug and the owners were applauding. We toasted our engagement with the OJ. The owner said he was pretty sure we weren't twenty-one years old yet. The applause spread to the other patrons and 'Congratulations' came from all over the restaurant."

Sister Charlotte said, "I could see it growing to that. Every time Bob took Arianna in his arms, I just knew. I had to wait until you found the right moment. Looks like Bob found it."

Sister Charlotte buzzed her secretary and asked her to bring Arianna to the office. She turned to Bob and Sara saying, "I think little Arianna should be a part of this celebration, don't you?"

"We should have an engagement gift for her," Sara fretted.

"That's what this bag is for. And, no, Sara, you can't see it until she gets here."

Sara said, "Dad and I were members at St. Jeans. Do you think Father Flanagan would do our pre-marriage counseling?"

Sister Charlotte replied, "I'll talk to him about it. Bob, are you of the Catholic faith?"

"I'm also a member at St. Jeans, so yes," Bob assured her.

"Have you talked about a date for your wedding?"

"Not until sometime this summer. We haven't picked a date yet. Will that give us enough time to get the wedding plans firmed up and the pre-marriage counseling done?

"I'm sure it will. Let me get to work on it."

The door opened and a nun brought Arianna to Sara. Sara said, "Daddy is here."

Arianna's whole face lit up when she saw Bob. She reached out her arms and leaned toward Bob. He took her in his arms in a big hug. "Daddy has something for you." He handed her the bag and she squealed for joy with a new white teddy bear almost as big as she was.

When things settled down, Sara told Sister Charlotte about the dinner tonight with Doug, Mr. O, Bob, and Sara, and asked if someone would be available to take care of Arianna. They were having dinner after stopping at the Rehab Center to see Maria to tell her the news. Maria couldn't come home yet but there would be plenty of time with her later.

"I need to run to see my parents. They don't even know I'm in town yet. Is there a way the three of us can have some time together tomorrow? We have so much to talk about," Bob asked.

Sister Charlotte said, "I'll have it all arranged for you when you come pick Sara up tonight."

16

The meeting room was all abuzz when the chief walked in. "Hello, everyone. All of you seem anxious, and even excited, to be working again. You already know some of the details of the fourth member of the Group, but I will summarize all of what we have when we begin. Before we start, I would like to introduce two more members of the group. First, Dave Smithson of the state police brought along their chief forensic analyst, Jeff Flanagan. Seems like we are getting a lot of Irishmen on the force. Welcome, Jeff, we need your knowledge and skills.

"The second new member is Doug McDermott. Doug and Tom here are good friends. Doug acquired a unique set of skills in the jobs he had before coming here to teach and direct Muskegon High School's orchestra. I've known Doug for some time as a friend of Tom's and a high school teacher. It was a revelation when he told me what he did before coming to Muskegon."

Jim continued, "Doug told me all this but wouldn't reveal who he worked for — you know, secrecy agreements and all. You all know the 'old saw' about that — that he'd have to kill me if he told me — so I didn't push him." Jim chuckled. "Doug will leave his job at the school and return to that life as of next fall. That is, if we have this business put to rest before then. He has already given his word that he is going to protect Tom and Maria. He's here until they are safe. I've put Doug on as a consultant who will be overseeing the protection detail for the remaining members of the Group. He can still keep his commitment to Tom and Maria to watch over them. So, welcome Doug.

"One last but important item. As of today, Mark is Lieutenant Mark Bergstrom. A well-deserved promotion, I might add." The room erupted in applause.

"I've asked Sheriff Bob Madison to be here as his office is the unit with jurisdiction of that stretch of Scenic Drive. Bob has graciously allowed us to be the unit of record since the killing relates to the Group of Nine case that we have been working on."

"Now let's get to the latest developments. Gerri finished typing up all the data that has come in from Mark and Sgt. Don Phillips. You'll have your copies of that before you leave. She is also taking notes of this meeting and will get those notes to you tomorrow early for review before Monday's meeting. Mark and Don were the first two on the scene after George Anderson's housekeeper called us this morning. We had a number of officers there later, mostly looking for footprints walking away from the cabin. The coroner was there about an hour after Mark and Don found the body. His preliminary report is being printed and you will have copies in the next half hour.

"Any questions before I start giving you my understanding of, and suspicions of, what happened?"

"None. So, here it is. The Group's attorney has been pushing for police protection ever since we let it be known that three members of the Group were dead. And now George Anderson is dead. We need to stop the killing while we try to find who is behind it. We have enough men on special hire to cover twelve-hour shifts giving us twenty-four-hour protection for each of the remaining members. Judge McVie is working on his schedule to see if some of his work can be postponed. If he could move the trial up, they might be in prison before they get killed. So, all are being picked up and spending the night in our custody here with a doubled-up shift. Tomorrow morning, Doug and I will assign two teams to each man, get them introduced so they know who their protection detail is. The goal is to get each man back home by 10:00 a.m. Saturday morning along with his 10:00 a.m. shift in place and the second shift crew coming on at 10:00 p.m.

"Now, on to details about George Anderson. I'll start off with the statement that we have no idea at this point who's doing this. We are starting from point zero. If each of the remaining members are in a cell here, they can't do anything so, if another dies tonight, that lets them out, at least directly. We know from the coroner's report that George was killed sometime early Friday. Their alibis seem to be airtight for that time period, but we'll check them out. I've read the coroner's report and here's what we know for certain. George tried to stand up, but was shot directly in the heart, two shots mind you. George just slid right back down to a sitting position. He was probably dead by the time he was on the floor. But the killer wasn't satisfied. He must have been angry since it appears he walked over to George, put his gun on George's head and shot him in the middle of his forehead. It didn't bleed much since the heart had stopped pumping. Any questions so far?"

Doug asked, "Were the first shots straight in or were they at some angle?"

"Good question, Doug. And right on the money. The coroner showed Don and me when we were at the crime scene. It was an upward angle. I don't have the actual number in my head. But what it seems to suggest is that either the killer is a short man or maybe a woman."

They all looked at each other with a question. "What motive would a woman have to kill George?"

"Maybe it is the wife of one of the others who have been killed already," Mark suggested.

"Let's not jump too soon that it might be a woman. It could be, but it also could be a short man who was hired by one of the members left."

There was a knock on the door. Sgt. Phillips came in with a blown up eight by eleven picture of a boot print. Don said, "Chief, here is a picture of a footprint I found in the woods. It was pointed away from the cabin. The other picture is a blowup of a larger area. There is some rough ground there and some stone. Whoever this was may have slipped on this rock and stepped harder than usual into the mud. Anyway, it is a good print, and it looks like a woman's boot print."

"I think you are right, Don. Good work. Do you want to stick around with us?"

"No, I have some things I have to finish before I head for home. But I thought this might be of interest to you and the task force."

"Thanks, Don. We'll see you tomorrow."

Dave murmured, "Now isn't that interesting. More evidence leading to a woman?"

"There's one more thing. There was a note, like the one we got in the mail when this thing started a few months ago. But this one has a difference. You'll notice that the upper part is made with the same crazy looking letters as the first one. But at the back, there is some handwriting that says, 'Before I shot him, he told me, he was the one who pushed Larry Olsen into the lake, and he was the man who poisoned Joe Antonelli. He kept saying he couldn't trust either one of them.'"

Jim turned to Jeff. "Do you have a handwriting expert on your forensic team?"

"We have someone we can bring in. Why do you ask?"

"Can he or she tell if the handwriting is by a man or a woman?"

Jeff replied, "Sometimes he can. If we can compare to a known sample, he could be more sure. Have each of the remaining Group members write this sentence, 'I was asked if I had gone out of the house on Friday morning and if so, where did I go.' Each man should sign the document. That will be the proof needed by their attorney that we stood by our word. And, we'll have a sample of the handwriting of each member."

"That's excellent, Jeff."

Mark asked, "Jim, are you leaning in that direction, that the killer is a woman?"

Jim replied, "Not necessarily, but I want to cover all the bases. I'll have our forensic person check it out and then send it home with you to have your people look at it. With that handwriting on the back, there might even be fingerprints."

"Now to your assignments. For all of you, please pick up your notes from the coroner, the summary of all we have at the moment, and the minutes of this meeting. Gerri will have them all done by 11:00 a.m. tomorrow. She is putting in some overtime in the morning, so they'll be ready for you then. Please read them carefully, keeping notes and questions for our next meeting, which will be at 1:00 p.m. on Monday. We need to keep moving on this."

Turning to Mark, he said, "Mark, can you be here at 9:30 a.m.? I have written permission from their attorney to ask them where they were and what were they doing if they went out. We'll each take two, then we'll switch and ask for clarification on some detail from them. Then we'll try to verify their alibis by the meeting on Monday. I'm not at all convinced that they are involved but we need to check it out. I'll be making an announcement for the papers Monday morning. We'll see what that stirs up."

"Tom, will you get your materials and do some analysis? See what comes up by the meeting on Monday. You can bounce some of this off Doug as he monitors the protection detail."

"Any questions? None, let's be ready with some on Monday."

The sheriff stayed until all were gone. "Anything we can do?"

"Have someone pick up the reports tomorrow at 11:00 a.m. And let me know if you think of anything else to do, I don't want any more lives lost here."

"Okay, Jim. Thanks for the invite to be here. I'll be in touch."

TOM AND DOUG stopped to talk by their cars. Tom asked, "Are you coming to see Maria yet?"

"Not yet, maybe on Sunday with just the two of us. Where shall we take the kids tonight?"

"How about Tony's? It'll be a good place for a celebration of their engagement."

"Good idea. We'll leave them early and let them celebrate over dessert."

"Doug, you surprise me. You have a romantic side I never knew about."

"You go ahead and meet with Maria. I'll make the reservation and meet you there at 7:00 p.m."

17

After the meeting, Tom called Bob at his parents' house. He asked Bob to pick up Sara and be at the rehab facility at 6:00 pm. They would have a half hour visit with Maria and then go to dinner. He arrived at the facility with a big bouquet of roses. Maria had just finished her dinner. He gave her the roses and got a quick hello kiss. Her aide took the flowers and went off in search of a vase and water. Tom and Maria took advantage of the privacy and shared a real kiss. Maria was getting much stronger, walking now to the exercise and therapy room with a cane. Her voice was stronger, her demeanor was much improved. She wanted to go to the dinner with Bob and Maria, but Dr. Franks vetoed that. He wanted her to wait another week or two for a first outing. And then only with Tom on that one.

Tom said, "Bob and Sara will be here at 6:00 p.m., so we have a half hour."

Maria asked, "Doug couldn't come?"

"He's also on special duty with the police department. He wants to come in Sunday afternoon with me."

"How did that come about, you know, the police duty?"

"Let's have that talk after we meet with Dr. Franks on Monday. Then I'll tell you everything if he says it is okay."

"I'm just so tired of being treated like a child with respect to some things. I think I'm ready! I'm hoping he will say I can come home sometime next week and come in for outpatient therapy. By the way, Mom and Dad and your parents were here this afternoon. It was good to see them. They all said how well I look and can't wait until I'm home."

"You do look well, mon amour," Tom held out his arms. She stood and they were still hugging when her aide came back with the roses. "Uh, oh," she said, "shall I come back later?"

Both said, "Yes!!"

"I can't do that. There's a couple of kids waiting to see you."

Tom and Maria looked at each other and smiled. "Send them in. We'll be standing just like this when they come in. We'll be good."

Her aide stuck her head out the door. "It's okay. Come on in."

Sara and Bob bustled in. When they saw Tom and Maria kissing, they burst out laughing and Sara said, "I think we should give them a little more time."

Tom laughed. "I like this girl. Here, Sara, you take my place, and then we'll all sit and talk for a while."

Tom and Bob settled into chairs, Sara and Maria sat on her bed.

Maria said, "I hear congratulations are in order! Tell me all about your wedding plans. When is it going to be? How many bridesmaids are you going to have? And what church are you going to have it in?"

"Whoa a minute," Sara said. "First of all, I can't answer all those questions yet. Bob and I are meeting with Sister Charlotte, Bob's parents, and Father Flanagan on Sunday afternoon to talk about everything. What I can tell you is it will be sometime this summer at St. Jeans and Father Flanagan will marry us as well as do the pre-marriage counseling with us. Sister Charlotte, who heads up the Home where I've been living, has set all these things up. Both Bob and I are parishioners there."

She continued, "Mrs. O'Banion..."

"None of that now, it's Maria."

"Maria, I have a special favor to ask of you. I would love for you to be my maid of honor if you are strong enough."

"I am honored to be asked. You don't have some family member who would do it for you?"

"No, I don't. Since Dad died, I am officially an orphan. I'd really like you to do it."

"Then I'm your gal. I'll be your matron of honor. I'm married, you know, to that handsome man over there." They hugged and both had tears in their eyes.

The charge nurse came in and asked, "What's this now, tears in my patient's eyes?"

"My friend Sara is engaged, and she has asked me to be her matron of honor this summer if I'm ready."

"Well, that's wonderful! And we'll know Monday morning about your progress. Just a little preview. Your numbers are all good. You are making remarkable progress. You'll be ready."

Maria looked at Tom with tears in her eyes again. "I'm ready now!"

The charge nurse said, "I think it is time for you to lie down and rest for a while now. It is also time for your meds. Tom, you have a feisty, spirited woman here."

"How about one more hug and kiss goodnight, Maria? We're headed out to celebrate with these two."

After the hug and Maria was in bed, meds taken, Tom sent the others out and spent one more fleeting moment with Maria. "See, darling, sleep well. Monday will be a good day. You'll see."

TOM TOLD BOB AND SARA, "Follow me. We have to meet Doug at Tony's restaurant in fifteen minutes."

Bob said, "I know where that is. It's my parents' favorite restaurant."

The three saw Doug at a booth near the back. He let Tom in beside him. He was on the outside of the booth facing so he could see both the main entrance and the door to the small room. The happy couple were across from him and Tom. When the waiter came to take their order, Doug asked Sara if she would like a Shirley Temple. Bob asked, "What is that, and what does it have in it?"

Sara chimed in, "I know. That's what Dad always ordered for me at his restaurant. It has some ice cubes in a Collins glass, a little grenadine, and equal parts of ginger ale and lemon-lime pop."

Doug asked, "How about you, Bob? What will you have?"

"How about a beer?"

Doug grinned. "Nice try, Bob. Let's stay out of trouble. How about an Arnold Palmer?"

"I know that one too. It's half and half unsweetened iced tea and lemonade."

Bob grumbled, "That will be okay. Just think, another year and a half and I can make other choices."

"Tom, how about you and I have Kir Royales?"

Tom licked his lips. "That's a great celebration drink to their engagement."

After the waiter left, Tom said, "Sara, tell me about your engagement. Were you surprised?"

"I was. Bob showed up this morning at the Home. I skipped school and we went to a restaurant in North Muskegon to have breakfast and there was Doug. He's the one who told me about the restaurant. There we were, enjoying ourselves when Bob asked Doug to get three orange juices. I looked at him in surprise. When Doug came back, I turned in answer to Bob's voice and there was Bob on one knee, holding out the ring. He asked me to marry him. I looked at Doug who said, 'It was all Bob's doing, I'm just a witness to the deed.' I said, yes! I've been ready for him to ask for a long time. So, here we are."

Tom asked, "How does Arianna feel about this?"

"She's already calling him 'Da.' I was outnumbered. I'm kidding, Bob. I've been ready for this."

Their drinks raised in toast, Doug said, "Here's to Sara and Bob and a long, happy marriage."

Tom added, "May you be as happy and as dedicated to each other as Maria and I are. I look forward to all of us having dinner together as soon as Maria is home and able to do so."

When the waiter returned, the gentlemen ordered steaks — Tony's was known for them — medium rare, of course. Sara ordered perch, telling them after the waiter left, "It isn't Doo Drop Inn's, but the perch is quite good here, too." They all went to work on the cheese and crackers, chattering away about Maria's progress, Tom's new Masters in Conducting. Tom asked Bob how his classes were going and was relieved that the stress of being separated from Sara hadn't affected his grades. Doug chimed in periodically, but he mostly cast a vigilant eye around the restaurant ensuring Tom was safe.

Doug asked, "Have you decided on a date yet for your wedding?"

"Sometime this summer. We're meeting at 1:00 p.m. Sunday to make some of those decisions. We'll pick our date, get our pre-marriage counseling scheduled, and get me a list of things to decide. I don't know how many attendants I want yet but it will be a small number. I've been out of touch with my girlfriends back at Muskegon High School. Maria is going to be my matron of honor. We'll know more about when she'll be home after the doctor's meeting on Monday. Tom and Maria and their families know how to get things moving in a hurry. We have enough time but have to get at it."

"Doug and I can help with the music and the musicians you might need."

"Thank you both. Another friend jumps in to help."

The waiter delivered their meals and, after a quick 'bon appétit,' the men tackled their steaks like they hadn't eaten in a month. Sara finished off her perch more sedately and enjoyed it just as thoroughly. She crossed her fork and knife on her plate when she finished and asked Tom, "Mr. O, what will you and Maria do after she is home? Will you be going back to teaching and will she be ready for the fall term?"

"We don't really know yet. You may not know yet, but you will on Monday. The task force is working again since there have been some new developments. I'll be busy with that for a while. We can't tell you much yet, but there will be an announcement Monday. I have applications at some schools for a choir director, but I haven't heard yet. Maria may not be ready to go back to teaching yet. We'll see."

He continued, "I ordered desserts for you two. The check is all taken care of. Doug and I are going to take off and let you celebrate alone for a bit. Enjoy the rest of your night."

Bob and Sara looked tenderly at each other and then Sara said, "Thank you for all of this, including the private time. We have to get back soon — I don't like to keep Sister Charlotte up too late. She has been so good to me and Arianna."

In the parking lot, Doug asked, "Tom, do you still have your weapon ready, or do I need to go home with you?"

"I'm ready, but I don't feel a threat yet. I'm supposed to be the last on the list. I have a lot of reading and thinking to do before our next meeting. I told the chief that I would be available if he wants tomorrow if I'm needed for the interviews of the women, you know the wives of the members who have been killed. I'll be seeing Maria in the morning. She will want some feedback on the dinner tonight and some assurance of her readiness to come home. Maybe you and I can get together on Sunday."

18

S aturday morning found Chief Jim and Mark waiting in two separate interview rooms. The security crew men were waiting in the conference room for their assignments about which one of the surviving members of the Group of Nine they would be protecting.

The remaining members were brought up from the holding cell at the same time and seated in a row of chairs outside the interview rooms. They looked at each other wondering what was going on. The chief and his lead detective, Mark, opened their doors, pointed to a man, and beckoned him into his interview room. When they were seated across the table from each other, each man was asked, "Did you leave the house on the Friday morning before you came in here?" No matter what he said, each man was then asked, "What did you do when you were out?" To a man, each said he didn't leave the house and then, with some indignation, said that they couldn't very well do anything away from the house since they were out on house arrest with substantial bail.

They were all put through the same procedure as before except the chief got Mark's interviewees and Mark got the chief's. This time each man was asked only one question, "What did you do when you went out of the house on Friday morning before you came in here?" And again, each man reacted, this time with some anger. Each said some version of "I already told one of you that I didn't leave the house." All the men thought the chief and Mark were demented.

All the men were then escorted into the conference rooms where they found their name tags on a chair between two policemen. The policemen acknowledged their presence but didn't say anything. Mark and the chief walked in, one carrying a coffee service, the other a tray of warm Danish with plates and butter for them.

The chief remained standing. "You are all angry and think that Mark and I are a little crazy. Don't be angry at Mark, this was my idea. You see something has happened to another of your friends. George Anderson was murdered yesterday morning. His killer put two bullets into his heart and for good measure one in the center of his forehead. No one in town knows this except the members of our police force. The public won't know until I hold a press conference on Monday morning. But now you know it and I see by the expressions on your faces that you are concerned, maybe even frightened by that knowledge."

The chief continued, "These gentlemen sitting alongside each of you are retired police officers from the various departments around Muskegon, men who have served their community with distinction. The two men beside you are two members of your personal protection detail and, after they have served their twelve-hour shift, they will introduce you to the men who will guard you for the next twelve hours.

"The gentleman at the other end of this table is Doug McDermott. Some of you may know him from Muskegon High School where he teaches instrumental music at the school and is the orchestra conductor. Before he came to our town, he had jobs where he learned skills that qualify him to be the man who will coordinate your protection detail's activities. We will make sure you get through this thing alive.

"I apologize to you for the strange questioning this morning. You must have thought it was a little odd. We, none of us on the force, didn't think that you had anything to do with George's death, but we had to hear what your alibis were for early Friday morning. We will confirm them, of course, but right now, we're convinced that you didn't directly have anything to do with yesterday's event. By the way, Judge McVie, the district attorney, and your attorney knew of our plans and approved them. There is a document in front of you signed by your attorney giving you permission to answer three questions. Please sign the document in front of you with the words, 'I was asked if I had gone out of the house on Friday morning and, if so, where did I go.' This is the proof for your attorney that you followed the instructions. Now, please relax and introduce yourselves to your protection detail and let's enjoy some coffee and Danish while I try to answer questions you might have. I may not be able to answer them all, but I'll do my best. Certain things we can't release yet."

One of them said, "I think I can speak for all of us. We are grateful for what you have done to keep us safe. Thank you."

All got Danish and coffee. The room was all abuzz with questions and comments. When they were done, cars with two officers and their charge drove off to his home.

The chief, Mark, and Doug had a short meeting in his office. Mark said, "Well done, Jim." Doug nodded his agreement.

"Thank you both. I wasn't sure it would work, but I'm pretty certain that they are not involved in George's death, at least not directly. What we don't know yet is if one of them hired someone to do it. I doubt it myself, but we must keep it in mind. Mark, can you do one more thing this afternoon?"

"Sure. What is that?"

"I'm going to call Mrs. Anderson and tell her about George. The housekeeper told me that she had been out of town visiting her sister since the first of last week. She is supposed to be coming home Sunday afternoon, but I don't want her to walk into this without knowing. And then Tom and I are going to stop in to see Mrs. Olson. I've talked to her before when Larry went missing and later when he was found dead. I will tell each about George. I'll tell each of them to keep it quiet until after the press conference. We don't suspect either of them — we just have to verify where they were on Friday. We know that Mrs. Anderson was at her sister's house in Indiana, but we don't know where Mrs. Olsen and Mrs. Samuels were. Somewhere in the conversation, I will ask Mrs. Olsen where she was Friday morning. I would like you to interview Mrs. Samuels and take Don with you. Tell her about George and ask her where she was on Friday morning. You know what to watch for. I don't have any strong feelings about any of them, but you never know."

AFTER MARK AND TOM LEFT, Jim called Harold Evans, the Group's attorney, and left a message that his remaining clients were now being watched over at their homes twenty-four hours a day by two police officers in two twelve-hour shifts. He asked him to call him as soon as possible as he had very urgent information to share with him.

He was thinking about what to say to Mrs. Anderson when his phone rang. *Now what*, he wondered, *who could be calling me on a Saturday afternoon.* He answered, "This is Jim Johnson, who am I speaking with?"

"It's Maria O'Banion, Jim. How are you? I took a chance you might be there."

"Hello there, Maria. I keep hearing good reports about you."

"I'm coming along nicely. We meet with my doctor Monday morning. Hopefully, I will have a release date when the meeting is done. I have a notion he might release me by the end of the week. I'm doing so much better and can't wait to get home."

"Well, young lady. What can I do for you on this Saturday afternoon?"

"Jim, I have a question and a favor to ask of you."

"First, what is the question?"

"Are there many, or maybe I should say, any female detectives in today's world, and a second part to it, are there any female private detectives?"

"What's up with this? What do you have in mind?"

"I'll tell you in a moment, Jim. How about the answers?"

"To my recollection, there are three or maybe four female police detectives in the state. I don't have a good handle on how many female private detectives. There are a few. It is new territory for us. But I'll say this, it is coming, and I welcome it."

"That's encouraging, Jim. I may need your help with Tom."

"What are you thinking? And have you said anything to Tom yet?"

"I haven't told Tom yet. It will be one of the many chats by the fire that we'll have early on when I get home. I watched and listened to Tom when he was on the task force last year. It is as though he has found a new mission in life, he was so energized during those times. And sure, I was concerned for him and later for both of us, but it is where he is headed permanently. He'll have to tell me that. I've seen it resurfacing since you've reconvened the task force. By the way, he hasn't told me of anything happening recently yet. He said he wanted to get your approval about telling me and also check with Dr. Franks to make sure I'm ready."

"Tom said that he told you he was working with us again. And he also said that he sensed that you wouldn't fight him about it."

"He always knows what I'm thinking. We've talked about where his ability to read people has come from. He has some ideas about it, but he doesn't really know. The thing is he has it and wants to use it."

"I've seen that in him. He comes up with insights that many of us don't see until he tells us. He has done well for us. So, now, what do you have in mind and what is the favor you spoke of?"

"I want to take the same training Tom did. I'll have to do much of the study work at home until I regain my full strength. I want to see us open up a two-person, husband and wife, detective agency. That may be a first in the state, but someone has to lead. So, the favor is, could you send me a set of materials to get started, that I could work on during my last days here? Most of the time I'm pretty bored between therapy sessions. I want to get moving."

"I didn't expect that. Tom doesn't know anything about this yet?"

"Not yet. But he will shortly after we get home and together again."

"I would like to see his face when you tell him. But no, that's between the two of you. Do you know if you will work in special fields like murders or robberies?"

"I don't know that yet, but I'll bet there are hundreds of cities across the country that have a cabal working in the background as they were in Muskegon. It might mean a lot of travel, but I think we would enjoy that. We'll see as we work through the details of it."

"Okay, Maria, I'll get you some materials. I'll drop them off myself, so no one else is involved and might let it slip."

"Yes, our meeting with Dr. Franks should be over by 11:00 a.m. at the latest. Tom will likely stay for lunch. By the way, I don't want Tom to know about the materials until I tell him. Is that okay?"

"The task force meeting is at 2:00 p.m., so I'll have time to drop them off just after lunch and miss Tom. I am doing a press conference Monday morning to let the citizens know what has happened. Once it is out in the evening *Chronicle*, there will be talk here about it. So, you and Tom will have to be careful if you talk about it much before you get home. There are things that we won't release to the public yet. Good luck with Tom, I think he will love your idea."

"Thank you, Jim."

19

Jim dialed the number the housekeeper had given him. "Hello, this is Jim Johnson, the police chief in Muskegon, Michigan. Are you Mrs. George Anderson's sister?"

"Yes, I am, I'm Jane Brown. What can I do for you, Mr. Johnson?"

"I need to talk to your sister — it's urgent. And Mrs. Brown, stay close to her, she may need you."

"My husband is a doctor. Should I get him here too?"

"That would be good. I'll hold while you get them both."

Jim could hear her calling her sister and then "John, would you come down? I have a question for you."

"Chief Johnson, this is Ann Anderson. How may I help you?"

"If you are not sitting down, Mrs. Anderson, please do so...I'm so sorry to have to tell you this, but your husband is dead, Ann. He was shot yesterday."

Jim heard her sister say, "John, she is passing out."

"Get my bag. I'll get her lying down on the sofa."

Jim heard some bustling around, then he heard, "This is Dr. Brown. What did you tell her?"

"Is she okay?"

"She fainted and she's coming to now. What did you say to her?"

"I told her that her husband was shot yesterday morning."

"Just like that, you blurted it out?"

"Dr. Brown, sometimes these things are best done quickly."

"Yes, I know what you mean. Tell me what happened so I can help her deal with it. And it's John."

"All right, John. Let me ask you first, do you know about George's problems up here?"

"I know enough about it to realize that George was in some serious legal trouble. I don't know much in the way of details, but I do know he was the alleged leader of a group of powerful men in Muskegon who seemed to be involved in some pretty shady dealings. So, what happened?"

"George was murdered yesterday morning. He was the fourth member of this group to be killed. The others were safe in our jail until I had my protection ready on Saturday morning."

"I thought there were only two dead. That's what I read in the paper."

"That was correct, but then things heated up. The third one was shot last Friday, and we received a warning that the rest would be killed before the killer was done. I immediately called all who were left, including George, to warn them, and let them know we were working on protection for them and that the task force on the case was being reestablished. George called me on Thursday to ask why we didn't have protection yet. I told him that the protection would start Friday night at the jail, then with a personal detail for each man Saturday morning. That was the soonest I could get it in place. George refused the night at the jail and told me where he would be. He was confident that no one would know about the cabin, and he would be safe. He wasn't."

"That sounds like something George would do. He always thought he was invincible. Excuse me a second... Ann, how are you doing? I'll ask him. Jim, she wants to know if you can tell me the details and she can wait until she is home on Monday to talk with you. Can you make that work?"

"I can. How long has she been down there?"

John said to the ladies, "Will you excuse me for a few minutes? Jane, I'll finish the call in my study. Please hang up this phone when I get in there. And Jane, fix both of you a weak cocktail. No, it won't interfere with her meds. Make it light and I'll join you in a few minutes."

When John got to his study, he said to Jane, "You can hang up now. I'll be out soon." He then closed the door.

"Jim, I'm back. To answer your question, she has been here two weeks. She told George that she needed to get away from the tension for a short time. We let her know she could come down and stay as long as she needed to. He flew her down the next day directly into South Bend on a small charter. Jim, I have not seen anyone so physically and emotionally stressed in some time. I fixed her up with a counselor and began to feed her well. She is a different person now, but this is going to throw her for a loop again. She tried to call George yesterday morning and couldn't get him. I don't know if she had a premonition or what.

"Here's what I'd like to do. I have a private practice with partners who can cover for me. I'm also on the medical faculty at Notre Dame. We are part of the I.U. School of Medicine. I can take some time off there as well. We'll all three drive up there Sunday afternoon and check in with you on Monday."

"That will work fine. That's very generous of you and your wife."

"These two sisters are quite close. Once we got Ann settled down, we've had a wonderful time. We'll probably stay a week or so, maybe longer. We'll see."

"John, how would you like to come to the press conference Monday morning? You'll get caught up on all that's happened and then some. The reporters from the local papers including Grand Rapids and the television people can be thorough with their questions. I'll have a twenty- to thirty-minute statement and let the questions fly. You'll get caught up in a hurry."

"I would like that, something I've never been involved with in person. I've only seen them on TV. Thank you for the invitation."

"My secretary, Gerri, can give you the exact time and get you a pass to get into the conference. I think it is set for 10:00 a.m. but Gerri will give you the exact schedule. And one last thing. I haven't told you any details of his shooting, it's a little gruesome. What do you plan to tell Mrs. Anderson?"

"I'll tell her he was shot and that he died instantly but beyond that you couldn't share details because it's an on-going investigation. I think that will work for now. She can hear the details on Monday."

"Okay, John. I'll see you on Monday morning. Safe travels."

Jim's next call was to Mrs. Olsen. She answered right away. "Well, hello, Chief Johnson. To what do I owe this call?"

"I have some news for you. It doesn't concern you directly, but I am informing all the wives of the Group about some recent developments. It won't take long. Could you spare some time this afternoon for Tom O'Banion and me?"

"I can't this afternoon. I'm getting the girls ready for a visit with their cousins down in Georgia. I'm putting them on an early flight tomorrow. It's spring break you know."

"I can work it out tomorrow afternoon. We get home from church at noon. Can we say 2:00 p.m., Mrs. Olsen?"

"I'll see you then."

20

S ara, Arianna, and Sister Charlotte arrived first at the Fowler home. Father Flanagan was right behind them. Sara introduced Arianna to Mr. Fowler, then Sister Charlotte to Henry and Sally. Henry let Sister Charlotte know he went by Hank. "Henry is a good name, but I've been Hank all my life."

Sally had prepared a lunch of several light hors d'oeuvres. When they were all seated with Arianna in her highchair between Bob and Sara, Hank asked Father Flanagan if he would lead the blessing. He was happy to do so.

Hank asked, "Sister Charlotte, will you join us in a glass of wine with lunch? I don't have to ask Father Flanagan. He likes the pinot noir that we often have. But we also have a good chardonnay chilling. Sally prefers the chardonnay. What would you like?"

"I'll have the chardonnay. Thank you."

Hank poured the four glasses of wine. Bob looked at his dad, "Don't you think that Sara and I could enjoy a small glass in honor of the occasion? Can we be a little French today?"

Hank looked around at the adults who all nodded, produced two more glasses and poured half glasses of chardonnay for Sara and pinot noir for Bob. "Just this and then it's lemonade.

"I would like to make a toast. Though we've seen Arianna a lot when Bob has been home from school and now here with Sara, this is a special time, a creation of a family. So, here's to Sara, Arianna, and Bob, a new family in our home, a new 'daughter,' and a new granddaughter. You bring joy to our home. Welcome."

Father Flanagan added, "And may I toast a new family-to-be. I spoke to the Bishop about Arianna. He says that after you are married, we can proceed to christen Arianna Fowler as a child of the church. She'll be, what, almost a year old at that point?"

"That's right, Father. Thank you for doing that."

Sally, ever the gracious hostess, said, "Let's eat before everything gets cold."

They chatted about what was going on in the community and their recent trip to East Lansing to visit Bob at college as they ate. When Sally's famous cherry pie was served for dessert, Father Flanagan asked, "What are you thinking about a date?"

Sara said, "Bob has to be back to college for his sophomore year. Even though we have a home here, we'll have to rent an apartment for the next three school years in East Lansing while Bob finishes his degree. Registration for classes is on Thursday, August 29 and Friday, August 30. Classes start on the Wednesday after Labor Day, so we need to be moved in the week before. Bob and I want a few days for a honeymoon, so backing the dates up means a wedding date of Saturday, August 17. That gives us time for a weeklong honeymoon and some time to move to Lansing before registration."

Bob added, "Actually, I've already selected my courses for next semester. Registration ought to go quickly."

Sally smiled at them with a twinkle in her eye. "I understand you have some friends who are kind of experienced at doing things faster than that. How would you like a June wedding?"

Bob and Sara looked at each other and said together, "That would be great."

Sara frowned, "There's just one, so far, little problem. I've asked Maria, Mr. O's wife, if she would be my matron of honor. It's looking as though she might come home sometime next week. It's March now. Will that give her enough time to get her strength back?"

"After we saw and talked to her on Friday and caught a glimpse of her spirit, I'd be willing to bet she will be ready," Bob said.

Father Flanagan added, "A June wedding in St. Jeans will be a lot cooler in the church."

Sister Charlotte said, "And, my children, it will give you most of the summer to adjust to being a family, grow together without the distractions of Bob's classes."

Sally smiled at the sudden turn. She was hoping for a June wedding, and they were liking it too. Sometimes things were just meant to be. She smiled again. Bob asked her, "Mom, what are you smiling about?"

"I'll tell you and Sara another time."

Hank hesitated, "I don't like being impertinent, but we can help with the costs of the wedding. You are talking about some dollars here."

Sara's turn to smile. "Thank you for your offer but I wouldn't want to deprive Dad of that pleasure. He left me well off so I'm doing this for him. If you will take care of the rehearsal dinner, I can cover the rest."

Sally asked, "How many bridesmaids would you want?"

"I don't want it to be too big, so maybe two plus Maria. I've lost touch with most of my high school friends. There is one I was quite close to so I will ask her. And then I'll figure out someone else. It also depends on how many groomsmen Bob wants. With no family, it's hard."

Hank replied, "Sara, we are now your family. You do have a family now."

Seeing Sara tearing up, Sally asked, "Anyone need more coffee?"

Sally laid a gentle hand on Sara's shoulder. "Have you thought about whether to have Arianna be a part of it? Or if you should. And also, who will walk you down the aisle?"

"Arianna. I don't know yet. We'll talk more about her later. And

I'm not sure what I want to do for an escort down the aisle. Something else to figure out."

Father Flanagan said, "Can the two of you come by around 5 p.m. today? I'd like to get you started on your pre-marriage counseling and work out a schedule."

At their nod, he said, "Good. See you at 5. Hank, Sally, thank you for this lovely lunch. I look forward to getting these two happily married. Sister Charlotte, let me drop you off and let this new family get to know each other better."

21

The chief and Tom arrived at Mrs. Olsen's house at the appointed time, 2:00 p.m. Sunday afternoon.

Mrs. Olsen greeted them at the front door dressed more for a beach or pool party in turquoise pedal pushers and a low-cut lace top with the ends tied up on her very tan midriff. "Come in, won't you? Would you like something to drink? I have some iced tea or lemonade or a glass of Coke."

Before she left, she continued, "Tom, I don't believe we have formally met." She gave him an up and down look and shook his hand, holding on to it too long for Tom's taste.

She went on, "Have a seat in the living room here and I'll be right back with our drinks."

After she left, Tom was about to talk but Jim held his hand to his mouth. "Shh." They looked around the room, nicely furnished with what looked like real art on the walls. *Larry and Anna must have been doing okay*, Tom thought.

Jim sat on one end of the sofa with Tom on the other end, forcing Mrs. Olsen to sit in an easy chair directly across from them, giving them both a direct view of her facial expressions and body language.

"Well, Jim, call me Anna. You said you had some new information for me?"

"There's no easy way to say this. So, here it is straight out. Larry didn't have an accident. He was murdered. We now have the forensic proof that he was pushed off that bridge by another vehicle."

She put her fist to her mouth and allowed herself to tear up. "I just knew it. What do you think happened?"

"We think someone in the Group wanted him out of the way. I don't have any idea why. We think the killer waited until he saw Larry come out of his office and followed him. We have testimony from the gas station owner where Larry stopped to gas up, but the attendant didn't see anyone suspicious pull in behind Larry. Were you going somewhere that weekend?"

"We were going to take a little weekend trip up north, you know, God's country up north of Traverse City. We were going to stay in Charlevoix, and then come back Sunday night. We never got there." She sniffled a little.

"Whoever his killer was thought you were going further since Larry filled the tank. Larry must have figured out he was being followed, so he tried to shake him and took a route he didn't know well. His killer pursued him at faster and faster speeds with his killer bumping him often until finally Larry lost control and went over the bridge. Our forensic team found dents and wood slivers in the back end of Larry's car."

She asked Tom, "Why are you watching me so closely?"

Tom replied, "Jim asked me to keep an eye on you. He was concerned that this might bother you so much that you could faint or something. That's all."

"Well, Mr. O'Banion, I'm not a fainter. I'm made of better stuff than that. You shouldn't have assumed that about me."

Tom answered, "Mrs. Olsen, you sound so hostile toward me. I don't even know you and didn't know your husband."

She gathered herself. "I'm sorry. This has me so upset."

"And something else you should know. George Anderson is dead." He stopped for a brief minute. Tom watched Anna carefully.

Then Jim continued, "George was shot Friday morning. Three shots, two in the heart and one, for good measure, in the forehead. His killer didn't like him."

"Well, I didn't like him, but I wouldn't kill him."

"We're not saying you did. We have no idea who his killer is."

"Well, I didn't like him because of the way he treated Larry. Larry would come home after each meeting they had very upset. He didn't like the way things were going and told George that. George doesn't treat him well."

Jim amended her words. "George *didn't* treat him well. Isn't that what you meant to say?"

She burst into tears. Soon she was sobbing. Tom thought, *she is a good actress. I don't believe her reaction. It's a little too much — the lady doth protest too much. Maybe it was to cover up her mistake when she said, 'I wouldn't kill him.'*

Jim stood and walked over to her. "Can I get you something?"

Sniffling, she said, "No, I'll be okay. Jim, do you have any idea who killed George?"

"Not a clue. But we'll find him eventually. The point is George is number four out of the Group of Nine. All died violent deaths. We're determined to find the killer, or killers, before they kill someone else. We've put all the remaining members under heavy police protection. That will continue until their trials."

"That's good. Police protection, that's rich. Why didn't you do that sooner? Maybe Larry would still be alive. Are they being held in their homes?"

"No, they aren't. Their location is being kept secret."

She started crying again.

"Anna. Is there someone who can come and stay with you?"

"Yes, there is. I'll call her."

"Can I do that for you?"

"No, I'm all right. Will you let me know what happens when you get this figured out?"

"I will. How long will your daughters be in Georgia?"

"Just a week. Larry's brother is a teacher in Athens, Georgia. So, my sister-in-law and the four girls will take a trip to Savannah. The girls all like that city, so they'll have a good time. I don't know how I'll tell them about their daddy when they come home."

"Will you be okay if we leave now?"

"I'll call my friend. She lives in the neighborhood, so she can get right over. I'll be okay."

"Thank you, Anna. I'll keep you posted."

22

J im and Tom drove back slowly, not talking at first. Jim broke the ice. "Tell me what you are thinking, Tom."

"She is one tough lady. Much of what she did in there was acting. She didn't react enough when you told her Larry was murdered and she overreacted to the news about George. And why would she immediately say, 'I wouldn't kill him.' She has a lot of pent-up anger at something. I wonder if she could be George's killer. I don't know yet if she killed Tim and plans to kill the others. What could her motives be? I say *motives* because I think the motive might be different for each case. I can't for the life of me figure why she wants to kill me if she is the killer. We should keep a close eye on her from now on."

"Do you think you are jumping too fast to these conclusions?"

"I don't but we are going to have a tough time getting enough evidence to be able to put her away. What I need now is a lot of time thinking about what she said in there. I sure wish I had a transcript of that conversation."

"You'll have one Monday afternoon."

"What are you talking about?"

"I had Doug wire me up this morning. He had the gear and knew how to use it."

"Is that legal?"

"I asked Judge McVie for a warrant to cover it. Gerri could transcribe it but getting her acquainted with Doug's system might take more time than she has. Besides, it would raise some curiosity at the office, and I don't want any hint of it out in the public. She still has a lot to do for the press conference in the morning and paperwork for the meeting in the afternoon."

"Jim, I bet Doug has what he needs to transcribe it."

"Where's Doug's house?"

"It's out of the way to the station. I'm supposed to meet him for dinner tonight after we see Maria. Doug hasn't seen her since she woke up. Jim, why don't you take it off when we get to the station? Then let us take care of the rest of it. That has a couple of advantages. It is out of your hands. Doug and I can take care of it and give you a copy of it. I'll pick Doug up, see Maria, and get right to it after we visit with her. Besides, while he is transcribing it, I want to listen to every word, every nuance and see what else it tells me."

"The judge said that it may not be admissible in court."

"We still need it. If I'm right, we have to stop her. It's worth the risk. One more thing, Jim. Can you use Doug to tail her? He knows how to do it without getting noticed. Have him take Don and teach him the ropes and tag-team her. They could start in the morning. I don't think she will do anything tonight. Hey, there's a pay phone. Let me call and see if Doug is home. Today was his first day monitoring the protection detail."

Fifteen minutes after the phone call, they were walking in Doug's front door.

"Welcome. So, the wire worked well?"

"I sure hope so. I didn't want to take it off myself, so that's part of why we're here. I could have Gerri do it. But it is different gear than we use."

"That's fine. It won't take long. What's the other part?"

"Doug, we can still make the trip to see Maria. I have a plan for the three of us to have a private dinner in the dining room."

"That sounds good. Set it up. Make the call while Jim and I talk."

Tom called the rehab facility first. He spoke with the charge nurse, Sandy, and asked if she could set up a special private table for three after the regular dinner hour. He explained that he was bringing a special friend that he knew Maria would love to see. He offered to bring dinner in so the kitchen wouldn't have extra work.

She asked, "What do you have in mind?"

"Can she handle Doo Drop perch, fries, and onion rings yet?"

"We had mashed potatoes tonight. Let's not do the fries and onion rings yet. Maria's digestive system is still adjusting to real food. Do they ever broil their fish?"

Tom laughed, "They would think that's a terrible thing to do to perch, but I'll see what I can do. Maria's going to complain about no fries and onion rings — you know Doo Drop makes the best ones in town."

Sandy chuckled. "Well, if you can bring the perch, I can get the table set up and provide the mashed potatoes and maybe some soft peas or another vegetable. Would that work for you?"

Tom went on, "Thank you. That's great. We'll meet her in the dining room at 6:30."

Jim explained what he wanted Doug to do. "We need to keep a tight tail on Mrs. Olsen. Can you start tomorrow morning? We're taking a little chance on tonight, but we don't believe she will move that fast."

"I can do that. Could I use Mark for the tag team when we have to do that?"

"I really need him elsewhere. How about Don? He has been riding with Mark and learning from him. He's a fast learner. We'll get you an unmarked car tomorrow."

"How are you so certain that you need to do this and that she is George's killer?"

"I was suspicious but when I listened to Tom's observations, he convinced me. He thinks she did it, but it is going to be hard to get enough evidence. According to him, she is one angry lady and I agree with that. I'll let him tell you the rest. Tom, can you pick up your car later? I'm just going home from here."

"Sure, Jim. I'll see you in the morning for the press conference. Hey, what if Mrs. Olsen shows up in the morning? It would be just like her to come and tell us that it is her way of keeping up."

"We'll just treat her as an interested citizen who has a strong interest in it because of what happened to her husband. If we play it right, she might even relax her mistrust from this afternoon. Doug, you could just happen to show up, too, if you want."

"I will, after I talk to the principal at school. It's time for him to get me a substitute on a regular basis."

23

After the chief left, Doug brought out two beers and the two sat talking about the developments. They had an hour or so before they had to leave.

"You really think she did it?"

"I do. I know I shouldn't jump too soon. But her general demeanor and her smooth way of talking to us. Wait until you hear. If I can, I'd like to listen while you are transcribing. I want to hear again how she speaks to each of us. She did one other thing that set me on edge."

"What was that?"

"When we were introduced, she held on to my hand too long for me and gave me a look that was too flirty. I was uncomfortable with it, and I think she saw that. And the way she was dressed — like she was going to a party instead of mourning her husband. And another thing, at one point, she asked me in a hostile tone of voice why I was watching her so carefully. Then when Jim said that George's killer didn't like him, she defended herself by saying, 'Well, I didn't like him either, but I didn't kill him.' Then she went into a story about why she didn't like him. She seemed to be following her script, no matter what Jim did or said."

"I'll be interested in listening to the recording myself to see what I pick up. Say, what time do we have to be there for dinner? What about things I shouldn't bring up while I'm there?"

"I'm going to call Doo Drop for some perch, perch only. The charge nurse didn't want her to have fries and onion rings yet — too much for her stomach. They will have some mashed potatoes from the facility kitchen and maybe a vegetable if we want. So, we have to leave in about fifteen minutes. As to what not to say, she knows nothing about what's happened with the case we're working. She doesn't know you are involved or what your future plans are. She won't find out until tomorrow morning when she can come home. And finally, she knows I'm working on the task force again and as I told you, seems to approve. I've told her that maybe I can tell her more after we talk to Dr. Franks tomorrow morning."

"So, what can I talk about? I'm not one to reminisce."

"Talk about school, how the year is going, what plays her substitute is doing."

Tom went on, "She may ask questions that neither of us can answer. We will just have to steer her away from them. She is doing so well physically though she tires quickly. She is still fragile emotionally."

They picked up the perch at Doo Drop, got to the facility and walked in the dining room to a softly lit area near the back. The staff had even found some flowers and a white tablecloth with real cloth napkins.

Tom walked up to Maria, gave her a kiss and a hug, and said, "I didn't get flowers today, but I brought you a big surprise." He motioned to Doug to come in.

Maria squealed in delight. "Doug, it is so good to see you." She stood up and hugged him.

The staff took the perch and put it together with the additions from the kitchen. Pitchers of iced tea and lemonade were already on the table. They poured their own and toasted Maria for a good result in the morning and a trip home soon. Three members of the kitchen staff came strutting out with a plate for each of them and a platter of dinner rolls. They were enjoying their show for Maria. They all liked her so much and were so happy about her recovery. They would do anything for Maria and Tom.

Maria exclaimed, "This fish is wonderful, how did you get them to approve this?"

"I talked to the head nurse. She arranged it but balked at the fries and onion rings. Too much oil. She tried to get me to bring broiled perch. I told her Doo Drop wouldn't approve of that. I thought about a glass of wine but didn't want to push my luck."

Maria was eating slowly, still hesitant with utensils but not spilling anymore. She asked Doug, "How is school going? How is my substitute working out?"

Doug smiled, "School is going well. I'm working on the show music already as well as getting ready for the spring orchestra concert."

"What show did she pick?"

"She found your planning list and selected *Guys and Dolls*. She is in early rehearsals. I think it is going to be good."

"I miss it. I miss the kids the most. But I don't know if I'll be ready by next fall. I'm feeling better all the time, but I have a ways to go."

Tom took her hand. "You are going to be just fine. We'll take it one day at a time and you will be where you want to be."

"I want to be wherever you are, Tom."

"Then we're together on that."

The ladies came back to bus the table. Kate, one of Maria's favorites since she was always slipping Maria an extra cookie or two, said, "We have the fixings for hot fudge sundaes and a fresh pot of coffee. Would you like to finish off with that?"

"Kate, you spoil me! And I love it. Thank you. Just a small one for me."

They devoured their sundaes, leaving the bowls so clean that it looked like they didn't need to be washed. Tom and Doug walked slowly with Maria back to her room. Doug said goodbye and told Tom he would wait at the main entrance.

"Kiss me, Tom. Quick before the aide comes in with my meds." They did and clung to each other, savoring the feel of their bodies close together.

"Sleep well, sweetheart. Tomorrow morning, we'll take the next step to moving on with our lives. I'll see you at 10:00 a.m. I love you."

24

_____

Doug arrived the next morning at 8:30 a.m. to find Jim and Gerri hard at it already. He waved the printout of the conversation with Mrs. Olsen. Jim excused himself, walked out to Doug, and took the printout as though it were a special gift. "This is going to help us nail Mrs. Olsen."

"You believe she is the killer."

"Yes, I do! I feel it in here!" He put his hand over his heart. "Now we just have to find the evidence, and this will help us. By the way, Don is already here and ready to go."

"Do you think he is up to it?"

"Yes, he is. I hadn't mentioned it before, but he completed the state police training in surveillance strategies. Doing it with you along will help him grow more. I would appreciate you mentoring him."

Don and Doug left the lot in an unmarked police car and drove to Mrs. Olsen's house. Doug told him, "I won't say much in the way of teaching you anything new unless I suggest another way to try. Deal?"

"Deal! I look forward to learning some new techniques from you."

They turned into Mrs. Olsen's Street. Don went on up to the next cross street, made a U-turn and parked where he could see her house and the garage door.

"Well done, Don."

"Thanks."

They didn't have long to wait. The garage door opened, and Mrs. Olsen took off back the way they had come from.

Don took off after her, keeping her in sight but not too close. As soon as there was other traffic, he put a couple of cars between them. She continued on through town and headed to the causeway.

"Looks like she is headed to North Muskegon. She's taking the left turn onto Lake Avenue. I'd better close in a bit. After we pass Ray & Sharon's Flowers, Lake curves north and there is a four-way stop at the top of the hill. We need to make sure we know which way she turns." They took the curve and noted that she was still stopped at the four-way. As Don approached the stop sign, he pulled in to park as if going to Ken's Five and Ten store. After she turned left, he pulled back out, made his left turn, and followed her west on Ruddiman Drive.

"Nice move, Don. There she is about a block up ahead."

They followed her until almost to Bear Lake Tavern when she suddenly turned right onto W. Circle Drive. She pulled into a driveway to a rather large house with a triple garage.

"Whoever owns this has money. That's a big house."

"I know whose house that is. It is the Anderson home. She is going to see Mrs. Anderson, George's wife. Why would she be doing that?"

"Is there a chance Mrs. Anderson could be a target?"

"Not likely. The bad business was all the men's doing. The wives knew very little what their husbands were up to."

"Maybe she's making a condolence visit? What do you think, Doug?" After a half hour watching from a corner on the other side of Circle Drive, they saw three women come out the front door. Mrs. Olsen headed for her car.

"The other two women look almost like twins. The chief told me that Mrs. Anderson was returning late yesterday from a long, two-week visit with her sister. That must be Mrs. Anderson's sister."

Mrs. Olsen turned back and gave them both a hug. She drove down the long driveway on to W. Circle Drive and turned left to go back east on Ruddiman Drive. Don pulled out after the school bus made its last pick up on Circle Drive and followed her back through downtown until she led them toward the police station and pulled up to park alongside the U.S. 31 Barbecue, just across from the police station.

Don turned into the barbeque lot and went around to the back. They sat there and watched Mrs. Olsen start walking to the police station.

"I told you I heard she was brassy, Don. I think she is going to the press conference. I'll follow and see if that's where she's heading. Is there a back door that leads to the auditorium?"

"There is. Once you see her go in and get seated, walk back out. I'll park back there, meet you, and walk you around to it. You cover the back and I'll take the front door."

Doug followed her to the auditorium. He noted where she was seated and hurried back out to the car. As Don drove around to the back of the police station, Doug told Don she was seated on the aisle just four rows from the back.

Don grabbed a pair of walkie-talkies from the trunk and then led Doug through the back door. He took a right turn to a door about halfway down the hall. He said, "That door leads to the backstage area. The stage manager will be there, and he can help you." Don took off for his station.

Doug said to the stage manager, "I need to get a note to the chief. He looks busy but could you get Gerri's attention and bring her over here?"

Gerri said, "Hello, Doug. What's up?"

"I need to let Jim know that we followed Mrs. Olsen here. Can you get him this note? She is seated on the aisle, Jim's left, about four rows from the back. Tell him we've got both entrances covered, so we can pick up the following when she leaves. And thanks, Gerri."

Jim took the note, read it, glanced over at Doug, and nodded. He buzzed Don to ask if she was still in the same spot. He buzzed back, no change.

JIM STOOD. "Good morning. Thank you all for coming." While the conversations were quieting down, he glanced around the audience and nodded to people he recognized from previous conferences as well as some newcomers like Dr. Brown from South Bend, George's brother-in-law. He also acknowledged Mrs. Olsen was there by a nod, and she answered with a smile and a little finger-wave.

"Good morning and again, thank you all for coming. I see all three TV stations are represented, as well as the *Muskegon Chronicle*, the *Grand Rapids Press*, and all three local radio stations. I appreciate you all being here. Let me introduce the people at the table. To my left are my lead detective Mark Bergstrom and Dave Smithson from the state police. On my right is a court stenographer and next to her is Gerri Pearson. She is my secretary and aide-de-camp. I couldn't run this department without her. But shh...don't tell her. She'll want a raise!

"So, let's get to it. Things have changed in a case that we first encountered about six months ago. So, here is how it will go. I have a statement in which I will review what happened six months ago. I'll cover that as quickly as I can, but I need to provide you with enough context that you will be ready for the new developments. Please, no questions until I am all done with the new info. Thank you for your cooperation."

Jim took a drink of his coffee, turned to his notes, and said, "Six months ago it came to my attention that the mayor had been threatened if he didn't stop trying to bring in industry that a group of men were opposed to. How the information came to the mayor was not important until he was assaulted as he left his office. He was not seriously injured at this time, but to be on the safe side, we assigned a police officer to follow him to and from his home. A short time later, he received a call from the company he was trying to bring in. They bowed out of the deal that the mayor had been working on for months. The mayor persuaded me to drop the police escort, to my regret.

"For a week or two, nothing happened. The mayor renewed his efforts to bring the company to Muskegon. He was assaulted again, and this time was kidnapped. He was found later to have been shot twice and killed. We suspected this group of men, which we later determined was a group of nine community leaders. We also wondered if the union was involved in thwarting the new business initiatives and possibly the mayor's death. After talking with the union, we were convinced that the 'Group of Nine' was responsible.

"We formed a task force that eventually grew to be eight people with different specialties including Mark and Dave, a state police detective whose specialty is assisting local departments in all kinds of cases. With a little luck and a lot of fine police work by all involved, we were able to tie the mayor's murder to all of them. As you remember, the Group hired a 'muscle man' to threaten the mayor, but he went too far and killed him. How we tied the Group to the muscle man will have to wait — their trial is due to start within the next two weeks.

"A private citizen, who was the mayor's best friend, came to us as a volunteer to help. It turns out he has some great detecting skills, so we accepted his offer. He was invaluable in helping to put the pieces together. The muscle man was put onto him by the Group and told to warn him to back off. When he didn't, he and his wife were shot at while they were up north on a honeymoon trip. His wife wasn't hurt, but he took a shot in the shoulder. It was only a flesh wound. They, too, went in hiding for a brief time, but when they emerged and went to be at one of their favorite places, the muscle man followed them there and shot both of them. He was hit in the leg, from which he is finally healing. But his wife was hit in the head and hit her head on cement when she fell. The trauma to her head put her into a coma. That was six months ago. The good news is that she woke up two weeks ago and is due to go home and finish her physical and emotional therapy as an outpatient." Applause broke out across the auditorium.

"Thank you for that. I'll be sure to pass on to both of them your concern and good feelings about her."

One of the reporters asked, "Who are they? With this good news, people will want to know."

"For their privacy, I am withholding their names. She still has a long way to go. Let's leave them alone until she gains full strength. Thank you for your respect for their privacy.

"So, back to my story. It's almost current. The muscle man was shot while he was trying to kill the couple. He was killed with a high-power rifle that we were able to track to another Group member. We arrested him, took his statement, and removed him from the jail to another location with police protection.

"A week after the shooting that killed the muscle man, someone got past our police protection and poisoned our prisoner.

"About a week before this, another Group member went missing. His wife notified me that her husband hadn't come home that night. I told her that we would start looking for him and put out a bulletin about his car. Nothing happened until a week later when a good citizen called the city to tell them about a hole in the fence on a bridge. We found this lady's husband in his car at the bottom of the lake that the bridge crossed. Our initial investigation looked like it just might have been an accident, driving too fast perhaps. But a more critical look at the car and the road across the bridge made us begin looking at foul play. Our forensic evidence pointed to another vehicle with a wooden front bumper that forced him off the bridge. The wife of that man is in the audience seeking answers as to who took her husband from her, and her two daughters, their father. You are welcome to be here. No, I'm not going to identify her. Again, let's give her the privacy she needs.

"At that point there were two members of the Group of Nine, Joe Antonelli and Larry Olsen, who are dead. The remaining seven, as I said earlier, are due to go on trial in the next two weeks.

"Now, the new developments. Two weeks ago, another member of the Group, Tim Samuels, was found dead in his office. He was in the habit of going in earlier than any of his staff. His killer was waiting, killed him, and got away unseen. At about the same time we received information that the rest of the members would be next. The remaining six members were assured that no one knew their names. The names of the group members were not released to the general public. We felt they were safe. We told them that we were re-convening the task force, which we have done, to investigate the most recent murder and to reexamine the earlier murders of victims one and two. We also told them that even though their names were not known outside of police, the judge, and the district attorney, we advised that they take a leave from work, and keep hidden. They did that, so we were confident we could get moving on the case. We set up a squad of retired police officers as a protection detail if it became necessary.

"We are meeting on a regular basis, reviewing evidence, but have no clue as to who the newest killer might be. Last Friday, we alerted all the remaining members about the warning and offered to let them stay at the jail that night and leave the next morning for their safe houses with their police detail officers, two officers per member. All but one member of the six agreed and spent the night in protective custody. They met with their protection detail the next morning and are now safe.

"The member who didn't accept told me he had a secluded cabin that not more than four or five close friends knew about. He left his home early Friday morning and went to the cabin. His wife, who was out-of-state visiting her sister, called him at their primary home to talk to him about her trip home. The housekeeper told her that he left early and could be reached later that morning when he got to the cabin. Mrs. Anderson asked the housekeeper to call him and ask him to call her after 11:00 as she was going out with her sister. The housekeeper couldn't reach him and thought the phone signal sounded 'funny.' She called me and said she was worried about him, and she needed to get his wife's message to him.

"Mark here and a sergeant in training for detective work went up to the second home. Without a lot of details, they found a fourth member of the Group, George Anderson, shot to death. And the same day, we received information that this man who was newly dead was allegedly the one who poisoned our prisoner and ran victim two off the bridge to drown in the lake.

"So, now we have four members who are dead. Two of them were allegedly killed by another member of the Group. The last two were killed by person or persons unknown at this point. You are now current on the case as of today. The task force is meeting this afternoon to begin analyzing what we have and figure out how to proceed from here.

"Your time has come. We have about fifteen minutes left for questions. Let me get some fresh coffee and we'll start."

He asked for coffee and signaled the stage manager to cut his mike. He turned his back to the audience and spoke to Gerri. "Gerri, don't look right this second but there is a woman wearing a white top and a pale blue sweater vest. She is about four rows from the back on our left. Okay, just casually now, shift your gaze and see if you can find her. Then tell me what she is doing right now."

"I see her. She wasn't hard to find. She is just sitting there, but with kind of a half-smile."

"Now write down three words, 'not a clue.' When you hear me use those three words in answer to a question, watch and remember any reaction you see in her face, in her body, or anything else you think might be of interest. Write yourself a note with those reactions so you can tell me later. Got it?"

"I've got it, Jim. What's this all about?"

"I'll tell you when we talk about it later."

He signaled for the mike to be turned on. "Alright, who's first?"

A hand shot up from the *Chronicle* reporter. "Harry Stone, *Muskegon Chronicle*. When are you going to release the names of the rest of the Group?"

"Their names will be released at their trial, which should happen very soon. The judge is moving the trial up given all that's going on."

The WZZM reporter asked, "Jason Wolf, WZZM, Grand Rapids.

Do you think these two killings were done by another member of the Group?"

"We don't know yet. We don't think so. All the rest seem pretty scared. If they did it, or hired someone to do it, they are pretty good actors. They are quite afraid they will be next."

"Cliff Woods, *Grand Rapids Press*. Do you think this will have any impact on the trial of the remaining members?"

"I don't see how. The judge, district attorney, and I have had long conversations about the legal implications of these new developments."

"Stan Black, WOOD, Grand Rapids. You really haven't told us much about how you will proceed. Why is that?"

"That's because this last one is so recent, and our task force hasn't met since that murder. We're meeting this afternoon."

"Harry Stone, *Muskegon Chronicle*. I'm asking this one because we've been talking. So, for all of us, do you have any ideas about who it might be?"

Jim bumped Gerri's arm. "Not a clue."

Gerri's hand began flying fast. Jim thought, *must be a big reaction.*

Jim stood up and signaled the conference was over. "Thank you all again for coming and for your interest in this. We'll have another news conference soon. In the meantime, we have a lot to do. See you next time."

25

D on saw Mrs. Olsen leave and let Doug know on the walkie-talkie. Don followed her out, hiding in a cluster of reporters. Doug came from the back of the station, and they followed her into the courthouse front parking area. She stood there for a while and took some pictures. She took off across the street where her car was parked in the U.S. 31 parking lot. Don and Doug went quickly to their car, keeping Mrs. Olsen in sight. She jumped into her car and took off in a hurry, squealing her tires as she turned the corner onto First Street.

"That was close. Good driving, Don. We almost lost her. She's moving really fast." She turned left onto W. Webster Street at the corner where St. Mary's Catholic Church was located. They followed but were surprised to find her nearly to the Hackley Library.

"Where is she going in such a hurry? And why?"

"Don't lose her, Don. This road will take her onto Seaway Drive toward the south side of town where her house is, won't it?"

"It will but she could turn off somewhere else," Don said as he closed in with two cars between them.

She turned off Seaway Drive onto Norton Avenue and took

another left onto Roosevelt Road. "Looks like she is going back home for sure. If she turns right onto Maryland Boulevard, we'll have her."

She turned right onto Maryland.

"You might have done this anyway, Don, but just on the chance she is watching us, pull into one of these driveways about halfway down. If she goes on up into the subdivision past McCracken, she won't have us behind her. This is the only way out of the subdivision, so we can't lose her. When we see her turn left onto Monteview Drive, we'll go up the hill and turn right onto Monteview. There is a spot where we can park up where the woods start and watch for her to come out." They drove up and parked by the edge of the woods facing Maryland Boulevard.

"If she spotted us near her house where Monteview turns into Hillsdale Drive and her house, she won't think to look up here. Nice, Doug. Thanks for the lesson. You must know this area well."

"I do. My house is off McCracken down by St. Francis de Sales Church. I often walk down to these woods and hike through them past the Waterworks complex to Lake Michigan. It's only a couple of miles but with some hills it is a good conditioner."

They sat there for a while. It was almost noon. Doug said, "I think you'll be okay to take over for a while by yourself. What do you think?"

"I'm ready. Where are you headed?"

Doug answered, "I have to check on the last of my protection detail and then I need to get to the task force meeting at the station. There is a 7-11 on the corner of Norton and McCracken and I know there is a pay phone there. I'll walk down, call the station and have them bring you a different car, full of gas and a different color. That should throw her off in case she noticed this car. Do you want me to pick you up a sandwich at the 7-11? They're pretty good. What would you like?"

"I'll have a ham and cheese, some chips, and a Coke, in a bottle please."

"I'll be back about 12:30 p.m. with our lunches." Doug took off down the hill and down McCracken. He called Gerri at the station and told her what was needed. "If they get here by 1:00 p.m., I'll have time to get my work done and get to the meeting."

Gerri said, "You should have seen your lady's reaction when Jim said that we don't have a clue who is doing this. Revealing!"

Doug replied, "I'm looking forward to hearing what Jim says about it. Thanks, Gerri."

He picked up their lunches, hiked back to the car. "Any action, Don?"

"Nope. Not a sign of her. She may be having lunch, too."

"Your new car will be here by 1:00 p.m. I hope she doesn't take off before then. We'll see what happens."

They finished their lunches and watched the new car come up the street. An officer in plain clothes jumped out. "Hey Sarge, here's your new buggy."

Doug and the driver headed out across the bridge to the south of Mona Lake to check his last member of the Group. According to his detail, all was well. The member hadn't left the house. His wife was just returning from grocery shopping as Doug was about to leave. One of the police officers introduced her to Doug.

Doug asked her, "Is everything good from your point of view, ma'am?"

"Yes, the policemen have eased the tension here. We feel safer. It took a little getting used to, but we're glad they are here. Thank you."

"Thank your officers, ma'am. I'm glad it is working out."

"Next stop, the station. We'll get you there on time for the meeting, Doug."

26

Tom arrived at the rehab facility about fifteen minutes early. He found Maria a little anxious. He took her in his arms for a kiss and a hug. "Don't fret, sweetheart. It's going to work out."

"I just want to get home. I'm ready to be back where I belong."

They sat, holding hands until Dr. Franks and the head nurse, Mrs. Jones, knocked and came in. The staff brought a couple of extra chairs, so the meeting could be in familiar territory for Maria.

Dr. Franks greeted her, "Good morning, Maria. How would you like some good news today?"

Maria brightened up. "I'm ready for that."

"Mrs. Jones and I have been going over your records and your latest tests. Everything looks good, both medically and emotionally. I sensed some anxiety this morning but that's natural. When I told you I had good news, I saw a change. You got less anxious and flashed that big smile of yours. I need to check some things this morning, a kind of mini physical if you will, and one more test that we will do early in the afternoon. I want you to have a chat with your neuro resident, and then he has some things to discuss with you. Tom tells me he has a meeting this afternoon that should be done about 4:00

p.m., so he says he will be here about 4:20 p.m. to get you home. How does that sound?"

"It sounds wonderful."

Mrs. Jones asked, "Tom, will you be having lunch with us?"

Tom looked at Maria. "I'd like to, but I have some errands to do now that I know you'll be home. What would you like for dinner tonight?"

"Surprise me, Tom. You're good with surprises and you know what I like."

"You've got it. Dr. Franks, I assume you will have some food restrictions for Maria. Could she have a glass of wine with that dinner tonight?"

"I don't see why not, but just one. Can you and I talk about it? Mrs. Jones needs to get Maria ready for her mini-physical. So, kiss her goodbye until tonight and let's step out."

Dr. Franks led Tom to a small room where they could talk in private. "Tom, I have a list of signs to watch for. I don't foresee them coming but you should be prepared. She is doing so well. Mrs. Jones will have a list for Maria, too, along with a suggested food list. Any questions so far?"

"She enjoyed the Doo Drop perch the other night, but I kept her portions down. You may not know this, but she has always had a good appetite. I'm looking forward to seeing that come back. She loves a broiled whitefish, so I thought I would put that together with a small portion of my mashed potatoes and a small salad. And, oh yes, since you okay'd a glass of wine, I'll have a glass of her favorite sauvignon blanc."

"I think she'll enjoy it. Any dessert?"

"Just a small hot fudge sundae. Will that be okay?"

"That will be good. And if I know you as I think I do, there will be candlelight and flowers."

"You've got it right — that's one of those errands."

"One more thing, Tom. Take it slow with her. Let her lead the way. I'm talking about your sex life. I assume you had an active sex life before this happened."

"We did, and I see signs that she is ready for that. But I'll take it slow. Dr. Franks, I don't know how I will ever be able to make you know how much we appreciate what you have done for Maria. Somehow, I always knew she would wake up. But that may have only been my love for her putting that in my head. But she is here, alive, and almost well. Thank you." Tom's eyes welled up with emotion.

"You are welcome, Tom. A lot of her progress was all the attention you gave her. I am convinced that what you did always makes a difference. Hers is a great case in point. I would like to do an article about her case. It's a good example of a lot of things that went right. Why don't you talk with Maria about it and let me know?"

"I'm inclined to. I'll see what she says."

"Take her home and treat her well. You have a great lady there."

AFTER THE MEETING, Jim walked through the audience to greet old friends. He shook hands with his friends from the press and worked his way to where Dr. Brown was still seated. Jim noticed on the way that Mrs. Olsen moved fast to get out of the room. That was all right, Doug and Don would pick up her trail again.

Dr. Brown stood as Jim reached his row. "Chief, that was masterful. I'm impressed by how you handle the press."

"It's Jim. Well, John, I learned a long time ago that if I treated them fairly and kept them in the loop, they would become my friends and respect what I could and couldn't say. It has paid off over the years."

"I can see that. I'm going to be here for a week. I would appreciate having an early breakfast or a lunch with you sometime during the week. This case fascinates me for reasons that would take too long to tell you now. Would that be possible?"

Checking his pocket calendar, Jim said, "I'd like that. I have Wednesday open. Do you like lake perch done just right? There are two places in town that fill the bill, Bear Lake Tavern, and the Doo Drop Inn."

"That sounds perfect. How about Doo Drop this time? Jane and I have been there a few times with George and Ann. We might have more privacy there if we can get a booth in the little bar room. They don't take reservations, but they might make an exception for us."

"I'll pick you up about 11:30 a.m. if that's okay?"

"I'll be ready Wednesday at 11:30 a.m. You know where we are staying, I would guess."

"See you then. I have to run. There is a special stop I need to make just before lunch. And then I need to get out to a spot to clear my head before the task force meeting. I have to run."

Jim drove to the rehab facility. Maria said Tom should be gone shortly after 11:30 a.m., so that would be a good time to stop by. He pulled into the lot and parked in the back of the parking lot facing outward. He had borrowed Gerri's car and was quite sure Tom wouldn't know it. He waited.

He saw Tom leave the building walking with a bit of a jaunty stride. He thought, *must have been good news this morning.* He waited for Tom to leave, then got out and walked right to Maria's room. There was a nurse aide just outside her door. "Hello, I'm Jim Johnson, a friend of Tom and Maria's. She's expecting me this morning."

"She's just dressing after her physical. Just a minute."

She poked her head into Maria's room. "Maria, you have a good-looking gentleman here to see you. Are you decent yet?"

"Just a second." She opened the door and threw her arms around his neck. "Hi, Jim. You came! I'm so excited to see you and to share our good news."

"Hello, Maria. You are looking a whole lot better than the last time I saw you. You're positively glowing. It must have been great news."

"Exciting news, Jim. Come on in and I'll tell you about it."

Her aide said, "Your lunch will be here in about fifteen minutes. Can I get you something, Mr. Johnson?"

"No, thank you. I only have a few minutes. Tell me about this morning, Maria."

"It couldn't be better news. I just had a physical, I have some test this afternoon and one more therapy session. Tom will be back around 4:30 p.m. and I'm going home!"

"That is good news!" Taking a folder out of his briefcase, he handed it to her and continued, "Here are enough materials to keep you busy for a while. This should keep you occupied until you can start the state police training. Has your doctor told you how long before you'll be out and about?"

"He said there will be physical therapy twice a week for the next six weeks at the house, of course, and a trip or two to the facility. He believes that just being home will make a significant difference. If this works as he has suggested, I should be ready to start that training sometime after the first week of June."

"That should work out well. There's a new session starting just after July fourth that you could make. When are you going to tell Tom?"

"Sometime this week. I'll let you know, but maybe Tom will get to you first. How much can he tell me about what's going on?"

"I think I'll let you and your doctor figure that out. From what I see, it shouldn't be long. You won't be able to avoid some of it after this morning's press conference. It will be the talk of the town for a while at least."

Her aide came with her lunch. Jim said, "I have to run and get ready for the task force meeting. I'm looking forward to seeing you and Tom soon. Take care."

"Thanks for these, Jim. We'll be seeing you."

JIM PICKED up a snack for lunch and sat for a while on a bench in Hackley Park. He always enjoyed this park. There was so much history around him. From where he was sitting, he could see The Hackley Library, St. Paul's Episcopal Church, the old Occidental

Hotel, still impressive but without many paying customers these days, the *Chronicle* building and, further down the street, the Masonic Temple. Then across W. Webster Avenue was the main campus of Muskegon Junior College. It was a mainstay of the community, but he had heard there were changes coming. He hoped they would fix up the Occidental Hotel — it was such a great building and an important part of Muskegon's history. Fred told him that he and Tom talked about that a lot. Tom loved the architecture of the Occidental and took his choir there every year at Christmas. He finished his lunch, filled Gerri's car with gas, and headed for the police station. He had a task force meeting to get to.

27

Gerri walked into the conference room for the task force meeting. "Jim is on his way. He said another five minutes."

Some were talking about the news conference this morning. Others were engrossed in Gerri's notes of the conference as well as the notes of the previous meeting and events since. Most of them knew what Jim covered this morning at the press conference and were looking for the rest of the story. *Shades of Paul Harvey*, Tom thought.

Jim came in a few minutes later, greeted them all, and was pleased to see Doug was able to get there. He asked Doug, "What happened with the person of interest you were tailing after the meeting this morning?"

"I'll give you a full report later when you want it. You know the person turned up here and went to the press conference. What's more, our person of interest took a lot of pictures of the people coming out of the press conference. We followed the person home, where Don is waiting to see what happens next. He is doing well, Jim. He must have had good training."

"Thanks for your help with that situation."

Jim looked around the room. "I saw all of you in the meeting.

Sorry I couldn't have all of you up front, but I think it's best that most don't know who you are. I see you all are reviewing what was said at the news conference. I'm sure you recognize that there was a lot left out. We don't want the press and the community to know everything we do as that could hamper our investigation.

"Tom, would you tell us quickly what happened this morning at your meeting with Maria and her doctor?"

Tom looked around the table with a big smile. "I'm picking Maria up at 4:30 p.m. today and we're headed home!"

The guys clapped wildly and hooted and whistled. Tom held up his hand to stop it. "Thank you. It has been a long time, the longest coma and recovery that Dr. Franks has ever seen. She is walking well, speaking well, eating food on her own. In short, she is a miracle. She still has a long way to go, more outpatient therapy at home, visiting nurses for a month or two. But my Maria is coming home! Thank you, Jim, for your patience with me during this time. Thank all of you for your support. You never wavered."

"So glad for the good news, Tom. Let's get going now." Jim called the meeting back to order.

"I'm sure all of you noted that I didn't share all the evidence we have. After consulting with Judge McVie and the district attorney, we worked out what I should and shouldn't say. We didn't want to upset the D.A.'s case. We didn't release the names of the rest of the Group because it helps us keep the remaining members alive. Doug tells me that the protection detail is working out fine. There is no suspicious activity, nothing unusual going on around the houses, and we don't even see the Group members, just their families.

"I didn't mention the notes at the press conference because they're important to our investigation. The second note included something new, a handwritten note on the back telling us that George was responsible for both Joe Antonelli's poisoning and Olsen's car being pushed into the lake.

"I didn't mention the second note for another reason. We have a suspect."

The room erupted into "Who is it? Tell us. Is it a man or a woman?"

"Who asked about 'a man or a woman?'"

"Me, Jim," said the state forensic specialist, Jeff Flanagan.

"Well, it is a woman. What's more she was in the audience this morning! Anna Olsen is our suspect."

"Larry's wife!"

"One and the same."

"You may recall that I wasn't convinced that the killer was a woman."

"What changed your mind? Some new evidence?"

"It was a lot of little things that I've been reviewing. The handwriting on the second note, a footprint that looked like a woman's boot, the angle. Little things that seemed to be adding up to a stronger possibility that our killer was a woman. We can't be one hundred percent sure yet — we need some hard evidence — but my instincts and experience are strongly suggesting it was a woman."

Jim continued, "I called Anna Olsen last Saturday afternoon and asked if I could come out to talk. I told her I had some news I wanted to share. She said she couldn't that day, but we made an appointment for Sunday afternoon. I talked to Tom and asked if he would come along to watch her reactions while I asked questions and passed along information. The next afternoon we went to her house. She was very gracious acting, a little flirty with Tom here, holding on to his hand too much when they were introduced. I was wired." He held up his hand at questions. "All legal. I got a warrant from Judge McVie for the wire. Gerri will be passing out a copy of the transcription of that conversation. We can't use it in court, but it may help us get some of the evidence we need to convict her. There was one moment of anger on her part when she thought Tom was watching her too closely. You'll see it when Gerri gives you all a copy in a moment. By the time we were ready to leave, she was back to her hostess mode and playing the distraught wife."

"As Tom and I drove away, we were quiet at first, both digesting what had just happened. I pulled over a few blocks away, we looked at each other, nodded, and almost simultaneously said, 'She's our killer.' Tom went on with, 'I know it. But she is tough, a brassy confident woman. We are going to have a real problem getting enough to convict her.'"

Dave Smithson asked, "On a scale of one to ten, how sure are you?"

"I'm at a ninety percent sure. Tom, what about you?"

"I put it a little higher, Jim. I'm saying ninety-five percent. But we are both open to any thoughts or questions you might have on our other possibility — a short man."

There were a lot of questions and comments. Jim and Tom shot each one down as it was registered. Finally Mark said, "Are you really still open to it maybe being a short man?"

"Good question, Mark. We are, but it's going to take a lot of evidence to move us in that direction. To me, the evidence points more clearly at a woman. But in the meantime, let's work on these clues. In a minute, I'll give each of you a specific assignment to focus on as well as reading all the info you have again and again to see if anything new jumps out at you. Review everything you've got with a fine-tooth comb. We need all your great skills to solve this. See where it takes you and we'll meet again on Wednesday.

"By the way, I have two more pieces to add to the puzzle. I asked Doug and Don Phillips, our new sergeant and budding detective, to follow Mrs. Olsen. They started this morning. Today she left her house about 8:30 a.m. She drove straight to the Anderson home in North Muskegon, pulled into the driveway as if she had been there before. She was there about a half hour, came out and gave Mrs. Anderson and her sister hugs and drove off. How did she know that Mrs. Anderson was home? And what did they talk about? And then she showed up at the press conference and Doug just informed me that she took a lot of pictures of the people exiting the police station. Why did she do that? What's her plan?

"I called Mrs. Anderson last Saturday to tell her about George's death. She has been out of town with her sister and brother-in-law. She wasn't dealing well with all the stress of what happened. I spoke with all three of them and she is still not doing well. Her sister and husband are, as of Sunday night, back here with Mrs. Anderson at the Anderson home in North Muskegon. She has a lot to deal with now with George's affairs. Her brother-in-law is a doctor and has helped a lot with her anxieties that returned with the news of his death.

"Doug informed me where she was sitting and what she was wearing. That's when my trusty aide-de-detective Gerri got to work." He pointed at Gerri, and all gave her a round of applause. She blushed. He continued, "I asked Gerri to watch Mrs. Olsen and write down her reactions when I said the words 'not a clue.' I figured someone would ask a question like 'Do you have an idea who the killer might be?' When I said the words, Gerri's shorthand worked. She has a transcript of that for you. In short, Mrs. Olsen's reactions were her eyes first widened, got big as saucers, she started bouncing in her seat until she must have realized that people might be watching. She then turned on her sober look, crossed her arms, and glanced around before turning to listen to me close the conference. What does that behavior tell us? We don't know for sure, but it seems like she now might believe we don't suspect her.

"Don is still on duty parked near the only entrance into her subdivision. We need to get him some more help. I'm going to assign a couple more officers to spell Don and Doug so we can keep her under surveillance twenty-four-seven. Doug has indicated he can help, but he has other responsibilities too.

"You have your assignments. Jeff, would you have your handwriting specialist look at the second note? And can you take the bullets from Anderson and compare them with bullet from Samuels? If they match, it will confirm that one person did both. I'd love to wrap this up and lock up the killer before she kills again."

_____

28

Tom and Doug stopped in the station parking lot to check plans. Doug said, "Everything is ready. We have your decorations, the big welcome home sign, the champagne chilling — your dad brought it — and the charcuterie board with light hors d'oeuvres and her favorite cheeses. It was a joint effort, your mom and Maria's mom. We're all meeting there just before 5:30 p.m. We'll have the fire going in the fireplace. Anything else?"

"Our favorite jazz station?"

"We'll have that on. Oh, and our cars will be parked around the corner out of sight. We're ready."

"Thanks, my friend. I knew I could count on you. We'll see you there at 5:30 p.m. or a little after."

Doug drove off to Tom's place. Tom headed to the rehab facility. As he walked in, the place seemed quiet. He went around to Maria's room. There was a cart filled with her suitcases. He knocked, her door opened, and there she was with a lot of the staff saying, "Maria, your man is here."

She stepped over and gave him a hug. Someone said, "Aw, go ahead and kiss him. It's okay!"

Maria's aide said, "Have a glass of punch and a cookie and we'll all escort you to your car." They all loved Maria. With tears in her eyes, Maria thanked them all, telling them that she would never forget them. Then she said, "Let's go! Much as I love you all, I'm ready to go home."

One of the nurses asked, "Tom, you can't keep this girl down. Are you going to be able to keep her reined in?" Tom shrugged and smiled. "I'll try, but her spirit and determination are what got her here."

They loaded Maria into the wheelchair for her last ride out — rehab policy — even though she could have walked it.

As they rolled down the hall to the main entrance, Tom ran ahead and brought the car up. While the aides loaded Maria's things into the car, Maria hugged everyone until Tom finally got her in the car.

"Thank you all for taking such good care of my sweetheart." He reached into the back seat and handed them a box of chocolates and a fruit basket.

"Aww, thank you, Tom. Maria, can we hug him?"

"Hugs. No kisses!" she admonished with a smile. Laughing, they lined up to hug and thank Tom.

Maria waved wildly until she couldn't see them any longer. She wiped her eyes one last time and then reached over and put her hand on Tom's. "We're headed home. I've never been so happy to be outside again. Can we go somewhere and get a look at Lake Michigan?"

Tom smiled. "I thought you might want that. We'll swing by Bronson Park. We'll just stand there at the main level and look at the lake. No climbing down to the beach or up onto the dune." He helped her out of the car. They stood for a while, watching the waves, and smelling the fresh air. Tom looked at his watch. "It's 5:15 p.m. We better get moving. I have part of our dinner simmering, so we better get you home."

"Do we have to?"

"No, we don't have to, but we should. The fireplace is ready to go with a cozy fire." He asked Maria, "What are you thinking?"

She smiled. "I have so much to tell you. I'm ready to start living again. I'm remembering things and want to share them with you. We have the time, we're so lucky to be here together."

"I know, darling." He took them down Beach Street, going in the back way to their home in the Bluffton area. When they were home, Tom said, "Might be a good idea to use your cane. This ground is a little rougher than the halls."

She grinned. "You just watch me go, Mister." She grabbed the cane anyway.

"You stand here for a second until I get the door unlocked. Then I'm going to carry you over the threshold again, like I did a few months ago." He rushed up the front steps and pretended to unlock the door, so everyone knew they were home. He came back and took her cane, picked her up and started up to the porch. When he got to the front door, he turned and started backing through the door.

Maria fussed, "Tom, what are you doing? Why are you backing in?"

Tom whispered, "Close your eyes, please. Just do it, please."

He turned around, set her on her feet. "Now you can open them."

There was her mom and dad, Tom's mom and dad, and Doug. All of them grinning, saying, "Welcome home, Maria," as did the big banner facing the front door.

"Mama and Dad." She walked straight into their arms for hugs. Wiping tears from her eyes she turned to Tom's mom and dad and hugged them. Finally, she gave Doug a little punch on the arm and then hugged him. "You! I can't believe you did all this. Looks like you've all been busy. Look at this charcuterie board, my favorite cheeses..."

Tom's dad held up a bottle of champagne. "And a celebration glass of champagne."

"Sweetheart, it was all their idea. When I called them all this weekend to tell them you might be able to come home today, they got to work. I have been so busy with what's going on that I haven't seen them much and they wanted to welcome you home and celebrate us being together. I didn't have the heart to say no."

They all got plates of the hors d'oeuvres. Maria gazed around the room in delight. It was so good to be home. It was just like she remembered only better because she could remember! She could see that Tom had moved things a little to make it easier for her to get around with her cane. She'd put things back where they were supposed to be as soon as she could, but he was so thoughtful. Tom and Maria cuddled on one end of the sofa, her mother beside her. Tom's mom and dad sat across from them in the wingback chairs while her dad lounged on the arm of the sofa next to her mom. Doug pulled up a dining room chair next to the fire. Tom's dad poured the champagne, nodded to Maria's dad who stood and said, "Here's to our young ones, ready to start rebuilding a life. Good health."

"Here, here, here" echoed around the room. Tom couldn't take his eyes off Maria. Her mom kept fussing over her, asking if she needed anything — A pillow? A blanket?

Maria finally said to her mom, "Mom, I love you and I'm so happy to be home. I'm just perfect the way I am right now, surrounded by all of you."

Her dad reached over and hugged his wife. "She's just so happy that you're home. We all are. She can't help but hover a little."

Maria's mom said, "Tom, what have you cooked for your bride her first night home?"

"Broiled whitefish and all the trimmings."

"My favorite! It's one of your best dishes."

Tom's dad asked, "What are you having for dessert?"

Before Tom could answer, Maria said, "I have my dessert right here," putting her arm around him.

Her mom exclaimed, "Maria! You shouldn't talk—"

Maria interrupted with, "Why not, he's my guy and it has been six months."

"Maria!" Maria's mother blushed.

"I'm not going to argue with her." Tom said. "Dr. Franks told me to let her lead the way and who am I to argue with her or her doctor."

Tom's mom said, "Tom!" Chuckling, they stood to gather their coats and pocketbooks.

Doug said, "I think that is our cue to head out."

"Doug is taking all of us to dinner. I think we should go and let these lovebirds have their way."

Saying "good night" and "enjoy your dinner," Tom and Maria waved goodbye. The remainders of the welcome home feast were picked up. The fire still felt good and looked cozy. Maria said, "I need to get a shower and..."

"But what about dinner?"

"I'm not really hungry for dinner."

Tom jumped up, "Just a minute, I'll join you. I'll make sure you don't fall until I build that handrail the doctor ordered."

"Well, come on, big boy."

Tom got in the shower behind her. Before she turned the water on, he stood behind her, ruffled her hair, and kissed the back of her neck. He whispered in each ear. She giggled at the first whisper. The second made her body go limp. "If you keep that up, I won't be able to stand up here." From there on, it was a fun shower, washing each other, caressing each other, kissing deeply.

Maria murmured, "Come on, let's dry each other off and..."

Later, they were still holding each other in the bed, cuddling. Tom asked. "Are you okay?"

She smiled, cuddled closer. "I'm fine. You said I could lead the way. Something is poking me. Does that mean what I hope it does?"

This time was slower till neither could wait longer. Afterward, Maria fell asleep first. Tom held her and finally fell off to sleep himself.

29

Tom woke first in the morning, put the coffee on, and started thinking about what to do for breakfast. The scrambled eggs were almost done, and the toast popped up when Maria came out in her robe.

"Good morning," she said with a kiss for him.

"How about some scrambled eggs and toast?"

"That sounds great. Just one piece of toast and a couple of sliced tomatoes if we have some."

"Of course, but you never asked for tomatoes before. What gives?"

"The facility kept bringing them in with my eggs and sometimes at night. I've come to enjoy them."

"No problem. I'll just slice this one up in a jiffy." Maria snarfed down her eggs and tomatoes while Tom made quick work of his eggs and toast. Tom was happy to see Maria's appetite returning. "Let's take some coffee to the sofa and just talk for a while."

"You don't have to go in to work?"

"No, Jim said to take the next two days off. I have some homework to do for the task force. And then I have to show up for the next meeting Wednesday afternoon. He told me we should just get reacquainted and spend a lot of time together."

Maria turned serious and asked, "How's our money situation?"

"We're fine. Jim has been paying me better this time. And I've played some in the clubs in Grand Rapids. That has covered me, so our savings are intact. The school is still paying you disability and health benefits since you're still on contract for another year. I expect they will be in touch with you when they hear you are home now. We'll see."

He continued, "And I told you when you were still in the coma that I finished my master's degree at GVSU. So, that opens up some new doors for us."

"I know." She smiled. "I heard a lot more than I let on. I couldn't reply but I heard a lot. I think the staff, especially my nurse aide, Jenny, has suspicions about it but never said anything. I don't know if that happens to everyone who is in a coma, but it did for me, especially the last month or two. By the way, you are singing well." And she smiled again.

"That reminds me of something Dr. Franks said to me in our little meeting. He wants to do a case study on you. He has never had a case where someone woke up after this long. He asked me to mention it to you, talk about it, and let him know."

"How do you feel about it? Do they put my name in the article?"

"No, they don't unless you and I give permission. How do I feel? Your feeling is what matters. But if you say yes, I wouldn't object."

"So, we don't have to settle it yet?"

"No, he said to take two or three weeks. He will talk to you about it after he knows we've discussed it."

"Did you talk with him about what is going on — the new developments? Can you share?"

"We talked about that. I think it should be soon. There was a news conference today, so the word is on the street and in the news. He said that I should watch carefully and if you appear to be getting upset, stop, and switch to something different."

"And you are good at reading me, so you will see it and know when to stop. I don't think I will have a problem handling it. My therapist and I became good friends and she told me she had not seen anyone get mentally stable so quickly. I told her that I thought it was because I was so well rested, comfortable... I knew I was safe where I was and that helped a lot."

"Let me get us some fresh coffee and we'll get started."

He poured the fresh coffee. "I spoke to Jim about it just before the task force meeting. He told me he trusts you to keep things between us. It kind of surprised me. I didn't think he knew you that well."

He noticed Maria's slight smile and asked, "What is that little smile about?"

"I'll tell you later. I want to hear what's going on."

"Okay, I'll get started. I'm going to follow Jim's new conference format but start with what has happened the past two weeks. I also have a transcript of the news conference that will help you get perspective from before. If you have questions as I go, ask away, and I'll answer them if I can. Okay?"

"Do we have a tablet or a yellow pad I can use to take notes?"

"Remember I have the transcription. Do you want to read the first part about what happened six months ago?"

"No, it will come back, or I'll ask."

"Here's what's new. On Friday night two weeks and two days before today, Doug dropped by with a pizza, and we were enjoying it when Jim called. He wanted to come by to talk. He didn't want to get into it on the phone and he was okay talking to me with Doug here."

"When I saw his face, I knew it was serious. He told us that Tim Samuels, one of the Group of Nine, was dead. He was shot and killed at his office that morning. There were no witnesses since Tim liked getting in earlier than his staff. When they came in, they found him lying in a pool of blood in his office doorway. Tim died almost instantly. They called the police and the police found nothing to identify his killer."

"Was it connected with the other deaths or something else in his life?"

"Good question, Maria. That same day Jim got a letter in the police department's mail. The note was big cut-out letters pasted to a plain piece of paper. He asked me to read it."

Tom took Maria's hand. "The note said, 'O'Banion, Samuels is number three. You are on the list as well and I want you to know I'll get to you after I get the rest.'"

Maria caught her breath, grabbed for Tom. "Why you? Has the killer tried to get you yet? Oh, that's right, the note said, 'after I get the rest.'"

"Hey, you're good. You were listening and caught what the note said. Besides there's now more evidence that suggests the killer is following that line. I'll be last. But our friend, Doug, isn't taking any chances. He got me armed and is watching me, and you. I'll tell you more about Doug later on."

"Were there any fingerprints?"

Tom looked at her with a question on his face. She said, "Well, that's the next question to ask, isn't it?"

"It is the next question and no, there were no prints. We think this killer is a very cool customer and doesn't seem to miss a trick.

"So, onward. Jim reconvened the task force. Mostly the same people as before but a couple of new faces I'll tell you about as we go. We reviewed the evidence we had, which was not much. We had no idea who the killer was but because of the note, we were sure it was tied to the other killings.

"Responding to some pressure for police protection for the remaining Group members, Jim put together protection details made up of retired police officers from all over the county. We wanted enough so we could cover them around the clock with two men at a time. We couldn't get the protection details in place until Saturday morning — paperwork and funding needed to be approved.

"On Thursday, we brought all the remaining members into the station. We offered to have them come in on Friday and stay in the jail and then go home with their protection detail on Saturday morning. All but one accepted. George Anderson said he had other arrangements. He was going up to his second place, he calls it a cabin, up on Scenic Drive, and take care of himself. Jim couldn't talk him out of it. The rest of the Group went home and agreed to come back the next day, Friday, and spend the night. We told them to be extra careful and not go out of their houses.

"On Friday morning, Jim got a phone call from the Anderson's housekeeper. She was all upset because she couldn't get Mr. Anderson on the phone at the cabin. Jim sent Mark and Don, a new sergeant up to check. Long story short, George was shot and killed and there was another note at the scene."

At this Maria sagged. Tom said, "It's time for you to take a rest from this. What do you think?"

"I agree. Dr. Franks told me I might need regular naps for a while. This is a lot to take in, so I think I had better get one now. Tom, would you come in, too, and take one with me? Even if you can't sleep, please just come and hold me while I do. We'll start up again after lunch."

Tom covered them with a colorful patchwork quilt that Maria's mother made them as a shower present. Maria fell asleep quickly in Tom's arms. Tom couldn't sleep, but just rested with her. His mind was filled with how Maria was taking it and thinking about what he would start with next. He finally gently removed Maria's arm from across his chest and went out to the kitchen to make some notes.

Dr. Franks called about a half hour later. "I just wanted to check in and see how Maria is doing."

"She's doing fine. I'm catching her up on events. She is taking it in pretty well for the most part. She told me when she needed to stop and get a nap. I thought that was smart of her to know when she's reached her limit. She is still sleeping but will be getting up soon for lunch. Do you need to talk to her?"

"No, that's all right. Just tell her I called. Her first visiting nurse visit is Wednesday at 10:00 a.m. Will you still be there?"

"I will but have to leave shortly after lunch. Should I have someone come and stay with her?"

"It would be good if you could. Do you have someone in mind?"

"I do. I'll either ask her mother or Sara. You've heard Maria speak of her. She is the former student who wants Maria to be her matron of honor at her wedding. I'll ask her who she wants in first. It will depend, too, on whether Sara is still on spring break."

"Great, Tom. We'll talk again at her first follow-up appointment with me next week. It's on her To-Do list she got at the facility. I'd like you to be there too. Bye for now."

Maria came in rubbing her eyes. "Who was on the phone?"

"It was Dr. Franks. Just a catch-up call to see how you are doing. He was glad you were napping. Your first visiting nurse visit will be Wednesday at 10:00 a.m."

"Yes, I remember. Shall we start again?"

"How about lunch first? A bowl of soup and some iced tea or lemonade sound good?"

"I want to fix it."

"If you are sure you are ready, okay. I was planning on cooking for another day. I'll get our drinks while you warm up the soup. Tonight is the broiled whitefish we didn't get to last night." He smiled, remembering why they didn't have dinner last night.

After they started on their soup. Maria asked, "Can we talk about Doug while we eat?"

"I think that would be okay. Let me finish and then I'll get my notes." He watched as she struggled a bit with the spoon. She was still a little slower eating, sometimes her hand didn't want to move the way she wanted. He picked up his notes and leaned toward her.

"Doug is a lot more than we knew him to be." He told her about Doug's time in the military and his time as an asset for one of the intelligence agencies. "He wants to go back to it. I'll let him tell you why sometime over a dinner with the three of us."

"Which one?" asked Maria.

"He wouldn't, or couldn't, tell me. Point is, he went to Mr. Mann and told him this would be his last year. When all this stuff started happening recently, he went back and told him that he could only be part time this semester due to some personal reasons, namely, protecting us, even though he didn't tell Mr. Mann that. Mr. Mann agreed, and they already have a long-term sub to take his classes."

"Doug also told Jim about his background and Jim asked him to be on the task force. He told Jim that he would if part of his time could be spent watching you and me."

"What an old softie he is. I didn't know he was like that."

"Neither did I. I think now that his jocular mode is a cover-up for it. I haven't told him that and likely won't. But a part of it also is his military background. The military says to him, you don't leave your friends when there is trouble. He is prepared to stay until this Group of Nine thing is all over and we are safe."

"We are lucky to have him as a friend."

"Yes, we are. Doug said something else to me too. He said Mr. Mann asked him if I might come back so at least the two of us would be together again at the school."

"What did you tell Mr. Mann?"

"I haven't yet. I want to tell him in person. We still need to talk about what we're doing next."

30

Maria finished her lunch and carefully carried her own dishes to the sink. Tom was pleased to see she was quite steady on her feet. "Ready to hear the rest of the story? It gets better now. I don't think there are any more big shocks. By the way, Dr. Franks suggested that we have someone be with you Wednesday afternoon while I'm at the task force meeting. I thought either your mom or Sara."

"I would like to see Sara and Arianna again. And we need to catch up on the wedding plans. I'll call Sara and ask her over Wednesday afternoon after school is out. Is that early enough?"

Tom got them some more iced tea, and said, "That should work since she's just doing half days.

"We stopped right after I told you George Anderson was killed. The new note was done the same way with the cut-out letters, except the number, calling Anderson number four. The big difference was a handwritten note on the back saying that George told the killer that he was the one who ran Larry Olsen off the road into the lake. He also confessed that he poisoned Joe Antonelli. So, now we have four of the nine dead — the first two allegedly killed by Anderson, and the third and fourth possibly killed by the same person, possibly not. The forensic people are checking the bullets from the last two and doing a comparison. If, as we suspect, the bullets are from the same gun, then we know it is one person doing the killing. We just don't know who it is...yet.

"The remaining members of the Group stayed last Friday night in the jail. The next morning Jim ran a little quiz session on them that convinced Jim of their innocence on the latest murders. They are frightened, scared half to death is more like it, so they are at home, hiding with police protection until their trial.

"Jim called Mrs. Anderson to tell her about George. It turns out she was down in South Bend, Indiana, staying with her sister and brother-in-law. She had been pretty upset about all that was happening. With her sister to help and her brother-in-law who is a doctor, she was improving but had a setback when Jim told her George was murdered. They are all three back here now in the Anderson home in North Muskegon.

"Jim then called Mrs. Olsen, Larry's wife. Larry Olsen is the one who allegedly ran George off the road. She couldn't see him that afternoon but made an appointment for 2:00 p.m. on Sunday. He asked me to go with him on that appointment and observe her.

"It turns out that some evidence and opinion from the coroner suggested that the person who shot George was shot by a short man or a woman. We talked about it at the task force meeting."

At this, Maria's eyes widened, "I can't believe it. A woman. What did the rest of you think of that?"

"Jim got lots of questions. We left it unresolved at this time but we're leaning toward a woman.

"Now back to the visit with Mrs. Olsen. When we got there, she was gracious, quite pleasant, a little giddy, maybe even a little flirtatious with both of us. She was inappropriately dressed I thought for someone in mourning. When we shook hands, she gazed into my eyes and held my hand longer than I was comfortable with. She did a similar thing with Jim as she handed him his lemonade. She took in the news about George and the confessions about her husband's death and Joe Antonelli. Then she caught me watching her closely and asked why. She got very agitated, turned to Jim, and said, 'I didn't like him, but I didn't kill him.' Then, like a switch, she was gracious and flirty again. Jim told her that Mrs. Anderson was home now, and she grimaced for a second, then went back to her gracious, pleasant hostess face. Jim thanked her for her time and said that he would keep her posted.

"When we got about fifteen minutes away, Jim pulled over and parked alongside the road. We looked at each other and almost simultaneously said, 'she's the killer.' Jim was ninety percent certain and I put it at ninety-five percent. But I said to Jim, 'She put on quite an act in there.' I told Jim that it would be very hard to get enough evidence to convict her. I told him that I wished I had a copy of that conversation. Jim told me that I would. He got Judge McVie to give him a warrant to wear a wire and Doug fixed him up with an agency wire. We called Doug, got the wire off, made the transcription and Doug took me home. We have a transcription in that pile of documents.

"Doug and Don, the new sergeant, started following her as per Jim's instructions. Monday morning, she led them on a trip to the Anderson home where she stayed for a half hour, came out, hugged Mrs. Anderson and her sister, and took off back to downtown Muskegon and went into the news conference. Doug let Jim know she was there, how she was dressed, and where she was sitting. Jim answered a question from one of the news people asking, 'Do you have any idea who the killer might be?' He answered, 'Not a clue.' Gerri was watching her reactions and there were many.

"There. You are caught up except for some details. I'm ready to relax a bit before dinner. If you have questions, I'll answer them now if you want, but I'd rather wait."

Maria said, "Let's just sit here and relax. Then while you are fixing dinner, I'll call Mom and Sara. I'll have a long chat with Mom and ask Sara if she can come over Wednesday afternoon. The meeting starts at 2:00 p.m., so if she can get here about 1:30 p.m., it will work out unless she has other plans. If she does, I'll ask Mom."

There was a knock on the door. Tom waved Maria back into the bedroom and took a look out through the window curtains. Tom called to Maria, "Come out. It's Doug, with two men standing behind him."

Doug introduced the two men. He said, "These men are the first shift of your protection detail. The second shift comes on in twelve hours. We'll let them get to their post and I'll tell you why they are here."

"Can I get you gentlemen something to drink, iced tea, maybe?"

"No, ma'am, we're all set for a while. Here is your walkie-talkie if you need to talk to us." They went out.

Doug said, "I'll have some of that tea, if you don't mind."

While Maria was getting the tea, Doug asked, "How much does Maria know of the situation?"

"I finished the update about ten minutes ago. She's a little anxious about it but she will be okay."

Maria returned with the tea and some cookies. Doug said, "As you may have suspected, there is a change. That's why your detail is here. It isn't that we think you are next but with what has happened, we're not taking any chances."

They nodded. He continued, "Our suspect is setting up her next victim. The pace seems to be increasing. It was just before dusk when she left home. Don followed her to Wendel's house — one of the older Group members. When Don got close enough, he alerted Wendell's protection detail to get out of sight so they could find out what she was up to. She pulled up about a block away and started walking toward the house. She took pictures from various angles, all around the house. Then she sat back in some bushes and watched the pattern of lights coming on. I got the feeling she was a little familiar with the house. This is one cool, plotting woman working her scene and planning. She strolled back to her car and took off home. Don reported she didn't go anywhere else."

Maria asked, "Are you sure he is her next target? She could be on to you all and may go off to someone else."

Doug looked at her. "That's a good question. Interesting you should ask it."

Tom added, "She's been asking questions all day long. Good ones, I'd say."

"You're right. And yes, Maria, we thought of that. We made sure all the others knew about her being at Wendell's and that's why we're here with your detail."

Tom asked, "Is there any chance she might come here next? She did say in both notes that I would be last, but she could change her mind. I don't want Maria to be in danger."

"We didn't want to take that chance. So, you'll have a team until this is settled. By the way, Jim said that you could skip the next meeting if you wanted to."

Tom looked at Maria. She shook her head no. "No, tell him I'll be there. I have some ideas I wanted to run by you all. Besides, Maria is going to try and get Sara and Arianna over here and catch up with their wedding plans. A little girl time, if you will. And now that our team is out there, we will feel safer. Thanks for that, Doug."

"Thanks for the iced tea and cookies. I better be going. Say, I wanted to tell you two. I really like your parents, both sets of them. I really enjoyed myself the other night having dinner with your parents. See you two later."

Tom got to work on his notes for the meeting on Wednesday afternoon. He had some thoughts for the rest of the team, and he wanted them to be just right.

While Tom was working, Maria called her mom for a visit. After chatting a while, her mom pushed her for a visit. "How about dinner next week at our house?"

Maria told her, "That sounds great. How about I call you back tomorrow with a firm date after my visiting nurse is here? Love you, Mom."

She then called to speak with Sara. There were only a few phones at the home, so it took a minute before Sara came on. "Maria, it's so good to hear from you."

"Sara, could you come for a visit tomorrow afternoon? Tom has to go to a meeting, and he wanted someone to be with me. I thought it would be great if you could come over." After a yes from Sara, Maria continued, "I have so much to tell you. How about 1:30 p.m.? It'll be just us girls. You can bring Arianna if you want."

Maria gave Tom a thumbs up about Sara. She dropped a kiss on the top of his head and let him know it was nap time. He nodded okay and kept working on his notes. Maria looked back at Tom and wondered when she should tell him about her plans.

31

Tom finished his work and went into the bedroom to check on Maria. She was still asleep, so he went back to the living room and called his mom. "Hi, Mom, how are you and Dad doing?"

"We're fine. Tom, how are things going?"

"Things are great. Maria keeps getting stronger. Her first time with the visiting nurse and the physical therapist is tomorrow. We'll see what they think about her progress. And Sara is coming to visit tomorrow afternoon. Do you remember her? She is our former student. Maria is matron of honor for her June wedding."

"Do you think she will be ready?"

"She'll be ready! You know Maria." They chatted on for a few more minutes and agreed to get together soon. "Say hi to Dad for me. I have a meeting tomorrow afternoon. If it ends early, I'll stop by to see you both and catch you up on what is happening. Love you, Mom."

Maria came out of the bedroom. "I'm getting hungry again. How's dinner coming?"

"The new potatoes are ready and I'm about to start the whitefish. Want to watch?"

"I do. I like to see you work your magic."

"I have been experimenting with a new olive oil. I like it better than what I was using. It gives a more delicate flavor."

Maria watched as he brushed the olive oil on the whitefish, sprinkled a little lemon juice, and finally some spices on one side and popped it in the broiler. In three minutes, he turned the whitefish over and repeated the process on the other side and added a light sprinkling of parmesan cheese and put it back in the broiler. He drained the new potatoes, and poured a mixture of butter, lemon juice, and spices over them. He covered them again to let the flavors work on the potatoes. He asked Maria to get the white wine out. He opened it and poured each a glass. With a flourish he got the salads out of the fridge and placed them on the table. Tom served up the potatoes and the fish. He lit the candle. "Dinner is served, sweetheart."

Gazing into each other's eyes, they toasted to a quick recovery. "This is an excellent Sauvignon Blanc. What's the occasion?"

Tom took another sip. "To us being together again. I can't tell you how seeing you here makes me feel. We're really here. This is like the rest of the honeymoon we didn't get to finish."

They made short work of the delicious fish. Maria couldn't stop moaning with pleasure at every bite. She told Tom that she thought the new olive oil was a hit. After dinner, Tom cleared the table, refilled their wine glasses, and set them on the coffee table. Maria went into the bedroom and came out with a large file folder that looked heavy.

"I'll tell you about this in a few minutes." She took another sip of wine. "I want to talk about our future."

She continued, "We need to start making our plans. I've seen the look in your eyes and the life in your face when you are working on this case. I see an excitement in you. Do you think you will be content going back to teaching?"

"I hadn't even thought about that. Getting my master's degree kept our options open. But as to teaching again, I don't know yet."

"Good. That's what I hoped you would say. I have another year on my contract at Muskegon High School, but I don't want to be there without you, and now, Doug. Are you going to see Mr. Mann soon and what will you tell him?"

"I will tell him no. I'll also add that he should remember that decisions have consequences, and you have to learn to live with yours."

"Wow, that's pretty strong for you. You're not usually like that."

"He fired me without getting the facts first with that whole Sara debacle. But I'm having second thoughts about the comment. That's why I may just call."

"Good! So, now our decision comes to, should we look for a place where we can both get a job at a community college or a high school? Or should we think about another direction?"

"What direction do you have in mind?"

"Are you ready for this? Have another sip of wine." She did as well. "I want to see if I can find the same excitement and joy that you have since you have been working this case. I saw the joy you got from it last year but didn't say anything. I want to see if I can find it!"

"You want to be a detective?"

"Yes! I want to follow a path like you did and see if it grabs hold of me as it did you. If it does, we could form a husband-and-wife detective agency and take on more cases like this one. You said it yourself, there are probably a lot of towns in the U.S. with similar problems."

"You have been thinking about this, haven't you?"

"Ever since I woke up and could think rationally again."

"Are there other female detectives, much less husband and wife teams?

"Jim says there are female detectives but knows of no teams."

"You've talked to Jim about this? He didn't say anything to me about it."

"I asked him not to. I wanted to surprise you with it."

Tom grinned, a big wide smile that covered his whole face, eyes too. "I say let's put our heads together and see what we can do."

Maria smiled. "That's how he said you would feel. And that's where that folder came from. Jim brought me the same files you had so I could start learning. I didn't get a chance to. He brought them to me the morning after the press conference. He got there about ten minutes after you left."

"Well, you are full of surprises. What else do you have up your sleeve?"

Maria had a twinkle in her eyes. "How about some dessert, big boy?" she said as she led him to the bedroom.

32

T om was up before Maria again the next morning. He took the walkie-talkie with him, brewed some coffee, put it in a thermos, and put on another pot. He beeped the walkie-talkie, "I'm at the door, coming out."

He walked to their car. "How about some fresh coffee?"

"That sounds good. Ours was getting low."

"How are your breakfast supplies? We have some stale donuts. My wife will be waking up soon and I'll make some toast and scrambled eggs. I can make a bigger batch if you'd like to share."

"We'll be glad to get them. Thanks."

"Just to let you know, Maria's visiting nurse and her physical therapist will be here this morning at 10:00 a.m. And then in the afternoon, one of Maria's friends is coming to visit while I'm gone. She may have her little girl with her. I'll be back later this afternoon. Let me go get started on breakfast and I'll be back shortly."

Maria was just coming out of the bedroom when he opened the front door. "Where have you been?"

"Just taking our guys some coffee. Ours is just getting done. I'm going to make extra eggs this morning and take them out to them. Is that okay?"

"Of course. It must be tough to sit out there all night. My appetite is coming back. I'm hungry this morning."

"Well then, how about pancakes for us instead of toast?"

"Yummy. I'll set the table and get the maple syrup warmed up."

Tom whipped up the pancakes first, filling the air with the warm yeasty smell of Pillsbury pancakes. While he scrambled the eggs, Maria made the toast. Quicker than scat, breakfast was ready. Tom carried breakfast out to the protection detail and then joined Maria for his own. They chatted about their day until Maria realized that it was almost 9:00. She jumped up to get a shower while Tom cleaned up.

Tom and Maria were finishing off their third cup of coffee when the ladies knocked.

"Good morning, I'm Joan, your visiting nurse for the duration, and this is Arlene, your physical therapist. Here are our cards. I'll be here every Wednesday for, we think, a month. If your progress is good, we may not have to extend. Arlene will let you know her schedule in a few minutes. Let's get some vitals. By the way, you are looking good, getting some weight back."

"It feels good. Tom is spoiling me."

After a few minutes, Joan said, "You are coming along just fine. Any anxieties?"

"Only a little when I learned what was going on with Tom's work with the police. You may have seen the reports in the paper after the press conference. But nothing since."

"Do the men outside have anything to do with that?"

Tom answered that one. "They are our police protection because of what's happening. We both feel better with them here. By the way, we would just as soon you didn't say anything about them to anyone."

"We won't. Any problems with your meds?"

"No, not a problem. How much longer will I have to be on them?"

"Dr. Franks will decide that when he sees you in about three weeks."

Arlene took over. She and Maria went over exercises that Maria could do at home to build up her strength. "We would like you to come Monday and Thursday for a session at the rehab facility. We'll see how you come along, but count on that for the first month and then we'll revaluate."

Maria asked, "When can I start walking around the yard and around the neighborhood, you know, on some uneven ground?"

"I would wait until next week to try that. Be sure to ask your therapists at the facility."

Maria then asked, "When can I start doing some cooking and some housework?"

"Have you tried lifted a frying pan or a saucepan yet?"

"I haven't, but my hands feel stronger so I thought I would try soon."

"Practice with some empty pans first before you cook. Be sure your hands are steady enough. How about in the shower? Do you feel secure?"

Tom and Maria looked at each other, smiled. Tom said, "She is doing fine."

When they were gone, Maria looked at Tom and grinned. "I wonder what they thought of your answer."

"They knew what I meant."

"Let's finish off the coffee and talk for a little about our new future. We have some decisions to make, and we should start doing some research. I'll have a talk with Jim about it. He might have some suggestions about getting started."

"You know this may mean some travel around the country, maybe not right away, but once we start advertising and get established. We need to figure out how to get known."

They spent the next hour or so working away at it, exchanging ideas. Tom saw Maria yawn.

"Aha, caught you. While you catch a nap, I'll reread my notes for the meeting this afternoon."

"When I get up, I'll make some lunch. Sandwiches and chips do?"

"Sounds great."

They had just finished lunch and doing cleanup when Sara knocked.

The two women hugged, and Sara asked, "Can I give Mr. O a hug?"

Maria laughed. "Of course."

"Bob and I have decided to adopt you two and Doug as our new best friends if that's all right with you."

"It's more than all right, but you must call us Tom and Maria."

Another knock sounded. "That sounds like a Doug knock."

It was. When he saw the ladies, he was all smiles and charm. "Two of my favorite people. How are you two?"

After reassurances that all was well, Doug said, "I'm here to escort you to the police station, mister."

Tom went along with the joke. "Now what am I supposed to have done?"

"All kidding aside, I needed to check in with the men outside and I thought I might as well take you to the meeting. How long will you be here, Sara?"

"The nuns at the home are watching Arianna until 5:00 p.m. Will you be back by then?"

"I'm sure we will. Say hi to that little girl of yours for me."

Tom kissed Maria. "See you later sweetheart."

As soon as Doug started for the station, Tom asked, "What's going on?"

"There's been another incident from our suspect. And not at Wendell's place as we thought. She is a shrewd operator, creating the stir casing Wendell's house, and striking somewhere else. She picked a different member's house. She didn't hit anyone."

"So, no one was hurt?"

"No, Jim and I think she did it just to let us know she could do it and get away with it. And she did. She put two bullets in the picture window of one of the other Group member's home with a high-power rifle, then pulled away and was gone before the guys could react. She was driving a different car, actually, a small black van. The guys went into the house after she was gone, checked that all was well and dug the bullets out of the living room wall. She shot well above the fireplace like she didn't intend to hurt anyone, least of all, the children and his wife. She was making a point to the police."

"Maria is going to be upset at this. Is there a chance she will try for me next?"

"That's why your protection detail is here. We still think her next target is going to be Wendell. The chief is already having the records checked for the car, the guys got the tag number. And they are looking at registrations for a hunting rifle."

Doug went on, "There is a good chance this will soon be all over. Judge McVie has moved the trial up. It starts on Thursday morning. By the way, you will get this again in the meeting. No one else on the task force knows yet. One more thing. Jim wants to have a short chat with you. It could be before or after."

"We are almost there, so let's do it before the meeting. I don't want Maria to be left alone too long. Sara has to be back at the home by 5:00 p.m. I would like you to come in, so you can hear it firsthand as well."

GERRI ANNOUNCED them and Jim motioned them in. "How is Maria doing?"

"She is coming along quite well. She saw her visiting nurse and physical therapist this morning and is ready to be off and running, well, not quite that yet. She thinks so but then she needs a nap. I think she will bounce back faster than the staff and her doctor think."

The chief asked, "Does Doug know yet?"

"No, I haven't had a chance to tell him yet. That's why I wanted him to be in on our chat."

"Okay, you two. What is going on?"

Jim started off, "In a quick version, Maria called me about a week and a half ago. She said she wanted some information. So, after the niceties, she started in asking questions about female detectives and husband and wife detective agencies. After answering her questions as best I could, I asked her if she had talked to Tom about it. She said no and wouldn't until she got home. Well, that happened faster than any of us thought. I didn't get her the study materials she asked for to her until—"

Tom interrupted with "About ten minutes before I came in to see her."

"You take it from here, Tom."

"We didn't get to it until last night."

Jim and Doug looked at each other with smiles.

"All right, you guys. Anyway, she made her case. And Jim, I appreciate you telling her you thought you knew how I would react to her proposal. You were right. Long story short, it is settled. As soon as she is up to more than reading the materials you got her, we will start putting together a plan to become a husband-and-wife detective firm."

Doug looked at Tom. "I didn't see that coming. We'll talk about this some more tonight."

33

Everyone was in the conference room and started asking questions the minute Jim walked in.

Jim held up his hand. "Hold on just a minute, gentlemen. I have news about Maria's progress and an announcement about the both of them."

Dave asked, "She is doing great, and they are pregnant."

The room burst into good natured laughter.

"You are right about the first part. She is doing very well. And that's the only thing I know anything about."

He told them about Maria's decision to become a detective and their joint decision to be a new husband and wife detective team. How fast this happens depends on how quickly Maria gains full strength and can work on her state police training. "I don't know her well, but I predict it won't take her long and they will be in business."

"Here, here, congratulations to Maria and to the team you two will form."

"Now, to the business at hand. There has been an incident with our suspect. Only a couple of you know of it. But for the rest, here's what happened. This morning a small black van drove past the house of one of the Group members. Our protection team watched it go by. Since it wasn't our suspect's car, they turned back to the house. Then three rifle shots in quick succession hit the picture window. They looked toward the sound and saw the van spin its tires as it squealed away fast. After a walkie-talkie 'Help!' from the house, they sprinted to the door, yelling, 'We're coming, open the front door.'

"They entered to find the Group member at the door and his family lying on the hallway floor. 'Anybody hurt?' The Group member, Mr. Jamison, and his family, wife and two children, said they were okay. All of them had been having breakfast in the kitchen and when our walkie-talkie call came in, they all hit the floor in the hallway as we had taught them. Our men got the family settled down and then checked for evidence.

"One of our men found the holes in the wall above the fireplace and said, 'Either he was a bad shot, or he didn't want to hurt anyone and certainly not the children or wives.'

"They called Doug, told him what happened. He and Mark rushed over there along with some patrolmen who heard the radio call. They dug out the bullets and put each into an evidence bag. Doug and Mark went outside with the protection detail and located the place where the van had been parked. All they could see were bad tire tracks on the pavement. Mark stopped Doug and pointed to a piece of white paper tacked to the telephone pole. It was another note, like the earlier ones. It said, 'See, I can get anyone I want, anytime I want. You won't know who is the next to die,' in the same block letters."

Jim asked, "Any questions or comments?"

"No question, just a comment. If we can tie this van to our suspect or her husband, Larry, we'll know for sure. This is one smart cookie, this woman. She is going to be hard to catch in the act and she seems to know how to conceal her tracks. If the van is registered in her name or her husband's, that could help."

Jim said, "We put out an APB quickly, Dave, but there's no trace of the van. This little 'gotcha' trick of hers was pretty well thought out."

"As cool and calculating as she is, she might make a mistake while she is taunting us. If we can believe that she doesn't want to kill family, maybe we can use that to somehow set a trap for her."

"And you all know me. I want to know why she is doing this. Is it something deeper than Larry getting killed that we don't know about it? Several times during our interview with her, I had the notion that she was just a little, maybe a lot, off up here," Tom said, pointing to his head.

"Tom, I had that same notion — that she doesn't want to hurt the families of the Group members — she just wants to hurt the Group members. I just don't know how we can use it."

"I've been wondering how we could just leak that we are putting them all in one apartment building. But we put a team of police in there instead," Dave said.

Jim replied, "Something is happening in a week that will bring them all together. Judge McVie has just moved the trial up to start next Tuesday. She has to know that if they all get convicted and sent to prison, she won't be able to get to them. The trial date isn't public knowledge yet. Is she crazy enough to try and get them all in the courtroom? Who knows? We can't let that happen. We have to get her locked down."

The phone rang. Jim answered and listened intently. "Thanks for the info. That was Don reporting that the state has a small black van registered to Larry Olsen. So, now the new question is was that his that she was driving?"

"Could we get a warrant to search her house and garage?"

"Maybe, but she will likely have it parked somewhere else. And serving a warrant on her will tip her off that we suspect her. That could change the game again.

"Come on, people, think!"

Jim continued, "Let's break for now and meet again tomorrow morning at 10 a.m. Take what we have, review it, and see what we can put together in the morning. One more thing, in the phone call with her or the interview with Tom and I, she said something that could only have come from the police. It is not coming from the people in this room. I trust all of you implicitly. I have a possible suspect for the leaker. I'm going to set a trap for him."

"That's all for now. Be extra vigilant. I think things are going to happen fast. See you in the morning."

34

Tom caught Jim before he went to his office. "Is it okay if I talk with Maria about what came up in the task force meeting?"

"I trust her to keep things close. You never know, a woman's perspective might lead us to something we can use. Caution her about the leak that I'm checking out."

"Thanks, Jim."

Tom called Maria from the station. "How was your afternoon with Sara?"

"It was great. I have a lot to tell you."

"We have something to share with you as well. Doug wants to buy us dinner and come to the house and help us eat it. Are you up for Doo Drop perch?"

"I'm ready for that, and some fries and onion rings."

"We'll see you about forty-five minutes. I love you."

"Love you too."

～

MARIA HAD the table all set when they came in. The platters on the table were soon filled with perch, fries, and onion rings. As a surprise, Maria served them Miller Highlife Beer. "I thought it was time to try something different."

Toasting and sipping brought comments like, "Not bad" from Doug and "Okay" from Tom.

"Tell us about your time with Sara."

"First off, she didn't bring Arianna, so it was just the two of us. And that was perfect. I've known Sara since she was fifteen and in tenth grade. I have never seen her so bubbly, so full of life. She is excited about this marriage. She is going to have two other bridesmaids to stand up with her and me as her matron of honor. Bob has to find three men for his side. He's still thinking about that. They are doing well in their pre-marriage counseling classes and should be finished about the first week of June. Bob will be home from college about the third week of May. They will have plenty of time to get a wedding ready for mid to late June. They haven't decided yet."

"She has a question that concerns you two."

Tom asked, "What could possibly involve us?"

"She has no family and can't decide which of you she wants to give her away."

"Here's a crazy idea. Why not both of us, one on each side? Would you go along with that, Tom?"

"I never would have thought of that. Have you ever seen that?"

Both shook their heads. Tom said, "Why don't you call her and tell her about our idea? Ask her to check with Father Flanagan about it. But what I really think is that we should just do it and set a new tradition. It's her wedding, she should be able to do whatever she wants...er, within bounds."

They adjourned to the living room and Maria asked, "Now, what is it you have to tell me?"

"Are you ready for some news both good and bad?"

"How about the good news first?"

"Jim told the task force about you wanting to take the state police training and that we were going to form one of the first in the state husband-and-wife detective agencies. The reaction from the group was all positive, even toasting with their iced tea."

"All right, what is the bad news?"

"There has been another incident." Tom went on to tell her about the van, the three shots that hit above the fireplace, and the note that was left. "We found out that Larry Olsen owned a black van. We have no way of knowing for certain that she was the one driving and did the shooting. We think that the fact that the shots hit high means that she didn't want to kill anyone at this time."

"What did the note say this time?"

"It said 'See, I can get anyone I want, anytime I want. You won't know who is the next to die.' It was in the same block letters."

"Doesn't the fact that the notes are the same mean that the driver is the killer?"

"I'm not sure what a criminal attorney would call that, but it's just circumstantial evidence. It takes more than that to convict her. We need to have solid evidence or catch her in the act."

"And at this point you don't have solid evidence? I would like to find out more about why she is acting in such a crazy way."

"A lot of us want to know that. You know me, I always look to the motive. It can often provide a way to get to them," Tom said.

"Tom, didn't you tell me that Doug and Don followed her to the Anderson home, and she spent a half hour there? And that when she left, it was like the three were old friends."

Doug said, "That's what it seemed like to us. What are you thinking?"

"A question first. Does Mrs. Anderson know that our suspect is Mrs. Olsen?"

Tom and Doug looked at each other, shook their heads together. "I think we both agree that she does not. Jim could confirm that. Right, Doug?"

"And didn't you tell me it looks like she had a chat with George

Anderson before she shot him? Also, that the final shot was into his forehead with the gun right on his head as if in anger?"

"All of that is right. So, what do you have in mind, Maria?"

"I want to talk to Mrs. Anderson in person, woman to woman. I have the sense there is something going on with the three of them. Mrs. Anderson just might say something to confirm that. And maybe that something is what is feeding her anger. She might have intended to kill only George but took out Tim Samuels first to cloud the picture. And now she may have gone off the deep end and is going to kill them all, including Tom."

Doug and Tom looked at each other and both started talking at the same time. Tom said, "Go ahead, Doug."

"Tom used to tell me that the task force thought some of his ideas were a bit strange and didn't seem like they would work. In the end, most did, as I remember. But this one seems to me to have a good chance to do some good."

"Do you see any chance of danger for me?"

Tom jumped in. "I don't see any at all. Jim has talked with Mrs. Anderson's brother-in-law who is a medical doctor. She was staying with her sister and brother-in-law in South Bend for almost two weeks. She was so distraught they hired a psychologist to work with her while she was there. Her sister is going to stay here with her, and her sister's husband will go back to South Bend next weekend."

"What time is it? Is it too late to call Jim with the idea? He would want to talk to the doctor to see if he has any concerns about Mrs. Anderson."

"It's only 7:30 p.m. I don't think he would mind." Tom reached for the phone.

"Jim, Tom here. Maria, Doug, and I have been talking. Maria has an idea that she wants to try. She might be able to find why Mrs. Olsen has so much anger pushing her."

"Put her on. Let her tell me about it." Maria laid it out for him. She stopped for his reaction but then continued with, "Jim, does Mrs. Anderson know that Mrs. Olsen is your suspect?"

"She doesn't unless it has leaked out. We have kept her name out of all discussions especially if there is someone outside the task force nearby. No, I'd say she doesn't know."

"Well, what do you think?"

"I like it. I want to talk with her brother-in-law and see what he thinks. How are you going to approach her?"

"I will tell her first about my time in the coma. Then when I woke up, I talked to my counselors about my concerns when Tom was working with the task force and how anxious I was about it. She should be able to relate to that."

"Is any of that true?"

"Yes, Jim, it is, Tom and I talked about it a lot, right away after Fred was killed and Tom was threatened. We didn't say anything to anyone except maybe Doug. And my anxiety about that came up in my conversations with my counselors at the rehab facility. Then I'll tell her that I'm talking to Mrs. Samuels and Mrs. Olsen next. I'm betting she will open up about her meeting with Mrs. Olsen and we'll see where it goes from there."

"All right, let me talk to Dr. Brown and I'll get right back to you."

She turned to Tom and Doug. "He's calling the doctor, Mrs. Anderson's brother-in-law."

Fifteen minutes later, Jim called back. "It's a go, Maria. Dr. Brown wants to meet with you and me in the morning before you go. He knows Mrs. Anderson well and can suggest what to say and what not to say, what trigger words to avoid."

"Can Tom and Doug go with me? I would feel safer with them sitting outside the house."

"They can. Tell them about that and that I will postpone the task force meeting until 2:00 p.m. so we can hear what you find out. Be at the office by 8:30 a.m. please. Good work, Maria. See you in the morning."

"We're on. He approved the two of you to be my escorts. I feel good about that."

"Does that mean we'll be with you when you talk to Mrs. Anderson? Won't that make it awkward?" Tom worried.

"No, you'll just be with me when I talk to her brother-in-law and then maybe Doug can drive me to their house. She won't know that he's involved with the task force. She might know that you are, Tom, so I'll make some excuse that you had to work or something and couldn't drive me. Or you could both just wait for me in the car."

35

Their meeting in the morning was in the little conference room connected to Jim's office. Jim introduced Dr. Brown to all of them. "I'm John, John Brown. I see from your smiles that you are thinking, 'I'll bet he gets some kidding about that.'"

He continued, "It bothered me when it first started happening. But now I try to have some fun with it. That defuses things."

"Now, Maria, Jim told me what you would like to do. Would you tell me again in your own words?"

Maria laid it out for him. "Do you have any questions, Dr. Brown?"

"No, I don't. Just some comments. Jim says he told you how fragile Ann has been because of George's business dealings. And then when George was killed, she nearly fell apart again. But this time she has come back more quickly. She is still fragile. I'll be there as well as you ladies, so I'll be watching her. If I say something that sounds like I am cutting the conversation off, I will not be, just diverting it temporarily. Can you pick up where you left off?"

"John, I have been a high school teacher for almost five years now. I work with drama students, and they know how to divert you. I'll get it going again."

He chuckled. "Good. Let's make the call. I'll start it off and then hand it off to you."

"Hi, Ann, I went out early this morning. I'm at the police station, visiting with my friend Jim. He's the chief. No, I'm not in trouble, no arrest. He wants me to ask a favor of you."

"What kind of favor?"

"One of Jim's friends, Maria O'Banion, is interviewing all the wives of the Group of Nine and would like to talk to you. She likes to be called Maria."

"How on earth did she get an Italian first name and an Irish last name? Never mind, I'll ask her. Is she there now? Put her on."

"Hello, Mrs. Anderson. I'm Maria."

"If I call you Maria, I expect to be called Ann. How do you happen to have an Italian first name and an Irish last name?"

"Okay, Ann. My parents are first generation Italians, and I married a wonderful Irishman. As John said, I am doing interviews of all the wives of the Group of Nine. I would appreciate some of your time this morning. I know it is short notice but I'm on a schedule to finish and I only have two to go. Would 10:00 a.m. work for you?"

"That will work. It will give us the time to get ourselves together. Can my sister Jane be there too?"

"Of course, she can. Thank you, Ann. Here's John."

"Thank you, Ann. This project means a lot to her. I'll be home soon, so can I sit in with you ladies? I'll be good."

"That will be fine, I'll have some coffee and petit fours, and oh, I have some Ryke's butter cookies. See you soon."

"It's all set, Maria. Don't be anxious. You will do fine," John reassured Maria.

"How did you know I am a little nervous?"

"I'm a doctor, remember." He smiled at her and she felt much better.

～

After John left, Jim said, "Maria, you will be fine. I have enough confidence in you to know that. Just relax."

Tom asked, "Do you want to stay here or run home before we go?"

"It is a few minutes after nine and we should leave by 9:35 a.m. or so. We should stay here. Do you have a cot where I could catch a short nap?"

"There's a cot in that closet. Doug and I will let you two relax in here and we'll talk in the conference room. The three of you can drive out to the Anderson's house together and let Maria go in by herself."

After a brief rest, the three of them piled into Tom's car and drove to North Muskegon. They parked in the Anderson's turnaround driveway. Tom said, "We'll be right here. The walkie-talkie in your purse will get us if you need us."

She knocked and was admitted by a lovely lady. "Welcome, Maria, I'm Ann. This lady behind me is my sister Jane and you've met John already."

"I'm so happy to meet you both. Hello again, John."

"Let's go into the living room."

Maria gasped softly as she entered the elegant room. Floor to ceiling windows were fitted with pale ivory water silk draperies. She admired the white marble fireplace with the brass andirons framing the peacock fire screen. The ivory grand rolled arm French provincial sofa was flanked with two matching pale floral wingback chairs. The marble coffee table was adorned with a silver coffee set and two crystal plates, one with gorgeous petit fours, and the other with Muskegon's famous Ryke's butter cookies. Delicate coffee cups were just waiting to be filled. Maria said, "You have such a lovely home. I love Ryke's butter cookies."

"I would be pleased if you tried my petit fours. I make them myself."

Ann served the coffee as John said, "Ann, why don't we let Maria start by telling us her story of her recent ordeal? This project she's doing is part of her recovery."

"Ann and Jane, I was in a coma since last fall. I just woke up about three or four weeks ago. Sometimes it feels to me like I just got up from a long nap. Other days I know I am a very lucky woman to have survived the brain trauma and resulting coma. I think my waking up and recovering is a bit of a miracle. I'm just so glad to be here. My doctor is going to write up my case for a medical journal. He says that people will want to hear this story. We think so, too."

"Did you say 'we'? I see the ring. Where was your husband during all that time?"

"Tom, my husband, was there the whole time, bringing my favorite flowers almost every day. I was told after I woke up that in the early days, he was there almost all day, singing to me, talking to me, holding my hands. The nurses said he was a man dedicated to being there when I woke up. The nurses and my parents finally convinced him to come less often and try to rebuild his life to what he wanted it to be when I woke up. He believed them and came less but was still there every evening and all day on the weekends. I told my doctor, Dr. Franks, that I remember some of Tom's words and all the songs he sang to me. We are both into theatre and vocal music and I believe it helped me to come back. I suffered from a lot of anxiety as I was regaining my memory and my physical strength. So, in a nutshell, that's my life for the last few months."

"You are a lucky woman. He must be a special man. How long were you married when this happened?" Ann looked at Maria with envy.

"About three months. So, we are now in a real sense renewing our honeymoon while I regain my strength and all the capabilities you lose when you're out that long."

Maria said, "Ann, you suddenly seem a little sad. Did something I said upset you?"

"No, nothing in particular that you said. I was just remembering the good life that George and I had during most of our marriage. It was really just the last couple of years that were not so good. I know what you mean about anxiety. Things were hard to deal with and then that whole business about George's business dealings came up last year."

"I'm hearing similar stories from the other ladies. May I ask how things changed?"

"Here, have some more coffee and treats. More for you, Jane and John? They know the story since I turned to them to get away for a while. I'll try to be as succinct as I can be but it's a long story. Is that okay with you?"

"Thank you for the coffee. I love your petit fours. And of course, it is okay. That's why I'm here. Do you mind if I take some notes?"

"That's fine. It might be a lot for you to remember. George and I, as I said, had a good life. We only have one child, a son, and he is all grown and moved away to the south. He has a good job down in Georgia and seems very happy with his wife and our grandchildren. George's business prospered and grew to be a dominant one in the automotive industry. We had some good friends, mostly leaders in other successful businesses here in town. He sat on several of their boards and some of them sat on the board of his company. Then one day he came home, we sat with a drink, and he said, 'a group of the other industry leaders in town and I have put together a new company.' When I asked what kind of company, he said, 'it is mostly for investment in local real estate especially along Muskegon Lake. We're going to develop it with industries of our choice and make them feed into ours, which would feed into theirs. We could grow to be a major industrial city.'

"I said to him, 'George, why do you want to do this? You've built a successful company. We have all the money we need. Why don't we just relax, do some things we've always wanted to do, like travel?' He broke in and told me abruptly, 'this is the way it is going to be. It is what I want.'

"I didn't like it, but I went along. I still loved George and didn't want to lose him over the new business." She paused for a few seconds, then went on. "He used to come home troubled from their meetings. They seemed to have a lot of meetings especially this last year or so. I asked him what was happening, and he told me to not worry, that it was 'just business.' That really upset me. We always used to talk about his work — he even told me some things that he probably shouldn't have. When he did that, he would always say, 'don't tell anyone about that.'" She paused.

"One time he told me about Larry Olsen and how he suspected Larry wasn't being true to the business. He told me that Larry seemed to know things that were happening in the police department. When George asked how he got this information, he said Larry told him, 'I have a contact in the police department. Pete owes me some money, so he brings me information he thinks I might want to know.' George told me not to mention that to anyone, but now that Larry and George are both gone, I guess it doesn't matter. George stopped talking to me completely the last few months about the business, nothing about what they were doing or the progress they were making. John and Jane saw me growing increasingly anxious and withdrawn." She paused again.

"There's more. Jane and John, you don't know about this…"

John jumped in. "Ann, would you like to stop for a little while?"

"No, John, I have needed for some time to get this out. It needs to be said now. And hearing how Maria's husband stood by her, it makes me even more angry and sad about how George had changed."

She continued, "It was shortly after our annual Christmas meeting at the Occidental — that was our tradition we always did with a group of close friends. I began to sense something going on. A different perfume smell, his being out of touch at strange times. Once I couldn't find him and needed to get a question answered. His office just said that he was out on business. I confronted him on it. He just said that he was out on some business. When he got home, I asked him, 'who is she, George? Who are you meeting with?' He told me it was just a woman who was part of the new business. When I told him I didn't believe him and I wanted him to break it off, he said, 'this is business.'

"I started following him. I rented a car he wouldn't know and parked it in a garage I rented. I waited outside his office until one day it happened. I followed him to his so-called business meeting and saw the two of them, laughing and talking, at the Holiday Inn. I took their picture with my old Polaroid camera. The woman saw me and told George. George came running out, but I was lying down in the front seat of my rental car. I heard him call my name. He never caught me, but I caught him."

John and Jane were shocked. They had no idea that Ann was going through this. Jane touched Ann's arm, but Ann waved her away.

"I confronted him when he got home. He denied it, of course. I threw the Polaroid at him. He took one look at it, started crying, and told me that he was sorry and that he would stop it. He promised. But I didn't believe him. I didn't see him for a few days. He came back and said he had been up at the cabin and asked for another chance. I said okay but not unless he had really broken it off with that woman. He stayed at the house, but we slept in separate rooms. I came to believe that he really was sorry, but it was too late. I couldn't really trust him anymore.

"Now you want to know the real kicker. The woman was Larry Olsen's wife, Anna. I had just about put her out of my mind until a day or so ago she called and wanted to come and tell me how bad she felt that George had been killed. I'm stronger now thanks to you, John and Jane, so I said yes. Can you believe the audacity of that woman? She spent about a half hour here putting on quite the show. She really is a good actress. She knew that I knew about her and George. I didn't buy her act for a minute.

"You might find it interesting that Anna Olsen mentioned talking with a man named Pete. Do you have any idea who that might be? I was going to tell the chief this when I speak to him.

"I'm so glad you were here, Jane. I might have done something terrible to that woman if you hadn't been here to support me. There, I think I'm done." Tears welled up in her eyes.

Maria stood quickly and took Ann in her arms. "You are one of the bravest women I know. And though you may not know it yet, I believe getting the story out in the open may turn out to be the best thing to happen to you. I won't write about this part. It will stay in this room. And may I offer some advice?" Ann nodded.

Maria continued, "When this is done and you feel you are ready, think of this time as the beginning of a new life for you, just as my waking up is my start to a new life. You'll soon find your way to doing some of the things you have always wanted to do."

"I hope we can be friends."

Maria said, "Count on it, Ann."

36

After they saw Maria out, John said, "I agree with her, the part about being a brave woman. I don't know how you got through that without losing it."

Ann smiled. "I couldn't have done it if you and Jane hadn't been here. Thank you both for all you have done for me. And there is something about Maria that said to me, 'you can trust her.' She just kept her eyes focused on mine and it felt as though she was reading my soul. I wanted her and you two to know everything. I'm sorry I hadn't told you about George's affair before. The next thing I knew a lot of things just came rushing right out of my mouth. I didn't say too much, did I?"

"No, you didn't. I'll tell you what, ladies. Why don't you two have some lunch and talk about fun things, maybe even those things that Maria suggested you might start doing in your new life? I know you're going to grieve for George and your good old life, but in time, you can remember the good and move on. Think about what you might want to do in the future. You know we'll support you every way we can.

"Tonight, I'll take you out to one of the best restaurants in Muskegon. Ann, you know the restaurants here. Why don't you pick one, make a reservation, and that's where we will go."

"I do have a favorite. I'll get it set up."

Jane asked, "Are you going out again, John?"

"Yes, I am. I was with Jim, the chief, this morning. They wanted to know if Ann would be okay before Maria asked to interview her. I told them you would be fine, and you were. You were amazing, Ann. I'm very happy you opened up to her."

"Do you believe her about becoming my friend?"

"Remember what she said, 'count on it.' If she said it, she'll do it. My confidence in her comes from what I have learned from Jim and how she handled herself today. I think you can definitely count on it, Ann."

John continued, "You remember that I went to Jim's press conference. I was so taken with his professionalism at the conference. I caught him that morning for a quick chat expressing my interest in what was going on in this town. He suggested that we have lunch before I go home. This morning he reminded me, and we set a time for this noon. I should be back about 1:30 p.m. or so. You ladies enjoy your time and I'll see you later."

MEANWHILE, Maria, Tom, and Doug were heading back to the station. Tom asked, "What happened in there? You were in there longer than we thought you would be."

"It was amazing, guys. I told her my story first. She was genuinely interested. She thinks you are quite a guy, Tom. Then I noticed a sadness come over her. I asked her about it. She refilled our coffee cups, offered us some more cookies, and said she had a story to tell. It wouldn't have the same happy ending mine did, but it was important to tell. Then the floodgates opened up. She talked about how things changed when George and his friends put together the group that the police called the 'Group of Nine.' At first, they talked about the new business. She would ask questions and he answered with what sounded plausible. Oh, and by the way, she said one of the members, a Larry Olsen, told him that he, Larry, had a contact in the police department. His name was Pete, but she didn't know the last name."

"Jim needs to hear that. He was suspicious that there is a leak in the department," Tom said.

Maria went on. "As the operation and number of meetings increased, George and Ann became more distant. She tried to discourage him from doing it, that they had enough money and didn't need another fortune. George refused to and their relationship worsened. I had the feeling John and Jane knew all this already. Her brother-in-law, John, asked her if she wanted to go on or stop. She told him no, this has to come out. 'It was time.'

"She started up again. She told us she suspected George was having an affair. He denied it and she followed him, caught them, took their picture, and confronted him with it. A few days later he convinced her that he had broken off the relationship. She didn't really believe him. You'll never guess who the woman was!" When they just looked at her with blank looks, she told them it was Larry Olsen's wife, Anna Olsen.

"What?" Doug exclaimed. "But how come they looked so cozy the other day?"

"Ann said that Anna came over to express her condolences and put on a good act. Ann didn't believe her for a minute. Maybe she was trying to throw suspicions off herself by pretending to comfort Ann."

"That's good thinking, Maria. If George really did break it off with her, that could be her motive. We still don't have enough solid evidence to convict her as the killer of Samuels and George."

"I told Ann that I would protect her name in all this. You have to be careful how you tell the task force about this. I don't want to break a promise to this woman. She trusts me and I think we will become friends. Tom, I'm suddenly very tired. Can we go home and let you two figure out how to tell Jim?"

"Take us home, Doug. She is pale. This has been a lot of stress on her."

Twenty minutes later they were home with Maria on the sofa and Tom on the phone with Dr. Franks' nurse. While he was talking,

Maria waved to him that she wanted to talk to him. He asked the nurse to hold for a second. He asked Maria, "What's happening?"

"I'm feeling better. It must have been the stress of the meeting, the telling of it again, whatever... But it is gone now. I'm hungry."

"Your color is better, too. Just stay there and I'll tell all this to the nurse."

He got back on the phone, but by this time, Dr. Franks was on the line instead of the nurse. Tom went through the scenario again, including the change in color and the fact that she was feeling better and even was hungry.

Dr. Franks asked what she had eaten for the day. Tom told him, "A good breakfast of eggs and toast, some Ryke's cookies and petit fours at an interview."

"Tom, get some soup in her along with a beverage, nothing sugary. Iced tea would be good and bring her in for a quick visit at 1:30 p.m. and I'll fit you in."

"See you then, Dr. Franks."

While Tom was fixing some lunch, Doug called Jim at the police station. He told Gerri, "It's important."

Gerri caught the chief just as he was leaving for his early lunch with Dr. Brown. Jim said, "Hang on a minute, John. I need to take this short call."

Doug told him that Maria did a great job on the interview and there were two pieces of information he needed to hear before the meeting this afternoon.

"Can you tell me the quick version now and fill in the details after the lunch hour? I'm on my way to lunch with Dr. Brown."

"That's good, Jim. He was at the interview and would have heard them too. The quick version is that someone named Pete was feeding Larry Olsen police information and George Anderson had an affair with Mrs. Olsen, Mrs. Anderson found out, and he dumped Mrs. Olsen."

No sound from Jim. "Are you still there, Jim?"

"I am. Just a little shocked. This is good information. I have to figure out what to do with it and think about whether I discuss it with the doctor. Thanks, Doug. Tell Maria, good job, and I'll see you at 2:00 p.m."

He was gone before Doug could ask another question.

TOM CALLED OUT, "Lunch is ready. Come and get it."

They ate lunch quietly, each mulling over what Maria learned in her interview with Ann. She answered some questions for the investigation, but she opened up a number of new questions that still needed to be resolved. After a few minutes, they cleaned up and Tom and Maria headed for the doctor's office. Doug left for the station to get ready for the task force meeting.

37

"We're headed to the Bear Lake Tavern. I know the owners there and they will fix us up with a somewhat private booth that's quiet. I use it a lot for one-on-one meetings with consultants. Good place to talk and good food."

John nodded. "I know the place. George and Ann used to take us there but that was a long time ago. We stopped going out with them when George got the investment group together."

"Can we talk about this morning on the way? I have some questions."

"Have you heard anything from Maria and her escorts yet? I saw them outside when I let Maria in."

"That's a precaution we've taken because of some developments in the case. I don't think our suspect will go after Tom and Maria right away, but we don't want to take a chance. That phone call as we were leaving was one of them reporting some names. Do you remember any names specifically that you hadn't heard before from Mrs. Anderson?"

"Yes, there were two. Ann described a conversation with George one time when he confided in her that a group member named Larry Olsen was getting police information from a man named Pete who owed money to Larry. Maria asked Ann about a last name, but she didn't have one. Funny thing is the name Pete came up during the visit that Mrs. Olsen had with Ann and Jane."

They arrived at Bear Lake Tavern, a not fancy pub on the Bear Lake Channel that was known for their BLT burgers and yellow-bellied perch. Jim greeted the owner and was shown to the private booth. The waitress came right away and took their drink orders — iced tea for both. Jim laughed at that. "I make it a habit not to drink in meetings like this. I hope we remain friends, John, and maybe can do this again with our wives and Mrs. Anderson."

"Mrs. Anderson won't answer to anything but Ann when that happens."

Their orders were taken, and John said, "Before we restart the conversation, I have a comment." Jim nodded. John continued, "I wanted to reiterate that I appreciated the way you handled that press conference. Not everything you know, only what you wanted them to have while still respecting their right to publish the news. Very professional."

"Thank you, John. I've had a lot of practice. I like to stay open to the community and yet I can't always tell them everything. I slipped a time or two during the learning process, but it is working well now. Now, what is the other name that got mentioned?"

"When Ann told Maria, and us, incidentally, about George's affair, she said that she caught them together and it was Mrs. Olsen that George was involved with. George broke it off after he and Ann had a big fight. The interesting thing I found was, let's see, how do I put this. I got the feeling that Mrs. Olsen didn't believe that Ann knew that she, Mrs. Olsen, was George's paramour. That's odd since Ann said Mrs. Olsen saw her when she was taking pictures of George and her. I wonder what game she's playing."

"That would mean that Mrs. Olsen thought George just broke it off on his own. That could have made her very angry at George. Good information that we can use."

"That's what it says to me, too, Jim. By the way, Maria promised

Ann that her name wouldn't be used or revealed as the source of the new inputs. Can you do that?"

"Not only can but will. We'll honor Maria's promise."

Jim saw their food coming. "Tell me how you and Jane met. How did you get to Muskegon from wherever you were?"

They were served their perch and started working on it before John answered. "I grew up in Fort Wayne, Indiana, and did my undergraduate premed studies at Indiana University. When I started looking for a medical school, I was fortunate to get into University of Michigan. Jane is a high school math teacher who graduated from U of M the same year I did from med school. We met in Ann Arbor, dated a couple of times and nothing clicked at that time. I got a cardiology residency at Butterworth Hospital in Grand Rapids, and she went home while looking for a teaching position. That first summer, I took what little time residents get and spent it at the Lake Michigan Ovals in Muskegon. Jane did too since she grew up in Muskegon. One day at the Ovals, you know as most of the locals call it, there was Jane with a group of women. As I walked by after a swim, she looked up, said, 'John!' I saw her and said 'Jane!' like we were long separated lovers. We started dating again that summer. The rest is history."

"Sounds like it was meant to be."

"It was! We've been married thirty-five years last January. I spent a few more years at Butterworth and then I got the position at Notre Dame, and we moved to South Bend. It's been a great career and life. Jane and I are very happy."

John looked at Jim. "How much time do we have before you need to be back?"

"Another fifteen minutes or so. Why do you ask?"

"I don't know anything about your business but I'm a curious sort. I noticed a little tic when the name 'Pete' was mentioned. And a similar reaction when you heard Mrs. Olsen's name. Can you tell me much about that interest or would you rather not?"

"I have a feeling that you know how to hold things close to the vest, so I'm going to trust you and tell you some things. This is strictly confidential — no one else can be told, not even Jane or Ann. How much do you know about what went on last year late summer and fall?"

"I have two sources for what I know. Ann told us a lot about the arrests, the arraignments, and the upcoming trial. The other source is what you covered in the press conference. There was a lot more there than I thought I would get. And to be straight with you, I think you didn't quite tell the audience the truth when you were asked, 'do you have any suspects?' So, being the curious fellow that I am, I asked myself why. Maybe I should just let you tell it if you still want to."

"You're very good." John nodded a thank you. Jim continued, "As you know then, there were three members of the Group of Nine who were killed last fall as things broke loose. Incidentally, the couple I mentioned who were shot at the same time as one of the Group is Tom and Maria O'Banion. She has only been out of the coma about three weeks, so she is still somewhat fragile. One of the reasons they were shot was that the shooter from the Group of Nine was threatening Tom in the same manner as the mayor whose murder set this whole thing off. Maria is going to be fine, but it means that Tom will miss some task force meetings as he sees to her needs. He was on the first task force last fall and made great contributions. He's an important member of the current task force looking into the latest murders and reexamining the ones last year. There's more going on with the two of them but that will have to be for another time.

"When Maria volunteered to do the interview with Ann to see if Ann knew anything that would help our investigation, we did so with some hesitation. But she insisted she would be fine, and she is very persuasive."

"She was terrific. Her eyes never left Ann's during the interview. She looks like a natural at it. She and Ann will become friends."

"I'm glad to hear that. In the case of the police officer named Pete, I only have one Pete, so I know where my leak is now. I'm working on a way to use that before I spring the trap on him. I'm still working through just how. As to the other name, Mrs. Olsen, we have been following her for a while now. We have a number of data bits that point to her as George's killer. The problem is that it is all what I would call 'circumstantial.' We need to set a trap for her and catch her with some hard evidence. We should be able to catch both Pete and Mrs. Olsen, thanks to Ann and Maria. And I'll make sure Ann's name will not be mentioned as the source as Maria promised her.

"All of this is complicated by the fact that the trial for the last members of the Group is coming up in about two weeks, maybe less if the judge's current case closes faster that he thinks it will. We don't want to be in the position of putting everyone in the courtroom in her sights. She seems to us a little irrational and quick on the trigger for various emotions."

"Sounds like a tricky balancing act," John mused.

"Let's get going, the restaurant will bill the city. Let's try to do this one more time before you go back."

WHEN THEY GOT to the station, John took off for his car and Jim went in the back door. Gerri stopped him right away to say, "Tom called. Maria had a stress complication from the interview this morning and her doctor wants to see her, just to be safe. Tom said if the time with the doctor is short enough, he'll come in late."

"Doug will be driving them. Try to get through on his police radio and tell him I said to stay put and I will call Tom later."

38

Tom and Maria were shown into Dr. Franks' examining room promptly at 1:30 p.m. Dr. Franks walked in right after them. "It appears that the two of you have been misbehaving."

"Not really, Doc. And certainly not on purpose."

"He's right, Doctor. I pushed Tom and his boss, Police Chief Jim, to let me do it. I was sure I could help and couldn't wait to step in. A friend, a doctor, advised me on how to approach the lady I was to talk with. This doctor is the lady's brother-in-law and he put her in the care of a psychologist while she stayed with them, so he knew what she could handle, and he also kept an eye on me. She has been through so much over the last six months and she is making good progress. But when she heard my story, she started telling hers and couldn't stop. There were tears a number of times. Both the doctor and her sister were in the interview with her. He asked if she needed to stop but she said she couldn't. She continued talking and eventually revealed some things that her sister and the doctor hadn't known. When she finished, she started crying. I couldn't help myself. I jumped up and took her in my arms until she stopped. That's where the stress must have started for me. I didn't even realize it then."

"When did you feel the symptoms of the stress?"

"It was on the way home. Tom said I looked very pale. I felt hungry but a funny kind of hungry. When we got home, Tom told me to rest on the sofa and called you. While Tom was talking to your nurse, I began to feel fine, and my color was back. I told him but when he got back on the phone, it was you there. You know the rest. Except that I am fine now."

"You still look a little pale to me. I'd like to check you out and run a couple of tests."

Later, after the examination and the tests were finished, they met again with Dr. Franks. "All your vitals were good, your glucose test was right where it should be, so I don't see any long-term effects. I suspect you had a mild sugar shock with all the cookies and, combined with the stress from the interview situation, it was just too much for you. I don't see it happening again, but we'll check everything at your next appointment and be sure. Is it likely that you will see this woman again?"

"I hope so. I like her and would like to be her friend. She seems eager, too, so we'll see. If we do get together, it will be with a different tone. I don't see a problem."

"Just be careful and keep me in the loop if something does happen. Take it easy the next couple of days. We don't want another episode like this one."

"Dr. Franks, Tom and I have talked about it. We would like you to go ahead and write the article about my case."

Dr. Franks smiled a big smile. "I was hoping you would agree. I'd like to schedule a longer visit next time so you both can get the feel of how it will go."

"Good, just let us know when."

39

W hen Jim and Gerri came into the meeting room, the discussion was already going on. It seemed that they had all taken his push seriously. Everyone seemed to have things to tell him. But their first question was wondering where Tom was.

"I sense a lot of energy in here and I don't want to change that. I have some information that I think will help us. I hear your question about Tom, and I will get to him shortly. Let me start with Judge McVie. His current trial ended today. He's taking the rest of the weekend off to rest and, I suspect, to refamiliarize himself with the original case. The trial for the remaining Group members will begin with the pleas of all the men. It is likely they will plead 'not guilty' as they did when they were arraigned. And he will start jury selection depending on their pleas. If they should all change their minds and plead guilty, Judge McVie will send them home. There won't be a trial, just a sentencing date later on. Keep that in mind while I tell you about the other new information.

"To the question, 'where's Tom,' the short version is that he is home taking care of Maria. Doug just dropped them off and he is now on his way here. I'll get Tom a copy of today's session, so when he comes in for our next meeting, he will be up to date. Your next logical question is likely what's happened to Maria. Our Maria brought it on herself. The condensed version is that she found a way to get some critical information. She asked Mrs. Anderson for an interview she was doing with all the women whose husbands were killed. She told her that it was a project her doctor thought might be good for her. And it was, but it caused her to have a mild stress reaction that alarmed her and Tom. Her doctor has examined her, done some tests, and she is now doing fine. But he wants Tom to stay by her side for a day or two just in case.

"In the course of that interview, Mrs. Anderson revealed two new pieces of information. Number one is that she identified my leak here in the department. It is none other than Pete Martin. Pete has been a good officer so far. He is working on his next promotion and a part of the required knowledge is to understand how our office works, the office regimen, so to speak. To that end, last year I assigned him more administrative work. Maria was told by Ann Anderson that George questioned Larry last summer about where he was getting his inside police information. He told George that he had a good contact, Pete, in the police department. He didn't tell George Pete's last name, so Ann didn't know it since George didn't know it.

"And further, Ann Anderson told Maria that when Mrs. Olsen called on Mrs. Anderson to supposedly express her condolences, she let it slip that she has been talking with Pete since Larry's death. We don't know why Pete was giving them information yet. We'll find that out when I set a trap for Pete and can question him."

There was a buzz around the room. Mark observed, "Jim, I noticed he always seemed to be asking questions of the station staff. I passed it off as just his style of getting familiar with procedure. But it just seemed like too much."

"I saw that too, Mark. In fact, he was my prime suspect. Now that I have this input from Mrs. Anderson, and secondhand from Mrs. Olsen, I'm still working out the details of how we can bait the trap. More about that later.

"Number two piece of information that Maria got direct from

Mrs. Anderson was that George Anderson had an affair with Mrs. Olsen. The fact that George broke it off with Mrs. Olsen seems to be a good possible motive and explains the anger we saw in how George was killed.

"The question now becomes after she killed George because he dropped her, why does she want to kill the other Group members and Tom? Or as we have discussed before, has she just gone off the deep end and wants to take out anyone directly tied to the Group?

"Our time frame has changed. We have only four or five days before the rest of the Group of Nine will be at the courthouse for their trial. We hinted around at one of our earlier meetings that we could try to catch her, but it will still put a lot of people in danger. So, what do you have for me and how does the new information change what you might propose? Mark, do you have something you'd like to share?"

"Yes. The airlines that serve Muskegon looked through their flight manifests for two teen aged girls. It appears that there were reservations for the two daughters, but they were for two weeks earlier than what she told you. And what's more they were no shows then. That got my curiosity going. I went to their school and asked if they were in class. I was told that they were no longer enrolled there."

"Then where are they?" Dave asked

"That's what I wanted to know. So, I checked the Greyhound buses and showed pictures. The bus ticket agent remembered two pretty girls and their mother. The girls got on a bus to Detroit where they would pick up another bus to go on to Cincinnati. When the agent asked if someone was meeting them, their mother said that her sister and her husband would pick them up in Cincinnati. The ticket agent said he was still a little concerned, so he called his counterpart in Detroit and was told the girls were picked up, luggage and all, in Detroit."

"It appears she is setting up a move to somewhere, but we don't know where. It could be Cincinnati or anyplace in between or beyond," Dave said.

Jim asked, "What is she going to do with the house? Can we find that out?"

Mark continued, "I wondered about that too. I asked a realtor friend to look it up for me. He said that he could tell if it was on the market or whether it had been sold. He found that the house went on sale two months ago and it sold right away. No details on how much and who bought it although it should be public record in the county tax office. He did say that it was sold with all the furnishings. The only things she wanted were their personal items. And secondly that possession couldn't happen until school was out. She wanted the girls to finish their year at this school."

Dave raged, "What is amazing to me is this woman. She is like a chameleon, one day putting on an act, another day killing someone, another taunting us. Who knows what else?"

Jim interrupted, "I wonder if she has the money for the house already. Follow up in county offices and see when the sale was recorded.

"And, Mark, see if there is any way you can find out where those girls of hers are. We have two girls who took a bus to Detroit instead of Cincinnati. Find out who really picked them up.

"What we have is a short time to set a trap for her. It means that we may have to use an idea that we've talked about before and rejected. I have some ideas about how we can tweak that plan, but I need your help in getting the details fleshed out. We can't have anything go wrong.

"Let's take a little break and we'll get at it. I'll ask Gerri to bring in some drinks and snacks — we are probably in for a long day. I think Pete is at his desk in the common area. He'll be watching, so take care."

After a fifteen-minute break, the team returned to an array of Coca-Cola, Orange Fanta, Dr. Pepper, and Seven-Up along with platters of chocolate chip cookies and brownies.

Jim started right in. "Help yourself. I don't know how Gerri always works her magic and takes such good care of us, but I sure do appreciate her. Thanks, Gerri, this department wouldn't survive without you.

"You all will remember that we talked about setting a trap for Mrs. Olsen at the courthouse. We abandoned it because it would have been too dangerous for wives and children in particular. I want to revisit that idea but with a twist. I want to move all the families out somewhere for that first day for certain and maybe the next day too. I know they won't be excited about not being in the courtroom with their husbands, but the first couple of days are not that crucial.

"We will double up on the team following Mrs. Olsen so that we'll know she is in her house the night before the first day in court. Then we'll have the families driven to the police station, loaded on a charter bus, and taken out of town somewhere. The problem is I can't figure out where to send them. The children, there are eleven of them (ranging in age from eight or so to sixteen or seventeen), wives, and we'll have some volunteer ladies to go with them. We'll also send along three or four police officers in plain clothes. It will, we hope, just look like a chartered fun outing. As I said, I just don't know where."

Mark said, "Jim, Gerri has been trying to get your attention."

"Sorry, Gerri, what do you need?"

"I have an idea for you. Why not take them to Chicago for a trip to the Museum of Science and Industry? They will love it. My kids did. And if you need more than one day in Chicago, they could do the Aquarium and/or the Field Museum."

"Gerri, that is a terrific idea. What would I do without you?"

A chorus erupted. "Give her a raise, boss." Jim chuckled with them and said, "I'll take it up with the interim mayor."

"There will be twenty-five to thirty people. We need someone to take care of the details."

The men started laughing again. Jim turned — there was Gerri with her hand up.

"Do you have time enough to get it done along with your regular duties, Gerri?"

"Just you watch me, boss."

Dave asked, "How will we let our suspect know that there won't be any family there?"

Jim grinned. "We'll use our newly found tattle — Pete. I'll arrange to have someone say to me when Pete is nearby that we'll have the men escorted into the court room that morning by the police. We will let her know the same way that the wives and children are not coming. But we don't want Pete to hear about this trip to Chicago. She will assume they are at home. We'll have someone at the houses bustling around."

Mark asked, "How will we know she has taken the bait?"

"As I said earlier, we have doubled her surveillance team. As we know, she is no dummy. She is a little crazy at times, but smart. Her surveillance team will know if she checks the site for the best shooting point. Once we know where she's going to be, we will be in place all around her with plain clothes cops. We'll also have vehicles blocking all the exits. There will be no way she can escape. When the Group members and their escorts start to come out, we'll get a signal. They will open the doors, one officer will peek out, look around, start waving the others out. One of our guys will be dressed in a suit like the Group members and he'll start to come out, but then the police officer will push him back in. She may try a shot then, she may not. But when they all duck back in, I'll be on the bullhorn and will start trying to disarm her. If she throws her guns out and comes out of her hiding place with her hands up and empty, we'll take her into custody."

"What if she starts blasting away?"

Jim frowned. "I hope that doesn't happen. But if it does, we do our job. We take her out."

He continued, "All right, ask questions and more importantly, tell me what's wrong with the plan."

"Are the Group members and their attorney actually coming out?" Mark queried.

"No, they won't even be near the door. The scene is all faked by the officer who sticks his head out the door and the plain clothes guy pretending to be a Group member. The police officer will have a police uniform on, so he won't be taken for one of the Group. And, by the way, I was able to get twenty of the latest version of military flak jackets. Both of them will have one of those on as will the rest of us. They have made big improvements since their first use in the Korean war, but they are not perfect, so we'll still have to be behind vehicles.

"Mark, that was more of an answer than you expected probably. But I thought you ought to know about the jackets. I don't want any more loss of life."

Dave wondered, "What about putting a sniper somewhere on the roof? I could probably get a sharpshooter from the state police pool."

"That would be good. Can he come for both Monday and Tuesday? We will be doing a dry run-through on Monday."

"He can."

"Won't she get suspicious if she sees a lot of cars around?"

"I think she would. How can we get the coverage we need without too many cars? All of you give some thought to that."

"Maybe a group of us should pay a visit to the courthouse and note natural cover, statuary and the like, and trees." Mark paused. "By the way, do you think she'll use that black van again or will she rent something else?"

"Good question, Mark. I wouldn't put it past her to have something new. But we'll have enough people on her that we'll know in plenty of time. Any more questions or comments?

"None. Good. Gerri will have your notes early tomorrow. Get some rest. We have some busy days ahead of us. We'll meet again Friday at 10:00 a.m. unless something breaks loose. Gerri will include a list of tasks to be done. Don't be shy about meeting without me to pick out what you want to be responsible for.

"If you have a brainstorm or two for me before we meet Friday morning, please let me know. I have several things on my own To Do list — talking with the judge, the district attorney, the Group's attorney, and I want to talk to Tom and Maria as well as Mrs. Anderson. I'm hoping they might remember something else from that meeting that can shed some light. Please call me anytime if you have a question or a suggestion, anytime at all. See you Friday morning."

40

As Jim walked to his office, he noticed Pete sitting at his desk reading and watching. He nodded to him and got a wave back. He called Gerri in and asked her, "Any reaction to the meeting that you didn't want to share while we were together?"

"You know me, don't you? Yes, I sense some uneasiness about the operation on Tuesday. That may be just a natural reaction and they may not be as uneasy as I thought. They all know they could get hurt in this business, so I guess it should be expected."

"They are all good men. I appreciate your input."

"I better get at those notes, and I want to make a couple of phone calls to Chicago and get that process started."

"Let me know when you go home. You'll get some overtime on all this. I'm going by to see Tom and Maria on my way home."

Jim called Tom and Maria from his office and asked if it was okay if he dropped by for a few minutes. He wanted to fill them in on the meeting and the new plan and see whether Maria had any more insights from her meeting with Ann Anderson.

"Of course," Tom replied without hesitation. "Doug's here, too. You'll be just in time for a glass of wine and some cheese and crackers."

WHEN HE ARRIVED, he waved to the protection team, knocked, and was welcomed in. After shaking hands with Tom and Doug, he asked, "May I give your wife a hug? Thanks to the inputs she gave us, we now have a plan."

Tom nodded. After Jim hugged Maria, he said, "You made some magic with that idea of yours. How are you feeling?"

"I'm doing fine now. I'm ready to hear about the plan to end this business. We were just about to have some wine and a cheese plate before dinner. Will you join us while you tell us?"

"No, well, I'm not officially at work now, so why not? How about a small touch of that red you have there? As usual, my wife will have dinner ready. We have friends coming, so I can't stay long."

Between sips of wine, he laid out the plan for them. He finished with, "I think I can talk her down. Then we'll get her into a police car and lock her up in our jail."

Tom jumped in to ask, "What if she starts shooting at all of you? What will you do then, Jim?"

"We should be relatively safe. Thanks to Doug here, we will all be wearing the latest version of what used to be called flak jackets in the Korean War days. Thanks, Doug, for the call to get the vests."

Jim went on. "To answer your question, I'll try to talk her into surrendering. But if she won't, we will do what we have to. We will shoot her."

When he saw the reaction on Maria's face, he said, "We will do everything we can to try to bring her in alive."

Jim continued, "By the way, Tom, I don't want you there on Tuesday. You either, Doug, unless you insist. I would like you all to look over the plan and critique it. And I would like both of you at the meeting Friday morning at 10:00 a.m."

He turned to Maria. "Can you spare them?"

"I guess I can. I'll have a little coffee klatch with my mom and yours, Tom."

The phone rang. Tom answered. It was Gerri asking if the chief was still with them.

"What's up, Gerri?"

"Sorry to bother you, but Dr. Brown called and wants to talk with you. Can you call him from there?"

"That's all right, give me the number please." Jim hung up and asked Tom, "May I make a phone call before I go?

"Hello John, this is Jim. How can I help?"

"I have to be back in South Bend, and I understand your schedule is pretty tight. I wonder if instead of a lunch you and your wife could join us Saturday night at Tony's. My sister-in-law would like to meet you. She has only talked to you on the phone and would like it if you could come. No talk of what has happened or any other business, just two families sharing some time, getting to know each other better."

"Thank you for the invitation. My wife doesn't do this very often — she doesn't like to talk about my business. But since we won't do that, she will likely come. I'll ask her and let you know or have Gerri do it. Say, I just had an idea. Would you mind if I bring Maria and Tom? And bringing them means I will have to bring Doug who is their friend and also their security. The city can pick up that tab. I'm remembering that Ann and Maria plan to be friends. Dinner together will be a good start."

"That's a great idea except that it is our party and I'll get the tab."

"Thank you, John. Hold on just a second, please..." He asked Tom, Maria, and Doug.

Back to John, he said, "They all said it sounds like a great night. That will make eight of us. The private dining room would be great for us. If you talk to the manager, tell her that I'll be coming along and to reserve a table for two where my security team can watch both the entrance to the private room and the main entrance. If you call tonight, the private dining room should be available. Sorry, John, here I am barking orders as usual."

"It's okay, I understand. I'll make the reservation for 6:30 p.m. We'll have a great time. I'll leave word that it is all set with Gerri. See you then."

41

Next morning when Jim got to the office at 8:30 a.m., Gerri came in to go over his schedule for the day. She said, "Pete is at his desk, studying one of the procedures manuals. Mark and the task force are at the courthouse doing a reconnoiter of the grounds and then they are coming back for their own meeting this afternoon. You have your meeting at Judge McVie's at 9:30 a.m. I'm thinking this might be your best chance to drop your fake hints. Pete will be listening."

"When I leave, I'll come by your desk and hand you a piece of paper, ostensibly a list of men for protection duty on the way to the courthouse with the five Group members. It's fake. But that's when I'll drop the hints. Watch what he does after I'm gone. I should be back just after lunch." Gerri went back to her desk.

Soon after, Pete got up to get a fresh cup of coffee. He stopped at Gerri's desk and said, "Seems pretty quiet around here today. Does that happen often?"

"Every now and then. We take them as a welcome lull and enjoy them. How's your reading coming?"

"I'm just about done with this set of procedures. Only have one more to go. Guess I should get back to it."

Gerri buzzed Jim with a call from Dr. Brown.

"Good morning, Jim. I wanted to let you know everything is all set for Saturday night. They were most cooperative. Ann is excited to meet you and your wife, and to see her new friend, Maria, and meet her husband. I think the meeting with Maria the other day was a good thing for her. She is beginning to talk about what she will be doing from now on. Jane is going to stay on for another week. Maybe when I come back next weekend, we can have that lunch.

"Glad things went well. My wife is looking forward to meeting you all, too. I'm counting on the lunch next weekend. Thanks, John."

Gerri buzzed again. "I have a call for you from Don. He has some new info for you."

"Good morning, Don, what is going on?"

"Mrs. Olsen went to the New Shores Bank early this morning — you know the one that has the Group account. She was in there about twenty-five minutes and came out carrying a big briefcase that she didn't take in."

"Did she go anywhere else?"

"She did. She made a quick stop at a coffee shop and came out with coffee and a bag of what could be pastries. I'm across the street ready to follow when she starts off. I'm in a pay phone. She's back to her car. Gotta go, Chief."

Jim came out of his office about ten minutes later dressed for his meeting and carrying a light briefcase. He said to Gerri, "I'm off to my meeting. I'll get some lunch while I'm out and should be back by 1:00 p.m. or so. Please get a message to Mark that I need to see him when he gets back in. Oh, and here is a list of the men who will be escorting the Group members to the courthouse on Tuesday morning. Please let them know to pick up only the men — the wives are not coming until later after the jury selection is done. You know where I'll be. Call me if you need me." There was a note on the paper he gave her: *Have Mark call me at the meeting — important.*

"Okay. See you this afternoon."

Jim nodded to Pete as he walked past him.

Pete appeared engrossed in his manual giving no indication he had heard a thing. But ten minutes after the chief left, Pete said to Gerri, "I have an errand to run. Jim said earlier it would be okay. I'll have lunch before I come back, see you about 1:00 p.m."

"Okay, Pete. See you later."

When he was gone, Gerri went to the pool secretary and asked her to sit at her desk and take phone calls. "The chief wants something done quickly, and I can only do it in person. I won't be more than a half hour or so. Thanks."

She slipped her coat on, took the paper with the phone number, and walked over to the courthouse. She found Dave quickly and asked where Mark was. Dave said, "He's just around the corner. I'll show you."

They found him and she said, "Jim wants you to call him at this number. This is for Judge McVie's private office, so it must be important to the case."

"Good morning, Judge. This is Mark, the chief got word to me that I should call him on this phone. May I speak to him please? Thank you."

Jim got on. "Mark, we have info from Don that Mrs. Olsen stopped by New Shores Bank this morning. She came out with a briefcase that she didn't have going in. We think she is taking all her money out. Judge McVie has given us a warrant that Mr. Strahan, the bank manager, will need to answer your questions about her transaction.

"Is Dave close by? Good, take him with you, come by the Judge's office and get the warrant from his secretary. The two of you get to the bank and see what she did. Thanks, Mark. I'll be back by noon or so."

Mark told Dave and Gerri what Jim said. Gerri said, "I have to get back to the office."

"I'll take you back while Mark walks in and gets the warrant. I'll pick you up in about five minutes, Mark."

∾

MARK AND DAVE walked into the bank about 11:00 a.m. and were
directed to Mr. Strahan by the security guard. They asked if they
could talk with him in his private office. When they were in his office,
he said, "May I see some identification?" After examining their
credentials carefully, Mr. Strahan asked how he could help them.

Mark said, "Chief Johnson would have called you himself, but he
is in a meeting with Judge McVie as we speak. This warrant was
issued fifteen minutes ago. He will call you this afternoon."

"May I see the warrant? This looks to be in order. What is going
on, gentlemen?"

"This is strictly confidential, Mr. Strahan. We need to know what
Mrs. Olsen did in your bank this morning. We know she was here
shortly after you opened. This is relating to recent events and to last
fall's happenings."

"How do you know she was here this morning?"

"We've been following her for some time now."

"Is she involved in crimes?"

"Yes, and please forgive me for repeating this, we have to keep this
quiet. If she finds out that we know what went on here, she'll be in
the wind, and we'll never catch her."

"All right, gentlemen. Here is what happened this morning. Both
Mr. and Mrs. Olsen's names were on the account until last fall. When
Mr. Olsen died in the car incident, we all read the will together, Mrs.
Olsen, her attorney, and I, and Mrs. Olsen assumed total control of
their assets — no probate. There was close to a half million dollars in
the account.

"She wanted me to close the account and give her the cash. I tried
to get her to let me wire it to a new bank wherever she is going but
she would have none of that. Mrs. Olsen is a gracious woman, but she
was very firm about how she wanted it. I was suspicious about her
motivations, but my hands were tied. I finally talked her into taking a
briefcase with $100,000 in it and a certified cashier's check for the
balance, nearly $400,000. She thanked me and walked out with the
check in her purse and the briefcase, a large one, in her right hand."

"We were right. She is heading to parts unknown." Mark nodded at Doug.

"Can I ask a question?" Without waiting, he went on. "Why can't you just arrest her? Don't you have evidence?"

"Yes, we do, but we need one more piece of evidence and we are about to get it."

"I still can't see why you don't arrest her." Mark and Dave looked at each other and nodded.

"The district attorney says we need to be sure we can get a guilty verdict. Mrs. Olsen may be gracious, but she is also a killer. We suspect she has killed twice already and has her sights set on several more. We don't want that to happen."

"I don't envy you. I think I'm glad she's no longer a customer of this bank. Good day, gentlemen."

42

Judge McVie, Jim, Doug, the DA Harvey, and the Group's attorney, Harold, were in the Judge's small conference room by his office. Having been informed that Mark picked up the warrant and was now at the bank, the Judge said, "Now tell me about this plan to get Mrs. Olsen doing her thing, whatever that is."

Jim started with, "Up to this time, our evidence, while solid, may not be enough to put her away. After some discussion with Harvey, we are adding to the direct evidence, but we feel we have to catch her in the act, so to speak.

"But she kind of forced our hand with her actions since we've been following her. The remaining Group members have had police protection since shortly after the killing of George Anderson. Even so, she drove up to one of their homes, parked her van so that she was ready to pull away fast, a van that we didn't know about. She shot into their house, but curiously in such a way that she wouldn't hit anyone. She then fled so fast that we lost her. Then she left us another note saying, 'See, I can get anyone I want, anytime I want.' The note matched the other two notes we received at the last two murders.

"My men hurried in to check on the family. They were fine

because the shooter aimed above their heads and fired into the fireplace wall. We have the bullets from that encounter and the bullets from the killing of one of the members to use for comparison. They match.

"She showed up at the news conference I gave last week looking pretty smug. She took several pictures of the courthouse, both inside and outside. It looked to us like she was casing the courthouse for her plan to take out the rest of the Group at the trial. We've redoubled our protection of the Group members and their families, so it will be harder for her to pick them off one by one. We think she's going to try to get them all at once and then leave the area. Her daughters are already in the wind — we're trying to locate them."

"So, what will happen on Tuesday?"

"I have a question first, Your Honor. Will you, depending on their pleas, start to impanel the jury?"

"I'm still thinking of not starting that until Wednesday. Why do you ask?"

"If you wait until Wednesday, then Tuesday's session should be short. When you dismiss for the day, we will have a uniformed police officer pop out of the door, look around and give a signal for others to follow. That signal will also be for my team of twenty armed men placed strategically around the courthouse to begin closing in. At the same time, I will get on a bullhorn and try to talk her in."

"What will you do if she doesn't come in? What if she starts shooting?"

"I can be persuasive, your honor, to help her see she hasn't a chance of leaving the parking lot. She'll come in. If not, we have a job to do."

"I have two more questions. Will the wives be there? And will there be any shooting inside the courtroom?"

"No and no, your honor."

"Okay then, let's do it."

43

After breakfast, Tom cleaned up and Maria called her mom. "Good morning, Mom. I'm fine, how are you and Dad?"

"We're good. When are we going to get together?"

"That's why I called. Tom and Doug have to be at a meeting at the police station Friday morning. I was wondering if you and Dad could come over for a visit. Tom doesn't want me to be alone very much yet."

"We could do that, but I have a better idea. I have been wanting to get together with Tom's parents. Let me set it up over here. I'll invite Tom's parents and you could bring your new friend Sara and maybe her little girl. I'll put together a little brunch."

"That sounds great, Mom. But I'll want a little time with you and Sara afterward. We haven't had much time to talk, just us girls. We can even do a little wedding planning with her.

"Mr. O'Banion, Tom's dad, will likely be at the office. If he can't come, what will you do with Dad?"

"Don't you worry about it. It will work out. See you all at 10:00 a.m."

When she hung up, she told Tom what was planned. "Mom will take care of the whole thing. I just have to get there."

"Do you feel comfortable driving yet? Dr. Franks said not to rush that."

"Do you suppose our protection team could take me?"

"I'll bet they would do that. They would need to be there as protection anyway. I'll check with them later."

"Mom will call your parents. I'll see about Sara and Arianna."

"Do you feel up to taking a ride, take a little break from your studies, get some fresh air, and maybe a little walk on a beach somewhere?"

Maria beamed at Tom. "That sounds terrific! Are we getting lunch out too?"

"We can put together a picnic lunch and run up to the beach near Duck Lake. We can sit there and enjoy our lunch while we watch the waves. We will put our toes in the sand and talk about...whatever. Nothing serious unless we want to."

"What about our protection? Will they give us some space?"

"I bribed them with lunch, too. I made it early this morning. Grab a sweater, I'll get the lunch."

44

When Jim got back to the office, Gerri was just finishing her lunch. "When you are done, why don't you come in and we'll compare notes and events of the morning?"

Gerri left someone to take calls and went to Jim's office. Jim asked, "What happened with Pete?"

"Ten minutes after you left, he told me he needed to run an errand. Oh, and that you said it was okay."

Jim shook his head. "Not so, but we are learning more about him each day."

"He said that he would be back by 1:00 p.m. He should be here any time now. I'm guessing he went out to call her."

"Anything else to report?"

"Oh, just that Mark said they were all going to lunch together but wouldn't be long and he'll be in to see you. They are all working on a plan to have cars set in such a way that she won't notice. He said he would explain later. How did things go with Judge McVie?"

"He wasn't happy with our plan, possible shooting near his courthouse and all. He had lots of questions, but we finally convinced him. I'm not as sure as I told the judge that there wouldn't be any shooting. In fact, I would rather she did fire at least one shot. More ballistics comparisons, you know."

"Doug stopped in to see you shortly after you left and said he would catch up with you later after his rounds. And he was a little put out by Tom and Maria. Tom called and left a message for Doug that he and Maria are at this moment having a beach picnic at the Lake Michigan beach near Duck Lake, with their protection along."

Jim chuckled. "It was probably Maria's idea. I don't know if Tom realizes what a strong woman he has. They'll be fine with their protection watching. What do you want to bet that Doug drove out by there just to check the situation out!"

"No bet on that, Jim. Last thing. The trip for the wives of the remaining Group of Nine and the children is all set. I got the wives of the protection detail to go along. It seemed like a more secure way to keep the whole thing quiet. The museum is expecting them on Tuesday and will have a special guide for the group."

"Good work, Gerri. Thank you. I have some calls to make, but I want to see Mark and Doug as soon as they come back."

Jim dialed John Brown right away at the Anderson home. "Hello, John. I have a question and a favor to ask."

"Anything, you only need to ask."

"Do you think Ann would talk to you about the meeting when Maria was there and/or at the meeting with Mrs. Olsen? I don't want to cause her any more stress. But you never know when some little something might help us."

"I think I can do that. I'll have to think on how to get into it."

"Just one thing, it has to be done before Saturday." Jim noticed a hesitation before John replied, and asked, "What is worrying you, John?"

"I'm thinking there is something big coming down. I'm wondering if Ann is in any danger from Mrs. Olsen."

"I think not, but let's not take any chances. I already doubled up on Mrs. Olsen's surveillance team and I'll have a team at the Anderson home for your protection. Maybe that is a good in for you to talk about things. And John, if Mrs. Olsen should call for another meeting with Ann and Jane, turn it down."

"Do you think that is likely?"

"I don't think it is likely but with this woman, you never know what is coming."

"All right, Jim. I'll get it done tonight and call you before your meeting in the morning."

Jim's next call was to Mr. Strahan at the bank. "Mr. Strahan, this is Jim Johnson, Chief of Police. I'm calling to apologize for not alerting you before my men were there this morning. I was with the Judge when this came down and had to act on it."

"I did think it was a bit abrupt and could have been done better. I appreciate you calling me. By the way, has Judge McVie decided regarding the bail money for the wives of those who are dead?"

"He has not. He is researching the statutes and will likely make the decision after the trial of the last members of the Group. Mr. Strahan, my apologies again, for the imposition this morning. I'll call you as soon as I have news."

"Thank you, Jim."

Gerri buzzed him. "Both Mark and Doug are here with news and the rest of the task force are busy working away in the conference room."

"Send them in, please." Jim greeted them with a firm handshake. "First, Mark, have you doubled up on Mrs. Olsen's surveillance team?"

"Yes, it's done. The second car and crew started this morning after she got back home from the bank."

"And Doug, do you think they were ready to do the job?"

"They are. I worked with them all last week after you told me you thought it might become necessary. She's covered."

"Good. Now how about the plans for Tuesday? Are we going to have enough cover to pull this off?"

Doug said, "May I go first?" Jim looked at Mark who nodded.

Doug continued, "In my past, which you don't know much about, I've been around a number of these kinds of situations. The only difference is that our goal was usually to take the person out as opposed to capture. But the principles are the same. Mark has his team right on point. They have good cover and know how to keep out of her possible line-of-sight. While they worked, I played the role of Mrs. Olsen in the two most likely spots she might choose. The only suggestion I had once we narrowed it down to a most likely spot was that we should keep her under complete surveillance. We will have binoculars on her as soon as she parks. Then when she goes to the backseat where she'll likely have the guns — she will have more than one — the cars covering any potential exits will move into position to block her from driving away. We walked through that routine twice to get the timing down. Mark and his team have it cold now. I recommend we not do the rehearsal Monday afternoon. She might be scouting around to see if there's anything unusual happening."

"What do you think about all that, Mark?"

"The man has it right, Jim. These things are seldom foolproof, but we are very close to that standard."

Gerri buzzed. "Jim, Pete is on the line. He says he is sick and wants to know if he can take the rest of the day off."

"Did he give you any idea of where he was, at home, or at a bar, or what...? Tell him I said he could take the day off and then ask him if he thinks he will be in by morning or is it more serious. See what he says and let me know."

"Now what do you think of that. Pete left shortly after I dropped the two hints I hoped he would pass on to Mrs. Olsen and now he has asked for the rest of the day off." Jim paused. "He says he is sick. I wonder if he is about to get more involved with her. Might be a mistake on his part.

"I want to step into the conference room for a second but before I do, I have one more thing for you, Doug. Do you have a protection team you can put on the Andersons?"

"I can do that. What's up?"

"I just got off the phone with John Brown, Ann's brother-in-law. I asked him to review with the sisters the two meetings, the one with Maria, and the earlier one with Mrs. Olsen. He asked if I thought that his sister-in-law Ann was in any danger. I told him I didn't think it was likely but told him I would get a protection team on their home. He seemed relieved."

"I've got four men, two teams, so I can get them covered. I'll do it this afternoon."

"Good, let's go talk to the team."

"Afternoon everyone. I've been hearing such a good report about what you all are doing. I wanted to let you know that I appreciate the effort you are putting in on this. I'm looking for a good meeting tomorrow."

Dave saluted. "For all of us, thank you, Jim. Atta boys are welcome."

Gerri followed Jim back into his office. "Pete said to tell you thanks and he thinks he will be in tomorrow morning. He didn't sound very sick to me."

"We'll see if he turns up in the morning. Thanks Gerri."

"By the way, Tom called in and said they were back home. He also mentioned how much good it did Maria. Did Doug say anything about it?"

"He didn't, but he might not. It was probably good for both of them."

"You really like them, don't you, Jim?"

"I do. They are both pretty special people. Now I have some more calls to make."

Gerri heard his door close and click locked. She thought, *he's going to take a short nap. He's been doing that more and more lately. I wonder how old he is. Mid-sixties? Will he be retiring soon? He deserves it. Almost thirty years on the force, the last eighteen as chief. A good man.*

GERRI HEARD HIS DOOR UNLOCK. She gave it a few minutes, then buzzed him. "I need to talk to you again."

"Come on in."

"One of Mrs. Olsen's surveillants called in for Doug. I told them I would track him down and he would be in touch. I signaled Doug on the radio with two beeps. He called right back from the Anderson's. Their protection is in place. He said he would wait there ten more minutes, so you can call him back there."

"Make the call, put me through, and stay on the line."

"Hello, John. Glad to see you are answering the phone. May I speak with Doug please?" Jim filled Doug in on the call from one of the men surveilling Mrs. Olsen.

"I'll head over there right now, Jim. I have a signal I can give them so one of the cars can follow me out and fill me in on what's happening. I'll get them back in position and call you back."

"Sounds like a plan. When you leave, put me back on with John please. I'll be waiting for your call."

"On it. Here's John."

"John, how are the ladies?"

"They are much more relaxed now. Thank you very much, Jim. Say, Doug is a great guy, he sure had the ladies laughing. We are all looking forward to Saturday night. You'll hear from me in the morning before your meeting."

45

P ete knocked on Anna's door and was welcomed by a smiling lady. *Hmm,* he thought, *this might have more potential than I have been thinking.* He greeted her, "Hello, Mrs. Olsen."

She gave him a hug. "Oh, Pete, you must call me Anna. Let's go sit in the living room. We can have a glass of a good white wine and some snacks. You do drink wine, don't you?" She pulled the living room drapes closed not noticing the car parked just around the corner where the occupant watched the entry proceedings. When the drapes closed, he drove by the house slowly, memorized the license plate number and drove around the block back to the hidey hole to watch for him or her when they left, if anyone did. Time was 2:30 p.m.

She poured some wine, gave him one, and toasted to a more complete partnership. "Well, Pete, what do you have for me? You said, it was good news when you called."

"I think it is. You'll see and make your own judgement. You know that the trial for the final members of the Group starts Tuesday, don't you?"

"No, that's news to me."

"Well, see, I'm telling you now. And more importantly, there will be a squad of officers who will take the men to the courthouse and in through a hidden back entrance. Depending on what happens in the initial stages of the trial, they will be released out the front door. The other piece of information is that the wives are not coming. They will be coming later after the jury is set. So, it will be just the men."

"Are the women staying home?"

"Nothing was said about that, so it makes sense that they would be."

She took another sip of her wine. "I don't care about the wives anyway. I figure we have all suffered equally from this business. Some of the wives have lost their husbands and are widows already. It is the men I'm interested in. How do you know they'll come out the front door?"

"I don't know for certain, but it seems logical and likely to me."

"I don't want likely, I want certain."

"How can you do that?"

She took another sip of wine. "You're going to help me get certain. How much money do you owe that gambling syndicate?"

"Just under $10,000. Why do you ask, why is that important right now?"

"Because if you do as I ask, I'll pay off your $10,000 debt and give you $10,000 more."

"That's very generous of you. What do I have to do?"

"I need you to create a diversion. I want you to make yourself a part of that team to take the members in the back door. You be the last one in, close and lock the door, then put a bomb that I'll give you at the bottom of the back door."

"How big a bomb is this? And how do I set it off without getting blown up?"

"The bomb placed at the bottom of the door will only jam the door and you set it off by throwing a switch that gives you ten minutes to get upstairs and into the courtroom. You can do the whole procedure in less than thirty seconds. And you can be upstairs in less than three minutes. When you get upstairs, position yourself so that you will be the first one out of the front door. A crowd will form after the explosion. Get out and blend with the crowd. I'll pick you up later and we'll get out of dodge."

"What do you mean 'get out of dodge'?"

"Why, Petey, don't you know this will be the start of something special for us?"

"I didn't know you were thinking that way."

"I didn't want to let you know until now. What do you say?"

"I'll do it."

"How will you get on the squad?"

"I already have it figured out. I faked being sick today. They are probably expecting that I'll call in sick tomorrow. So, I will and instead I'll scout out the back entrance, so I know how to find it outside and inside, get all the timing done, I'll be ready."

She got up, poured him some more wine, and bent over and kissed him on the lips. "That's just a sample, Petey. Please call me tomorrow to let me know you got everything worked out."

"Shouldn't I come over to let you know?"

"No, I don't think we ought to take any chances about meeting. I'll get you the bomb right now and show you how to use it."

After the lesson on the bomb, she said, "See it's big enough to get the job done on the door, and small enough to carry in your uniform pocket." When she was sure he was okay with the bomb, she kissed him again and whispered, "Until Tuesday."

"How will I find you afterward?"

"As I said, come out the front door, first one out and I'll be waiting for you in the van. Don't be late now."

The front door opened and both Pete and Anna came out. She reached out, touched his face, gave him a kiss on the lips and sent him on his way. He walked slowly to his car, holding the bomb as though it was something alien. He opened the passenger side door, put it on the seat, took off his jacket and covered it. He drove away carefully.

It was 3:15pm. The observer noted what happened and thought that the guy looked pretty anxious about whatever he was carrying.

DOUG STOPPED at the second surveillance station on Belmont to talk to Lenny. From here Lenny was in position to go wherever Mrs. Olsen went if she left. He told Doug that Don was right around the corner watching while Pete was in the house. There was a squawk on his walkie-talkie. He said, "That means Pete is just leaving, but Don won't be following."

"We don't want him anyway. I'll go up and wait for Don in our little cove just up the hill. I want to get Don's report right away. Once I get that, I'll head for the station and report to Jim. You two just go back to watching and following her. This is almost over, hang in there."

Doug got the report from Don. At the end of the 'just the facts' part, Don said, "He got here at 2:30 p.m. She let him in with a big smile. She pulled the drapes shut not long after he went in. They were open long enough for me to see a bottle of wine chilling and a plate of snacks. So, it seems that they have more than just a casual relationship. And, one last thing, when Pete came out, he walked slowly, carefully to his car, put the boxy looking thing on the passenger seat and covered it with his jacket and drove away slower than he usually drives. Here is a Polaroid picture of what he was carrying. It is a little fuzzy. He left at 3:15 p.m. and she has been in there since. She opened the drapes."

"You did well, Don. This will soon be over. I'm headed back to report to Jim. He may have more questions for you when you go off shift."

As Doug came down the hill, he turned left, stopping for one more chat with the other man on the team. He asked, "Did you see him leave?"

"I did. He came down the hill, driving kind of slowly as he turned onto McCracken. I got out and pretended to be washing off the car hood. I could see him down past Seminole and then Norton. I'd say chances are good he kept on going down McCracken to Lakeside. That's where he lives you know."

"Yes, I know. You did well. See you when I come by for my next rounds."

~

Doug asked Gerri, "Is the chief available?"

"He said to get you in as soon as you got here." She buzzed him in.

"Hello, Doug, fruitful trip?"

"Yes. The Andersons are happy. And the men on Mrs. Olsen's detail did a great job on Pete's visit. You were right, he's not sick. Don was in the usual position where he could watch the front of her house. When Pete parked in her driveway, she was waiting and watching at the front picture window. She met him at the door with a big smile and invited him in. Don got a Polaroid of him. The drapes were still open, Don saw a bottle of white wine chilling, but she closed her drapes before he could see much more. Pete left about 3:15 p.m. That forty-five minutes is enough to settle something between them but not extended enough for anything else. Besides, what happened when he left is more telling."

"This much is pretty good. Tell me more."

"When the door opened, Pete came out holding what looked like a little box. She came out and stood alongside of him talking. He nodded and she reached out, touched his face, and gave him a kiss on the lips. Pretty cozy for what we thought their relationship was."

"I think she is playing him. She is very good at that."

"Don said that Pete walked slowly and deliberately to his car and put the box on the passenger's seat. He went around to the driver's side, looked back at her and waved. She waved back and blew him a kiss. She went back in, opened the drapes, and made a telephone call."

"I wonder what was in that box. I thought at first it might be money, but why would he walk so gingerly with a box of money?"

Doug agreed. "That was my thinking too. But what I think now is it may be some kind of bomb. If it is, it is not so large as to do major structural damage. So, I wonder what it could be for?"

"Maybe the others will have some sort of idea when we meet in the morning. Is there anything else?"

"Don's partner didn't follow Pete when he left but did the next best thing. He got out of his car, started faking polishing the hood of his car. He watched Pete go down McCracken, past Seminole Rd, past Norton Ave... He thought that even though he could have turned off on one of the less major streets, he said that he thought Pete went on to Lakeside where he lives."

"I agree. But I'm going to call him to see how he handles a phone call about his sickness." He buzzed Gerri and asked her to get him Pete's home phone number. She brought it in.

"Hello Pete, this is Jim. I'm just calling to see how you are doing. Gerri said you called in sick and took the afternoon off. How is it coming?"

"Nice of you to call, Jim. It is getting better, but I just stayed in this afternoon and slept off and on. I would like to stay home tomorrow as well. I'm sure after the weekend, I'll be over this bug. Thanks for the call, Chief."

Jim hung up. "He lied to me. Said he was home all afternoon trying to sleep it off. She persuaded him to do something for her, but I can't quite figure out what yet."

"It may be some kind of diversion, but I don't see where it fits yet."

"We'll share it and a lot more with the others at tomorrow's meeting. Maybe we'll get some ideas."

"Jim, I hope you don't mind my saying this but here goes. You look tired. Why don't you take off early and get a good rest? Nothing is going to happen tonight."

"Thanks for your concern. And yes, I am tired. It has been a long stretch with things changing almost daily. I think I'll take your advice. My wife will be surprised, I think I should call her first and let her know."

46

Before Doug left the station, he called Tom. "Hey there, my friend. How are things going?"

"Great, Doug. We spent a very relaxing day, which was so good for Maria. A little beach time, a nap for Maria. What's going on at the office that I should know about before the meeting tomorrow?"

"That's part of why I'm calling, to catch you up. Some interesting stuff going on. Things have changed a bit."

"Why don't you come by and brief us in person? It seems like we haven't seen you in a bit. After her nap, Maria put together her famous lasagna and I've got a good red to go with it."

"Sounds good. I have one more stop to check up on a protection detail. I should be there about five or so."

"See you then."

When he got to Tom and Maria's, Doug stopped to talk with their protection detail. When he asked why he wasn't notified about the beach trip, they looked a little sheepish. "The way we understand it, Tom proposed it, Maria jumped right on it, and the next thing you know we were on the road."

"Maria can be impulsive and she's a strong woman. But I need to know when things like this happen. Just a phone call from the house before you go. I don't like surprises."

"Sorry, boss. It won't happen again."

Doug smiled at them. "Now I'll go in and face the music inside. I won't mention our conversation in there."

Tom saw him outside and called from the door, "Hey, Doug, get yourself in here. Maria's hungry and you know how that goes if I don't feed her."

Doug gave his men a last grin. "See what I mean." Then he went in and greeted them both.

Maria already had the wine poured and the cheeses and crackers on the coffee table. Maria raised her glass to toast, "Here's to an afternoon at the beach, soaking up sun, to do a girl a world of good."

When Tom noticed a slight frown on Doug's face, he said, "Sorry we didn't get word to you."

"It's okay. I just don't like surprises when it comes to my two best friends. I can see it was good for you both."

Maria added, "Tomorrow when you are in the meeting, I'll be at my parents' house for all morning. Mom invited Tom's parents and Sara. We're going to work on the wedding plans. I'll likely be there until just after lunch. How's that, my friend?"

Doug laughed. "Touché. I guess I had that coming. If you are ready for a briefing, let's get started. Here are the most recent notes. There is a lot that has happened.

"First of all, Maria, there were two pieces of information from your interview at the Andersons that were important. First, Mrs. Anderson, without knowing she did it, alerted us to a possible motive for Mrs. Olsen's anger toward the men. She was angry at George for dumping her, so she killed him, but not before getting him to confess about Joe and Larry's murders. She shot Tim Samuels because, we think, she thought the leaders in the Group had planned her husband's death instead as she found out later, it was all George. George told her he had to take her husband out. She had a lot of anger building up."

Maria asked, "If she was so angry, why didn't she go to the police and tell them everything she knew and/or suspected before she killed Tim and George?"

"We don't know for certain. I suppose we won't know until we get her in custody. We can get her with a psychologist who might be able to shed some light on it. At the moment, it seems that this is when she started losing control of herself and laid out her plot to take vengeance.

"The second big break was finding out, as you did, that Pete had been leaking information to Mrs. Olsen's husband for some time. When Jim heard this, he told us he suspected Pete was the leak.

"And there is another event that gave us some insight. We didn't tell you about this because Jim thought you were too fragile yet. She fired shots at the home of one of the remaining Group members. She did this from the back of a van that we later found out was her husband's. She got away but on examination we found that she deliberately fired high. We believe that she didn't really want to kill anyone at that time. And especially she didn't want to kill his wife or any of the children. We are taking this and the visit with Ann Anderson and her sister to conclude she isn't interested in killing the women, just the men of the Group of Nine."

"What if you are wrong about that? She just might fool you and take out a wife or two." Maria had tears in her eyes even thinking that might happen.

Doug was quick to say, "That's why we are taking precautions as you'll see."

"Can we finish this after dinner? I'm getting hungry. How about you two?"

Without waiting for an answer, Maria took the lasagna out of the oven and put the garlic toast in. Within five minutes, she said, "Let's eat, gentlemen."

After dinner, she and Doug went back to the living room while Tom cleaned up, only fair since Maria cooked the entire meal.

Doug said, "I'm going to condense this next part a little bit. You'll get all the details at tomorrow's meeting, Tom, and you can pass it along to Maria tomorrow afternoon. When Judge McVie sent word that the trial for the remaining members would start next Tuesday, Jim revived the plan to draw her into trying to get the last of them at one time on Tuesday when they came out of the courthouse. The task force yesterday spent time enough to plan where they would be and to anticipate where she would most likely park. To draw her in, Jim let Pete overhear him. There were two items he let Pete hear. One was that the men would be taken to the back entrance to the courtroom by a detail of five police officers. These officers would remain in the courtroom until the pleas were entered. The judge said it was not likely he would start empaneling the jury that day. It should be a short session. The second item leaked was that there would be no wives there on the first day, Tuesday."

Maria asked, "Will the wives and children be protected?"

"Better than that, they won't even be in town." He went on to outline the plan to have them on a 'field' trip to Chicago's Museum of Science and Industry. They wouldn't be coming back to town until sometime Wednesday.

Tom asked, "That is a good plan. Who thought that up?"

Doug grinned. "It was Gerri, and she even took care of all the details. They will be safe."

Maria just smiled.

Doug continued, "We met this morning with the judge to fill him in on the details and have him approve the plan to get the last piece of physical evidence we needed, according to the district attorney, to convict her. The next thing that happened convinced us that we were right in moving on the plan. While we were with Judge McVie, we got word from Mrs. Olsen's surveillance team that she went to her bank and walked out with a big briefcase that she hadn't come in with. With the judge's warrant, Dave and Mark went to the bank. The president, Mr. Strahan, said the briefcase was filled with over $100,000. She also carried a certified bank check for nearly $400,000. She is a very wealthy woman as well as an angry one."

Tom whistled. "That is a bunch of money. She must be getting ready to run."

"That's what we figured. And one more thing. You'll remember that in our time with her, you and I heard her say she sent her daughters on a little break to Atlanta to her aunt and two cousins. Mark was suspicious about that. He did some amazing detective work and found that she put them on a bus the day before with tickets to Detroit and a transfer on to Cincinnati. They never got on the bus to Cincinnati. They are somewhere near Detroit waiting for their mother to pick them up and go to who knows where. We don't have a clue. What this means is that we have to get her Tuesday in the parking lot of the courthouse."

Tom asked, "How will you try to take her?"

"Jim is going to get on a bullhorn and try to reason her in. He will let her know that she is surrounded and can't get away."

Maria asked, "What will you do if she doesn't surrender?"

"We'll do our job, Maria. We don't want any more killings, even and especially hers."

"But..." She couldn't continue.

"Trust us. We have a good team, well-protected. When she sees them all pointing their guns at her, even in her state, we think she will surrender."

Doug continued, "Jim doesn't want either of you involved. He told me so this afternoon when he knew I was coming by here. He feels that you, Maria, are just not strong enough yet to be there, and you, Tom, for two reasons. One is that as good as you have gotten with a gun, you're just not ready to be involved yet. But the most important reason for you is that you are both very special to him, and to me, as you know. He wants you to move on with your new life you have planned."

Doug looked at Maria. "Will you be able to sleep tonight? Jim and I talked about this possibility and wanted me to ask. So, I have. What do you think?"

"I just don't like the feeling of helplessness that I'm having right now. I know there is nothing I can do, but I feel a bit of sympathy for this woman who is so lost and doesn't know what to do except kill people. And Doug, as long as I have Tom here with me, I'll be all right."

"Good, I'm going home. I'll see you, Tom, in the morning. And Maria, you ladies have a wonderful time planning a wedding for two young people that I happen to like a lot. Goodnight, you two."

When he was gone, Maria turned to Tom. "It's true, isn't it? There is nothing I can do to change things. So, take me to bed and just hold me until I fall asleep."

47

Gerri was already at her desk when Jim bustled in. "You're looking chipper today. Looks like taking some time to refill the bucket did you some good."

"Yes, thanks to you and Doug. I stopped and got Martha flowers on the way home. She was so surprised. We had a light dinner and then took a walk in the woods behind our place. The spring wildflowers are in full bloom and the sand was still warm from the sun. We are only a half mile from the Lake Michigan beach. We sat and watched the sunset. They are gorgeous this time of year. All that and a good night's sleep."

"You show it. It's good."

The phone rang. It was John Brown with some news.

Jim answered in his office. "Good morning, John. What's the good news?"

"Ann, Jane, and I were reflecting on the session with Maria. At first Ann was doing all right, but as Ann thought about all she had revealed, she became more agitated and concerned. After Jane and I reassured her that she was very brave and had done the right thing, she began to brighten up. Then she started remembering the meeting with she, Jane, and Anna Olsen. She thought there was something that Mrs. Olsen said that bothered her, but she couldn't quite remember it. I asked her to close her eyes, imagine that time in the conversation, and try to recall what was said. She sat quietly for a moment and then it hit her.

"She remembered that Mrs. Olsen said she and her husband had a big fight over him even getting into the Group of Nine. She told him that she felt as though she couldn't trust any of them. She said her husband told her that seemed to be the case with a lot of the wives — that a number of the guys had mentioned that their wives weren't in favor of the group nor the project about Muskegon Lake.

"She went on to say that the Christmas party at The Occidental only served to increase her distrust. She was concerned that the men were getting too enamored with their power and how much money they were going to make. They had another fight when they got home from that party. She wanted her husband to back out of the Group and he told her he wasn't about to.

"Then Ann got a sad expression on her face and almost teared up. I encouraged her to tell us. Ann continued with 'I just feel so sorry for her, Mrs. Olsen.' She told Jane and I that Mrs. Olsen seemed to be angry at the men in the Group, angry at her husband, and feeling sad that all she had was herself and her girls. She just seemed lost."

John continued, "What I read into that was, Mrs. Olsen let that anger grow and began then to plot how she could break it up, make them fall apart. I suspect that she never told the other ladies about her thoughts and eventually plans. And then when her husband was killed, her anger grew and festered but only at the men. Seems to be motive enough."

"And also verifies for us that she has no thoughts to harm the women or children. This is useful information. We'll see what the task force thinks at the meeting this morning."

Jim hung up, sat thinking for a moment. *I forgot to say something to him.* He buzzed Gerri and asked for the Anderson home phone number. Gerri said, "I'll get him for you."

John answered, "Did I forget something, Jim?"

"No, I did. I meant to ask you. I know you are a cardiologist, but it keeps occurring to me that you sound like a psychologist or a psychiatrist."

"I was at one time thinking of following that career path. I had a good rotation in psychiatry, did a lot of study in the field, but finally decided I wanted cardiology instead. Why do you ask?"

"I have a favor to ask. I would like to invite you to sit in on the task force meeting this morning and then we'll have lunch somewhere and you can tell me what you observe and see. I will introduce you as a cardiologist who has been following this because of Ann. I'll tell them how you have been involved. Are you interested?"

"Interested! I would have asked but thought that my asking would have been an imposition. Yes, I'd love to be in there listening and answering any questions they might ask me."

"Good, I'll see you at 10:00 a.m."

THE COFFEE KLATCH began at 9:00 a.m. at the Vitale home. There was Maria's mom, Sally, Maria, Tom's mom, Mary, and Father Flanagan. Mr. O'Banion couldn't make it, he had appointments to keep at work. Hank Vitale, who was already retired, was thinking *what am I going to do while all these ladies, and Father Flanagan, plan a wedding.*

The doorbell rang. "That will be Sara," said Maria. "May I let her in?"

Maria greeted her and looking behind her saw Sister Charlotte carrying Arianna. Father Flanagan brought up the rear carrying a big bouquet of white daisies and pink carnations.

"It looks like I have some introductions to make. Everyone, this is Sara, the lady behind her is Sister Charlotte, the head of the Home where Sara has been staying for a while now, and this little cutie is Sara's six-month-old daughter Arianna. Does everyone know Father Flanagan? The flowers are so lovely."

Pointing to each, Maria introduced the new arrivals. "Sara and Sister Charlotte, this is Tom's mother, Mary. Mr. O'Banion couldn't be with us today because of work. This is my mother, Sally and my dad, Hank. There, I think everyone knows everyone now."

Sara interrupted, "Mrs. Vitale, I hope it is not an imposition to have invited Father Flanagan and Sister Charlotte. They weren't in the original list but were needed for reasons you will hear later."

Sally took the flowers from Father Flanagan. "Sara, there is no problem. We only have the one child, Maria, but we have lots of other family. A big dining room table comes in handy. I even have a highchair for Arianna. Let me get some more coffee and we'll get this gathering going."

Hank joined in, "I was wondering what I was going to do while all this wedding planning was going on. Sister Charlotte, if you and Sara would permit me, I'd like to help with Arianna, that is, if she takes to me."

"I'd be happy to share with you. She is a little sweetheart. We have enjoyed her being at the Home." Everyone played musical chairs until Hank and Sister Charlotte were seated next to Arianna in the highchair.

"Thank you, Mom, for pulling this together so quickly. I'm so happy to see all of you. Tom and Doug have a big meeting this morning and they are both pretty protective of me yet. I thought this would be a great time to spend with all of you. And it seemed like a good time to do a little wedding planning since the wedding is just a few months away. Sara, do you want to take the lead?"

"Thanks, Maria. I really appreciate everything you and Tom are doing for me. And I am so grateful to you, Mrs. Vitale, for inviting me to brunch this morning. Some of us have already met and taken care of some basics. All of that is coming along nicely. Bob and I will finish our pre-marriage counseling next week. I have a matron of honor, Maria. When I asked her, she said yes without even thinking about it. I was concerned about her rehab progress. But from what I see and what I have heard, you are ready."

"I wouldn't miss it for the world. I'm your gal."

"And one more thing I want to let everyone know now. Bob and I discussed what you and Tom proposed a while back. We also spoke with Father Flanagan about it. Tom and Maria have agreed to be Arianna's godparents." When everyone started applauding, Arianna tried too, which brought smiles and chuckles to the group.

"To go on, I have my other attendants chosen. We are looking at color schemes and gowns. Bob has his best man picked but doesn't know who the other two will be yet. Father Flanagan has been so good to us. He has the dispensation from the Bishop, so we can get married in the church, his church. We still don't have a complete guest list ready, but that will come quickly when we settle down to do it. We do have some RSVPs from the sisters of the Home. They are a big part of my family now."

Mary asked, "What are you thinking about a reception?"

"Oh, yes, that. We can talk about that later. First, I have a couple of questions." She looked at Mrs. Vitale and Mrs. O'Banion. "I know you have a little experience putting a wedding together in a hurry." There were chuckles around the table as Sally and Mary looked at Maria.

She continued, "Bob and I want to make our home right here in Muskegon. Fortunately, I own the house that I have lived in most of my life. There are only good memories in that house. Dad raised me from the time I was eleven when my mom passed away. He was a great dad. Now that he is gone, everything is mine. Bob and I will move into the house as soon as we can after the wedding. Bob is done with classes on May third since Michigan State is on trimesters. So, here is the question. Will you all help Bob and I move this wedding up to mid-May, so we can get into the house in late May? We would like it to be Saturday, May eighteenth. Can you do that?"

The three ladies looked at each other. One said, "Piece of cake." Another said, "Nothing to it." Maria said, "I'm sure we can do that, *dahling*," in her best Dolly Levi voice.

Sally laughed. "That's Maria's acting coming out. She played the lead in *Hello Dolly* in high school."

"One more question. Since I'm an orphan, there is no one to walk me down the aisle. I want either Tom or Doug, but I can't choose without maybe hurting one of them. What do I do?"

Father Flanagan said, "Sister and I have talked about it. Why don't you have them both? I'll let her finish telling you."

Sister Charlotte added, "Child, when you first raised the issue, I could see you were struggling with this. I asked the Father if he thought that would work. One on each side of you, walk you down, a kiss on each cheek, and go to their places. You are a rebel enough, so go ahead and do it even though it has never been done before. We'll support you and you don't have to hurt either one of them."

"Thank you so much. That relieves my anxiety. I don't know how I got so lucky to have you all in my life. I think we've talked enough about the wedding now. If you're willing, could we get together again next week to make a To Do list?"

"Of course. Why don't we meet Tuesday late afternoon at my house — just the girls? Tom is pretty tied up with work at the police station right now. Do you think we should include Bob's mother? She might like to be in on the preparations, and they'll need to start thinking about the rehearsal dinner."

"That sounds like a plan. And now, let's eat before all this food that Mary and I prepared gets cold. Father Flanagan, would you say grace, please?" Sally bowed her head and joined hands with Maria and Mary.

The ladies served the brunch — breakfast casserole with eggs, bacon, and spinach cooked by Mary, homemade cinnamon rolls that Maria contributed, tossed salad with a light Italian vinaigrette that Sally made, sourdough toast with orange marmalade or raspberry jam that the nuns at the home made and sold at the farmers' market in Muskegon. Arianna liked the cinnamon roll the best and then made do with Gerber strained peas. Maria took two plates out to her protection team along with a carafe of coffee and two big glasses of orange juice. The room grew quiet as everyone enjoyed their brunch.

Arianna's eyes started to drift closed when her tummy was full. Sara realized she needed to get her home for her nap. She and Sister Charlotte bade the group goodbye and thanked them profusely for the plate of cinnamon rolls to take back to the Home. Father Flanagan excused himself, saying that he needed to get back to the church. Tom's mom stayed on to help clean up and then she, too, thanked the Vitale's, hugged Maria, and told her that she and Tom needed to come to dinner soon.

Maria and her mother spent another hour talking, just catching up. Maria told her mother that she was thinking about a career change and that she would fill her in later when she and Tom had more details. Finally, she told her mom that she needed a nap and headed home with her protection. The protection called in with a message for Tom that she was home safe.

48

A
t ten sharp, Jim and Dr. John walked into the meeting room. The buzz in the room quieted down until they got the scoop on the newcomer. Jim said, "I'd like to introduce John Brown. He is a cardiologist and professor of medicine at Notre Dame Medical School."

The members of the task force went around the table and introduced themselves — Dave Smithson, Michigan State Police, Lieutenant Mark Bergstrom, Sergeant Don Phillips, Gerri, executive secretary, Tom O'Banion, consultant, Doug McDermott, consultant. They waited for Jim to tell them why Dr. Brown was here.

"John's first introduction to the case we are working on came by way of his sister-in-law, Ann Anderson. You see, he is married to Ann Anderson's sister, Jane. He followed the case in the paper and through conversations with Ann and Jane. About three or four weeks back, they invited Ann to South Bend for a visit. It was obvious to them that Ann needed some help. Ann was working with a psychologist to help her deal with her anxiety and get through the trial. When I called Mrs. Anderson to tell her George had been killed, I talked with Dr. Brown about what happened since Mrs. Anderson was so emotionally distraught. John was planning to be a psychiatrist until he discovered he liked dealing with the heart instead of the head. As a keen observer of human behavior, he was well-prepared to help Ann during this time. So, put that time together with what he has learned since bringing Ann back home, he has some insights that may be useful.

"You all remember Maria's interview with Mrs. Anderson. John was there during the interview. Just recently he reviewed the interview with the ladies. Something else came out. John, why don't you share what you found?"

John first filled them in on what he had told Jim this morning, focusing first on how Mrs. Olsen and her husband, Larry, fought after every meeting. Larry told her things that had happened in the meeting, and she would start the argument again. Larry said he was coaxed to join the Group because they needed another investor. But, as her husband confessed, he was afraid of being involved, but didn't feel like he could get out. In the meantime, she started an affair with George to try to get more information and to see if she could help Larry find a way to leave.

John went on, "Then her husband was killed. She didn't know George was responsible until she noticed the wooden bumper on George's truck matched the scratches on Larry's bumper. She put it all together and about that time, George ended their affair. By now she was really angry at him and the whole group because they stole Larry from her and left her daughters fatherless. It is my belief that all that anger is what is driving her killing of all of them. I'm not a practicing psychiatrist, but I think the woman needs help."

Dave inquired, "How often does this much anger lead to what she is now doing?"

"More often than we know. In the face of so much anger, it is hard to figure out what a person might do. She chose to kill the men. And that bears on the other point that came up again last night. She only wants to kill the men. She won't kill the wives. She is in the same boat they are. Nor the children either; in her eyes, they are the innocents."

Tom asked, "Doesn't she realize that she is still hurting the children?"

"No, the anger has such a hold on her, she likely doesn't think of that. Now, gentlemen, I'm just going to sit quiet as a mouse, listen, and if you'll permit me, ask a question now and then."

"Thank you, John. I know you mean 'quiet as a mouse.' John subscribes to the Will Rogers maxim, 'Never pass up a chance to be quiet.' Now, two more items, this afternoon after the meeting, Mark is going to run through a dry run on how Tuesday morning will go. Before we break, Doug will catch you up on our leak, Pete Martin. What he will tell you may mean a slight change for Tuesday. Doug, take it away."

"Pete has been a busy guy. He called in sick yesterday. But he wasn't sick as we found out later. Yesterday, he was in touch with Mrs. Olsen, at least once on the phone and then in person at Mrs. Olsen's house for about forty-five minutes. There was a happy greeting at her door, wine on the coffee table that we saw before she pulled the drapes. We don't know what happened inside during those forty-five minutes. It is what happened when he left that has us most concerned. He was carrying a small package. She kissed him passionately goodbye, watched him go to his car, put the box carefully on the front seat and covered it with his jacket. He then waved goodbye, and she blew him a kiss.

"All of this suggests that she has co-opted him for something before she leaves town. We have no idea what she wants him to do, but we need to take it seriously. We've discovered that Pete has some serious gambling debts. And we know that Anna Olsen just emptied out her bank account and walked away with about $100K in cash and another $400K in a certified check. We think she's getting ready to flee. Her daughters are gone. The house is sold, so she can go anywhere and start over. She likely promised him enough money to pay off his gambling debts and maybe even more. The possibility exists that he may be going with her, but we didn't think that they were that close until we saw the kissing yesterday. That could still be an act on her part and Pete may be in for a rude awakening or worse.

"One more thing, we have a Polaroid picture of Pete and the item he was carrying, babying is a better term. I'll pass it around. Look carefully and you'll see it is a small box-like package about the size of a pack of cigarettes that could fit in his pants pocket or shirt pocket. Pete smokes, so it wouldn't look out of place on him.

"From my experience and the way that he was handling it gingerly suggests the possibility it is a bomb. If it is a bomb, it's a small one. It may be a diversion on Tuesday, or something else entirely. If it's just a diversion, it could draw our attention away from the real action. It could be used to open or jam a door, maybe at the courthouse, like the door where we are going in with the members of the Group. I went by the courthouse yesterday afternoon to check it out. It would be easy enough to jam the door and give Pete enough time to get away and give her time to get off a few shots. That's what we know or can guess. What we don't know is what is really in that box and where it will be used. And we don't know exactly what Pete's role is going to be. Any ideas?"

"I think we ought to play to the facts we have. I think this is going to be used somehow at the courthouse. She can't get the rest of the Group before that. They're in their own homes and won't be together until they get here Tuesday morning, so she would have to pick them off one at a time. A question for you, Jim. When will Pete be back to work?"

"He promised he would be in on Monday morning. Knowing him, and knowing that something is up with Mrs. Olsen, I wouldn't count on that."

Doug jumped in and said, "I put a loose tail on him this morning. I made it loose since he might have had some training in spotting a tail and I didn't want him to know we're on to him. I think tomorrow morning I'll double up on it. Mark, do you have any more men who are trained surveillants?"

Dave spoke up. "I can get you some from the state police."

"Could they be here early in the morning?"

"What do you think, Jim?" Doug looked at Jim expectantly.

Jim said, "Please call them with our thanks."

Mark asked, "One more question, Jim. Is Pete in uniform when he is in the station studying procedures?"

"Yes, he is. What are you thinking?"

"If he is in uniform, he could try to get into the courthouse ahead of time and try to join up with the squad inside. Or he could try to join the officers bringing the members and say to them that you, Jim, okay'd it."

Doug piped up and said, "All the more reason for the double tails."

"Doc, I mean, John. You have been true to your word and haven't said a word yet. Any comment you'd like to add now?"

"Thank you, Dave. Thank you, gentlemen, for including me. It has been good for me to be here both for the update and for letting me see pros at work. From my limited experience, it looks like you've covered all the bases."

Jim stood up. "It is almost noon. How about lunch at US 31 Bar-B-Q?" Jim looked around the room as the men nodded their assent. "Fine. We'll get them in and take a little break until about 1:30. John and I made plans to get lunch out to thank him for his help. Your run-through this afternoon shouldn't take more than an hour or hour and a half. I'm going to have the other officers that will join us Tuesday come in about 1:30 p.m. so they can be briefed on the new developments. They need to be filled in on the Pete situation. Mark will take everyone through Tuesday's agenda, a dry run rehearsal if you will. If you have any questions that you think I should answer, I'll be back in my office around 1:30 making phone calls and dealing with other matters. When you are finished with the run-through, feel free to head home. Have a good relaxing weekend. Tom and Doug, you don't have to be here this afternoon unless you want to sit in."

"Why don't we take my car? I want to take you to The Occidental to get the best hot fudge sundae you ever had. They have sandwiches, too, if you want something before your sundae. We could walk but I need to be back for some phone calls at 1:30."

"Jim, I've heard of those famous hot fudge sundaes but never had one. Great idea."

After a short five-minute ride, they walked into the Occidental lobby. Jim started to go to the ice cream shop, but John stopped him. John was looking around the lobby like a tourist in a new place. "This is great architecture. Those columns, the Tiffany style lamps near the easy chairs, the balcony around the two sides and the back — it's all so elegant. It is a treat just to see it. Thanks for bringing me here. I could just sit here and enjoy the ambiance, but I admit to being a bit hungry."

Jim grabbed his favorite seat so he could watch out the window toward Muskegon Lake. He said, "Wait, let's switch sides, I want you to see this view of the lake and the Clipper at berth there."

"Hi, Chief," said his favorite waitress, Marlene. "Your usual?"

"You've got it. I always have the perch lunch with fries and coleslaw. Then finish with a coffee and my hot fudge sundae."

Marlene turned to John. "And you, sir?"

"He prefers John...instead of 'sir.'"

John nodded at the waitress. "Yes, I prefer 'John!'"

"All right, John. What say you?"

"And to that Shakespearean phrase, I say the same as the other gentleman."

She said, "Gentleman, hah..." She grinned at Jim.

"I think they like you here, Jim."

"They do. I eat here more than I should. You can see it," he said as he patted his stomach.

She brought their coffee and water. Jim asked, "Any thoughts you want to share on the meeting this morning?"

"They are as well prepared as they can be with all the variables you face. They are all a little edgy. You have no idea how she will act when she knows you are all there. You don't know what Pete will do, but I believe your team will do fine. How about you, Jim? Are you a little nervous?" John watched Jim closely.

Their perch lunches came, so they tabled the question. They chatted about the weather, their upcoming dinner with the wives, and John's trip back to South Bend. Marlene was attentive as usual and was there to take the dishes, bring the hot fudge sundaes and fresh coffee as soon as they finished their perch.

"Well, that was terrific. I'll have to bring Jane here before we leave. Okay, Jim, back to my earlier question. You are going to be a part of the team, aren't you? Are you nervous?"

"I am, and I will confess I am...a little. But I believe that I am the right one to try and talk her in. She knows my voice from our interview with her. I think what Pete might do is the more complicating factor. Problem is, we have to leave him in the picture. If he didn't show, that might scare her off and she would vanish. I don't want that to happen. And I don't want to have to shoot, but we will if we have to. We will be somewhat protected with flak jackets, but they are not foolproof. Sometimes the stress of this job gets to me, and this would be one of them."

"Jim, have you ever thought about retiring? I'm not sure you are old enough, but I know you've been here a while."

"I have enough years in, and Martha and I talk about it now and then. The time is coming. We'll see." Jim stared off into the distance. "We better get back. I have things to do."

When they parted at the station, they shook hands and looked at each other for a minute.

"Be careful out there. Maybe I should be there Tuesday hiding in the bushes or something. I wouldn't want anything to happen to you. You've become special, a good friend."

"Maybe so, although I don't think it will be necessary. I plan to be very careful. I wish it had been under different circumstances, but I'm glad I met you. See you tomorrow night at Tony's."

Gerri caught Jim right away. "The district attorney wants to talk with you. The team is also back, and they want to see you for a few minutes."

Jim called the DA. "Hello, Harvey, something new?"

"I think you will be happy to hear this news. Harold Evans, the Group's lawyer, Judge McVie, and I have worked out a plea deal. We should be out of there in less than one hour on Tuesday morning."

"I am happy to hear that. That may make stopping her and getting her in custody go a little smoother. We'll talk about it with the task force this afternoon. Harvey, can I know how it came about?"

"I don't see why not. Apparently, Wendell, the oldest remaining member, played an important role in making it happen. He talked with the others and told them that the judge might show some mercy if they would plead guilty. He might take some time off their sentences. They all finally came to an agreement to ask their attorney what he thought. Wendell told all of them that it must be all of them, or it wouldn't be accepted by the judge.

"When Harold Evans brought it to me, we discussed it. I told him I would need signed documents to that effect, and they would individually have to repeat their guilty plea on Tuesday. We worked out a time last night and all of us met at Wendell's house."

Jim interrupted, "Without letting me know! I would have appreciated a phone call at least. That could have put them all in danger."

Harvey agreed. "Evans was insistent that we not tell you, and I couldn't change his mind. Sorry, Jim. We got them together, got the documents signed simultaneously, and got them back home safely with their protection along on both trips."

"It actually will be better for us. Now that we have a more specific time frame, I will arrange a signal so that everyone knows when the action is starting. Thanks for getting this done, Harvey. By the way, I'm suggesting that you and Harold Evans stay with the remaining Group members and the protection detail that will be with them until you get an all clear from me. That will be someone coming to the back door. Wait a minute. The back door. That's it!"

"What's it? What about the back door?"

"I'll call you back later. I need to get all of this to the team. We will have to change our strategy about Pete."

"I'll be in all afternoon and will be waiting for your call. Who is Pete anyway?"

"He's the leak in my department who has been passing information first to the Group of Nine and now to Mrs. Olsen." Jim said goodbye and told Harry he would call him within the next hour.

49

Tom and Doug got to Tom's house with a Scrib's pizza. As they walked to the front door, Tom said, "That sure smells good. I'm so hungry I could eat it box and all."

Tom went in first and saw Maria fast asleep on the sofa. He shushed Doug, pointed to her. They went into the kitchen and got some beers from the fridge, some plates, and went to the dining table. A head poked up over the back of the sofa, sniffing, and asked, "Is some of that for me?"

Doug and Tom looked at each other and laughed. "She is getting better."

Tom got her a beer. "I thought you might not be hungry after your mom's brunch."

"That was two hours ago. Now I'm hungry again."

"That's my girl!" He gave her a hug and a kiss.

"Not in front of your friend, you two."

Between bites, she asked, "What happened at the meeting this morning?"

"Not so fast. We want to hear about the wedding plans. Did our moms agree to help get it done by June?"

She finished her slice, then, "No, they didn't... They agreed to get it ready by May eighteenth."

Doug asked, "What! Do they need to? Maybe she's pregnant again."

"Doug, don't say that. She is a different person and so is he now. I would be willing to bet a lot that they are not even doing it."

"Really! I might take that bet."

"Oh, you guys."

She snagged another piece of pizza, took a bite, and when she finished it, she said, "There's more to tell. She asked me a while back about the two of you and what role you might play. With no father or relative, she wanted to ask one of you but couldn't decide which to walk her down the aisle. She didn't want to hurt either one of you. Sister Charlotte and Father Flanagan solved it for her. They told her she was a rebel, and she could have both of you do it. One on each side as you walk her down the aisle, two kisses, one on each cheek, and then take your places as groomsmen. The only problem is she now has to find one more bridesmaid."

"How about Nancy?" Doug said.

"Do you think she would? I haven't spent much time with her since last fall."

Doug said, "I'll call her tonight and ask her. I'll tell her it was your idea if you want."

"No, it was your idea. That might get you on her good side."

"Not interested. Remember I'm out of here in a month or two."

That thought brought a sad look to Maria's face. "We're going to miss you, friend."

"Me, too," Tom added.

Doug looked at both of them. "I'll miss you both. Who knows, maybe we'll get together on another case in the future? And you won't be able to get rid of me completely. I'll still come back and visit."

"Now I want to hear about the meeting," Maria insisted.

The phone rang. Tom reached it first. "Hello, Jim."

"I have some news, but I need to tell Doug as well."

"He's here having pizza with us. I'll put him on the extension."

"That will be good. I need feedback from both of you."

Jim said to them, "There are two new items. Judge McVie, Harvey Svenson, and Harold Evans worked out a plea bargain with the rest of the Group. That means that what happens on next Tuesday will be just entering the new pleas of guilty, submitting new documents, and setting a time for a sentencing session. They will be done in no more than forty-five minutes to an hour. It should make what we have to do go more smoothly."

"That's great news. What's the other item?"

"When I was talking to Harvey, something came up about the back door. That triggered a reaction for me. I believe you are right, Doug, and the little box that Pete has is a bomb, too small to do a lot of damage or kill anyone unless they are standing right there by it. But it is enough to damage the door so that it can't be opened. Everyone would be trapped in there and the only way out is through the front door where she will be waiting."

"I think you might be on to something. And that would give her the opportunity to pick off the Group members as they come out the front door," Doug agreed. "So, Pete is the key because he has to set the bomb to blow up the back door."

"I agree. The question is how best to stop him. Do we grab him Monday morning when he comes in? That might not work for at least one reason — we have no guarantee that he's going to come into the office. He may, instead, go directly to the courthouse and get in by the back door early, lay in wait, and be ready to drop the bomb after the Group has all gone upstairs. He wouldn't look suspicious to anyone else because he'll be in uniform. Or Mark suggested at the run-through that Pete might try to join the Group and their detail after they get out of the cars and just say that I said it would be okay and then hold back while they go up and be the last one in. He doesn't know the detail has been briefed about him, but if he got suspicious, I think he'll try to get into the courthouse early."

Doug said, "I think the former is right."

"So do I, gentlemen. Thank you. The only change I will make is that I will put two more men outside the door in case he tries to get out before the bomb goes off. Tom, tell Maria I said hello, and we'll see all of you tomorrow night."

After they told Maria what Jim had said and what he was going to do to stop him before he did any more damage, she looked sad. Tom asked her why. She said, "Are you sure they are not going to shoot her? She needs help more than she needs a bullet."

50

Jim walked into the meeting. "I understand you needed to see me for a few minutes. Can I give you some news first?"

"Actually, that's what we wanted to see you about. We heard there were some new developments. What has happened?"

"Quite a bit, Mark. First, Judge McVie, the D.A., and the Group attorney have worked out a plea agreement. All are pleading guilty and asking for a reduction of sentence. Apparently, the judge bought their argument that the older members pressured them to sign the document saying they were in favor of killing the mayor. Some tried to back out of signing but were not allowed to. The older members, who are no longer with us, threatened them and they finally signed. As I said, the judge bought it.

"The signed new plea agreements are in his hands, and they only have to make the new plea in person next Tuesday morning. Judge McVie is studying the Plea Guidelines to decide how much time he can take off their sentences.

"What this means to us is that we will have only a short session on Tuesday morning, and we'll know that going in. The Group and the squad will still take them out the back door, hopefully before

Mrs. Olsen knows what's going on. I will have one of the men give a wave as they leave that it's a done deal."

Mark's next question was, "They can't change their mind once they are in the courtroom, can they?"

"Not only can they not change their minds, but it is also believed by all of them that throwing their case on the mercy of the court is their best bet to get a shorter sentence and with good behavior, they won't spend a lot of time behind bars. They won't change. Any other questions?

"None, good. Now, to the second item. During my conversation with the D.A., the back door of the courtroom came up. That triggered a strong hunch about the plan Mrs. Olsen and Pete worked out. I think Pete is somehow going to get at the tail end of the line going into the back door. I believe that he and the squad will make sure he is the last one in. He may fake having to pick something up or just wait until they are all up the stairs, place the bomb at the bottom of the door, and scoot upstairs. The bomb is to be both a diversion and a jamming of the door. No one can get out that door, the only exit is the front where she will be waiting to pick them off one at a time. I plan to have a man on each side of the door who will disarm him, take the bomb away, put it in a bomb box, and cuff him before going upstairs. Questions or comments?"

Mark again. "We better have some eyes on him so he doesn't place the bomb and switch it on just before he goes in. Can we just wallop him on the head, catch him before he falls, and then take the bomb from him?"

Jim replied, "Much as I would like to see him get walloped, I think that might be dicey about the bomb. And the other thing is the uncertainty on all this about how he gets in the line. He might even ask me sometime Monday if he could tag along for the experience. And he might not even show up here on Tuesday but just go the back door and join in telling them I said it was okay. He still might get into the courthouse early and arm the bomb. That's why I'm going to have a guy on both sides of the door to take Pete down and make sure the bomb doesn't go off. Let's think about all this over the weekend and talk it through Monday when we are all fresh."

"Jim, won't Mrs. Olsen realize that something's wrong when the bomb doesn't go off? I agree with your basic plan that getting that bomb without it going off is the smart thing to do, but what about Mrs. Olsen? She may retreat if she doesn't hear the bomb go off."

"Good point. We may have to create a distraction of our own — that we control. Everyone head home now and think about this over the weekend. See you Monday."

Jim called the D.A. back. "Hello, Harvey, I'm ready to tell you about that flash thought I had. You'll remember that the back door came up in our discussion and I reacted. Well, here's the backstory on that." He went on to outline the situation with Pete, being the leak, and now being in with some sort of arrangement with Mrs. Olsen. "We are all set after the meeting to stop him before he can set the bomb off. Harvey, hold on a second..."

He buzzed Gerri and asked her to get Dave to wait until he was off this call.

"So, Harvey, we feel pretty confident about how we are going to get the bomb away from him. But there are some uncertainties about when he may show up and get in at the end of the line of squad members. We are working on it."

"How sure are you that bomb isn't so big it can bring the building down?"

"Not to worry. I have already had an explosives expert study the picture we have. He knows the size by the comparison with Pete's hands. He says the most it will do is jam the door so it can't be opened. He tells me that even for the most effective explosives available today, something that size can't do major damage. The state police explosives lab agrees with him. I'll arrange a signal to all that the bomb has been neutralized."

"Okay, Jim. I trust you."

51

They were all gathered in the private room at Tony's — new friends and old. John arrived early and arranged seating to help everyone get to know each other better. John had asked for a round table big enough to seat eight with each having plenty of room. He put Ann next to Maria on one side with Jim and his wife, Martha, on the other. Tom was seated next to Maria. On his other side were Jane and then John. Doug completed the circle between John and Martha. The private dining room was warm and cozy with red velvet patterned wallpaper, overstuffed chairs, heavy wood dining table, and a roaring fire to take away the spring chill.

Tony's special cheese dips, crackers, and shrimp cocktails were at each place. Two overflowing baskets of bread and breadsticks were placed on each side of the low flower and candle arrangement. The champagne was already chilling in ice buckets. As soon as all were seated and the champagne poured, John stood. "This is, for most of us here, a special evening. So, here's to new and old friendships. May we all get to know each other better, cheers to us all." In the best French tradition, they locked eyes around the table as they clinked glasses and sipped their champagne.

"And let's raise our glasses to two special ladies. They have faced problems, beat them, and will soon be off on some new adventures that we may hear about tonight. To Ann and Maria, cheers." Cheers and clinks of glasses all around the table.

"Now..."

Jane said, "Enough, John, I'm hungry."

Maria laughed. "My kind of gal. Let's eat."

Their two waitstaff quickly took their orders. Maria started by ordering the wedge salad and Steak Diane with mashed potatoes and a side of asparagus while Jane, Ann, and Martha decided that the chop house salad and a petit fillet were just what they wanted. Tom and Doug argued about who could eat the most prime rib and finally ordered the 20 oz slab — medium rare, of course. They didn't bother with the salad. Jim settled on a house salad and the 8 oz fillet wrapped in bacon. John looked shocked at the orders. "It's a good thing I'm not here as your cardiologist tonight. I'd have to give you all a good talking to. But since we're here as friends and it's okay to indulge in moderation, I'll let it pass this time." He ordered the house salad and the 8 oz piece of prime rib. He also ordered two bottles of Inglenook Cabernet Sauvignon, a very fine wine judged by many as one of the finest cabernets made.

The waitstaff topped off their champagne glasses and left them to their conversations. John was watching Ann and Maria. They seemed to be hitting it off just fine. He thought it was a good thing that Ann would have a new friend since Jane would have to come back to South Bend at some point. Ann said, "And this is your Tom that you spoke of."

"Good to meet you, Ann. Maria told me how much she enjoyed meeting you the other day. When you feel up to it, we'd love to have you come over for dinner."

"That would be lovely. I want to hear more about how you supported Maria through her coma. What a thoughtful husband you are."

The conversation continued around the table until the salads arrived. As they tucked into their salads, Doug and Tom made do with the breadbasket. Doug told John that he should come up for one of the Muskegon Lumberjacks hockey matches. John admitted he was a huge fan of Notre Dame's hockey team and went to as many matches as his schedule allowed. "I don't like a lot of pro or semi-pro hockey. It seems like all they want to do is fight." Doug defended the Lumberjacks vigorously. "They play good hockey and sometimes that means fighting."

Jane and Martha discovered they were both avid gardeners. Martha's garden was just beginning to wake up after a long, cold winter. They engaged in a lively disagreement about whether the new lilac bushes were better than the heritage trees.

Jim listened in on Maria, Tom, and Ann's conversation. He could tell that Ann was quite taken with the young couple and hoped that they would provide good support for her in the next few months.

Soon the group became somewhat boisterous. It might have had something to do with the wine, or it might have been they all seemed to be enjoying each other. By the time dessert was served, John and Jim congratulated each other on a great evening.

JIM STOPPED Doug as they were leaving. He asked, "Are your protection teams alerted to the gathering of the wives and children?"

"They are. The Greyhound charter will be waiting for the school buses to drop off their packages. We thought it would be better if it looked like the kids were going to school as normal. We put police officers in as substitute school bus drivers, and they'll take the kids to the Greyhound terminal where their mothers and the wives of protection detail will be waiting for them. We put a few extra police officers on their bus so they will be safe. The charter bus will be en route by 11:00 a.m. and with a lunch stop, be in their hotel in Chicago by 5:00 p.m. latest, Chicago time. The protection teams will remain here guarding the men."

"Good. I need you Monday for a possible assignment following Pete. It may not happen, but it is important that he not be lost or for the follower not to be spotted if he leaves. I'll get you data on his personal car."

"I have it already, thanks. I'll make sure he's never out of my sight. And he won't know I'm there."

52

Monday looked to an outsider as just a normal day at the police station. If Pete showed up, Jim didn't want anything to alert him about any aspect of Tuesday's business. Pete wasn't yet at his desk when Jim came in. Jim beckoned Gerri to follow him into his office.

Jim asked, "No sign of Pete or call from him yet?"

Gerri answered, "Neither. How do you want me to handle it?"

"If he comes in, treat Pete as though things were normal for a Monday. Leave the door to the conference room where the task force meets open. He will likely notice that, make up some excuse to walk by the door as well as note that most of the offices are empty. When he asks where everyone is, just say I have them all chasing down leads and information that I asked them to do in the meeting on Friday.

"I'm pretty sure that he will want to talk to me. Buzz me and I'll make him wait ten minutes or so while I finish a fake phone call. Then I'll have you send him in. I'll give him the same story and add that there might be another meeting this afternoon or maybe not until tomorrow afternoon. I'll see what develops."

Jim asked her one more thing, "Is everything all set for the wives and kids?"

"It is, Jim. The packages — the wives and children — will be picked up by school busses, taken to the Greyhound station where they'll meet the wives of their protection teams along with a few other police officers who will travel with them. We didn't want them to be completely unprotected if their protection teams are staying with their husbands. They should be on the road by 11:00 a.m. I've also told the ladies they can call and let their husbands know that they are safe in their hotel. And one last thing, all have been told to maintain strict silence about why they're doing this and where they're going. It is just a field trip."

"Good job, Gerri. I knew I could count on you to take care of all the details. Sorry to ask, but I just had to hear it. There's so much riding on this."

"I know, boss. I can see the strain in your face lately. Take care of yourself, Jim."

When Gerri started back to her desk, she saw Pete come back from the direction of the conference room with coffee and a couple of donuts. He went to his desk. She smiled at him. "Good morning, Pete."

"Morning, Gerri. Say, where is everyone?"

"They are out running down leads and looking for new information. Jim gave them their assignments after Friday's meeting. How are you feeling today? That bug you caught about gone?"

"I'm feeling a lot better. The doctor wants to see me again later this morning. I have to ask Jim for one more bit of time off."

"He's doing phone calls now. I'll buzz him and let him know you want to see him. I'm sure he will fit you in."

Pete went back to his desk, ate his donuts, and refilled his coffee cup. He started reading his manual while waiting for the chief. He heard Gerri's buzzer and looked over at her. She told him that Jim could give him some time now between calls.

"Good morning, Pete. How are you feeling?"

"Much better, Chief. That's part of what I wanted to talk to you about. The doctor wants to see me this morning. Just for a final check that it is gone."

"How much time do you think you will need?"

"My appointment is at 11:30 a.m. I might as well grab some lunch while I'm out. Maybe get back by 1 or 1:30 p.m."

"That'll be fine. Just get back as quickly as you can and keep your studies going. You are running a little behind. We want to get you moving on."

"That's the other thing. I was wondering if there might be some kind of assignment I could be a part of now. Any action that is coming down or anything that would let me build some experience?"

"There's nothing going on right now, Pete, but I'll keep you in mind...wait a minute."

Jim appeared to be thinking on something. Pete leaned forward, looked earnest and eager.

"How would you like to take part in a protection detail? I would not be able to allow you to carry your sidearm. We need to get a group of men into Judge McVie's courtroom. We will be taking them in through the back door and upstairs. It should go without a hitch. The protection team are pros, you can learn from them. Can you handle that?"

"Of course, I can, but no sidearm? How come? I'm a good shot. I did well in training."

"I know you did, Pete. But regs are regs. No sidearm for first timers on this kind of detail. Wear your standard uniform without the sidearm."

"All right, I'll do it. Thank you, Chief."

"Don't let me down now, Pete. Be here by no later than nine tomorrow morning. I want you to meet the other officers."

"I won't, Chief." Jim couldn't miss the excitement that showed all over him. Pete left his office with a strut.

As he walked past Gerri's desk, he said, "Guess what, Gerri. I get to be on a special detail tomorrow. Part of my training, the chief said."

"That's great, Pete."

"Should I park in some special area?"

"No need, just your usual spot in the officer's lot."

"Okay, thanks, Gerri."

Jim buzzed Gerri. "Any new calls I need to add to my list?"

"I'll bring you a copy of your list with the new ones added."

"Pete, we're on short staff today. Would you keep an eye on things while I run in and talk to the chief? I won't be but a minute."

"I've got it, Gerri."

She stepped into Jim's office. "I squawked Doug. He'll be calling any minute from the pay phone inside the back door. I'll make sure Pete stays put. When is he leaving?"

"About 11:00 a.m. His doctor's appointment is at 11:30 a.m. That is, if there is one. Ten to one there isn't." The phone rang. "That will be Doug. Please close the door on your way out.

"Sorry for the delay, Doug. A little thing going on with Pete. It went as I hoped. He will be the last man into the back door. The two men just inside the door will detain him, cuff him with his hands above his head, and secure the bomb."

"Are the two men at the door trained for this, Jim?"

"They have been. But it still is a concern for me. We don't know where he will have the bomb. There are pockets in the front of his uniform jacket. The only problem is that they are not very deep. And there is an inside pocket on the right, his right. That's the most likely place. He will have to be careful how he gets it out as will whichever officer takes it out."

"Jim, I would like to be the man to take that bomb out and disarm it. I've done it before...successfully. It is not that I don't trust your men, but I know I can get it."

"Okay. Once you get done following Pete here, will you have time to get to the courthouse before they come?"

"I can. I can be there in five minutes."

"Okay, Doug, thank you. You've eased my mind a lot. Be careful, will you? We don't want anyone hurt."

"Got it, Jim. What time do you think Pete will be coming out?"

"About 11:00 a.m. You have his car in sight?"

"I do and I'm ready to set out after him. Later, Jim."

WHEN GERRI TOLD him Pete had left, Jim came out of his office. "Well done, Gerri! I'm off to see Judge McVie. He is still a little nervous about tomorrow, so I need to reassure him. I'll have some lunch and then be at the conference room in the courthouse for the final briefing. You have both those numbers. After that meeting, I'll make a quick stop here and then it's home and Martha. See you later."

53

Jim knocked on Judge McVie's office door. "Come in, Jim."

"How did you know who it was?"

"You are always on time. I admire that in a person. You've never let me down."

"Thank you, Judge."

"So, are you going to help me get rid of this uneasiness over tomorrow?"

"I am. As it turns out, there is a new development just before I came that makes me even more confident. A short time ago, I hired a new man to help us with certain kinds of problems where we had no experience. He has been immeasurably effective for us. The task force trusts him as do I."

"What is his background?"

"I can't tell you everything because I don't know everything. He is a friend of Tom and Maria O'Banion. You remember them."

"Isn't Tom the one who was on trial in my courtroom last summer?"

"He is, and his wife is only recently out of a coma nearly six months long."

"You sound almost like a proud parent there."

"I have come to respect and like them a lot. Yes, they are special to me."

"Anyway, back to their friend, Doug McDermott. Last year they were all three teachers at Muskegon High School. The three are inseparable friends. To make it a short story, Doug was in the army, attracted the attention of certain agencies, and became part of an elite team who does specialty things for an agency that will remain unnamed. Doug wouldn't, and perhaps couldn't, tell me which one it is. After several years of that, Doug left the service and struck out on his own as an asset for one of the agencies. Again, he couldn't tell me who. He spent some time doing that and decided he was ready for a quieter life. He became a high school teacher. Now, when all this is over, he is going back to his life as an asset but refuses to leave here until he knows his friends are safe. It is the way of the service, he told me. You never leave a friend in need. So, he came to work for me. This morning I learned of another skill that is in his kitbag, as he calls it. He is an explosives expert. He volunteered to be the one taking the bomb and defusing it. He assured me it will not go off in your courthouse."

"I would like to meet him and thank him for his service."

"I can likely arrange that... Judge, how would you and your wife like to be invited to a wedding the third weekend of May? Let me tell you another story and you'll see another side of Tom O'Banion."

"We'll need more time than we allotted for our meeting. Would you like to have lunch in my private dining room through that door over there? Oh, and do you like US 31 Bar-B-Qs?"

"Yes to lunch, and yes to US 31. Thank you."

"Good. I'm a secret aficionado of the US 31 Bar-B-Qs." He called his secretary who took their orders. "Of course it's legal, my guest is the police chief. My bailiff walks over and picks them up for me. He doesn't mind, he always gets one too. They'll be here in about fifteen minutes or so. So, while we wait, what's your other story?"

"Do you remember the young lady who accused Tom O'Banion in your court?"

"I do. She was most penitent when she was caught in some lies. I gave her probation because of her condition. What ever happened to her?"

"Sara changed completely after her father, Joe Antonelli, was killed in that business last year. She is Catholic and her priest put her in touch with the Catholic Home for Unwed Mothers. Sister Charlotte of the Home put in a good word for her at Catholic Central High School. She studied at the Home with materials the school sent. Sister Charlotte told me she worked furiously on her high school studies and finished her high school work on time with this year's senior class. She graduates next month. She had her baby while she was living at the Home and brought the little girl with her back to the Home. Sister Charlotte and the other nuns who staff the Home love her little girl. Arianna is now six months old and is a joy for all of them.

"Sara and Bob, her boyfriend in high school and the real father of Arianna, are getting married the third weekend in May. That's the wedding I referred to that I can get you invited to. The great thing about this story is what happened next. When Tom is asked how he feels about Sara, after what she put him through, all he says is 'Sara is a good friend to my wife, Maria, and I. What happened in the past is just that, in the past.' Long story short, Sara asked Maria to be her matron of honor, Doug and Tom are in her bridal party. When you come to the wedding, you and your wife will be able to meet them all. Will you come?"

"Thank you. Of course we'll come and happy to be there. Jim, would you mind a personal question from an old friend?"

"Ask away."

"You look tired. I see the strain on your face and in your eyes. These recent events have taken their toll. Have you thought about retirement?"

"Yes, Judge, I have thought about it. I hate to admit, but I'm tired. You remember my secretary, actually my right hand 'man,' Gerri? She recently asked me the same question. I'm in my early sixties and have enough service hours. Martha and I will make that decision soon after this affair is over."

"I'm glad to hear that. You've done an excellent job here and deserve the thanks of the city...and if you'll keep it quiet, my wife and I have been thinking that way too. There are some up-and-coming attorneys in this town and I think they would make good judges. I'll never campaign for anyone, but I will encourage the good ones to run. The people have to elect their judges. So, for me too, sometime in the next year I'll announce it. You and I should sit down and talk about our futures over lunch when all this is over. For now, let's eat some barbeque. We have a big day tomorrow."

54

———

Jim walked back to the station thinking about the visit. *I will miss him.* He walked into the office and asked Gerri if there was anything new. He didn't see Pete at his desk but decided to wait until Gerri's report.

"Several things, Chief." She asked one of the office pool to pick up her calls and forward the chief's calls.

"What are they?"

"First, I received a phone call from one of police officers on the Greyhound. He said that they had a good trip — lunch at the Russ' restaurant on the south side of Holland and an ice cream cone from Sherman's Ice Cream and Dairy Bar in South Haven to let them run off some steam. They are now safe in the motel not far from the Museum. Mission accomplished, boss."

"Well done! Next."

"You have two phone calls to make. Doug is home waiting for your call with some info about Pete. And Tom and Maria would like a call from you. They'll be in all evening."

"Did Pete show up this afternoon?"

"No, and that's part of why Doug is calling. Interesting things Pete did this afternoon."

"I'd better get to it then." He called Doug's home. "Hello Doug, what did our boy Pete do today?"

"He was busy, but not with a doctor's appointment. He made a stop at his bank in the downtown area. He went to Federal's Department store and came out with two bags of what I took to be clothes. He then stopped at a real estate firm for about a half hour. His last stop was at Etterman's Market in Lakeside. He left there with a small bag and then it was home."

"Later he came out with two large suitcases, put them in his trunk, and took off. With me following, of course. You with me so far? Where do you suppose he went?"

"Mrs. Olsen's house!"

"You've got it. Don was parked where he could watch her house. I parked my car near the other half of the surveillance team, Don's partner, and asked him to drop me off at Don's car. Don's partner was to watch for Pete's car and follow him home when or if he left. I also asked him to stay on him until Pete got to the station in the morning. By the time I got there Pete was already inside after being met with a kiss according to Don. The drapes were pulled again. So Don and I waited. About a half hour later, Pete came out to his car, took the two suitcases out of his trunk. She opened the garage door and he put them in the trunk of her car. They kissed again and Pete left.

"I told Don to sit tight for a bit to see if she had anything planned. She did. Don followed her while I hoofed it back through the back yards to get my car. I got behind them just in time to see Don turn right onto Lake Harbor Road. We piggy backed each other until she took a left at Mt. Garfield Road. We hung back until we had to use binoculars to see her. After a time, she turned into a two-lane road to what looked like an abandoned farmhouse. She took the suitcases into the barn and came out without them. I watched all this from my car as I drove past her turn-in. Good thing there was a big ol' tractor in front of me, so I had plenty of time to watch what was going on.

"I got a good look at the farmhouse and the outbuildings. I turned around a little east of the house and watched her go back the way she had come with Don following a good distance behind. When they made the right to go back north on Lake Harbor Road, I pulled into the farmhouse drive. When I checked inside, I found her van, only now it was a dark green, but it is the same van. If you look closely, you can see where they missed some black in hard to get at places. I looked but couldn't see any guns inside. She may be bringing those in the morning. There you are, Jim."

"That's excellent work you two did. She could still pull a trick on us, but I doubt that."

"Don will be watching Mrs. Olsen all night until she gets to the courthouse. His second will be on Pete until the same time. I'm going home to get some sleep so I can be fresh for things tomorrow. Good night, Jim."

"Good night." Jim hung up and dialed Tom. "Hello, Tom, Gerri said you had a question or two."

"I do. Maria has been pushing to somehow be on the scene tomorrow. She wants to be there in case she is needed."

"That's not a good idea, Tom. If she popped up at the wrong time, she could be hurt."

"I told her the same thing, but she is adamant. How about if we get there very early? She and I could be there standing by one of the windows. We could be your spotters. Anything that we see that looks like a problem, we could let you know on a walkie-talkie."

"I just don't know. Let me think on it and I'll call later tonight, and we'll talk some more about it. It will give me time to think about it."

"All right. Until tonight. Thanks."

Jim called Doug. "We have a little problem." He went over the phone conversation between him and Tom.

"Not a good idea, Jim."

"That's what I told him."

"How about this? I'm planning to get in early to get a good look at Pete. I want to make sure I get the right guy. When I finish with that, I'll take them over, put them through a crash course on how to watch from a window without being seen. And get a flak jacket on each of them."

"Okay, I'll let the courthouse team leader know they are coming."

"And I'll let Tom and Maria know to be here about 8:30 a.m. before anyone else is around. We don't want to tip anyone off that something's going on."

55

Tom and Maria showed up Tuesday at 8:30 a.m. They stopped at Gerri's desk. Gerri said, "Jim set Doug up in that office over there. See him? He will wave for you to come in, get you seated as though you are filing a complaint or making your statement."

Doug watched Tom and Maria at Gerri's desk and beckoned to them to join him. He shook their hands and said, "Please close the door, sit in those chairs facing me. I'll be looking for Pete. I need to get a better look at him before things start."

"I can point him out to you."

"No, Maria. Keep looking at me as though I am taking your statement, normal police business. I'll be watching for him. When I have him spotted, I will nod to you as though I'm listening to you. Once I'm satisfied that I can pick him out in a crowd, I will ask you to leave by the front door and head toward the courthouse. I'll exit from the back and catch up with you. We'll all enter through the back door, go upstairs where I will put you through a crash course on watching through a window without being seen. I'll then outfit you each with a flak jacket and go back to my post. Clear?"

They both nodded and were just chatting when Gerri signaled to

Doug that Pete had arrived. Doug watched him, faking talking, and saw him leave to get his coffee. When he returned, the first of the escorts for the members of the Group arrived. Pete walked over to him and began talking with him. Doug signaled to Tom and Maria to leave. They did and he left going out the back. Ten minutes later they entered the back door of the courthouse. Doug grabbed the flak jackets he had stashed there, helped Tom as he talked him through it. "Tom, you get Maria's on. Both of you put your dark jackets on over them. I'll be waiting for you at the top of those stairs."

They joined him and walked to where he thought would be the best location for them to observe and taught them how to stand back away from the window and still see where Mrs. Olsen would likely be parking. "You are on the north side of the building, so the morning sun won't be a problem. Still, Maria, you should take off your earrings and the necklace. Finally, here is a pair of military binoculars that are designed to be non-reflective. The sun won't be a problem for them."

He left them with the final warning, "If you have to leave and sit for a bit, back up slowly — no fast movements, she'll see those. There are benches over there and restrooms are just around that corner. Remember, slow movements. Here is your walkie-talkie so you can talk to Jim's aide. I'm going downstairs to my post, and I'll connect with you as soon as I have Pete in custody."

Maria and Tom took their positions. Maria asked for the binoculars and began to scan the north side parking area and entrances to it. She couldn't see the police officers that were hidden in various spots in the front area of the courthouse grounds.

BACK AT THE POLICE STATION, the Group members were brought in by their protection detail and placed in the conference room. The five-person squad assigned to escort them to the courthouse arrived and were introduced to the members. Gerri walked in with one more officer, Pete. "Good morning, all, we have one more member for your protection on the way to and at the courthouse. This is Officer Pete

Martin. He is going along to observe the procedures your protection detail uses. Chief Johnson has allowed him there as one of his requirements for his sergeant promotion process. He, by department rules, does not have a weapon so he, in a way, is being protected as well. He will be the last officer to enter the back door where you are going in. You will be escorted up to your courtroom and they will stay there with you. Any questions?

"None, that's good. On your way, gentlemen, you need to be in place in twenty minutes. It will only take five minutes to drive over there and another five to walk upstairs into the courtroom. Thank you for your attention."

They left in two vehicles, pulled around on the east side of the courthouse and stopped about twenty feet from the back door. One man from each car got out, checked out the scene, opened the back door, and went back to have one man with each member of the Group. Pete brought up the rear, watching the procedure. Pete came in the back door, closed, and locked it. When he turned around, there were two men with guns pointing at him. "What is this?" he said.

The taller of the two men said, "Make another sound and I'll blow your head off. Hands over your head."

The second man took his hands down and cuffed them behind his back.

Pete blustered, "What is going on here? I'm a police officer. Why are you doing this?"

"I told you to keep your mouth shut." Doug smacked him on the side of his head with a hard right. Pete staggered a little but recovered.

"You aren't hurt that badly. Not even any blood. Now here is what I will be doing. I'm going to search you. You can save me a lot of trouble and you a lot of discomfort by telling me where that package you got from Mrs. Olsen is hidden. Even if you don't tell me, I will find it and disable it. Sam, my friend behind you, is watching every move you make. If you make a move that he doesn't like, he will hit you with his Billy club. He hits a lot harder than I do."

Pete said, "Don't hit me again. It's in my inside jacket pocket, right hand side. Be careful when you reach for it. It has a touchy switch. I don't want to be blown up."

"Not a move then. I would hate to have an accident." Doug reached inside Pete's jacket, found the pocket, and the package inside. He shielded the switch with the cupped palm of his hand. Holding onto the sides with his fingers, he began to move it out of the pocket. "Don't move now." Doug drew the package out. "Well, look here at what we found — a bomb."

Doug set the bomb down on the table, turned back and took a chain out of his jacket. "Sam, thread this chain through the cuffs around to the front where Pete's hands can move only a little." He then proceeded to search Pete more thoroughly and found his hidden gun in Pete's leg holster. "One more find. I suppose you thought we wouldn't look for this. But we knew we couldn't trust a betrayer of the police department. Now, I need to disarm this bomb and Sam will take you upstairs. We'll keep you in a little room until things are over and done."

Sam started up the stairs saying to Doug, "Good luck out there." When Sam and Pete got to the first floor, they turned right, went a few feet down the hall, and unlocked the door to a small holding room. Sam said, "I'll be right outside. Don't go away now."

"Look, Tom. There she comes in her van. It is green now. She pulled into a parking space right across from the front of the courthouse so that the rear double doors are facing the front door of the courthouse. She believes that is the only door available and will be where the men would come out after the hearing."

Tom got on the walkie-talkie and said, "The package has arrived."

The chief's aide said, "Thank you. We have eyes on."

Mark said to the chief, "Jim, all the vehicles are in place blocking her exit. Some plainclothes guys are pulling into parking spaces surrounding her. One of our guys who backed his car in can see through his tinted windshield that she got out of the driver's seat and went to the back of the van."

Maria saw the back door open about a six-inch crack. She could make out the muzzle of a rifle just inside the van aimed toward the front door of the courthouse. *She's setting up to take out her targets when they come out after the hearing.*

IN THE COURTROOM, there was a quiet expectation of a quick hearing of the new pleas and a setting of the sentencing hearing date. The judge entered. "All rise. This court will come to order. The honorable Judge McVie, presiding."

Judge McVie was seated and said, "It is my understanding that a new agreement has been reached and that there will be new pleas entered."

Harvey Swensen, the district attorney, rose and said, "That is correct, your Honor."

"Mr. Harold Evans, you are the attorney for the Group. Is it your understanding that all are agreed they are changing their plea to guilty?"

"It is, your Honor."

Judge McVie motioned to Mr. Swensen for him to bring the copies of the new pleas to him. He read them again, including the attached statement of lesser responsibility and pressure from the older senior members of the Group of Nine. He said to the defendants, "I need to hear each of you one at a time as your name is called to state, as you have signed, that you plead guilty. The bailiff will read the charges against each of you and then call your names."

A few minutes later, all the pleas had been made. Judge McVie said, "This court accepts the new pleas and declares that each of you is guilty as charged. Sentencing will be done next Tuesday at 10:00 a.m. Court is adjourned."

PETE FOUND his handcuff key in his back pocket. It was a bit of a struggle, but he finally fished it out and unlocked the cuffs. He then untangled the cuffs from the chain and not having a key to the chain lock just left it on the cuffs. He balled the cuffs and chain inside his fist so he could hit Sam with it as soon as the door opened. He went to the door, banged on it, and shouted, "Please let me out to go to the bathroom. I really have to go bad."

Sam said, "Just hold it. It shouldn't be much longer."

"I can't hold it any longer. Please let me get to the bathroom."

Sam unlocked and opened the door. Pete jumped him, hit him in the head with the balled-up cuffs and chain, and then dragged him into the room. He hit him again, knocking Sam out cold. He grabbed Sam's gun, relocked the door, and started down the hall to the front door. As he passed one of the windows, he stopped briefly to check. There was his lady love in the green van. He continued toward the front door and heard all the buzz about the new pleas and saw the big contingent of policemen. He realized he had to warn her. He ran to the main doors, knocked the policeman there to the floor, and went out the door.

He stopped at the top of the cement stairs and shouted, "Anna, it's a trap. I'll be right there. We need to get out of here." He came down the stairs as fast as he could and started running to the van. A shot rang out. Pete went down. Mrs. Olsen turned around inside the van back to the steering wheel but stopped when she saw the two policemen standing with rifles aimed at her through the windshield. She froze as she heard a loud bullhorn.

"Mrs. Olsen, please come out with your hands up. Give yourself up. You are surrounded by over twenty police officers with guns aimed at your van. Come out with your hands up and you won't be harmed. I promise you that. Let us help you."

Slowly the back doors opened. She stepped out and raised her hands and started walking toward where Pete was lying. The bullhorn came alive again.

"Mrs. Olsen, Chief Johnson here. Please keep your hands up and stop where you are."

She continued walking but with her hands up until she was standing over Pete's body. She collapsed on his body and as she did, she pulled her most powerful handgun from the back of her pants, then started sobbing and wailing.

Maria turned from the window and ran for the door from the courthouse with Tom right behind her. Doug took off on a run toward Mrs. Olsen. She stood up. Doug saw the gun and stopped. Tom saw it and stopped Maria on the steps. Mrs. Olsen cried out, "Tell my girls I'm sorry." She then put the gun barrel to her head and blew a hole in her head, falling back across Pete's body.

Maria collapsed at the top of the steps. Tom held her as she said, "I couldn't get to her. I couldn't help her."

Doug walked to the two bodies, checked both pulses and said on his walkie-talkie, "They are both gone." He looked over at the chief, shook his head and said, "This is one scenario we didn't count on."

56

Chief Johnson came out from behind his police car. "You're right, Doug. I never thought she would do this."

Maria walked up with Tom beside her. Jim blocked their way. "They are both gone. Don't get closer, it's pretty gruesome and we need to preserve the scene for the coroner. Mark has gone inside the courthouse to call him."

Mark came back. "The coroner is on the way. Do you want me to start checking the van for evidence?"

"Do that. Be careful. No telling what will be in there. Look for her purse. There may be something in there that could explain why she did this, why she shot Pete and then herself."

Mark returned with the purse saying, "The rifle we saw was in a stand for steadier aim. There was luggage, four big suitcases. They were packed to run after she killed the last Group members. I haven't checked her purse for any notes yet. There may be some clue about where the girls are. Shall I go through it?"

Jim said, "No! Mark, log it in as evidence. We'll have the state police lab search it."

"Good idea, Chief."

Maria started crying softly again. Tom said, "I'd better get her home."

Jim turned to Tom and Maria. "Thank you both for your part in this business."

As he turned back to Mark, Jim stumbled slightly and put his hand to his chest. Doug and Mark held his arms, one on each side to keep him from falling. Mark said, "What's going on, Jim?"

"I'm not feeling well. I better sit down." They sat him down on a nearby park bench.

"Get one of those EMTs over here to take a look at the chief."

The EMT Derek came over quickly. He checked the chief's vital signs: blood pressure up, heart beating rapidly. His color was not good. "We better get him to emergency at Hackley." He called the other EMT, told him to call the coroner's office and stay until he picked up the body. "We have to use this ambulance. I'll need one of you to drive the ambulance so I can tend to him."

Jim stopped him. "Two things. Mark, I would like you to get back to the station and take over as acting police chief. You all heard that. Mark is now acting chief. And second, my cardiologist, Dr. Brown is over there. I would like him to ride with us to the hospital."

Derek said, "Gladly. It will be good to have him along."

Doug offered, "I can drive the ambulance for you. I've had experience with this in the service."

Maria stopped crying, grabbed Tom's arm, and said, "Let's get to the station. I need to get Jim's home phone and let Martha know." She said to Jim, "I'll call Martha. Tom and I will bring her to the hospital."

"Good. Tell her I'm going to be fine. Just a little slow-down."

They put the chief on a stretcher and got him into the ambulance. Derek went to work putting in an IV. He had the IV in place and had it connected up to a Ringers Lactate solution while Dr. John Brown observed Jim as the ambulance headed for Hackley ER.

Dr. Brown asked Derek, "May I examine your patient?

"Please do, Doctor."

John observed that Jim's color was a little grayish. John asked, "What are you feeling?"

Jim said, "I feel weak, I hurt in the center of my chest, though not as much as when I first went down."

John said to Derek, "Can you get the ER on your radio?" Derek got connected with the ER, told them what was going on, and that he had a cardiologist on board with him. They wanted to know who it was. Derek said, "Why don't I put him on?"

John got on the radio, introduced himself, where he practiced and that he taught cardiology at Notre Dame Medical School. He told the ER doctor that he didn't want to do anything without permission from them.

The ER doctor said, "Our cardiologist will be here any moment now. We know your work, Dr. Brown. It would certainly be all right for you to take some actions, but the hospital cardiologist has to give permission. Here he is now..."

"Dr. Brown, what a pleasure. This is Eric Jones. I heard you at a conference in Cleveland last year. Good to have you on the job in the ambulance. What is going on with our patient?"

John ran through the symptoms with him. Eric asked if he had any nitro with him. John replied that he had a full kit and said, "I'll explain why later."

"Do you have an IV in place?"

"Yes, Derek did that first."

"Do you have nitro in pill form with you?"

"I do, all doses. I can give it to him sublingually right away."

"Good. Do that. Do you also have morphine?"

"I do."

"Use your own judgement. If he needs it, do it. Derek, no more delays, get him to the ER now. And thank you, Dr. Brown. I'm glad you are there."

Maria told Gerri what was happening. "We need to call Martha. Tom and I are going to take her to the hospital. It might be better for you to call her and then I'll speak with her."

Gerri got Martha on the phone and told her about Jim. She said, "I'm putting Maria on. You know her, Tom's wife. Here she is."

"Mrs. Johnson, Maria here. Everything came off fine this morning except when it was done Jim said he was not feeling well. The EMT told everyone he needed to get Jim to emergency at Hackley. His friend, Dr. Brown, is also with him in the ambulance. Tom and I will come pick you up and take you there. We'll be there in..." She looked at Gerri. "Twenty minutes."

"Let me tell Mark where I'll be, and I'll lead the two of you over there."

They followed Gerri over to the Johnson home. All three rushed in. Martha was already standing at the door with her pocketbook. Gerri gave her a hug. "He's going to be fine. He's a strong man."

Martha said, "I've been after him to get a checkup. He kept saying when this is done. Well, it's done, and he is getting checked out whether he wants it or not."

They all left, Gerri back to the station, and in about fifteen minutes, Martha was in the ER. Dr. Brown met her and told her what was happening. He told her they would know more when all the test results were back in about ten minutes or so. He said, "Come on, I'll get you in to see him."

John walked into the examining room and said, "Jim, I have someone who wants to see you."

"Hello, Martha. I'm getting a little rest."

"Jim Johnson, you just get better. Can I kiss him?"

"As long as it is a kiss we can watch and not something we'd be embarrassed to see," laughed Dr. Brown. He continued with, "He needs his rest and not have his heart overstimulated."

"Can I sit with him a little time?"

Dr. Eric Jones came in and was introduced to Martha. He said, "Sit with him, hold his hand, and let him rest. Dr. Brown and I need to confer." They walked out into the hall.

"What do your tests show, Eric?"

"The best news is that the initial cardiac enzymes were only slightly elevated. His pain is gone. The second set of cardiac enzymes are nearly normal. I believe he did not have a heart attack. I believe that much of this was brought on by the stress of the situation in front of the courthouse this morning. Would you look at his results with me?"

"If you are sure you want me to do so."

They went over the tests together. John told Eric he agreed with his opinion. He recommended a few days' rest, some low doses of medication, and maybe some cardiac rehab. No work for at least a month. Eric said, "I'm grateful you were there when it happened. You likely saved him from a worse problem."

"Nonsense," said John. "I'm glad I was there. You and your team did all the right things, and he is going to be fine. Your community is lucky to have you...Jim and I have become good friends. I have suggested he consider retirement. He told me he has the time in and that he and Martha have talked about it. This may help him make that decision."

"Let's go in and give Mrs. Johnson the good news."

When they went in, Mrs. Johnson immediately asked, "How is he doing, Doctor Jones?"

"He is going to be just fine. There was no heart attack, but he was lucky he came in. He'll need to be here for a few days, some rest at home, and then some medications which will be only minimum by the time he is home. Can you handle all that in a week or so?"

"Dr. Jones, I've been taking care of my man for over forty years. I'll be able to handle it. Thank you, Dr. Jones. And thank you, John."

In unison, "You are welcome." He continued, "Let's go tell the others."

57

A fter getting the good news, Maria went in to tell Martha that they were going to the station to spread the good news. "We'll be back to take you home when you are ready."

Doug asked John if he could come by for a few minutes. He said, "I'm sure some people are going to want to thank you for your role in his treatment."

They all assembled in the conference room. Doug started by telling them the basics, no heart attack, but some heart stress. He asked John if he would say a few words and answer questions.

"It is pretty much as Doug says. No heart attack, some heart distress likely brought on by the stress of the activities of the morning. Jim is a lucky man. He will have the luxury of slowing down and having a good life in retirement whenever he decides to do so. He will be off work for about a month or so."

Clapping started with one person and soon grew to a loud roar.

John said, "Thank you, I'm glad I was handy when my new friend needed me. The EMT, Derek, and the hospital did their work well and he's going to be fine. I'm happy my new friend will be around for a long time yet. May I leave now? I have some people to notify." Dave shook his hand, and he left amid calls of "See you doc."

Maria was standing beside Gerri who was in tears. They shared a hug.

∼

MARK TOOK THEIR ATTENTION. "Jim ordered me before the EMT got there to take over as acting chief. I've notified the mayor and the city council. I emphasize that it is temporary and only until Jim is back. I've taken some steps already. Doug agrees with me that we can pull in all the protection details, and I have done so. I've also called in the task force for one more short meeting on Thursday afternoon at 1:30 p.m. to finish reports and they've agreed. I hope you, Doug, as well as Tom and Maria can be here for that meeting also. I called Judge McVie to tell him what happened this morning and to tell him about Jim. Finally, I'm told the courthouse grounds have been cleaned up and we have left no traces of any of our activities there.

"Gerri told me she heard from the museum tour people. The wives and children had an enjoyable day and are about an hour out of Chicago. Their husbands have been advised that they are free to meet them at the bus station and pick up their families in another two hours or so. Gerri plans to be there when they come in to tell them all the good news. And for all of you, job well done. Thank you on behalf of the whole community.

"Doug disarmed the bomb that he found on Pete when he came in the back door. Dave is going to take it back to the state police explosives lab for a thorough investigation. He will bring the bomb and their report back with him.

"I'll be making a more formal presentation of appreciation for all of you. Let me say right now though, great work, all of you. It is my hope that after the meeting on Thursday afternoon, I will be able to disband the task force. I'll see most of you then. Tom and Maria, could I see you in my office before you head for home? And Dave and Doug, could I see you now? I'll have one more question for you before you leave."

~

WHEN THEY WERE all assembled in his office, Mark asked Doug and Dave, "Before I left the scene this morning, Jim handed me Mrs. Olsen's purse. He and I believe Mrs. Olsen is crafty enough to have left a booby trap in the purse. For you two, how do you propose we handle that?"

"Doug, you appear to know more about explosives than I do. What would you recommend?"

"I think to preserve the chain of evidence, Dave, I will bring everything to your lab in Lansing tomorrow morning. After your people are finished analyzing everything, I'll take them with me. I'll be staying overnight with my parents who live there and leave there in time for the afternoon meeting. I haven't seen them for some time. I need to tell them about my future plans. Will that work?"

Dave answered, "That will work, Doug. When will you tell us about your future plans?"

"I'm going to be around here for a couple of months yet. There will be some meetings with people in the D.C. area to formalize my new association as an asset for one of the government agencies. I promise that I'll let you know as much as I can before I leave for training and an overseas assignment. They want me overseas by fall. In the meantime, I have a wedding to be in. Not mine." He laughed "I'm helping to walk a friend down the aisle with Tom. And I want to spend a little time with Jim. He gave me an opportunity to serve here. I want to see if there's anything more I can do for him. So, Dave if I can have the address of your labs in Lansing, I'll see you there tomorrow morning."

Doug added, "I would like to meet with the protection teams. They were professionals all the way, did what they were told, and never an argument or a problem. I want to thank them in person some time before I go."

Mark turned to Tom and Maria. "Now to you two. I have some questions. Maria, what progress have you made with your state police training? And Tom, how long will it be before you set out on your own?"

"Let's hear from Maria first. The time she needs to finish the training and get her private detective license is the critical factor."

"I am caught up on my reading and after some review, I need to meet with the state people soon to see how to work out my in-person studies at the Grand Rapids Operation. And finally, we meet with my doctor next week for a thorough check up on how I am doing in the medical sense. If my doctor gives me a free rein, I think I can be ready for field training some time mid-summer. So, I'll know more next week."

Mark said, "It sounds like a few months if all goes well." At her nod, he went on, "What about your part in getting your company up and running?"

"Mark, it is like this. There's a lot for us to learn about the business end. We want to open for business with both of us ready to go to work on a case. It may take a few months to get ready to launch. I've learned a lot from working on the task forces and from you and Jim during this time. I still need to earn a living until we get the business up and running."

"I think I can help with a plan that Jim and I hatched a little while ago. We would like to offer you a six-month contract as a detective on a beginning detective salary plus expenses. And we would have an option for renewal for another six months. We like having you around, so there it is."

"That is terrific. It will help me build some more experience and keep us afloat at the same time. Thank you, Mark. I accept."

"Good. Now I want to sweeten the pot a little. Maria, we can't put you on full-time until your rehab is done, and you are ready to work. What we can do is offer you an as-needed position and, as you are able, put you on a per diem basis plus expenses. We'll count your days in the Grand Rapids State school. You'll have at least two days of per diem per week. And what do you think?"

"This is so very generous, Mark. I accept as well. Thank you.

Please take the message to Jim as well that we are honored to be a part of the team."

Mark smiled and said, "He will be happy with the news, as am I. You should know that we have hopes you will stay on for a long time. We applaud your plan and dreams about your own husband and wife team. We hope it is a success for you but in the meantime, you will be quite an asset to the department. Those are Jim's words, but I echo them. Shall we set an official start date on the Monday after next? Gerri will take care of all the paperwork when you come in for the meeting Thursday afternoon. Now I suspect you have things to do. I know I do, so I'll see you on Thursday."

58

When they left, Mark called Jim. "Hi Jim, this is Mark. How are you doing?"

"I'm doing fine. I'm ready to get out of here. They are keeping me another day or two just to observe. How are things at the office?"

"It is all good. We have a final meeting of the task force Thursday afternoon. The team has all promised their final reports."

"If I get out of here tomorrow morning, I would like to make that meeting. I want to give them my final thoughts and thanks. If I don't get out until Thursday, could it possibly be Friday afternoon?"

"I'm sure everyone would make it Friday if needed. Jim, I saved the best until last. Tom and Maria have agreed to stay on for a six-to-nine-month period while they get ready to get their business going. I'm thinking we may have them for at least a year before they make a move. We'll see after that. They told me they will need a month off maybe this fall. They want to do the honeymoon in Paris that they had always planned. I agreed to that. I hope I haven't overstepped my responsibilities?"

"Good work, Mark. This makes it easier for me to tell you this. Martha and I have been talking and here it is. I will be retiring soon, but before I do, I have a plan to make you permanent new chief. That is, if you want it."

"I'm flattered, and yes, I would like to have a shot at it. What is your plan?"

"I'd rather not tell you over the phone. How do you think your wife, Elizabeth, will feel about it?"

"I think she will be okay with it. I'll talk to her tonight and let you know."

"Could you and Elizabeth come for dinner some night next week? We can hash out the plan then and work out the details."

"That would be great. We'll work out the time and day. Thank you, Jim, for your vote of confidence."

"My pleasure, you deserve it. We'll make it happen. Talk tomorrow."

59

D r. Jones came in around 9:00 a.m. and said to Jim, "How are you doing this morning?"

"I'm ready to go home."

"Well, Jim, I think we can arrange that sometime later this morning. We have a few tests we want to do, and you'll be set to go. The nurse will have some instructions for when you go home — what you can and can't do. You can call Mrs. Johnson and have her come here about 11:00 a.m."

"Do you think I could go by the office tomorrow afternoon? Mark will be closing up this case and the task force. I would like to be there for a few minutes to say goodbye and thank them for the excellent job they did."

"If you'll promise to keep it to a few minutes, I think that would be alright."

As soon as Dr. Jones walked out of the room, Jim called Martha and gave her the good news. She was so ready for her man to come home and would be there with his 'coming home' clothes.

He had just hung up from his call when Dr. Brown popped in. He told Jim, "We're leaving for home, and I wanted a final chat with you, not as your doctor, but as your friend."

"I'm glad you did."

"Jim, have you considered retirement? Maybe it is time for you to find your next passion, something you have always wanted to do but didn't have the time. And let someone else take the reins of police chief. What do you think?"

"Actually, I'm ahead on that already thanks to your words of wisdom during the ride to the hospital. This has been a scare. Martha and I have been talking and we agree that it is time. I need to get a couple of things done first."

"What are those? Not cases, I hope."

"No, nothing like that. I think that Mark will make a great police chief. He has all the credentials, an undergraduate degree in Criminal Justice and a master's degree in Public Administration. He has taken over for me every year for a few years now when we take vacation. He is making good decisions now as acting chief. He is a natural. I have a plan to convince the city administration to appoint him without a big search."

"When are you going to spring this?"

"Dr. Jones suggested that I take at least a month off, maybe two months. During that time Mark will be building a record of leadership. We don't have any big problems to solve right now but you never know what may show up."

Jim continued, "This is something like a case of 'Sometimes we are forced to do things that we should have known to do ourselves' and I take the lesson to heart. It is time Martha and I start enjoying the things we like to do. Our house is paid for, we have some good investments, and my pension is adequate if not generous. We don't know what we will do yet. Travel is at the top of the list. We'll find our path together."

"Jane and I hope that your travel plans include a visit often with us in South Bend."

"That it will. I won't be making the announcement until my doctor mandated period of rest and relaxation is done. That also gives Mark more chance to build his experience at the job."

"I am so happy that you have taken this seriously. I like you, my friend, and want to see you around for a long time. I better get going — Jane is ready to be home. Let's stay in touch."

W{HEN} J{OHN} {LEFT}, Jim's nurse came in to do an EKG on him and while she was setting that up, a lab nurse came in for a blood sample. Jim thought, *this is good. Dr. Jones isn't wasting any time.*

When those tasks were done, Jim called the police station. Gerri answered. "Hey, Gerri, this is your old friend Jim."

"Hi, Chief, how are you doing? It is so good to hear your voice."

"It is good to hear your voice too. I am doing just fine. In fact, they're sending me home later this morning. I'm ready to be home. I will be home doing R & R for a month or maybe two. We'll see. How is Mark taking his new responsibilities?"

"Jim, he has jumped right in and is doing a fantastic job. He's terrific. Oh, oh, maybe I shouldn't have said that. No one can come up to you, Chief."

"That's all right. It is exactly what I wanted to hear. Do you remember the conversation we had a few weeks ago? Martha and I are agreed. It's time for me to retire. But mum's the word, I'm not ready to let the word out yet. And by the way, why don't you get used to calling me Jim instead of Chief?"

"Okay, Chief, er, Jim, I will. Do you want to talk to Mark?"

"I do, but before I go, my doctor says it is okay if I come to the meeting for about five or ten minutes, so I'll see you tomorrow."

"Great! I'll ring Mark."

"Hello, Jim. What's the good word?"

"My doctor has given his permission to come to the meeting tomorrow for five or ten minutes. I have a few words to say to the task force. What time would be good?"

"Why don't you take your time settling in at home and come in at 3:30 p.m.? I'll have the meeting all finished by then and you can have the floor. I'll have Gerri come out about 3:25 to bring you in."

"Sounds good, Mark. I'll see you there."

Mark walked into the meeting with Gerri by his side promptly at 1:30 p.m. He said, "It is so good to see all your faces again. I see that you are all here, even those of you who were on the first task force. Thank you for coming. This meeting is kind of special. We are finally all done with this case that started early last summer and just wound up a couple of days ago."

"We have six of our own officers here, seven members of the state police, some from the first task force, the rest from the second task force. Finally, we have three pretty special people — Tom, who was on the first task force, but could only be part-time on the second. Maria, who is Tom's wife and part-time member of the second task force. I think she came out of the coma just to get on the force. And then, there is their friend, Doug, who played a strong role in this second task force. His skills he learned elsewhere played a significant role in letting us close off this case. Last but not least is a new member of the second task force. Don Phillips is a newly minted sergeant and turned out to be so valuable, we have him on course to become a new detective for the department."

Don jumped in and said, "Where's the food? You said not to eat lunch because you would provide it. I'm getting hungry."

"See, he is already coming right to the main point. Let's eat! Any minute now, Don. I'll finish my overview after we eat. Aha, I smell perch." In walked two Doo Drop Inn staff with perch dinners for all. "I thought we needed a little celebration of a job well done. Finally finished."

They all settled into eating their perch dinners. Conversation was loud and exuberant — so much energy for having finally stopped the killer and the murder of several more men. Now the remaining Group members could pay for their crime in prison. Justice had been served.

When they were finished, and the table was cleaned, Mark brought the meeting back to order. "You will recall that last fall, we thought our work was done except for the trials for the Group members who were left. There were three expensive funerals last fall. Harry, the muscle, was killed by Joe Antonelli out at the Ovals. In that same fight Tom was wounded and Maria was put into a coma by Harry's gun. We now know that Larry Olsen was killed by George Anderson who ran him off the road to a drowning death."

He continued, "So, here we were with three expensive funerals and six members arraigned, charged, and waiting for a trial. Our district attorney persuaded Judge McVie to give him more time to consult with us and build his case on the evidence we had and what we might yet find. Judge McVie was about to assign a trial date when things changed. Another Group member, Tim Samuels, was shot with a rifle in his office. We had no clue about who or why.

"George Anderson, the leader of the Group of Nine, came to Jim demanding police protection. The chief assembled a small protection detail who were assigned to watch over the remaining members. Except that George told Jim that he wouldn't need one, he could take care of himself. Three days later he was found dead in his second home on Scenic Drive. He was shot three times with a handgun. This was when Doug came into the task force. He told Jim that he had some skills that might be useful. Jim hired him as a special consultant, first to supervise the protection squads and then later to do training like what our state police friends do for us. He has been a valuable asset. By the way, in his other life that he is returning to, he was also known as an asset. He won't tell us who he is an asset for."

Doug jumped in, "And if I did tell you, I'd have to kill you... Bad old joke, I know. Sorry!" Laughter around the room.

"To continue my story, we still were clueless but had some suspicions. We suspected but couldn't prove it yet that a woman was the killer of these two members, Tim and George. After an interview with Mrs. Olsen by the chief and Tom, we were convinced our killer was her. The evidence was strong, but we and the district attorney felt we needed more solid evidence. She taunted us with cryptic notes left at the scene or sent to the chief essentially saying, 'I will get them all plus Tom.' Why Tom, we don't know but her real focus was the remaining members of the Group. She wanted there to be nine expensive funerals. We doubled security on the remaining Group members, but she still tried. This was witnessed by two of our protection details.

"Jim's plan was to bait a trap through Pete after we discovered he was feeding her information. The evidence suggested she and Pete were leaving together after she killed the remaining Group members at their new plea hearing. As we all know, she shot Pete when he failed to get her bomb diversion plan to work. We know what happened next. She looked like she was surrendering but walked to Pete's body and threw herself on him, pulling a hidden handgun as she fell on his body. Her suicide ended the case. We don't know what motivated her to try to kill them all nor why she killed herself. We believe she was driven by anger, obsessed with revenge, and thought that all the men of the Group were responsible for her husband's death. We will never know for sure.

"So, we ended up not with nine expensive funerals but with several expensive funerals and the rest of the members will be in jail with lighter sentences because of their plea. We'll see next week when Judge McVie does the sentencing. By the way, that was the way the chief wanted it to end and why he beefed up their security. He wanted no more killings, but we got two anyway. The last Group members will still get, we think, long stays in a Michigan prison for their role in the death of the mayor.

"We have no case to prove anymore and just need to have all the reports from each of you for the records. Please do so and the task force will be done as of today. We have most of the members of the protection squads who are ready to join us.

"And here they are now." Mark paused to welcome the newcomers.

"I have one more announcement to make before we are done. As some of you know, Tom and Maria are setting out to become a husband-and-wife private detective agency. They can't get that going until Maria completes her training with the state police. They have agreed to our offers for Tom to be starting next week as a detective for us and Maria to be available on a per diem basis while she recuperates from the long coma and finishes her training. They have both agreed to a six-month contract with an option to renew. We hope they will be here for a long time."

The room erupted with cheers and applause. They knew this was a good move for the department.

Mark then said, "We have a little surprise for you." Just then the door opened and in walked the chief. They stood and gave him an ovation.

He waved them quiet and said, "Thank you, all. My doctor said I could come today but only for a few minutes. I'm supposed to be at home relaxing, but I'd rather be here. I want to congratulate all of you on a job well done. Thanks to outstanding efforts by our state police friends, especially Dave Smithson who has been with us on both task forces. He and his colleagues have been invaluable throughout the time of both task forces. And of course, my officers, Don, Tom, and Maria. A big thank you to our protection squad members. They are all former officers of various police forces who came out of retirement to do an excellent job of protection. I hoped we could avoid more killings and you helped make that happen. I have to tell you all that the suicide by Mrs. Olsen was a twist I didn't see coming.

"Finally, a big thanks to my chief detective, Mark. As you all know, he is now acting chief. From what I have heard so far, he is doing well at the job, like a natural to it. The doctor said no more than ten minutes and I'm beginning to feel it. My wife, Martha, is outside waiting to take me back home where she can watch over me. I'll be back on the job in a month or so. Again, thank you all for all you have done. See you soon." As Jim shook Mark's hand at the door, he handed him a small invitation-sized card. Jim walked out to another round of applause.

Mark said, "Meeting dismissed. My thanks as well."

Mark went into his office, opened the card, and read, 'Will you and Sally please come to dinner and conversation about your future here, Wednesday or Thursday at 6:00 p.m.? Your choice. Please call and let us know. Best, Jim and Martha.'

60

As they drove home, Maria said, "I think we have time for a quick nap before our parents come. My lasagna is all ready, an extra big one for six of us. Mom is bringing a big salad and some Cole's garlic bread. Your mom is bringing appetizers and, as she puts it, a surprise dessert. She wouldn't tell me what it was."

"It will be good to have them all over. We can tell them the good news about the department's offers and our decision to honeymoon in Paris for thirty days. Say, could that nap include ..."

"Not a chance, but later tonight. Can you wait?"

"If I have to."

They were back at the house by 4:30 p.m. As they walked in, Tom said, "You set a gorgeous table here. But the Kir Royale flutes aren't on the table."

"I've read that you should chill the flutes, so I thought we would try it tonight."

"Nap time. Set the alarm for 5:30 p.m."

"That will be good. The lasagna needs about a half hour. They will be here at 6:30 p.m."

Tom woke up first and preheated the oven. He had installed a dimmer switch on the decorative light over the dining room table. He adjusted it to what he thought was just right. He turned on some jazz music and set it to a low volume and was sitting there listening when he felt arms around him from behind and a kiss on his head. "Hi there, lover."

In his best Humphrey Bogart voice, he said, "Later doll, later..."

She came around and sat beside him on the sofa. "What do you think they'll say about our plans?"

"I think they will be a little apprehensive about the husband-and-wife agency but happy about the offers from the police department."

"My mom will be the one who questions us the most about the danger involved."

"We'll soon see. I hear one car and I bet the other is probably coming down the street. They both have a thing about being on time. How's the lasagna coming?"

"Another fifteen minutes and then I can set it to a warm temperature. We need enough time to enjoy the appetizers."

When they opened the door, she found both sets of parents with their hands full of goodies. "Come on in. Let me take something. I have a sideboard over here to set things on."

Tom's mother exclaimed, "What a lovely setting! You have a gift for this, Maria."

"Thank you."

His dad said, "Pretty lush for an ordinary bunch of people."

"Dad, nothing ordinary about this group. How could we be anything else with parents like ours?"

"Here, here. I wanted this to be an extra special time. Our lives have been so roiled since we got married that we haven't had time to do this. It is the first time we've all been together in our home. Welcome. Tom, will you do the honors?"

Tom took the Crème de Cassis and champagne out of the refrigerator while Maria took the chilled flutes out of the freezer section. He started by pouring in the small amount, just a splash, of Cassis in each flute. Then he popped the cork on the champagne and poured it, going from glass to glass until he topped them all off. As he brought them to the ladies first, he said, "Did you know that the Kir

Royale was invented by a Catholic priest in Dijon, France? His name was Canon Felix Kir. He started first with white wine and cassis, but then upgraded it to champagne and cassis. It quickly became popular throughout the Burgundy region. In time, it made its way to America, mostly on the east coast. We decided a while back we would bring it to Muskegon."

He returned to his seat, raised his glass, and said, "Here's to an extraordinary group of people! Now let's get after this charcuterie board. It is amazing, such variety of cheeses and meats, Mrs. Vitale."

"Oh no, not Mrs... You can call me Mother Sally or just Sally."

The conversation while they ate was mostly about Maria and how she was recuperating.

She told them, "I'm doing just fine. I still tire fast but even that is getting better. At the rate I am progressing, I'll be ready for our trip in September."

"What trip is that?"

"We're finally going to take our honeymoon trip. We're going to Paris for almost a month, late August through most of September. We have an apartment reserved in the sixth Arrondissement. It is one of the most centrally located districts and will let us get to places on our list with ease."

His mother asked, "How are you going to afford it? Neither of you has been working."

"Don't forget we had saved for this before the wedding, and I added to our savings while Maria was in the hospital and long-term care. We're okay for the trip and beyond. The rest we'll tell you over the surprise dessert. Now, how about some lasagna, salad, and garlic toast? We have some excellent Chianti to go with it all."

Tom's dad said, "I'd like more of the Kir Royale. Who else wants another?"

Tom got three takers and the rest wanted their Chianti. He served the lasagna from the sideboard, Maria put the salad and garlic toast family style on the table. Everyone loved Maria's lasagna saying, "Tom, it is as good as you were telling us it would be." They finished their dinner. Tom's dad patted his tummy and asked, "Can we hold the dessert for a bit while that great meal settles?"

Tom topped off their wine glasses and said, "Everyone can just sip their wine while we tell you what our plans are." They cleared the table of all but their wine and waters. Maria started a pot of coffee to go with dessert.

Tom started it off. "You all remember that I got my private detective license this past spring. And I was working with the police again at least until Maria came home. Then my job took second place."

Maria jumped in. "Yes, and he took such loving care of me while I was regaining my strength. Gradually I started doing more things here at home, but it was mostly Tom during those early days out of the coma."

Tom said, "Maria is well into her studies to get her private detective license. It will take a few more months to finish and pass the exam. We told you we have plans for a husband-and-wife detective agency. That takes time to get going, develop the right business plan, drum up some cases. In short it will be a few months before we can think about that bringing in any income. The question became one of what to do to make a living. You all know about the incident in the courthouse grounds. The way it ended there is no more reason for a task force, so no more pay from that.

"By the way, Jim, the chief, showed up at the end of the last task force meeting but only for ten minutes. So, Mark, the lead detective, is acting chief until Jim comes back. It could be anywhere from one to two months. Then we got a surprise. Mark took the two of us and our friend Doug into his, well, Jim's office. We were both offered jobs with the department. Monday I start in as a full-time detective. The salary is enough to take care of all our living expenses. They couldn't hire Maria yet in that kind of position, but they set her up on a per diem basis with her state police training days in Grand Rapids two days a week counting as per diem days as they did for me. We said yes, of course, and signed six-month contracts with an option for another six months if we need it."

The parents were so excited knowing that Tom would be gainfully employed full-time for six months to a year. "Hooray! We'll drink to that!"

Tom's mom said, "How about celebrating with my new special dessert?" She retrieved a tall box from the refrigerator since the surprise dessert had to stay properly chilled. She took the filled parfait type glasses out of the box while Maria poured the coffee. "Here it is! Chocolate mousse."

"She hasn't served it to anyone else except me while she was perfecting it. I was very happy that she had to test it a lot," his dad said as he patted his stomach. "I can guarantee it is fabulous."

"In doing my research for the recipe, I discovered that the French have it with no toppings. I brought along whipped cream, chocolate shavings, and cocoa if some of you want it. We can do it our own way."

"Let's celebrate our upcoming Paris honeymoon and all have it French style," said Maria.

Tom tried his with a sip of Chianti, mousse, and a sip of coffee. He exclaimed, "What a great taste combination!"

They all agreed that the meal was an immense success and a perfect celebration to their new jobs.

61

The next day was another rainy day in late April. Tom and Maria were sleeping in. It was just after 10:00 a.m., they were still in their pajamas enjoying a third cup of coffee. The phone rang. It was Sara.

"Good morning, Maria. This is Sara. How are you two doing?"

"We're good. We are being lazy. It is the kind of day for it."

"Could I come by later and talk about the wedding? It is only a little over three weeks until the big day." Maria turned to Tom and asked if there were any plans. He shook his head.

"We have no plans today. Tom and I have some great news to share with you as well. Will Bob and Arianna be with you?"

"No, just me. Bob is taking his last final today. He'll be home tonight. And Arianna will be with Sister Charlotte and the other nuns. It's one of the last times they'll get to baby-sit. They are not happy we are leaving. Could you see if Doug could come over too?"

"We'll call him right away. What time are you thinking?"

"How about 2:30 p.m.?"

"How about 1:30 p.m.? We'll have a little lunch. Nothing fancy. Just sandwiches and chips. We will eat, catch up on things, and talk wedding plans."

"That sounds great. See you then."

TOM AND MARIA got moving and while Maria was cleaning up, he went to Etterman's to get some sandwich fixings, potato chips, beer, pop, and lemonade ingredients. When he returned, Maria had the house ready. Doug showed up about 1:00 p.m. The three of them were sitting on the porch with a beer when Sara drove up.

Maria gave her a hug and asked, "What can I get you to drink? Pop, tea, or lemonade?"

"I've got about two and a half years before I can have what you have, so I better have lemonade."

They all went inside to eat. The three of them switched to iced tea, Sara smiled and said, "Thank you, but you didn't have to do that. I don't mind if you have beer. My dad enjoyed a glass of wine with dinner every night while I had milk."

During lunch, the conversation turned to what she and Bob were doing to get the house ready for them to move in. Sara said, "We're on target to get all our things in there by the weekend before the wedding. My best friend from high school will be coming in on the Wednesday before the wedding, so she will stay with Arianna and me. Bob will stay with his parents until after the wedding. We'll move the majority of his things in before the wedding and just leave what he needs for the wedding and the honeymoon at his house."

"Have you decided where you are going?"

"We are splurging and staying at the Grand Hotel on Mackinac Island. We're staying in the honeymoon suite. The wedding is at 11:00 a.m. The reception should be over by 3:00 p.m. or so. We should be on the island by 6:30 p.m. roughly and the hotel will have a special dinner for us about 7:30 p.m."

"That sounds great. Who is going to take care of Arianna?"

"I'm sure the ladies at the home will if we ask them."

Tom and Maria looked at each other, nodded. Maria said, "Tom and I have been talking. We think it is about time we got acquainted with our goddaughter. We'll take good care of her and if we run into any problems, we have two mothers who will pitch in if we need them. How does that sound?"

Tearing up, Sara said, "It sounds wonderful. You could also call on the nuns at the home in a pinch. They would love it."

"We should probably try to see her two or three times before the wedding, just to get acquainted."

"That's a good idea. I'll make that happen. You said you and Tom have some exciting news as well."

Tom said, "I'll make it short so we can get to wedding plans. Both Maria and I start at the police department as of this coming Monday. We have six-month contracts with the possibility of renewal. You'll remember we told you about our plans for a husband-and-wife detective agency as well. But we need some time to get everything ready to go and Maria needs to complete her training. Our best guess is that we'll be here for at least a year. We will see what happens after that. Oh, and by the way, we're going to Paris in the fall for a long-postponed honeymoon."

"That is so great. I'm happy you will be around for a while longer. How about you, Doug?"

"You remember that I had another life in the military before I became a teacher and orchestra director." She nodded.

Doug continued, "I have had some conversations with the government and, long story short, I am returning to that shortly after the wedding. My country needs me again, so I am going."

"Will you ever come back this way?"

"Of course, I will. I have some friends I need to see occasionally, these two and now you, Bob, and little Arianna. And who knows how many more there will be when I come back."

"Doug, let us get settled in a marriage first. Then we'll see."

"Well, it worked pretty well the first time!" Doug laughed.

Sara blushed. "Doug, you are embarrassing me."

Doug smiled. "I'm just teasing you a bit. You and Bob have become special to me. I want to see how you turn out. You two are going to be just great together."

Maria jumped in with, "How about some hot fudge sundaes and coffee while we talk about the wedding?"

After they enjoyed their desserts, Sara told them about the wedding. "As you know I will have three ladies, Maria, my best friend from high school, and Nancy."

Doug interrupted. "Excuse me. I hadn't heard that yet. It will be good to see Nancy again."

"I have the dresses all picked out. I brought Nancy's along to show you what they look like." She took it out of the box and held it up to herself.

Maria exclaimed, "It is beautiful. I like the color and the style. Where do I have to go to get it fitted?"

"I have the address right here. They are expecting you sometime early next week."

"We have to go for my two-month checkup next Tuesday. We could do the fitting right after the appointment."

Sara continued, "And you gentlemen need to be fitted for your tuxedos. They may have to order yours special, Doug. You are such a big guy. You should get in soon as possible. Here is the address for the tux rental place. They have all been paid for, gowns and tuxes."

Doug asked, "Can we help pay for all this?" Tom and Maria echoed the sentiment.

"Absolutely not. Dad left me very well off. He would have paid for the entire thing and would expect me to take care of it now. Thank you for the offer."

"How about all the instructions about what we have to do?"

"That will come on rehearsal the Friday night before. And before you ask, Bob's dad is covering the rehearsal."

"You've done a great job, Sara. Your dad would be proud of you. He'll be watching over it, won't he?"

They said their goodbyes, Sara got three hugs, and she was on her way.

62

Tuesday morning at 9:00 a.m., Judge McVie met with the district attorney, Harvey Swensen, and the Group members' attorney, Harold Evans, to discuss the sentences.

Judge McVie said, "I wanted to meet with the two of you. I have sentences in mind but would like to get your feedback. I know you will each have opinions and I want to hear them. So, here it is. I am sentencing each of them to fifteen years in a minimum-security prison to be named later. They are to show up by the end of May for the terms to start. That should give them time to get their affairs in order. Mr. Evans, they are your clients and be frank, tell me what you think."

Mr. Evans stuttered, "Your honor, with respect, the sentences are too harsh. I suspect you figured I might say that. Here's my thinking. Four of the men are fairly young with young children. They were low men on the whole in the Group and were pushed into signing the document that they approved the killing of the mayor. That is the major charge against them. My argument is that they had no choice but to sign it, even as they, one and all, said in the meetings that each said on the record, 'I didn't sign on for this.' That should mean something about the length of their sentences. As for Wendell, the oldest of the bunch, if he served the full sentence, he would be an old man of sixty-six when he got out. His life will essentially be over after that."

"That is about what I thought you would say. I didn't expect the 'I didn't sign on for this' comment and I'll take it under consideration. But the fact that they 'didn't sign on for it' doesn't eliminate their role in the mayor's death. They didn't stop it. Harvey, what say you?"

"I can empathize with Mr. Evans' position on them all. I'm willing to concede that even though it is not the maximum you could hand down, it is pretty stiff. With good behavior, they could all get out in eight or nine years. That is still a lot for all of them. I would not argue against a lighter sentence."

"All right, here is what we'll do. I will drop the sentence to ten years and include my comments in the decision document that it is my wish that they be considered favorably for an early out for good behavior. I won't suggest what that time could be. That is not in my purview."

Both said that they believed that was a fair and just decision and thanked him.

THE COURT SESSION was called to order, Judge McVie came in. He looked at the men and their wives behind them in the next row back. He started with statements about his knowledge of the family situations and the fact that they all had businesses in the community. "I hereby sentence each of you to serve ten years in a minimum-security prison as close as possible to Muskegon. I have included in the document that each of you should be considered favorably for an early out based on good behavior. These sentences will not start until the first of June to give you time to get your businesses into the hands of someone who will do well by it while you are gone. As for your families and how they will get by, I have conferred with other trusted judges as well as Michigan Supreme Justices as to the 'cleanness' of the monies you all put up for bail. I will be releasing those monies when you have started your sentences. Your families will not be destitute. Court is adjourned."

63

Wednesday at 6:30 p.m., Mark and Sally knocked on the chief's door. When it opened, there were Jim and Martha, both welcoming them in. "Come in, welcome to our home. We should have done this a long time ago."

They went into the living room where they saw appetizers on a coffee table along with an open bottle of pinot noir. There were cheeses, crackers, and some of those tiny seedless green grapes. Jim said, "I have never asked if you drink wine, but we decided to take a chance that you might on this special occasion." Mark and Sally both said that they would take a little and then see how they felt.

Jim poured the wine and gave a toast. "Here's to a new police chief coming up." Glasses clinked.

"If I may, I'd like to toast the best man I have ever worked for. It has been my pleasure, Jim. And here also is to many happy and fun years in retirement."

Martha was beaming at Mark's words. She wanted this for some time.

"What a lovely home you have." Sally admired the warm green and blue tones in the living room.

"Thank you. We like it a lot. We've been here for forty years. Our children have grown up here. This is where we'll stay."

After finishing some snacks, Martha left to get things on the table. Sally followed along to see how she could help. Jim and Mark began to talk about his upcoming time as chief.

"I am going to try and not come back for almost two months. My doctor said at least a month, maybe two, and I'm going to use it all. I want you to get as much attention and time in office as acting chief to strengthen my case to show how right you are for the job. And that there is no need to do a search. I know the city council and acting mayor well enough to know that they would lean toward you and would prefer not to have to do a search. You've been on the job here for some ten years. Now, I don't want to see anything real bad happen but if a situation came up that called on you to solve it and you did so post haste, that would help. In short, I'm going to sell you to the city council."

He continued, "You can call me if you have to, but I hope you won't. I'd rather you solve whatever comes along and I'll make sure that you get the credit you deserve. I won't announce my retirement for at least six weeks."

Martha and Sally said, "Dinner's on."

They had a sumptuous meal of baked ham with a raisin sauce, mashed potatoes, salad, and for dessert, Martha's homemade coconut cream pie and coffee.

THE NEXT MORNING, the interim mayor called Jim. "Hello, Jim. I heard you stopped in at the last meeting of the task force. And on strict orders from your doctor, you were only there for ten minutes."

"That's right. He told me not to overstay my welcome. So I didn't. I could see that I wasn't needed there. From what some friends of mine tell me, Mark has things well under control. He is doing what I would have done if I were there and without asking me what he should do. He'll make a good chief someday."

"Are you going to retire soon Jim?"

"Why would you ask such a thing? I will let you know when my time comes, and it is not there yet."

~

THE INTERIM MAYOR went to the city commission meeting that afternoon intending only to be there and contribute to the discussion on some minor issues. One of the city commissioners asked him, "Have you heard how the chief is doing?"

"As a matter of fact, I talked to him just this morning. He says he is getting better. His doctor wants him to stay away from the job for a month or maybe two. He said, not to worry, that Mark is doing an excellent job as acting chief. The cleanup after last week's incident outside the courthouse went well. In short, the department is running along very well and will do just fine until he can come back."

"So, you don't think we should be looking for a new chief right now?"

"No, I don't. I even asked him if he was going to retire soon. He got a little huffy, saying that he would let us know when his time comes, and it isn't now. So, my feeling is he'll come back when he has recuperated, and things will go along like they have since he became chief."

Several commissioners nodded and said, "We can take that off the agenda until something changes."

The city council chairman said, "The meeting is over. Let's have a drink."

64

Sara knocked on Sister Charlotte's door. She said, "Come in. Good morning, Sara. What a pleasant surprise. What can I do for you?"

"Sister Charlotte, you, and the nuns have done so much for me. I find it hard to say the right thing to convey my thanks. You have taken me in, helped me finish my schooling, taken care of me when I had Arianna, and now love her like one of your own."

"Thank you. Those are kind and loving words. We have loved having you here, watching you grow into a mature and smart young woman."

"Oh, and we, Bob and I, would like you all to come to the wedding. I have an offer from Arianna's godparents, Tom and Maria O'Banion, to care for Arianna while we are on our honeymoon up north. We'll only be gone about two days. Then we're moving into my parents' house and start a new life together as a family."

"I understand you wanting Arianna's godparents to have a chance to get to know her. What if they need help with her?"

"They have two mothers who will jump in and help if needed. I told them they could also call you if they felt the need. I hope that wasn't too presumptuous."

"No, not at all. We would be happy to go if needed and may stop by for a visit. And thank you for the invitation. If nothing happens to demand our attention, we'll be there. I enjoy Father Flanagan's messages. I look forward to your wedding."

"May I bring up one more thing?" Sister Charlotte nodded yes. "My father left me very well off. In fact, some more money just turned up. So, Bob and I will never hurt for money. That means that I can do something that I have been wanting to do for some time now."

She took an envelope out of her purse and said, "This is for your ministry. I know you all well enough that you will put it to good use. My attorney cleared all the legalities, so it is all legal for you to accept it." She handed Sister Charlotte the envelope.

Sister Charlotte took the envelope and asked, "May I open it now?"

"If you wish, of course."

When she opened it and saw the amount on a check, her eyes filled with tears. "Child, are you certain you can do this? This is a lot of money."

"I can do it and so maybe you can do for more young women like me, what you did for me."

"Thank you, Sara."

65

On Friday afternoon, the wedding party, Tom and Maria's parents, Sister Charlotte, and Father Flanagan were at the rehearsal at St. Jeans. That was over by 2:00 p.m. The early dinner after was held at the restaurant Sara's dad once owned. The new owners closed the restaurant from 2:30 p.m. until 5:00 p.m. just for them. Sara opened the festivities with a toast to her dad, saying, "He would have approved having it here. He is smiling with approval somewhere up there now."

There was lots of conversation, getting better acquainted, and questions.

Nancy asked, "Is Arianna going to be at the wedding?"

"Yes, she is. She likely won't remember much of it, but I think she ought to be there. We can show her the pictures when she gets older."

"Who will have her during the ceremony?"

Sara said, "I asked Tom's parents to be master and mistress of ceremonies. They agreed. I asked Maria's parents to pick up Arianna at our home on Saturday morning and bring her to the wedding. They agreed, so it all worked out."

The ladies of the bridal party all returned to Bob and Sara's home along with Arianna. They had a big night planned with mani-pedis and facials. They would dress in the morning at Sara's house and then all go together to the church.

The men returned to Tom and Maria's house for a quiet bachelor's party. They teased Bob a bit about the honeymoon, but Bob just smiled and told them it was none of their business. Since Bob couldn't drink, they let him go home early with his college buddy who was his best man. Tom and Doug enjoyed a beer on the porch before they turned in for the night. Festivities would start early in the morning.

SATURDAY DAWNED as a beautiful sunny spring day, a perfect day for a wedding. The ladies in the wedding party bustled around with Sara at her home. Since they spent Friday afternoon and evening just getting to know each other better, catching up on their lives, it was like a two-day slumber party. Arianna was the star of the party, entertaining them with her giggles and antics. Maria really appreciated the time she got to spend with Nancy — they had so much to cover about what was happening at Muskegon High School. The ladies all vied for the single bathroom and the full-length mirror, but eventually they were all dressed and ready. Maria helped Sara adjust her dress and veil.

Mr. and Mrs. Vitale came at 9:00 a.m. to pick up Arianna. She was all dressed in her yellow organdy dress with little black patent leather shoes and white lace anklets. At first, she was not sure she wanted to go with them. Mr. Vitale brought some of the toys that Arianna played with at the planning session. When she saw them, she didn't even look back at her mom.

All were at the church in their respective corners by 10:00 a.m. in plenty of time for an 11:00 a.m. wedding.

Bob and his best man came out with Father Flanagan. The bridesmaids and then Maria, the matron of honor, came down the aisle. The organ segued into the wedding march and Sara came down the aisle with Doug on one arm and Tom on the other. All the people stood and smiled at the different arrangement. As they went past Arianna, she said, "Ma Ma Ma" and all smiled. Sara stopped long enough to give her a kiss. They continued down the aisle to the altar. Tom and Doug kissed her cheeks at the same time. She surprised them both by kissing each one in turn. The two men took their places in line with Bob and his best man.

A mass was read. The vows that they had written themselves were said. When Father Flanagan pronounced them man and wife, Bob kissed his bride. They turned and Father Flanagan introduced Mr. and Mrs. Bob Fowler. They started down the aisle only to hear again, "Ma Ma Ma." Bob and Sara stopped, Bob took Arianna in one arm, took Sara's hand in his other hand, and finished the walk to applause all the way out to the front steps of the church.

They all convoyed up to the Lakeside Inn in Whitehall for the reception at 1:00 p.m. When it came time for the bride and groom to leave for their honeymoon up on Mackinac, Arianna was fast asleep in Mr. Vitale's arms. Bob and Sara both gave her a quick kiss. Mr. and Mrs. O'Banion hushed the crowd for a last word from Sara. "Bob and I want to take just a minute to tell you all how happy you have made us by sharing this day with us. We love you — thank you for being here. We'll see you again soon."

Mr. O'Banion held up his hand for quiet. "Just one word from all of us who love Bob and Sara, Arianna too. We would add our thanks. This is a special day for a very special couple. We have this place until 4:00 p.m. Enjoy and be careful going home."

66

Al Svensen, interim mayor, was enjoying another cup of coffee and reading the notes from the last city commission meeting when his secretary buzzed him. She said, "Jim Johnson, Police Chief, is on the line for you."

"I wonder what he wants. Maybe he is coming back to work. It has been six weeks. He ought to be ready. Put him through." After she connected them, Al said, "Good morning, Jim. To what do I owe this pleasure? And how are you feeling?"

"I'm doing well, thank you. Have you fixed your agenda yet for tomorrow's city commission meeting?"

"We have not. There's not much that we need to deal with. I have a rough draft that I will be sending to them before noon today. Why do you ask?"

"Would you please set aside about thirty minutes for me after your regular business?"

"Can you tell me what it is all about?"

"I could, but I would rather wait and tell you all at the same time. It is important to me personally and I would greatly appreciate the courtesy."

"Alright Jim, I'll do it."

∽

THE NEXT AFTERNOON, Jim was waiting outside the meeting room until the Commission completed their regular business. The door opened, and the mayor beckoned him to come in. "We're ready for you. Come on in, Jim, and welcome."

"Good afternoon, gentlemen. I first want to thank you for making time for me today. What I have to say to you is important to me. I know many of you and would like to get to know the rest. For all of you, I want to share a little of my journey to where I am today.

"As most of you know, I grew up here. We lived out on Henry Street not far from the old float bridge. This was a great town to grow up in and our location was the best. Lots of woods to explore. I played sand lot baseball in a big field near where I lived. Our favorite opponents were the fellows from the new Roosevelt Park homes built just after the war. Lots of nostalgia.

"I went to Maple Grove School through eighth grade, went on to Central Junior High, and graduated from Muskegon Senior High School. My dad always told us to respect the police and the work that they do, and I grew up with the police as my heroes. I wanted to be like them. I earned a degree in criminal justice and was proud to be asked to be on the force after graduation. I had come back home. That was over forty years ago, the last twenty years as your chief. My goal always was to keep the people of Muskegon safe.

"Now why am I telling you all this? This last year and a half, we have seen difficult, tough times that started with Fred Thomas being killed last year and finally ended just a few weeks ago. I was devastated, my city was hurting, but we finally put it to rest. How did we do it?

"I can see in your faces that you are wondering where I am going with this. My Martha has finally convinced me that a sixty-seven-year-old man needs to hand over the reins to someone else. So, effective June thirtieth, I will be retiring. I'm not retiring immediately. I have one more task to accomplish before I go..."

The mayor used the slight pause to jump in. "Jim, we don't want to see you go but we saw how these last few months have taken their toll on you. What is the one more task you have to get done?"

"I hope I can convince you gentlemen that the best way to replace me and do it without all the hassle and expense of a long search is to take the easy way to a new chief. I'm speaking of Mark Bergstrom, the man you allowed me to appoint as interim chief. Let me just summarize his qualifications. He has the degrees, a B.S. in Criminal Justice, a Master of Governance and Public Policy, he has the experience, fifteen years here after a five-year stint on the east side of the state, and last, he is well respected by the men of our department. Finally, and most importantly, he is well respected all over the state. He has the respect of the state police with whom we have been working of late. I have my sources and I know he has had offers from departments all over the state. He doesn't know that I know, but I do. He hasn't said anything about becoming chief, he doesn't know I'm here today. So, I'm urging you to offer the job to the best man you are likely to find. He will accept and make you proud of your choice. Now, I have to stop talking. I'm sure you can hear the tiredness in my voice. Let me step out so you can talk among yourselves about this. I've brought along summaries of his background and his experience if you need them. It's in your hands, gentlemen."

"Wow!" the mayor said. "Thank you, Jim. Give us a little time and we'll let you know."

"I'll be waiting just outside."

"Comments anyone."

John Martin, one of the senior commissioners, said, "I've known Jim Johnson most of the twenty years he has been chief. I have never known such a fine man, a man whose opinion I trust. If he says Mark Bergstrom is the best man, I believe that to be true."

"Any arguments? Anyone?"

"How do we know he didn't set this up with Mark?"

John said, "If he says Mark doesn't know he is here, I trust that to be true."

Al asked, "Shall we put it to a vote, a voice vote?"

The answer was unanimous. Hire Mark Bergstrom.

Al asked, "Shall we get Jim back in and ask him if a two-year contract with a ten-year renewal would be accepted? Or shall we just say we want you for chief?"

The entire group said, "Just hire him."

Jim was called back in and asked that question. "Why don't you call him and ask him to come over?"

"Do you think he'll come?"

"Of course, he will."

There was a phone in the meeting room. Al called and Gerri answered, "Hello, Mr. Mayor."

"Is Mark there and may I speak to him?"

"Mark, this is Al Svensen, the mayor. Would it be possible for you to step over here? The city commissioners and I would like to speak with you. We have some questions."

"Of course. I can be there in about five minutes."

While they waited, John Martin asked Jim, "What are you planning for your retirement?"

Jim said, "Get my health back. Do a little traveling. At first just short distances, but maybe see some more of this country."

"Is there a chance you'll become a snowbird?"

"No. Martha and I love Muskegon. It is our home and here we stay."

Mark walked in a few minutes later. He looked directly at Al and asked, "What kinds of questions?"

All the commissioners turned toward Jim. Mark said, "Jim, what are you doing here?"

They all laughed. Jim said, "These gentlemen have a question for you."

Al said, "We would like to offer you the job you are doing already. We want you to be our new chief of police. Do you accept?"

"Of course, I do. It's what I have been working toward for a long time but couldn't say anything. After all, we had Jim. He's the best."

John said, "That's what he said about you."

Laughter and congratulations went around the room.

Al said, "We'll make the announcement to the press tomorrow and have a more formal ceremony later in the week. But consider yourself the new chief."

"Thank you, gentlemen. I won't let you down."

"We know!"

67

I t was in late June that Jim was home and napping when the phone rang. He woke quickly, remembered that Martha was out shopping. He picked up the phone and it was Mark. "Afternoon, Jim, did I wake you?" But there was a smile in his voice. Jim knew he was kidding.

"Hello, Mark. I *was* napping as it turns out. How are things with you?"

"I'm doing well. I'm putting a final wrap on the brouhaha a few weeks back. But I have some questions that you can answer for me. Could you come down to the station for an hour or so? I'd like to run some things by you."

Jim felt a twinge of disappointment. He knew Mark could handle things. But why not, it would be good to see him in his new office. He said, "I would, but Martha is out shopping, and I have no vehicle."

"I could send a car...wait, suppose I send Gerri to get you."

"That would be great. It will give us a chance to catch up."

"Good. She'll be there in a bit."

～

JIM FRESHENED up and put on a clean shirt. Gerri knocked on the door. Jim opened it, gave her a hug, and said, "Let's go."

They had a great visit on the way to the station. Gerri said she was happy with Mark as chief but that she missed him.

"I have missed you as well. We were a good team, weren't we?"

Gerri pulled into the back lot where she usually parked. "Maybe I should have let you in the front door."

Jim said, "Nope. The back door employee entrance is just fine. Thanks for coming to get me."

Ever the gentleman, he let Gerri in first. They walked through the big open office area past her desk. "Mark said to bring you right to the conference room. Everything he needs is in there."

"Lead on!"

She opened the door and stepped aside to let him in first. As he walked in, there was a chorus of *For He's a Jolly Good Fellow* from a room full of officers, council men, and Martha walking toward him. There were tears in his eyes that he hid by giving her a big hug. Martha turned to the crowd, "How about that? I go shopping and he comes strutting in here with another woman." The tease got a big laugh, all of them knew better.

There were congratulations being shouted to him as he and Martha walked over to their table by the lectern. "Get that man something to drink and bring him some cake. Take a good look at it before we cut it. 'Congratulations. Happy Retirement.'"

The mayor stepped up to the podium, flanked by four members of the city commission. "Jim, here is a plaque engraved with the words you used recently. 'You spent your life making sure the people of the city of Muskegon were safe always.' Thank you with the gratitude of all the people of Muskegon."

John Martin, the dean of the commissioners stepped up to say, "You never let us down and you set up safeguards while you were chief that we see as preserving what you gave the people. Here is your first retirement check and a bonus for your final act of making sure we saw the wisdom of bringing in Mark as the new chief. We already are seeing how right you were. Now here is the new chief with another surprise."

Mark stepped up. "Jim, we didn't know what we could get you as a gift until we spoke to Martha a few weeks ago. So, here come our newest detectives on the force with a gift from all of us on your team."

Tom and Maria pushed a cart with a big box on it up to the podium. Tom said, "Enjoy this in good health for many years to come. We love you."

Jim said, "I can't imagine. I'm overwhelmed."

There was a chant of 'Open it, open it."

He did and found a new rock tumbler, the very model he had been looking at for a while. "How did you ever know? Aha," he said and turned to give Martha a big hug.

Jim stood, was quiet for a minute while the room quieted. He said, "I am so humbled by what you all have done. I had a wonderful career here. It has been my privilege and pleasure to have served. Thank you for this day and for what it represents."

68

Tom and Maria slept in that Saturday morning. They awoke to a beautiful day — sunny, not too warm, no humidity — typical of the end of June in Muskegon. After a leisurely breakfast, Tom turned to Maria and said, "How about a walk to one of our favorite spots?"

"I know what you are up to Tom. You have taken me to see the big lake often since I woke up, but you have avoided the Ovals. Why is that?"

"Dr. Franks and I talked about it. He suggested that going to the place where you suffered the brain injury that put you in a coma too soon might be a problem for you. I was just following his guidance."

"That's what I figured. I think I'm ready. Let's go."

They walked up the little hill and around the curve to see Lake Michigan, Coscarelli's concession stand near the lighthouse pier, and of course, the iconic red lighthouse. They stopped at Coscarelli's to get soft drinks and a bag of popcorn to share.

Maria said, "I'm okay, Tom. Being right at the spot where we got shot is not the upsetting thing now that it could have been earlier. I feel like justice has finally been served even though it took longer than it should.

I'm sorry that four of the group members were killed — they should have gone to jail, too. I don't feel bad about Harry's death — he killed your friend. I still miss Mayor Thomas. He had such vision for the city before he was killed. We didn't have the nine expensive funerals that the consultant predicted would be needed before change could occur, but nine overly powerful, self-centered men were taken down. Now we must move on. We're going to build our new business and help other people."

"Let's go over to the swings and just sit and watch the waves roll in. Let Lake Michigan heal us."

They were sitting there when a car honked from the oval drive behind them. Tom looked. "It's Doug. I knew he would find us."

Doug walked up. "Hey, you two lovebirds. Let's get some lunch and talk."

Maria said, "I have lunch ready at the house. We'll be able to talk better there."

"Then hop in and we'll get back there."

Maria prepared roast beef sandwiches, small salads, and they enjoyed a glass of cabernet sauvignon while talking about Doug's return to his previous life.

Tom asked, "When do you fly out?"

"Monday morning. When I leave here, I will head to Mom and Dad's place in Lansing. I'll spend tonight and all day Sunday with them. We'll get what little I'm taking with me unloaded from my truck and stored in their basement. Dad will park my truck in his extra garage until I return. I'll be picked up when I get to D.C. and taken to my assigned location for refresher training. After about six weeks there, I'll have my first assignment — just a little fire to put out."

Maria smiled. "And where is that?"

With a waggle of his finger, Doug said, "Non, non, non..."

They all laughed.

Doug asked, "When will you be in Paris?"

Tom handed him a three by five card. "Here is the address of the hotel where we are staying in the sixth arrondissement along with the dates we'll be there. We'll be there for the month of September. Do you think we'll be able to connect?"

"I'm hoping so. If I know in advance, I'll figure out a way to let you know. More likely, my visit will be a surprise since I don't usually have much notice about my schedule."

Maria exclaimed, "I love surprises. I hope it turns out that way."

Doug asked, "Any extended time away from Paris or mostly there?"

Tom said, "We have such a long list of what we want to see and do while we are there, I doubt we'll find time to get out of town. Maybe a side trip to Giverny to tour Monet's gardens and his home."

"Good. That will make it easier to get together." Doug continued, "Well, the time has come, mes amis."

"Stay safe, wherever you end up. We want to see you back here."

After hugs and farewells, Doug drove away.

They stood on the porch watching him drive away, both with tears in their eyes. But they had a feeling they would be seeing him sooner than they expected.

A SNEAK PEEK AT INTRIGUE IN PARIS

COMING SOON

Tom and Maria had been in Paris for a week on their much-delayed month-long honeymoon trip. They were staying in the bridal suite at La Louisiane on the Left Bank in the eclectic 6th arrondisement. This historic hotel was right in the intellectual and literary center of Paris. Writers like Hemingway, Satre, Simone de Beauvoir, and Antoine de Saint Exupery loved the location. Simone de Beauvoir said upon discovering the Hotel La Louisiane that she "never lodged anywhere that fulfilled my dreams as that place did; I would have happily stayed there for the rest of my life."

Tom was in love with the fact that many of his favorite jazz musicians like Miles Davis, John Coltrane, Dizzy Gillespie, Billie Holiday, and Charlie Parker also stayed at La Louisiane. The hotel was not fancy, but it had been good enough for Jean-Paul Sartre and George Sand. And the location couldn't be better — just a couple of long Paris blocks to the famous literary cafés — Les Deux Magots, Café de Flore, and Brasserie Lipp — as well as the beautiful church, Église Saint Germaine de Prés.

Tom and Maria spent the first week doing the things new visitors to Paris do. They started with a tour on a double-decker bus for a first look at the sites they wanted to return to. The museums were superb — The Louvre, Jeu de Paume, and the L'Orangerie covering both classical and Impressionist art. On a memorable walking tour of the Montmartre district and Sacré Coeur Cathedral, they had a great lunch at a lovely pink restaurant, La Maison Rose, a favorite of many artists. On Wednesday morning they toured Notre Dame and then wandered around the Île Saint Louis. They lunched at La Brasserie de l'Isle Saint Louis and finished the meal with delicious Berthillon ice cream.

This morning they had taken a bus tour to Giverny and Monet's gardens and home. Pleasantly exhausted, they felt they had done almost all of what they had wanted to of the touristy pleasures. There were still sights to see, but for now, they wanted to see another side of Paris, the real Paris with its neighborhood bistros, and get some feeling for the people of Paris.

They were relaxing in their suite before venturing out for a late dinner when there was a knock on their door. They looked at each other wondering who could that be. Tom put his robe on, went to the outer door and saw an envelope on the floor just inside the door. He quickly looked in the hallway but there was no one there. It was addressed to 'My dear friends.' Tom showed it to Maria. "Were you expecting any mail? I wonder what this is all about. Maybe it got delivered to the wrong room?"

The mystery deepened when they read the note. It said, "You have a reservation at 7:30 p.m. at La Citrouelle. Your hotel manager will know where it is. You will be seated at the table near the picture of Edith Piaf, the chanteuse of France. Please leave the seat facing the front of the restaurant open for me. You will be served by a waiter named Chabon. You'll like him. Order three Kir Royale drinks and tell Chabon you have someone joining you. Please don't show any recognition when I walk up. I will ask you, en français, if I may join you. Please say 'veuillez le faire' or 'please do,' as if you don't know me, but are being polite. Please dress for the occasion. See you soon, mes amis."

Maria said, "Who could this be? Someone we met on a tour, that couple from Australia?"

Tom said, "Maybe, but I have a hunch it is Doug. 'Mes amis' is the term he used last summer when he left Muskegon, Michigan. I think we should go and see what this is about. I wonder what 'dress for the occasion' means?"

Maria changed into a soft beige wool dress and low-heeled tan shoes. She threw her new scarf from Galleries Lafayette, the huge French department store, over her shoulders and draped it in what she hoped looked very Parisian. Tom added his tweed sport coat to his grey slacks and long sleeve white shirt. After checking with the front desk for directions, they walked the three blocks to the bistro. They didn't notice the man with the full beard watching them from across the street, checking to see if they were being followed. They presented themselves at La Citrouelle. The host seated them near the picture of Edith Piaf just as it was supposed to happen. Their waiter, Chabon, introduced himself and then asked, "May I get you something to drink?"

They told him they were waiting for someone and then ordered three Kir Royales as had been suggested. While they waited for the drinks, a tall man with a full beard and mustache and dressed in a Saville Row pin stripe suit approached and asked if he could join them, en français.

"Veuillez le faire." Tom responded as instructed.

The man was seated so he could see both the front door and the rear exit. He said, "As I recall, you are American, so can we speak English."

"We can," answered Maria. "Didn't we meet on our tour of Giverny?"

"We did, indeed. But we've met many times before. Do you know who I am? If you do, just nod. I thought I caught you looking at me quizzically earlier as if you thought you should know me," he said sotto voce.

Tom nodded. He looked at Maria to make sure she recognized Doug. She nodded.

"Please allow me to introduce myself. My name is Sir Douglas McDermott from Ireland, but please call me Doug," Doug continued in a loud enough voice that anyone eavesdropping could hear. "I am here on business for a couple of days in Paris and I enjoy finding dinner companions who speak English. Is this your first trip to Paris?"

Playing along, Tom introduced himself and his lovely wife, Maria. "Yes, it's our first trip to Paris. We're here on a month-long honeymoon and we've been here just a week so far." He murmured so just Doug could hear, "Great to see you, Doug."

"Let's toast to a great honeymoon trip for the two of you. Tell me about your first trip so far."

Maria exclaimed, "Doug, it is exciting, so much to see and learn. We have been the typical first-time tourists so far. This restaurant is the first new experience for us as we begin to get to know the real Paris. My French is not as good as Tom's but we're trying to learn it by being immersed in it."

"That is the best way."

Chabon returned to take their orders and said, "Ah, Sir McDermott, bienvenue ce soir. Welcome."

Tom said, "You have been here before."

"Oui," Doug said, "many times. This is one of my favorite restaurants in Paris. I highly recommend the Soupe de poisson — fish soup — as a starter. And for your main course — le magret de canard — duck — or the poulet fermier — roast chicken — or moules marinières — mussels — are all delicious." Tom selected the poulet fermier and fish soup while Maria chose the mussels and French onion soup. Doug started with the fish soup and selected the duck. He ordered a bottle of Beaujolais for the table.

"Merci. I'll bring you a basket of bread." Chabon left to take the orders to the kitchen.

Doug scanned the room and did not see anyone paying particular attention to them. He continued quietly, "I would like your help, both of you. I need more eyes to help me watch over a personage that is important to current events in Viet Nam. The problem is that the

Sûreté Nationale is on its way to becoming the National Police of France. They are on to me. The Sûreté Nationale doesn't want anything to happen to him while he is in Paris, so even though we're on the same side, I'm working 'off the books' and they don't want me interfering with their job. And factions from Viet Nam are also on to me. These factions don't want the personage to be successful. I am here to prevent his injury, capture, or something worse. He is a high-level personage from Viet Nam, here to connect with the French president and we want to make sure he gets in and out of the country safely. A sightseeing couple will be a great cover for you. Will you help? It should take no more than a week or so."

Tom and Maria looked at each other, turned back together to Doug. "We're in. Let us know what we can do. Can you tell us who it is?"

"I'll tell you who it is later. One more question. Have you seen the Palace de Versailles yet?"

Tom answered, "No, but we want to see it before we leave."

Doug said, "Here comes Chabon with our starters. Let's enjoy our meals and we'll talk more later."

They spoke of the places they had seen. Doug was listening as though he were a new friend learning about their lives. Doug told them stories about his "business" in Ireland. When they finished, Chabon persuaded them to have coffees, along with desserts — profiteroles for Tom and Maria and Baba au Rhum for Doug.

Doug finished the conversation about the Palace de Versailles. "Our VIP wants to visit the Palace also. Let me book it for you. I'll join you and we'll have some time in a secure room so you can get to know him. It will give him an opportunity to be comfortable with you around all the time."

As Chabon arrived with the desserts, Doug stood quickly, moving behind Chabon.

Doug spoke quietly but urgently. "Both of you stand up, right now please, and stand close together. Sûreté officers just came in the front door. I don't think they will know me in this getup. I don't want to take the chance, so I'm leaving through the back door. Chabon is tall, so the three of you will shield me from their sight. The bill is all paid, so stay as long as you want. If the Sûreté officers ask you about me, just tell them we met on our tour to Giverny and we just enjoyed a dinner together in English. And he is late for another engagement. He had to leave quickly."

Doug finished with, "I'll be in touch. Thanks to you both."

ACKNOWLEDGMENTS

I have so many people to thank. Let me start and end with my children and grandchildren who are first, last, and always my encouragement and inspiration. Thank you all.

Thank you to all my teachers of writing craft beginning with my hometown writing group, Stirrings. Thanks to Angie Maloy who brought me in, who continued to teach and inspire, who set up the structure of the sessions so that we all got lots of feedback, both good ideas to correct problems and praise when we had done well. You all taught me so much about how to tell stories. I appreciate all the comments made by all my editors. Any errors remaining are mine alone. All review comments on the first page are from Amazon reviews or personal emails. Thank you all.

Thank you, Charlie Brice, for your comments in the reviews page and the back cover. They are much appreciated.

Thank you to my teachers and friends at the Bear River Writers' Conference who taught me with your praise and critiques. Laura Kasischke earns special praise. I was in your class for three straight years. You awakened the writing muse in me and look where it has taken me. To those Conference teachers with whom I have not studied yet, patience, I'll soon get to your class. I have learned so much from all of you during your readings and our private conversations.

Thank you to my teachers and mentors for various aspects of the writing craft and the business of writing when I attended the University of Madison Writers Institute. Thank you, Christine DeSmet, for your Master Class in novel writing. I appreciate your time generosity after the session when you critiqued my early pages and led me in a new direction. You said, "Try again and do this." I did that and it worked as you said it would.

Thank you, also, Phil and Jean, Michael and Cheryl, my brothers and your wives, for your unwavering support and encouragement in my writing efforts. Your big brother is taking a new step. Who knows what's next!

In a Bear River staff presentation, Keith Taylor, then director of the conference said this, "Get yourself a good editor and listen to her/him. He/she will help you make it a better book." I took your advice and did just that. My daughter, Deborah Smith Cook, edited the book and as you said she would, made it a better story. She caught things I missed and helped me find a better way. Thank you, Deb.

Once again, Kitty Bucholtz was my self-publishing consultant and Deborah was my coach while I was learning the independent publishing side of the business. Kitty and Deb are such good teachers and editors, and brought my second book to where it needed to be. Thank you, Kitty and Deborah.

And finally, again, thank you to my children and grandchildren. Your constant encouragement and support helped me bring this book to reality. I love you all.

ABOUT THE AUTHOR

After a satisfying and productive career as a research physicist, Hayden Smith came home to Muskegon to be near his children. Not content to rest on his laurels, he started a new career as a physics and mathematics instructor at the local community college. Working with his students and interacting with his colleagues was one of the most fulfilling times of his life. However, he would often say at lunch with colleagues that he would like to write a novel — that he had an idea for a story.

Two things happened to make that dream a reality. One of his daughters, who knew about his wish to write, told him about The Bear River Writers' Conference and sent him to it. At about the same time, a dear friend and former colleague remembered the lunch conversations and suggested he join the writing group that she led. He did both, attended the Bear River Writers' Conference and joined the writing group in his hometown. He is so grateful for both suggestions. His life was changed forever. He found a new passion that he didn't know he had. In addition to all the other writing he did along the way while learning his writing craft, his novel began to shape up. That dream was fulfilled with his debut novel in 2020, *Nine Expensive Funerals*.

Now he has five passions that feed and gratify him. The first and foremost passion is to stay close to his children, grandchildren, and great-grandchildren. They are his joy. What else? He is getting back to his roots in music and theatre, both performing and attending. Look for his third cabaret show in 2023. He is passionate about travel — especially to France, Ireland, and Italy, and around this great

United States. He particularly loves the wine regions in California, Oregon, and Virginia. Hayden continues doing research in physics and physics-related subjects. And of course, writing fiction and the stories of his life. He often says, "It is a great, full life!"

Connect with Hayden today!
HaydenMSmithJr@gmail.com

a amazon.com/Hayden-Smith/e/B08PC1XRTM

in linkedin.com/in/hayden-smith-3b195714

Made in the USA
Monee, IL
19 October 2022

16132308R10198